IFRIT

IFRIT

D. L. Wilburn Jr.

ISBN: 979-8-9912868-9-3 (eBook)

ISBN: 979-8-9912868-8-6 (Paperback)

ISBN: 979-8-9912868-7-9 (Hardcover)

Library of Congress Control Number: 2025918618

Any references to historical events, real people, or places are fictitious. Names, characters, and places are products of the author's imagination.

Printed in the United States of America.

Cover by Suvajit Das, Architect of Design

Edited by Elaine Wilburn.

Beta Readers: George Engel, Cheryl Barger, Jennifer Schneider

First printing edition 2025.

W-III Publishing

Permissions@W-III.org

For my father, Don Wilburn Sr.
My love of the horror genre started with
Jaws and Halloween.

by D. L. Wilburn Jr.

The God Protocol: Dragon

The God Protocol: Worshippers

The God Protocol: Judgment

Vulture House

Steve's Alien Rescue Club

Co-Author as Leilana Rae

The Meaning Between Us

HAKIMAH

In the Persian tradition, the Hakīm was the wise one. The keeper of hidden knowledge, healer of spirit, interpreter of the unseen. Rarely named, rarer still a woman, yet their counsel shaped kings and caliphs alike.

Chapter 1

Nafara stood at the edge of the ornate carpet, swirling the red wine in her glass. Sitting before her were the five wealthiest donors in the state of Texas. Oil and energy-rich. Her long, black, curled hair flowed over her shoulders and halfway down her back. She wore a wrapped, green and white dress that hung from her neck, around her breasts and continued around to her back. The ornate gold rope belt secured the dress at her waist and legs, following her curves to her ankles. Its elegance extended to a daring slit up her right side. The colors highlighted her tanned Persian skin. She could read their expressions, and the dress had the desired effect, until they found themselves in the position they were in now.

Three men and a woman sat on the center couches, facing each other, but angled away from where she stood. Their fear permeated the air as they sat fidgeting, their drinks untouched. A young man knelt in the center of the rug, his eyes downward, his body trembling as he sobbed.

Tanya watched intently from the side of the room. Her ivory and forest green designer dress was more conservative, elegant, leaning toward business vice dining. Her light brown hair was back in a professional ponytail, as she had become accustomed to while studying at Rice University. Despite her neutral expression, she felt empathy for the group, the young man kneeling before her aunt, the Jinn Ghul, Nafara Al'Hiyal, or Kavioni, as she had adopted five years earlier. They were out of their element. Used to being in power, controlling every room they entered, they were silent, eyes on Nafara, unsure of what was about to happen. Tanya shifted her gaze to focus on the woman. Almost imperceptibly, the glass in her hand was shaking. The confidence of her silver, Park Avenue chic hairstyle, and her triple-strand pearl necklace contrasted with the look of fear in her eyes. The men were no better, all with clenched jaws and frowns of displeasure. She could almost read the thoughts in their heads. 'How dare this woman, a nobody, threaten us.' It almost drove the thread of empathy from her.

The younger man kneeling between the two pairs was attractive, with well-groomed short blonde hair swept to the side, blue eyes, and dazzling white teeth. The tailor-made clothes accentuated his athletic build. Clad in gray slacks and a white shirt, he embellished his attire with diamond cufflinks. His jacket lay at the feet of the man he bore a striking resemblance to. He kneeled on a large circular rug. The configuration of ornate red and gold Persian patterns on an ivory white background was mesmerizing and intricate. Beyond the rug and the leather sofas, no other furniture adorned the open round room, making the young man the current centerpiece on display.

Nafara stepped forward, reaching out to touch the cheek of the man to her right. Tanya noted the thin red line left behind by the brush of the woman's hand. Defiantly, he didn't flinch at the cut.

"Tomorrow, you four will hold a press conference to announce your support for the Republic Unity Party." The deep, confident voice of her aunt commanded them calmly, as a mother would her children.

A man on the opposite couch, a billionaire immersed in the new energy sector, straightened. "I will not. It doesn't matter what you threaten us with. I won't be bullied by a nobody looking to make a name for herself. I'm leaving." He stood, looking for support from the others, but received none.

Nafara closed the distance between them, her hand resting on the outspoken man's cheek before he could react. A wicked grin appeared on her face.

"Get up," Nafara commanded the kneeling man without looking at him, her eyes locked on the challenger. His body relaxed, then straightened as he regained control from whatever force held him in place. He scrambled away from her, and across the room, toward the door, like a beaten dog. His eyes darted back and forth between the people present.

Nafara leaned in, her grin widening. "And I thought the youngster would serve as my example." She slid her hand under the older man's chin. He tried to pull away but shuddered as her nail extended through his chin and into his mouth. He gagged, blood staining his lips and running down his neck. The woman screamed, and the others tried to get away. Nafara ignored them and lowered the gasping man, choking on the blood filling his mouth. She slid her hand down, just above his heart.

Tanya felt a vibration in the air and heard the accompanying flat note hanging in the room. She knew the others were oblivious to the sound. The guests stared in shock as tiny red dots appeared on his exposed skin and dripped from his eyes, nose, and ears. The blood pooled around the man, forming an expanding crimson stain, soaking into the ornate rug. Years ago, she would have fled in terror at the sight of the ritual. She still wasn't comfortable watching, but she had a role to play.

After a few moments, an intense light formed beneath the Jinn's hand. Tanya felt the hum increase in frequency, its pitch rising, feeling the energy moving around her. The man's body absorbed the spreading heat from her touch. His body dried and cracked like a piece of paper left out in the blistering summer sun, its edges holding the glowing spark of fire. The cinders floated upward, swirling into Nafara's open mouth.

As the man's body disintegrated, the group lost all control. The young man and older woman cried as the other two men tried to open the locked door, struggling to turn the large brass handle, the door rattling in its frame. Tanya stood motionless on the other side of the room, observing the scene unfold.

A flash of light filled her vision, then darkness ensued. Tanya no longer stood at their home in Austin. She was in a round room, a

3

picture of George Washington hung before her. Blood covered the floor, and the smell of burnt flesh filled the air. As she turned to look around, she found herself back in her home. Another vision.

"Sit down!" Nafara's voice cut through the chaos.

All four terrified guests turned their gaze back to the Jinn. They stared wide-eyed at their hostess standing with her arms spread, indicating the two ornate reddish-brown Chesterfield sofas. They moved back to their seats, the younger man taking the open spot.

"As I was saying. Tomorrow, you will jointly announce the formation of a new political party. One that seeks to heal the divide that plagues our great state. After the press has had a few days to digest your enthusiastic goal to unite Texas, you will announce me as your candidate for governor in the fall."

There were no objections.

"You will work together to message the necessity of forming a third party to repair the damage caused by the long-term manipulation by the majority parties. It is time for our great state to stand united behind a single party, with the interests of the people at its forefront. My staff will handle the coordination of all other messaging."

They nodded in resignation.

Nafara reached out and slid her hand under the chin of the young man. "Cheer up, young Asher. Fate has smiled upon you today. You'll live and receive your father's inheritance sooner than expected." She let her hand drop from his quivering chin. Nafara looked around at the sullen, frightened faces, biting her lower lip in mock sympathy. "Look on the bright side. You're about to change the world. We're going to take this election by storm, and that is only the beginning of what we'll do together." She laughed lightly, frighteningly.

She moved with sinuous grace to the door and turned the handle, opening the door. "I hope you're in the mood for dinner. We have a wonderful meal planned." She smiled, motioning her guests to follow, and stepped out of the room. Tanya strode after the Jinn, not sparing a further glance at the gathered party.

Her phone vibrated in her jacket pocket. As she entered the spacious hall, she glanced at the screen and froze.

Imam Yusuf Ahmed Al-Fortwani.

He's alive?

Yusuf: Tanya, we need to talk.

Chapter 2

Yusuf sat at his computer, Tanya's image appearing beside an article about her graduating class at Rice University. It was mostly a local piece, something parents might keep for a scrapbook. The article described the ceremony as being focused on hope for the future. Tanya had graduated as valedictorian with a double major in applied mathematics and music.

His hand ached. He let go of the mouse and rubbed his curled left hand, holding it close to his body. Tanya's speech addressed the hopes and dreams of her classmates and encouraged each of them to take an active role in changing the world. The accompanying photos showed her accepting her degree from the dean and faculty, as well as one alongside her aunt, Nafara Kavioni, a tech entrepreneur.

"Sayyidi, do you need your medicine or a cup of tea? I could run down to your office and get it." Farid's gaze dropped to his teacher's hands.

"Ibni Farid, I'm fine. My hand is acting up. Allah has blessed me with a means of predicting bad weather. In case you are interested, there's a storm coming." He smiled, not receiving the desired response from his assistant, and gave in. "Yes, I would like a cup of tea."

Farid Amirzadeh, a long-time student and protégé of the imam, shook his head, got up, and stepped out of the room. Yusuf heard the clinking of dishes and the teapot and smiled. Farid kept the office more organized than he did, though he would argue that he could find anything he needed, regardless of the clutter. Whether anyone else could was another matter.

He let go of his aching hand and pushed back from Farid's sleek white composite desk. It looked like a set piece from a science fiction movie, unlike his antique rosewood desk. Farid's shelves were neat, every book arranged by height from left to right, gaps marking the few that were missing. Farid had his own style, and it pleased Yusuf that he felt comfortable making this section of the office his own. Too many times, he had seen assistants lose who they were, doing what they thought would please their teacher. He had chosen well.

Yusuf returned his focus to the image of the young woman on the screen. He rubbed his left hand again, a habit he didn't notice, as he stared at the image. *Why hadn't she responded to his text or calls?* He changed tabs back to the homepage of Kavioni Neural Sciences. Tanya's aunt had founded the company three years ago based on a breakthrough during her doctoral research at Stanford. She hypothesized that brain-computer interfaces could heal psychological trauma and mental health issues by manipulating neural pathways related to emotions and memories. Her device, the Eunoia Neural Therapy System (ENTS), promises to address the ongoing mental health crisis affecting the country. The article talked about partnerships, funding, and ongoing FDA testing.

"Sayyidi, what are you looking for? You've been on that page for over half an hour. What's troubling you?"

"Talib Farid. This woman, Nafara Kavioni, what do you notice about her?"

Farid rolled a chair beside his teacher, sat and looked at the screen. After a few moments, he answered, "Her name and features look Persian."

"Very good. She's Tanya Janessy's aunt."

"The girl from Cedar Ridge? The one hunted by the Ghul?"

"Yes."

"We've looked at this before. The case was closed. The murderer was a grief counselor."

"Do you believe that?"

"No, Ghul don't let their prey go easily. Forgive me, teacher, but couldn't you have been mistaken? The mythology describes Ghuls as decrepit souls associated with graveyards and ruins. She doesn't look like a Ghul. Could it have been a different type of Jinn?" Farid sat back, looking expectantly at his teacher.

"I don't know, but with the Jinn, anything is possible. I know what I saw, what she did to me." The imam's eyes were distant, and he clutched his arm. "It's a sight I'll never forget."

"Sayyidi, I know you seek closure on this. We don't know how you escaped after she left you paralyzed. Maybe Tanya helped you. She seems happy. Are you sure you want to dredge up those emotions?"

"I don't know."

Yusuf thought back to his encounter with the Jinn. He remembered everything until the point she left him lying on his back, staring up at the vultures on the roof. Their piercing black eyes watched him as he lay paralyzed at the base of the cypress trees. He recalled the fear and the blinding light of the sun emerging from behind the clouds. Whatever she had poisoned him with left him unable to close his eyes from the burning light.

He had prayed, resigning himself to his fate. Despite the pain in his eyes, the threat from the vultures, and his paralysis, a sense of calm had engulfed him as he embraced Allah's will wholeheartedly.

He woke from a coma months later in a hospital. Farid had filled him in on the news stories of Tanya's house burning down, and her graduation that summer, but after that, they lost track of her.

Yusuf still had nightmares of the Jinn, standing over him, unaffected by his prayers or invocation of faith. Her burning gaze bore into him. Yusuf would never forget the image of the Jinn. He shook his head, clearing the memories. There was no similarity between Tanya's aunt and the Jinn, but it felt too coincidental that Tanya would have a Persian relative show up just in time to help her reconstruct her life after the death of everyone she cared about.

Tanya had no social media presence. Farid had done a thorough search. She kept a low profile throughout her four years at school, without notice, except for the graduation article, which would have been difficult to avoid.

Farid set a hot cup of tea down in front of him. He inhaled, letting the smell of the spices fill his nose. Yusuf took a sip of the hot tea. "Farid, well done with the temperature. It's perfect."

"It's a skill I've been working on for years now."

Yusuf smiled before taking another sip. He pushed back from the desk and turned his chair to face Farid.

"Maybe you're right. Maybe she doesn't want to remember."

He picked up his phone. Still no message from her.

A flashing notice reminded him he had a faculty meeting soon. He stood, an ache across his lower back made itself known, and he flinched. "Ibni Farid, thank you for the tea. I'm going to grab a pill from my office before the morning faculty meeting. If you have time, please check the mail. I am waiting for a manuscript from Qom."

"Yes, Sayyidi."

"With Allah's blessing, the occult studies course will receive approval from the committee today."

Chapter 3

Tanya slid her hand along the smooth wooden railing of the curved stairway in the large rotunda. To her right, a beautiful multi-layered chandelier hung from a long chain on the distant ceiling. Their home's entryway was warm and bright, creating a welcoming atmosphere. The main floor boasted white marble, while the stairs, walls, and handrails followed suit in their pristine whiteness. Only the light, sand-colored smooth wood railing was an exception.

The home was newly completed, a sharp contrast to the past four years. The pair had lived in a nondescript suburban home close to the campus. Her day had become routine, with classes and study throughout the week and weekends focused on her music. The persona of Yasmin disappeared when they left Cedar Ridge. They had settled on the image of Nafara Kavioni, her aunt and benefactor, who swooped in to rescue her after the tragedy with her family and friends.

It would be naïve to believe that they settled into a routine of normalcy. Tanya knew what Nafara had to do to survive. She tried to forget the scene from inside the Vulture House of her father being consumed by the Jinn. She could still smell burning flesh. Afterwards, others suffered the same fate, though Nafara assured her that only those who deserved justice received her wrath. Did the oil baron deserve it? Nafara insisted he did. Politics was messy, and there were often illegal deals to get things done. He was a human trafficker.

Nafara embraced her, but she understood her aunt had ulterior motives. Her encouragement was always positive. The Jinn loved to hear her play, often asking her to replay songs multiple times, each time with more passion or emotion. Nafara urged her to connect with the music, let it touch her, and strengthen her feelings. Tanya would get lost in the music, just like she did with the song from the fall recital, but that perfect feeling never came back, no matter how many times she tried.

Tanya crossed the home to a set of large glass doors framed in polished brass. The doors displayed an ornate symbol split between them, resembling a cursive capital B. It represented the house Al'Hiyal. Tanya had moved past the sense of regret and loss the symbol brought to her. She didn't know if she would ever relinquish it entirely, but she had accepted her position as hakimah, whatever that meant. Nafara was her teacher, friend, and yes, her family.

Tanya slipped off her house shoes and stepped through the doorway to the garden enclosed within the house. The area, larger than her house in high school, was landscaped with flowers and plants selected by her aunt. She crossed the open space to a five-foot-wide ring of rich soil encircling a ten-foot patch of pinkish-red sand.

The soil felt warm under her bare feet. The air was cool with a mist from a system Nafara had installed to help protect the tropical plants in the Texas summer heat. Tanya closed her eyes for a moment, centering herself, and breathing in the scents of the garden, strong with hyacinth and jasmine. She embraced the familiar, relaxing routine, letting her muscles release any tension she felt. After a few moments, she heard and felt her heartbeat.

With eyes closed, she raised her flute to her lips and began playing an ancient Persian song, written for the ney flute. The ethereal tones of the music led her through joy, tenderness, and loss. The serene song shifted, flowing like a river nearing its flood peak, about to ebb. As she continued to play, she concentrated on an image of a beautiful city made of brass, its curving Arabic architecture challenging the surrounding desert. She pulled from images she had seen in books, and in her online searches of how the city might appear, but it felt off.

"You're fighting the flow," came the silky voice of her aunt.

Lowering the flute, she shook her head and opened her eyes to see Nafara sitting across the circle of sand opposite her in the wide dirt ring. She was holding a simple blue teacup.

"I can feel the music. I understand the balance of the underlying frequencies. It's the image of the city I have trouble holding in my mind."

"Would you like some tea?"

Tanya grimaced at the memory of Nafara's bitter tea. It was a carefully balanced mixture of saffron threads, rue, licorice root, wormwood, basil seeds, and sumac berries. All ingredients Nafara grew in her gardens. She was about to decline, then changed her mind. Maybe the shock to her palate would help. "Sure, I'll try."

"Excellent, I'll make you a cup." Nafara got up and went to the glass doors, pausing before pushing them open. "You played beautifully."

"I know it's not the ney flute, but it's what I love to play." Tanya shrugged.

"Have I ever complained? Harnessing your gifts, I believe, is all about aligning with your natural energy flow."

"I know. I have to learn to develop concordance." Her aunt had told her this several times over the past few years.

Nafara smiled. "Good."

"You know, it would help if I understood what you want me to do."

"It's not time. You have much to learn, and don't need the distractions. Keep practicing. I'll be right back. I want to go over the results of our initial efforts to test the waters for the campaign."

Tanya closed her eyes and repeated the relaxation technique. She played the song through again. Her connection to music had deepened as she learned to imprint her emotions in the songs. Throughout her time with the Shepherd School Symphony Orchestra, she had grown in her understanding and feeling of the emotional flow possible in music. She had added a Bachelor of Arts in music in her sophomore year. Math and music, her two loves. Music for her, and math for Sheri. A pinprick of sorrow pierced her heart.

Nafara returned with a cup of tea, handing it to Tanya before assuming her seat across from her in the sand circle.

Tanya laid her flute across her lap and sat cross-legged, mirroring the Jinn's position.

"Would you have killed him?"

"The son? Yes," Nafara said matter-of-factly.

Tanya sipped her tea, hiding her expression as the bitter taste filled her mouth.

"Is he as guilty as his father?"

"Nothing compared to what the father allowed, but . . ." She paused; her eyes focused on Tanya. "I see your unease, but it was necessary to provoke the father into revealing his intentions. The others needed to understand the consequences of their actions, should they choose to oppose me."

"How can you be sure they won't go to the police?"

Nafara laughed. "They have too much to hide."

"I still don't see why you must enter this race. Why politics? Couldn't you run the company and be happy? Look at all of this." She motioned to the garden and house.

"Tanya, this is nothing compared to what my family, my people, had before it was taken away from us. I want to return what's rightfully ours."

"And politics is the way to do that?"

Nafara looked past her, as if seeing something in the distance. "Not the way, but it's a first step."

Tanya took another sip of her bitter tea, a fitting reflection of her aunt's cryptic inferences.

Chapter 4

Yusuf shook his head and tossed the letter toward his desk. It spun in the air, rested on the edge for a second, and slid off. "Narrow minded fools!"

"Sayyidi, what's wrong? Is that not what you wanted?" Farid asked from the doorway.

"It's not. I have been corresponding with the lead scholar at the seminary focused on occult studies, Sayyid Reza Al-Majlisi."

"I'm not familiar with the name," Farid said.

"Few know the name, unless they seek knowledge of the occult. It's becoming less common in the modern age, though I would argue it may be more relevant today than in the past hundred years."

"People often blame the Jinn for their misfortune, but usually it's their own poor decisions or the actions of another person who cause the stress." Farid entered the office but didn't sit. His eyes showed the concern Yusuf had grown accustomed to.

"Multiple verses in the Quran highlight their existence and nature, as well as their capacity for good or evil, like humans. The Quran provides guidance on understanding their place in the world and their interactions with humanity."

"Sayyidi, I'm ashamed to say that while I understood their place in our world and the writings of the Quran, it was your encounter that truly grounded my belief."

Yusuf stepped closer and rested his hand on Farid's arm. "Without my experience, I wouldn't blame you."

Farid nodded, resigned. "What were you hoping to get from the seminary?"

"In our discussions, Ayatollah Al-Majlisi referred to a tome, Al-Tasfir fi Mawajihat Al-Jinn, *Interpretations in Confronting the Jinn.* The title is self-explanatory. He said that it was the most thorough collection of stories, tales, rumors, and eyewitness accounts of humans defending themselves from Jinn. It's essential to our new course, and they didn't provide a copy as I requested."

"What reason did he give?"

Yusuf turned and picked up the paper from the floor and handed it to Farid. He checked his watch. It was almost time for Maghrib, evening prayers.

"This looks like a form letter. *Thank you for your inquiry. We take all requests to expand the knowledge of our teachers seriously, etcetera.* What about the note at the bottom? It's handwritten."

"I saw it. He can't be serious."

"Sayyidi, he invited you to take up your request in person, to better explain how this knowledge will benefit you in serving Allah, Inshallah."

"Yes, and drop all we have going on here?"

"Sayyidi, I think you should consider it seriously. What if the Ghul reappears? I, for one, would prefer to have proven defenses. You were saved by the grace of Allah."

Yusuf waved him off. "I'll consider it. You'd better hurry along. I'll see you after Maghrib."

Farid nodded his head in deference and retreated from the room.

Yusuf felt troubled. Prayers had gone well. He felt the connection he always did, but his mind kept getting drawn to his confrontation with the Ghul. He remembered the vivid details of Amara pausing, looking at him, knowing he would follow her. The Ghul had lured him into the house for their inevitable confrontation. He hadn't told Farid, but he shared the same doubts. While the faithful believed in Jinn, he put little credence in modern stories of Jinn influencing a person's business, home, or family. Earthly concerns frequently caused a person's troubles. Now he wasn't sure.

Did he see her in her true form? If the old stories were to be believed, she should have been a hideous monster feeding on the flesh of the dead in abandoned graveyards, but that wasn't what he had experienced. He didn't need to close his eyes to see her. The Jinn's movements were sensual, like a serpent. She toyed with him and left him to the vultures. He expected to die, so he called out to Allah, asking for mercy and strength. Allah answered his prayers. He did not notice at the time that his encounter paralleled that of his namesake, the Prophet Yusuf, and the betrayal of his brothers, as well as his later imprisonment. He did not mention this to anyone, even in his correspondence with Ayatollah Al-Majlisi.

Yusuf sat alone in his dark office, the only light coming from the small reading lamp on his desk. The dark didn't bother him. It pleased the younger students when they visited. They found it mysterious. He felt it was more practical to take an active role in preserving the environment. He sat forward, elbows on his desk, holding the letter under the dim yellow light.

Esteemed Yusuf Ahmed Al-Fortwani,

I hope this message finds you in the best of health and faith. Should you wish to appeal this decision or examine the books you have requested, I would be honored to host you at the Seminary. I look forward to our continued correspondence and hope you will consider my invitation.
With respect,

Sayyid Reza Al-Majlisi

Yusuf set the letter down on his desk and opened his laptop. He looked at his schedule. His newly permitted occult course was among the classes offered. Yusuf felt torn between his responsibilities to the institute and, more importantly, his students. While the Jinn threat seemed to have ended with the death of the counselor in Cedar Ridge, something still felt off. An ominous feeling hovered just over the horizon, like a storm building. Farid could cover his class while he was gone. It would be a quick visit, and he hadn't been back in over a decade.

"Oh Allah, blessings be upon You. Grant me the wisdom to see the path You have laid before me, and the strength to choose it wisely," he said aloud.

Yusuf closed the laptop and gathered his things, tucking them into his leather satchel. Hopefully, he would sleep tonight, with no dreams. Tomorrow he would talk to Farid. He never had the fortune of having a son, but his protege had filled that void. Scanning the dark office, a sliver of fear pricked his heart. He tried to brush it aside, but it hung on as he made his way out of the office.

Chapter 5

Tanya lay back in the spacious bath. Sweat ran down the side of her face and into the water. She relaxed as the scent of hyacinth surrounded her. Opening her eyes, she counted the candles at the edge of the oval tub, pointing her big toe at each one. She adjusted, letting the bubbles from the miniature jets massage her. Hoping to avoid having to wash it, she had her hair up, but the hot water felt too good to turn down, and now she was sweating in a bath too hot for the summer in Austin. *But it felt so good.*

She picked up her phone, scrolling through her messages. The week was filled with meetings, fundraisers, and exploratory committees. Nafara hadn't shared her plans over the past four years beyond encouragement to study and excel in school. During her time at Rice, Nafara traveled quite a bit and brought back ancient mathematical texts, several linking the manipulation of numbers to magic through numerology, astrology, or some other concept. Despite her benefactor being a Jinn, she still struggled with which stories were real, and which were fantasy. Nafara often deflected the question or told her that more would become apparent when she needed to understand. Currently, math and music were the focus.

Sweat was running more freely, and the pink tone of her skin told her she should get out. She let herself sink under the hot water, feeling the heat on her face. She held her breath, letting the silence surround her. After a minute, she emerged and stood. She dried off and headed to her room to get ready for the evening.

As she came down the stairs, she saw Nafara standing at the glass doors to the enclosed garden.

"What are you looking at?"

Nafara turned, flashed a quick smile, and returned her gaze to the garden. "The garden. You said something the other day that has been nagging at me. I think I may have influenced you inadvertently." She turned to face Tanya. "I love that color on you."

Tanya blushed. "Thank you." She knew Nafara was old, but in her mind, she associated the powerful woman before her with her cocky friend from high school, Yasmin. "What do you mean by influence?"

"The City of Brass. The books, the art, all of it. You said you were trying to imagine the city, when in reality there is no known depiction of the city. You may be trying to connect with a fairy tale not grounded in reality, instead of the actual city."

Tanya watched as Nafara looked past her, lost in thought, before the Jinn motioned her to follow.

"Almost three thousand years ago, King Sulaiman locked away and banished my people because we wouldn't bow to his will."

They continued through the kitchen. Nafara's fingers were more animated with her hand movements, a sign of agitation.

Nafara boiled water for tea and prepared two cups. "Look at all that your people have accomplished in the time we have been gone. I don't know what the city looks like today. Three millennia have passed. You've discovered the entire world. You can fly, go to space, crack the atom, and so much more. This is," she paused, pouring the water into the cups, "something we need to think about."

"I don't know what you're expecting me to do using instinct alone. I don't have powers like you."

"Ah, but you do, my young hakimah, even though the knowledge has been forgotten. I felt a connection when you played the song I gave you."

"Yes, but what does that mean? I've done everything you've asked." The image of the blood-covered room and the picture of George Washington flashed before her, followed by a sense of dread.

Nafara looked up from her tea and stared into her eyes. The confusion in her expression disappeared. "I want you to help me free my people."

"From the City of Brass?"

"Yes. I searched a long time for the object used to seal the gate, but I am convinced it's lost."

"So, how am I supposed to reopen the gateway? What is this object?" Tanya stood, arms out.

"It's a ring. The Seal of Sulaiman, the West calls him Solomon. It's mentioned in at least a dozen historical and religious texts. It is said that Sulaiman could do many wondrous things, including command Jinn."

"Like slaves? But you have free will." The statement hung in the air. When Nafara didn't answer, Tanya continued, "How do we open the gateway?"

"I believe your control of music and understanding of mathematics will lead to a solution. You need to unlock what the modern world has lost."

Tanya leaned back against the counter, stirring her tea. She took a drink, her mind at work with the new information.

"Why are you shaking your head?"

Tanya snapped out of her thoughts. "I didn't realize I was. I'm trying to piece it all together. Trying to recall the feelings or thoughts I had when I saw the beautiful scene at the concert or when I tried to picture the city. One was clear, the others were not. It's like something is pushing back." She didn't want to tell her about the recent vision.

Nafara perked up. "But there was something. You're feeling the threads of creation, the binding filaments that tie everything together within the weave."

Tanya wanted to push for information. Nafara hadn't been this open, even considering the ancient texts she had gifted her. "Is this within the realm of what a hakimah can do? Do you have any texts, scrolls, or anything I haven't studied?"

"I'm working on it. You need to focus on creating a doorway. The key is in your music."

"I know."

"We need to work harder." A flicker of flame flashed through Nafara's eyes as they shifted to their true form. "We each have our roles to play. Concentrate on the gateway. If you need to step away from the campaign to complete this task, so be it."

Tanya felt a wave of disappointment wash over her. "No! I'm fine. I can do both." The feeling lingered as Nafara held her gaze.

"I'm pleased to hear your commitment."

Nafara set her teacup on the marble counter. "I'm starving. I think we should go out for dinner."

Tanya maintained her composure. "Where would you like to go?"

"I've been told there is a dinner party at an exclusive steakhouse, Cut. The mayors of Austin, Dallas, El Paso, and a few state representatives are meeting to discuss political strategy. Despite losing the funding from our backers, they are discounting our campaign as an attention-grabbing stunt."

Tanya watched Nafara's expression shift from amusement to predatory focus. She felt no remorse. Nafara had convinced her that most politicians had stepped on someone or broken a few rules to get their power. "If we're going to make a statement, I should make a call to the local media to let them know where we'll be dining tonight."

Nafara tilted her head slightly, a smile spreading. "Very good. I like it. Make the call, then have the car brought around."

Her imagination raced with visions of how an entire city of Jinn might have evolved over three thousand years. Could she even comprehend it?

Chapter 6

Tanya stepped out of the midnight-blue Extended Audi A8, flashing a quick smile to the driver, who was holding the door. "Thank you, Barry."

"Yes, ma'am."

Tanya was conscious of her expression, keeping it cheerful as she followed Nafara into the studio for an interview. She would watch from the side, paying attention to the host's reactions to Nafara's answers. Lucy, the new campaign manager, walked beside her aunt, providing last-minute details. Tanya admired the woman's poise. She was attractive, with straight blonde hair that hung over the shoulders of her off-white business suit. Her blue eyes popped, accentuated by the royal blue blouse. She wore an amazing women's Rolex watch that sparkled in the slightest light. Tanya picked up the pace and stepped to Nafara's side, opposite Lucy.

"Aunt Nafara, is there any—"

"Excuse me. We need to finish our last-minute preparations," Lucy cut her off.

Nafara stopped, and faster than anyone could react, grabbed Lucy's wrist, pulling her closer. Her eyes shifted to burning embers. "Don't talk to her that way. She gets the same respect as I do. Do you understand?"

Tanya looked at Lucy's wrist, where Nafara had a grip, seeing the extended black pointed nail pressing into her skin.

"Y-y-es, I'm sorry."

Tanya didn't relish the rebuke. Lucy was new, having been "persuaded" by her aunt to leave the frontrunner's campaign after he announced his re-election bid. The news had shocked the political pundits in the state and even garnered a national mention for a day. Tanya wanted to put a hand on Nafara's arm, to move them forward, but waited for her aunt's ire to fade.

"Good." She looked at Tanya. "What do you need, dear?" She had changed the way they spoke in public to reflect the relationship the public believed they had.

"Dr. Gutierrez just texted me. The FDA approved Eunoia for limited human testing. You were busy with Lucy. It's trending on social media. He expects the media to pick up the story soon. I wanted you to know before you go on, in case you're asked."

"Thank you, Tanya." She smiled, placing a hand on her arm.

Nafara continued toward the main entrance to the studio, motioning for Lucy to keep up. Tanya let the pair move ahead and fell in behind them. The studio staff showed them into the green room and informed them they would be called soon. Tanya walked around, looking at the wall of famous former guests. They included politicians, celebrities, and two presidents. Each one had autographed their pictures. Tanya wondered whether Nafara's picture would be on the wall in the future. Local politics still considered her an outsider, as she was a first-generation Texan, born in America to parents who fled the Middle East and died after her birth.

The large screen in the room showed the live feed from the set. Camila Navarro was interviewing a local business owner and grilling him about the recent hike in prices. She was smooth, talking the man into a precarious position. Camila had a reputation for keeping her show light-hearted unless she detected a hidden agenda, or an attempt to hide the truth. Several politicians over the years had their careers ended on her show, some without knowing how it had happened.

"She seems relaxed. In her element. That poor man doesn't know that he's in the center of the viper's nest," Nafara mused.

Tanya sat down on the small sofa next to Nafara. "What do you mean?"

Nafara's smile remained in place. The interviewer earned her respect. "Look at her eyes. The saying 'look a person in the eyes to really know what is in their soul' is truer than people give credit for. He's looking at her, but he's distracted by her appearance, and that top. Watch his eyes. When she moves, he can't resist the urge to look down. She's got him wrapped around her finger."

Tanya could see Lucy nodding along at Nafara's words. "You're going to meet many people who do that. The media's full of them."

"This is going to be more fun than I thought." Nafara leaned back on the cushion with an amused grin.

Tanya didn't know what to make of the comment. All she had shared was that becoming governor was an essential stage of her plan. She usually took it more seriously. Tanya's thoughts flashed back to her father lying on the slab of rock in the basement of her house, the Vulture House. Yasmin/Nafara had enjoyed the slow revelation of her plans to save Tanya from her father before killing him. She wasn't often light-hearted or as playful as now.

Tanya observed the host's mannerisms, reminding her of a cat toying with its prey. She shook her head. That woman did not know what she was about to dance with. She'd better hope she has the reflexes of a mongoose.

A young man stepped in. "Ms. Kavioni, you're on in five, just after the commercial break. If you'll follow me." He held the door and waited for the three women to leave the room. They went down a narrow hallway to the studio set.

The producer waved them over. Another assistant came close and began getting the microphone set up and clipped to Nafara's lapel. "Ms. Kavioni, you'll be sitting to the right. Camila will open with a quick introduction and a few softball questions to help the audience get to know you before shifting to your run for governor. Do you have any questions?"

"I don't."

Their escort held his hand toward the set. "I'll introduce you to Camila."

Camila wore a comfortable pastel yellow business suit buttoned up enough to look professional, while providing a view of the space between her breasts. Her black, curled, silky hair hung over her shoulders and was halfway down her back. Tanya watched the woman sizing Nafara up with her dark brown eyes.

"Hello, Ms. Kavioni, welcome to the show. I'm happy to have you here with us."

"Please call me Nafara."

"Of course, Nafara."

"What do you think?" Lucy asked, leaning over her shoulder.

Tanya adjusted to bring Lucy into her periphery. "It's going to be interesting. Camila isn't sure how this is going to go. She's trying to get a read on my aunt but hasn't yet."

"Well, your aunt can be persuasive." Lucy rubbed her wrist.

"Yes, she can." Tanya turned back toward the set. Her vision shifted to a similar but different scene. She was in a studio, the cameras focused on Nafara.

"My fellow Texans, we will overcome this plague in our cities and make them secure for all people." As Tanya watched, she felt the Jinn's presence, commanding attention while portraying concern. Outside the camera shot were a pair of bodies.

Tanya shook off the vision as the studio came back into focus. She struggled to maintain a stoic demeanor. Nafara leaned in and whispered something to the host. Tanya was worried but didn't see any physical contact. When Nafara took a step back, there was a change in Camila's expression. Like a lioness who smelled a fresh kill. Tanya shifted her focus to Nafara. She was calm and confident. This was going to be an interesting chess match.

"Thirty seconds! Everyone take your places," the producer called out.

Chapter 7

"Sayyidi, you're going now?" Farid stood inside the door to his teacher's office watching Yusuf rummage through drawers and search his bookshelves. The wind battered the window as heavy rain pelted the glass.

"I must, Ibni Farid. Something is off. I feel an impending sense of doom."

"It could be the tropical storm." He pointed to the window. Thick clouds plunged midday into darkness. Yusuf didn't look up. "Take me with you. If it's as bad as you say, I should be there."

"No, I'll be fine. I've contacted Ayatollah Al-Majlisi. He's looking forward to my visit. He opened his schedule to discuss my encounter and listen to my concerns." Instead of searching his desk, he looked at Farid. "I'll be fine. I haven't been back to the seminary in almost four decades."

"As you wish. Allah watch over you."

"I appreciate your concern. May Allah watch over all of us."

Farid shifted his weight, his shoulders dropping in resignation. "Sayyidi, is there anything I can do here?"

"Yes, I'm going to try to contact Ms. Janessy one more time before I go. If I cannot reach her, I'll leave her number for you to continue our efforts."

"Is it necessary? She seems happy. Do we need to drag up her memories?"

"I've considered that, and while I don't want to cause her any more distress, we must know if the threat still exists. The police believe the counselor was the killer and that she and the girl's father killed each other. But it doesn't line up. If the Ghul is alive, why did it let her live? That is out of character from all that I have studied. There are too many questions."

"Sayyidi, you know I believe you, but maybe our understanding of the Jinn is incorrect. Many of the beliefs associated with them can be explained away with reason."

Yusuf stepped around his desk and closed the distance with his student. "Ibni Farid, are you telling me you don't believe in the Jinn?"

Farid straightened up and looked into the determined eyes of his teacher. "No, Sayyidi, I believe all that is written in the Quran. Peace and blessings be upon the Prophet. But, in ancient times, this storm," he pointed out the window, "would be considered a raging group of Jinn punishing the city for insulting them with their misdeeds."

Yusuf looked at the man before him. "I understand how this sounds. Something about this Jinn is different. Why, after remaining hidden for thousands of years, would she draw so much attention to herself?" He turned away, rubbing his left arm with his healthy hand.

Ding!

Tanya: Yusuf?

"It's her."

"What are you going to tell her?"

Yusuf leaned over the phone, typing with a single finger.

28

Yusuf: Tanya, hearing from you is a welcome surprise. I have been worried.

Tanya: Is this really you? How is that possible? I was told you passed in Cedar Ridge.

Yusuf: My injuries put me in a coma. I have important news and questions. Can we meet?

Tanya: I don't know. I want to put all of that behind me.

Yusuf: I understand, but it's important. I'm leaving the country for a few weeks. I would like to visit once I return.

The pair stared at the phone.

"I was right. She doesn't want to think about that time. She lost her whole family." Farid shook his head.

"No, have faith."

Tanya: I'll think about it. Text me when you get back, be safe.

"Do you see?" Yusuf pointed at his phone.

"I will once you get back." Farid quipped.

Yusuf: I will text you when I return. Take care.

Yusuf sighed. "That's a load off my mind. She seems of sound mind and is willing to entertain a conversation."

"To change the subject, in case you decide to stay longer than the two weeks. I registered your course with the registrar's office. It's on the fall schedule. You'll have at least one student in attendance. The office assistant got excited when he read the course description."

29

"Two weeks should be fine, and that will give me a week to prepare. Thank you, Farid. I'm going to finish here and then go back to my room to pack."

"I'll drive you to the airport, so you don't have to go out in the storm. Let me know when you are ready, Sayyidi."

"Thank you." He went back to searching through his desk, his assistant disappearing through the doorway.

Yusuf reached into his drawer, normally used for files, and pulled out a small cigar box. He unlatched the top with his thumb and opened it. There were three small red tassels, resembling the large knots tied with threads at the end of rugs or curtains. These weren't from either. A colleague gave him these talismans of protection before Amara and her family were killed. He set the box down on his desk, took a talisman out, and studied it. He felt a dull pain in his chest at the thought of her family. The murder was the work of the Ghul, meant to send a message.

It was old news by the time he awoke from his coma. He rolled the talisman in his hand. The woven threads fell between his fingers. An iron ring bound the knot above the threads. The inscription read *Bismillah-ir-Rahman-ir-Rahim*, in the name of Allah, the Most Gracious, the Most Merciful. He had been too late, delayed by a day. Enough time for their murder. Placing the talisman in his pocket, he carefully slipped the box back into its place at the bottom of his desk drawer.

A bright flash and a thundering crash of thunder pulled his eyes to the storm outside. His flight would be delayed, which was fortunate because he needed extra time to pack. With his journal and prayer rug, he collected the small pile of books and went off to pack.

The wind howled outside his window. Next week, it would be peaceful clear skies. This was Texas weather.

Chapter 8

Tanya followed the scent of baked orange-cranberry something through the house. It smelled like her mother's recipe. As the memory of her mother came back to her, a poignant image of her taking a fresh pan of muffins from the oven flickered before being overshadowed by the scene of her murder. Tanya shook her head to clear the image. She focused on the smell, summoning happy memories of sitting at the kitchen table, Jackson beside her waiting for his share of the delicious treat. Tanya always slipped him something. She missed the little guy, her resilient little Scottish Terrier with the enormous attitude. He had survived everything and had made it most of the way through college with her before succumbing to old age.

She wanted to get another pet, but Nafara was against it. She didn't say why, beyond insisting they would be a security threat. When asked any further questions, Nafara would brush it off. *Roses.* The scent hit her, pulling her away from the trail of baked goodness. The intense, fruity richness evoked smelling salts, but its texture was smoothly velvety. What was going on? Why was her nose acting up?

She entered the kitchen and saw the muffins sitting on the island, fresh from the pan.

"Morning, Maria!"

"Morning, Miss Tanya."

She walked over to the muffins, closed her eyes, and took a deep breath. "Mmm, these smell amazing. Did Nafara ask you to make them?"

"No, ma'am. I thought you might like something different from cereal."

"Normally, no, but for these, a resounding yes. May I?"

"Of course. Let me get you a plate."

"Thank you!" As Tanya took a bite of the muffin, she savored the perfect mix of tart and tang. She resisted the temptation to take another and left the kitchen instead, heading to her office on the opposite side of the house.

She sat at her oversized desk and scrolled through her email. Turning on the news, an amber alert scrolled across the bottom of the screen. The news anchor was talking about an increase in child abductions in the area, stating that the police had no leads to report. She was certain it wasn't Nafara or another Jinn. Her aunt assured her she would focus only on feeding on those deemed unworthy or guilty of grave harm to her fellow humans. She understood Nafara's needs.

Was she complicit in murder? Yes, society's rules forbid killing. Her guilt rose, and she pushed it aside. It wasn't the same. Nafara, not she, committed the murder, a killing Nafara deemed justified and essential for her survival. Was she Renfield? The vampire's loyal assistant, caught in a life of serving a monster? No, Nafara wasn't a monster, not anymore. She had saved Tanya from the actual monster, her father.

A deep, warm, earthy smell caught her attention. She turned her head, following the scent coming from her leather chair. She hadn't noticed it before. The leather? She turned back to her desk and leaned forward to smell the glass. Nothing. She got up and walked around the office, inhaling the smells of books, flowers, trinkets, and paintings. All of them had a unique smell she could distinguish. Once aware of each smell, she became overwhelmed by them. She picked up two books and took a small oil painting off the wall. After grabbing her muffin, which she held in her mouth, she departed the office.

Tanya sat in the center of the sand circle surrounded by the objects she had gathered: her muffin, an oil painting, an Assyrian text, an Egyptian papyrus, a handful of roses, and hyacinth. She spread the objects equidistant from one another around the perimeter at the outer edge of the sand. Tanya sat in the center, her eyes closed, trying to focus on each smell. She wore a light cotton shirt and yoga pants, both of which smelled of the detergent used by the staff. While she wanted to explore the surrounding scents, she was not willing to sit naked in the garden in the center of the house. Nafara might think she was losing her mind. She concentrated on isolating each scent, keeping them separate from the detergent smell.

She relaxed her breathing, slowing, yet deepening her inhalations before exhaling as she had learned from YouTube meditation videos. Not surprisingly, it worked. With her eyes closed, she could trace a scent back to its source, and she could feel how prominent, or strong, it was. She visualized each scent as a thread extending from the object toward her. With her eyes still closed, she reached out with her hands and touched the "scent" of the muffin. The pleasant, sweet-tangy scent grew stronger. As she examined the thread, she noticed smaller threads wound inside. She eased them apart, careful not to break any. As she touched the separate threads, she smelled the orange, cranberry, wheat flour, milk, butter, eggs, and oil. With a growing sense of excitement, she relinquished her hold, leaving the distinct scent to permeate the air.

Shifting her attention to the rose, she pulled the thread closer. She separated the threads. Sweet, earthy, fruit, citrus, honey. She pulled the citrus from the muffin and the thread from the rose. Holding each in a hand, she felt the difference in strength, texture, and potency. It was exhilarating. Tanya could feel the essence of the objects. She repeated the process for each scent, breaking them down, and comparing their qualities. She reached out and welcomed the smells from the garden, the plants, and flora around the outer ring. Each unique.

A foul odor crept in. Focusing, she discovered several similar threads radiating from the outer ring of the garden. They smelled of decay, rotting meat, wet earth, and blood. The image from the massacre at the church center filled her mind, and she pushed everything away.

Tanya fell back, trying to get away. She felt something dark around her closing in. Opening her eyes, she scanned for the threat. Her heart was racing. She jumped up, ready to run.

Emptiness followed the receding fear. She was at the center of the garden, alone. She brushed herself off and collected the items. Her heightened sense of smell was gone. She scanned her surroundings as she left. Something dark was buried here.

Chapter 9

Tanya sat across from Nafara in the back of the Audi. She looked out the window, watching the city landscape as they passed through the affluent Westlake Hills. They were on their way to the Vista Veranda, an exclusive Mediterranean fusion restaurant 'Nestled in the hills with a panoramic view of downtown Austin and the hill country, offering a sophisticated ambiance and top-tier service.' At least, that is what the website stated.

"You're quiet this afternoon," Nafara mused.

Tanya broke free of her thoughts. She took a breath and shook her head.

"Tanya," Nafara said her name sternly but with concern. "You know you can be open with me. What's bothering you?"

She turned her head and looked at her aunt. "I'm afraid sometimes."

The expression on Nafara's face flickered from concern to unhappiness. "Of me? I'm still the woman who befriended you." She shifted, changing her appearance to that of Yasmin.

Tanya sighed. "I know. You'd think after five years, I'd be accustomed to you as Aunt Nafara."

Yasmin leaned forward, taking her hand. "What brought this up?"

Tanya looked down at their hands. "A few days ago, I was overwhelmed by smells or scents. Everything was strong. At first,

I thought it was the muffins Maria made. They reminded me of my mother. Then it was rose, leather, and then everything. When I concentrated on the smells, I could," she paused, looking up to her friend, "feel them."

"That's interesting progress." Yasmin observed.

"I think part of it might be me gaining an understanding of the weave, but I looked it up and there is a condition called hyperosmia. It's a neurological disorder that genetic anomalies, hormonal changes, stress, or a dozen other things can cause."

"Maybe you should come down to the lab. We can look at it."

"No. I don't think I have that. I was just searching for alternative explanations. I don't know why."

"What do you mean?"

Tanya looked over her shoulder to make sure the divider was sealed to the driver. "Is this your curious doctor hat or Jinn?"

Nafara laughed. "It's me trying to help you." She transformed back into the image of her aunt.

"Okay, this may sound out there, so let me know if this is familiar to you. I could break a scent up into its components. In the muffins, I could smell the distinct ingredients. I could feel them, touch them, feel the strength. It was different."

Nafara sat silent for a few moments. "It sounds like a connection to the weave. I can't tell you what a human would feel. It's innate to us. We are born connected and, as a result, our senses are more focused. What you describe seems ordinary to me, but I can see how it would be overwhelming to your kind."

"I smelled death in the garden." She raised her eyes to watch her aunt's reaction.

Nafara's expression shifted to stoic dismissal. "Things die in gardens all the time, eat the wrong thing, get caught by something else. Sometimes, it's being in the wrong place at the wrong time, as the old cliché states."

"You promised."

A small spark appeared in Nafara's eyes and grew. "Hakimah." Her expression changed as she struggled to control her emotions. Her eyes returned to dark brown. "Tanya, I have kept my promise. But be aware that you humans make that rule an easy one to live by. Most humans have something bad they're hiding. At least those who come snooping around, led by someone else's dirty money, do."

"So, there *are* dead people buried in our garden?"

"Yes."

"I thought you *disposed* of them."

"Do you expect me to consume every person I kill? Do you eat everything that's brought back from the grocery store?"

"That's not the same!"

"It most certainly is, but fine! I won't bring more bodies to the garden. But in my defense, the human body is an amazing fertilizer."

Tanya set her jaw and looked out the window. She was Renfield. They sat in silence for the rest of the trip. Thankfully, it was brief.

The car pulled up to the restaurant, which was impressive in design, reflecting a large home from the beaches of Europe on the Mediterranean. Large windows in the spacious room showcased a stunning cityscape. The host directed them to their table, where they joined Mayor Billy McWilliams of Austin.

Nafara reached the table and took the hand offered by the mayor. "Mayor McWilliams, it's a pleasure to meet you at last."

"The pleasure is mine, Ms. Kavioni."

Nafara stepped aside. "This is my assistant and niece, Tanya Janessy."

He took her hand in his. Its vastness enveloped hers yet remained gentle. She could feel the calluses on his palm. He came from a cattle family and had worked his way up on the expansive ranch before shifting to politics almost a decade ago. "Nice to meet you, Tanya." He held her gaze for a moment before shifting back to Nafara, motioning both of them to sit.

"While I appreciate the opportunity to get out and enjoy a fine meal with a pair of beautiful women, you know that my endorsement, when it comes, will align with that of my party."

Tanya watched her aunt maintain a pleasant demeanor, though it was the worst-case scenario they had discussed. Lucy had briefed them earlier that he was a true-blue Democrat with aspirations of sitting in the White House someday. And that meant that he voted party line every time and was a pain in the current governor's backside.

"Bill, that is disappointing. I had heard that you were open to progressive ideas that benefit your constituents."

He chuckled, biting his lower lip and nodding. "Of course, I am. But I also recognize that I plan to sit in that seat someday, and if I put my support behind you. Well, then it will be difficult to replace you in four years. You'd better turn and smile. People are taking pictures." He directed his eyes toward the kitchen, offering a wide smile.

Tanya looked around and saw a young woman had a camera pointed at their table from a hall the staff were moving to and from. She smiled, glancing around to see if anyone else was taking pictures with their phones. They weren't, not with this crowd. A power play was in action, and she was sure they were watching with anticipation of the outcome. She wondered herself whether her aunt would scratch the poor man, inflicting influence or a deadly disease on him. To her surprise, her aunt remained reserved.

"I have to say, Bill, I'm disappointed that you aren't even open to discussing the matter." She shifted in her chair. Her blouse shifted, revealing more of her cleavage. The mayor didn't bite. He kept his eyes locked on Nafara's.

"Well now. I'm not saying there isn't an opportunity to work together. I'm thankful that you chose Austin for your company. From what I've read, Eunoia is going to do some amazing things, especially with our veteran community. My daddy was in the Army in Vietnam, and I wish we had something for him."

Nafara feigned a look of compassion. "I was sorry to read about your father. It's difficult to lose someone close to you, especially at such a young age. You were twelve, correct?"

"Yes, I was, and it was tough on the family. But my brothers and I stepped up, and here we are." His grin spread wide across his face.

"Well, I hope to prevent that from happening in the future. The Eunoia treatment will help more people than you can imagine. If you believe the news, we're in the middle of a mental health pandemic."

"How about we continue this over lunch? My treat, of course. I don't want your trip to be for nothing."

"That would be lovely. Perhaps we can find more common ground."

He motioned to the waitstaff to take their orders.

Chapter 10

Yusuf inhaled the aromatic smells of prepared dishes, spices, and everything at the Qom Market. The din of barking merchants filled the air, working to garner the attention of shoppers. The bazaar teemed with vibrant colors of woven clothes, set beside traditional blue and white architecture. Despite the early hours, the market was busy. He had a few hours before his first meeting and was working to overcome the last of his jetlag.

The heat wasn't too bad. Still, he opted for a white turban and a light brown robe, with a darker cloak over his light khaki pants and white shirt. He felt a difference from Houston despite the lack of humidity. At home, he usually wore less except on occasions that required the traditional garb.

He smiled at the locals as they moved about shopping. The smell of fresh bread was welcome in every part of the world. He turned, searching for the bakery, and spotted the shop front a little way back.

As he neared the shopfront, a black-bearded man in a light gray business suit accepted his order, a small bag from the baker, and turned to leave. He collided with Yusuf and offered an instant apology. "My apologies, Your Eminence." Though his words were respectful, his expression lacked sincerity. Without waiting for a response, the man hurried away.

The young were losing their reverence, even here in the heart of Shia Islam. Yusuf didn't let it bother him as much as he should have. Over the past few decades, exposure to the West broadened his perspective on his place in the world.

He looked around the shop, awaiting his turn at the counter, and saw that loaves and sweets, among other baked goods, still filled the shop.

Stepping forward, he was ready to order. "Please, I would like half-a-dozen kloocheh with dates and two Barbari breads."

"Yes, certainly. Six kloocheh with dates and two Barbari breads." The baker selected the items, taking the bread from the freshest batch, and wrapping it in paper. "Here you go."

Yusuf paid and took the small bag. He reached in and pulled out a round, dark brown pastry and took a modest bite. The version with dates was his favorite. He moved through the bazaar, observing the people. Most were respectful, allowing him to pass unobstructed. He came to a branch and realized that he had passed where he had entered the market. Searching for a sign, he noticed the man in the business suit who had run into him a little farther back. The man appeared to be looking at scarves. Something wasn't right. Yusuf looked around, not recognizing anyone else. He put the last of the pastry in his mouth and started walking away. As he moved through the shoppers, he resisted the urge to look over his shoulder.

Yusuf chose the path to the right and picked up the pace, passing ten shops before stopping by a drink vendor. He took his time ordering, chancing a glance back the way he had come. After a minute, he saw the man round the corner, glance down the path, and then focus on the corner shop.

Yusuf felt his pulse quicken, resisting the urge to flee. He spotted an exit and headed toward it. Once free from the market, he looked around for a teahouse. With open outdoor seating, he spotted one. He walked down to the corner and waited for the traffic to stop before making his way across the street. He saw the man exit the bazaar from where he had. The server directed Yusuf to a seat in the open under a large, beautiful awning.

"Two chai, please," he ordered. He didn't feel the anxiety he would have had before. Instead, he waited for the man to look at him from across the street, and he waved him over, showing the seat at the small table. The man looked confused by the act but made his way over. Yusuf watched him approach.

"Please join me."

The server appeared, setting the cups before each man, took the teapot and filled each two-thirds full, and set the pot down between them.

"Thank you." Yusuf nodded at the server. When he left to attend another table, Yusuf turned his full attention to the man across from him. "You're following me?"

"Sayyid Al-Fortwani, my apologies for intruding on your time. I was ordered to ensure your safety. I'm Mehrdad Rahimi."

"Why wouldn't I be safe here?"

The man scanned his surroundings. "There are some that don't want the information you possess to get out."

Of the Jinn? People blame Jinn for everything. Why would they be concerned with something that happened so far away? It was a local matter in the west. It registered a minor blip on the national news.

"Mehrdad, I don't know that my story would be a cause for concern here. Can we talk in the open?"

"No, it is not safe."

"Well then, perhaps we should enjoy the chai." He checked his watch. He still had a few hours before his first meeting at the seminary.

Mehrdad sipped his chai and seemed to relax. His eyes wandered to their surroundings, searching.

"Is someone else following me?"

"Not that I have detected. But not everything is visible to the naked eye."

That piqued his curiosity. The Ayatollah's decision to send someone to watch over him already raised his concern. It had been over five years since his encounter with the Jinn. Was there anything else? He wanted to finish their drink and head back to the seminary so that he could get more answers, but if someone were watching, it would look suspicious and impolite. *I'm a scholar doing research, not a spy.* He took another drink of the spiced chai, enjoying the warm beverage.

"Are you going to follow me around throughout my visit? My meeting with the Ayatollah isn't for a few more days."

"Probably."

"My assistant in Houston, Farid, will be pleased to know that I am safe, not that I had any doubts."

Mehrdad leaned in, taking the teapot to refill their drinks. He kept his eyes on the cups as he poured and lowered his voice to a whisper. "Sayyid Al-Fortwani, your friend *is* right to worry. Not all is as it seems. What happened to you is of grave concern to the Ayatollah."

"What do you mean?" Yusuf lowered his voice to match the level of the man.

Mehrdad threw back his head and laughed as if he had heard something funny, then lowered his voice before speaking. "I can't say any more." He sat back, adjusting his cup. "Do you have more shopping to do or anywhere you would like to see?"

"I have a meeting in just over an hour. After that, though, I'm free. I would like to visit the Fatima Masumeh Shrine."

Yusuf sipped his tea, as his guest did. While he watched the odd man across from him, the man watched everyone else.

Mehrdad's phone rang. He answered and listened. "It's all set. After Dhuhr, the midday prayer, and your meal, I'll escort you to the shrine."

Yusuf sipped his chai. Someone is listening and tracking his movements. He wouldn't be able to tell if anyone else was following them. His unease returned.

Chapter 11

Tanya checked her speed as she neared the hill. She was always wary of someone trying to pass in her lane, concealed. Cresting the hill at just over sixty, she saw fields of yellow flowers glowing in the sunlight and an empty state highway stretching out in front of her. The sun was setting, resting just above the horizon, the orange becoming more vibrant and holding the light as the night sky took over, shifting to a deep purple.

Tanya pulled over and parked. Stepping out of the car, she was greeted by a light, cool breeze. The air was warm, but not uncomfortable, and the breeze carried the smell of wildflowers. The fields on either side of the highway stretched a good distance to a lush tree line. Surprisingly, there were no fences along the field's edge, a rarity in Texas. As she took a deep breath, she felt an urge to walk among the flowers.

Stepping off the road, she waded into a sea of yellow. The plants were at waist level but not bunched so much that they impeded her progress. Their smell was sweet, with a hint of musk. As she pressed further into the field, the breeze dissipated, and stillness prevailed. Bees flitted about, gathering pollen, their buzzing a soft addition to the serene scene. Smiling to herself, she continued through the field, her fingertips brushing the flowers, imagining the scene from the movie *Gladiator*, where Russel Crowe was walking through the field of wheat at the end.

She walked for a while longer before coming to an open round area, maybe fifteen feet across. Tanya kneeled and ran her fingers across the top layer. It was dark brown and fertile. She scooped a handful of dirt, feeling the moist, rich soil. *This is strange.* She stood and looked around for any more circles like this one. She didn't see any, but wouldn't anyway, because of the height of the flowers. If she had veered off only a few degrees, she may have missed this one. Her car sat parked in the distance. She thought about continuing across the field to the trees, but something in the circle tugged at her to sit and relax. It was a familiarity, like the garden at home.

Tanya moved to the middle of the circle and started to sit, but a feeling of unease stopped her. She backed until the feeling was gone. The warmth of the sunlight, coupled with the smell of the flowers and the sound of the bees, was relaxing. She closed her eyes, took a breath, and sought the weave. Warmth enveloped her. She opened her eyes.

Across from her sat an old woman. She wore a tanned hide wrap, was barefoot, and had no jewelry. Her hair was long and gray, bound and hanging behind her. *She's a shaman.*

Tanya remained calm. The woman's eyes were closed as well. Her arms reached up and around her, picking small strands of gossamer threads floating in the air. She looked to be conducting an orchestra, each movement marked by smooth fluidity.

Tanya watched as the woman selected the threads. Initially, they looked similar in appearance, but she knew better from her experience in the garden. Focusing on the filaments, the finer details became apparent. Tanya extended her hand, her fingers brushing the threads, feeling their essence. The vibrant yellow flowers boasted three filaments: color, texture, and smell. The wind existed as touch and sound. Color, sound, taste, and touch defined the bees.

Refocusing on the woman, she saw a feature she hadn't noticed, a third eye in the center of her forehead. It directed the woman's hands to specific threads. Tanya reached out, taking hold of a woven thread the woman had released. The connection between flowers, bees, and wind became clear to her as she watched pollination, the bees' drive, and the wind's creation of scented bee trails. She lost herself in the vision.

Startled awake, she felt a sense of unease wash over her. The sun had set, and the sky had darkened further, filled with foreboding storm clouds. She didn't know how long she'd been asleep, but she was surprised at how damp her skin and clothes felt. How had she not awakened when the rain started?

A nearby howl chilled her blood, interrupting her thoughts. Fear gripped her. The dull roar of rain hid the direction of the howl. She looked around for her car, but the field was dark. The rural state highway was also devoid of lights. She couldn't tell if the wolf was between her and the road.

The smell of wet dog wafted near. Tanya held her hand in front to determine the wind's direction, but it shifted. If she smelled the wolves, they would be upwind. Were they smart enough to get between her and her car? Polar bears hunted people, placing themselves between a village and the person, pushing the person to exhaustion as they tried to escape. She couldn't remember whether wolves did the same. She hoped for a flash of lightning to help her get her bearings, but none came. Another howl, this one lower in pitch, sounded from somewhere to her left. There was more than one.

She patted her pockets. They were empty except for her keys. Her pulse increased. Attempts to suppress her fear were failing. As she turned, she steadied herself and focused, listening for sounds outside the rain. She heard it. The sound of rain on the trees, their wet leaves, and branches brushing together. She turned, putting her back to where she thought the tree line was, and started walking. Another howl, closer this time, reached her, followed by another on the opposite side. Fear gripped her and she ran.

Her pace was slowed by the wet flowers that seemed to bend, wrapping around her legs. She felt a feral presence on her left. Despite her attempt to duck, she was struck by a heavy weight and tumbled into the flowers. She scrambled and struggled to get up. A guttural growl came from her right. Tanya bolted as fast as her legs would carry her, away from the sound. Heat and pain erupted in her calf. It felt like a knife punctured her calf and pulled her aside, dragging her down. In a panic, she thrust her hand and keys down toward the piercing pain and was rewarded by a yelp and release. She got to her feet and felt the crunch of gravel. She was at the side of the road.

Lightning flashed, and she saw her car was only twenty yards away. Hearing a pained howl nearby, she realized it would attract the rest of the pack. She tried to ignore the pain in her leg, but her leg wanted to give out with every other step. A high-pitched warble sliced through the night as she hit the car alarm button. She stumbled the last few steps, grasped for the door handle, and jumped in, closing it behind her. As she started the car, the cold air from the vents hit her and sent a chill across her body. The headlights illuminated the road before her, and six enormous wolves, spread across the road, blocked her path. One was missing an eye, blood running down the side of its muzzle. With the car in gear, she took off down the road, causing the wolves to move at the last possible second before she passed. Instead of turning around and heading back to Eunoia, which was only half-an-hour away, she decided to press on the forty minutes to her home. She would stop at the next service station and get something for her leg. She gripped the steering wheel, her knuckles white, her fingers crushing the leather.

Chapter 12

Tanya sat in the garden. Her legs crossed, she opened her eyes, and forced herself to relax. Her vision shifted, almost like augmented reality. She saw the garden as normal but could also see and sense the threads of everything in the garden. Her calf ached with a dull throb. She ignored the pain.

Tanya reached out and pulled the thread of scent spreading from the outer ring of the hyacinth flowers. As she held it in her hands, she felt the plant's potential. Her mind shifted its perception to make sense of the alien feelings. It joyfully fulfilled its purpose, drawing in solar energy, air, and extending its roots. Reaching out, she took the filaments from other plants, rocks, and insects in the soil. Mimicking the woman in the field, she pulled on the threads and weaved the filaments together, nudging the plant back through the thread.

"Impressive," Nafara's voice interrupted her concentration. She stepped into view, taking a seat across from her.

"What is?"

"The flowers." She pointed to the side of the garden.

Tanya turned her head and saw the hyacinth was now twice the size of the surrounding plants. She was surprised.

"I'm still trying to understand how this works. I didn't know I did that."

"What did you do?" Nafara asked with serious curiosity.

"If I relax, I can see the filaments of the weave, connecting everything. I assume the filaments are my mind's interpretation of what my senses are relaying to me. Sight, sound, taste, touch, and smell. I think there are more. For instance, I could feel the potential of the flower. And others, satisfaction at taking in the light, nutrients, water, everything."

"Interesting."

"Is that what you experience?"

"Not quite. All the things I do with plants are innate. They come naturally. I know what I need to do, and based on that need, it happens, like walking."

Tanya ran her hand over the bandage on her calf. Nafara wasn't telling her everything. She wasn't trying to deceive her. It was more like protecting knowledge she wasn't ready to share.

"What happened to your calf?"

"I was attacked last night."

Anger flashed in her eyes. "What?" Her posture shifted. "Who did this? Why didn't you tell me?" She stood and looked ready to react.

"I stopped on my way back from the lab. There was a beautiful field of flowers. Something drew me to it. I think I had a vision."

Nafara relaxed. "A vision? What did you see? Are you sure it was a vision?"

"Ok, maybe not a full vision like others I've had. More like a feeling. I was sitting in the field, and meditating as I do here, and a woman appeared. She was older, wearing a leather hide wrap. I think she was a Native American shaman. She didn't speak. I think she was showing me how to change the weave. It felt like influence and guidance instead of forced manipulation. There was a flow to her movements. I don't know what she was doing, but it made sense. So, I tried it today."

"Tell me about the attack. Was she responsible?"

"I don't think it was her. I must have fallen asleep. It was raining when I woke up. I sensed danger nearby. I was disoriented, and it was dark. Once I heard a howl, I knew it was wolves."

Nafara shifted her stance. "Are you sure it was wolves?"

"I'm positive. I saw the one that bit me. They were big, definitely larger than coyotes. When I got ready to drive away, there were six of them standing on the road. I put out an eye of the one that bit me."

"Wolves hunt my people," her voice trailed off as if she hadn't meant for the comment to be spoken aloud.

"Do you think they smelled you on me?"

"Maybe. Of all the shapes we can take, wolves are the ones we can't assume, not even our best shapeshifters, the Jann."

Tanya's vision shifted. Despite the darkness, intermittent flashes illuminated the surrounding sky. It reminded her of a war movie. The smell of smoke and death filled the air. She heard a low, guttural growl from her left. She turned to see a large wolf creeping toward her. A dark shape stepped out with a kind of weapon raised. She snapped back to the present.

"Tanya! Are you okay?"

"Um, yeah, I had another vision of a wolf. It was weird, like it was a war zone. The wolf was different. It was almost as tall as a person, huge."

"Wolves will eat whatever they find. Nasty beasts. How do you feel? Are you stressed from the attack?"

Tanya didn't want to mention the other visions yet. "I feel fine. I mean, I was scared last night, but now that it's over, you know. Like I said, I'm fine. What about you? I thought you'd be out on the campaign trail."

"I'm curious about the sudden increase in visions. It could be added stress, or your improved connection to the weave." Nafara ignored her question, staying on her train of thought.

"I'm not sure." She intended to be truthful, but her thoughts drifted to Amara and Sheri. Could she ever tell her everything?

"I left a package on your desk in the office. It's a scroll discussing the mathematics of magic and manipulation of the weave. It could be helpful. We have an engagement tonight, so dress for dinner, not business. I want the meeting to be short." Nafara turned away, heading for the doors opposite them. She was thankful Nafara hadn't shown the ability to read minds.

"Of course."

"You'll let me know if you have any more visions?"

"I will."

"Okay. Don't forget that we have the prototypes for Eunoia working and preliminary tests are positive. If you're dealing with trauma, even though you feel fine, there is help. No one needs to know. We could examine you without installing the device."

Tanya agreed. She wanted to stay as far away from the devices as possible. She didn't want anyone or anything poking around inside her head. "I'll think about it if it gets worse."

"Tanya, well done with the flower. Just so you know, it didn't escape me that the plant you enhanced is my favorite." She smiled with approval. "I'll see you in a few hours. I have another meeting."

Chapter 13

Yusuf removed his reading glasses, setting them on the edge of the small desk. He placed his finger on the page to hold his place, his attention drawn to the window. The building and its east and west wings surrounded the area outside on three sides. It differed from the Darul Hikmah Institute in Houston, where he would see students sitting in groups on the grass, discussing whatever topics they had for the day. Here, they had paved the grounds and decorated them with stonework, small gardens, and fountains. He had fond memories of sitting near the fountain during his time here as a student.

Knock, knock!

"Come in." He stood up, stepping away from the desk to greet his guest. A young man with a short trimmed beard entered. "Sayyid Al-Fortwani, Ayatollah Al-Wajlisi, has asked if you could join him in the primary library."

"Thank you, I'll be right there."

The young scholar left, not waiting for him to follow.

Yusuf gathered his glasses and pulled his cloak from the small closet, donning it and checking the mirror. It wouldn't do to meet the Ayatollah covered in wrinkles. He left his room and made his way to the library. Unhurried, he took time to appreciate the Persian architecture he sometimes missed back home.

Heading toward the side door, he went up the steps. It was next to the ornate glass doors, which remained closed except on special days. As he entered the building and stepped into the main hall of the Great Library of Ayatollah Al-Uzma Mar'ashi Najafi, a sigh escaped his lips as he took in the room's beauty. Bookshelves extended down both walls of the long room, from the decorated tiled ceiling to the floor. Tomes in glass cases extended along the length of the bookshelves.

A tall, thin scholar dressed similarly to him excused himself from a conversation with several younger men and approached.

"Assalamu Alaikum, Ayatollah Al-Majlisi. It's an honor to see you."

"Wa Alaikum Assalam, Ayatollah Al-Fortwani. The honor is mine." Using his new title still sounded foreign to him.

Reza stepped closer and extended his hand to guide him toward the entrance. "Yusuf, I have looked forward to meeting you. How was your flight?"

"Reza, it was good. I enjoy long flights. I find the silence, when most of the passengers are sleeping, an opportune time to read. Thanks be to Allah."

The tall scholar was older than Yusuf but looked immaculate in his dress and in the maintenance of his beard. He had achieved the status of Ayatollah over two decades prior and appeared unaffected by the passage of time.

Yusuf followed Reza out the main entrance to a door on the side he assumed went to the staff offices. He was mistaken. Reza unlocked the door with his fingerprints and a code on a keypad.

"Are we going into a vault?"

Reza chuckled. "Partially. Our oldest manuscripts are down here, but we're passing through that area to one more interesting."

True to his word, they passed by a large hall that mirrored the one above, with filled bookshelves and more glass cases. Six scholars worked and studied in the room. At the other end of the hall, he again opened a biometric lock that led to another stairway down. He paused in the small circular room, admiring the pictures of previous scholars, none of whom he recognized.

"What secrets are you keeping behind such security?"

Reza nodded. "That's not an uncommon question. See for yourself." He pushed the door open and stepped aside for Yusuf to enter, a knowing smile on his lips.

They stepped into a room that was a quarter of the size of the rooms above. The walls were plain white marble tiles with none of the elaborate design from the floors above. The shelves in this room contained ancient tomes, parchments, and scrolls. There were no glass cases here. Ornate yet comfortable chairs and desks were available, however.

"I assumed these would be some of the oldest documents, but there seem to be plenty of new books and manuscripts here." He motioned to the right side of the room.

"You are correct. Your story is among this collection."

"Mine?"

"Yes, Yusuf. Your encounter with the Ghul was thorough and provided enough detail to allow for confirmation and validation as a significant historical event."

Yusuf didn't know what to think. He had received a form letter telling him that his account had been received and forwarded to the Department of Occult Studies for review.

"I didn't receive confirmation."

Reza cocked his head. "Do you require it? You told the truth about what you experienced. Nothing sent in response would change that."

"You speak the truth, Reza, praise be to the Lord. I don't know what I was expecting. I'd never have predicted I would encounter a real Jinn."

"If the stories are to be believed, they live among us in plain sight. There are very few confirmed reports anymore, and none involving Ghul."

Yusuf thought about the revelation. His thoughts returned to Tanya. He didn't believe the official report, placing blame for the murders on the counselor. There was more to her story.

"I think she's still out there."

"The Ghul? What makes you think that?"

"It's too convenient. All the killings solved and wrapped up neatly. I saw the Jinn." He gathered his thoughts, with the image of the Jinn in his mind. "She was confident and powerful. Tall, beautiful, fierce and fearless. I prayed, and she was unfazed." He rubbed his arm. "With a scratch, she paralyzed and infected me. She reveled in the thought of killing me, mocking our faith. The Jinn taunted me and left me to die."

Reza observed him with an empathetic look and uttered, "By the grace of God, you were spared. I'm sorry for the trauma." Sorrow filled his eyes.

Yusuf smiled weakly. "Allah does not place challenges before us we can't overcome."

"Praise be to God."

Yusuf refocused. "Reza, I know she is out there, and I believe that the girl, Tanya, is still in touch with her."

"Are you sure the girl is human? Perhaps they were a pair of Jinn working together."

"I'm positive she is not a Jinn. I didn't see any signs."

"This is an interesting time. From the historical records, it would be a rare occasion for a Jinn, a Ghul, to befriend a human." Reza turned and led Yusuf further into the room, to a shelf labeled *Prophet Sulaiman*. "Are you familiar with the works of the Prophet Sulaiman?"

"Yes, I'm familiar with the writings in the Quran, including the verses concerning Prophet Sulaiman (peace be upon him). His wisdom and the stories of his interactions with the Jinn are indeed profound and insightful."

"I assumed as much. I would like you to study the accounts of his interactions with the Jinn." He turned and showed two shelves of the bookcase. "This particular tome contains stories and accounts of the life of the Prophet. Take your time. We can discuss your targets in a few days, once you've had time to read through."

"Thanks be to God. I'll do my best."

"If you'll follow me back upstairs, I'll have an assistant help you with the administration. You'll need a card. We have your information. We need record only your fingerprints and facial images."

Chapter 14

Tanya shook the hand of each Dallas City Council member. Her cheeks ached from the forced smile she held through the two-hour meeting. She watched her aunt moving with ease through the chamber, stopping to chat with each member. The reception was good, as she had expected. Nafara talked about her move to the DFW area five years prior and how she had stepped in to help her niece recover from the trauma of the serial killings. Her discussion of family and family values, commitment to mental health and recovery from trauma led her to seek further education and led to the development of the Eunoia device. By the end of the meeting, the atmosphere was positive.

She waited on the side after most of the council had left. Nafara was talking to the mayors of Dallas and Fort Worth. The latter had made it a point to meet the newest candidate, as she shared Nafara's concern for education, the homeless, and the problems associated with an open border. Tanya resisted the temptation to walk to her aunt's side, as she didn't want to attract more attention to herself and divert from their conversation. She watched the body language of the Dallas mayor and shook her head. He was polite, but his body language, added to the comments he made during the meeting, was strongly partisan. He wanted to know what she could do for him, and it looked like he had decided that "nothing" was the answer. Nafara excused herself and walked toward Tanya.

"I don't think there's going to be any convincing of that man."

"What are you going to do?"

"I'm going to try one more time. We'll have to extend our stay until the morning. I'm going to meet him for dinner." Nafara looked toward the Dallas mayor, who was roaring with laughter in discussion with his counterpart from across the metroplex. Tanya watched her aunt, noting the feral look in her eyes. She wanted to ask more but knew there was nothing to be done. He had sealed his fate.

"If it's okay, I'll just stay at our house in my old neighborhood." Tanya shuffled in place, nervous to see her aunt's reaction.

"Are you sure? We've got a room reserved," Nafara said.

"I'm sure." Tanya reaffirmed her decision with a half-hearted attempt at a smile.

"That'll be fine. We'll swing by and drop you off before I leave for dinner."

"No, I'm ok. I'll order a car. I want to clear my head. I'll just grab my flute from the car. I want to practice."

"Alright, call if you need anything. I shouldn't be too late." Nafara moved closer, and Tanya hugged her. *She is my friend.*

The Uber dropped her off in front of the house. She thanked the driver and turned to stare down the street toward the lot that had held her old home. An empty spot that stuck out in the crowded suburban setting. The lot sat vacant, a bare foundation surrounded by an overgrown yard. It clashed with the neighborhood. She suspected Nafara had something to do with the delays that had prevented construction.

She continued past, walking a few houses further up the street. Her heart ached as she got closer to the house that had been Sheri's. A copper-colored minivan sat in the driveway. She didn't get very close. A few rooms glowed with light. She imagined Sheri coming outside. Sorrow tugged at her heart.

Tanya turned back down the street toward the Vulture House, their house. A few black vultures perched on the roof, and two others circled overhead against the darkening sky. The birds didn't call out a warning, the dry raspy hiss that made her skin crawl. She went up the steps to the front door and punched in the code. As she stepped through, the interior lights came on. She smiled at the added convenience, given the primary occupant was over a thousand years old.

Tanya went to her room, noting that her luggage was beside the bed. Nafara must have had it sent ahead. She opened her flute case with the same care she had since sixth grade and assembled the instrument. She raised the instrument to her lips and played through a series of scales. Satisfied, she headed downstairs, to the last resting place of her father.

Under the stairs, she made a turn and entered the oversized laundry room. She unlocked the door to the basement and followed the stone steps down into the dark, earthen chamber. As she rounded the corner into the main room, the scent of flowers greeted her. She took in the ambiance, walking to the raised stone dais and altar in the center of the room. She ran her fingers along the top, where her father had finally paid for his crimes.

They didn't come back often, but when they did, her emotions were a jumbled mess of happiness, fear, anger, and resolve. She placed her hand on the altar. The stone was cool, with a rough texture. She pictured her father lying before her, panicking, pleading for mercy, before Nafara dealt him justice. Sadness threatened to overwhelm her as she remembered finding Sheri's necklace. Had her friend died here? Had she betrayed Sheri in the end by pledging herself to Nafara? Was there another choice? There was nowhere for her to go. Tanya allowed the emotions to clash inside, embracing the inner turmoil. She raised the flute, letting the first few notes hang in the air.

As she played, the surrounding air shimmered with new life, fed from the plants throughout the room. She could feel the music affecting them. Joy. She balanced it with thoughts of Sheri, and the mood of the room fell to misery and loneliness. Nafara came to mind, and Tanya allowed herself to imagine the loneliness she must feel at being cut off from her people, and the joy she might experience if she could reunite her with the Jinn. As she played, the weave reacted. Tiny filaments floated in the air, carried on by the melody of the song. She didn't play a particular tune, feeling the need for musical freedom as if she were in a jazz ensemble and it was her turn to riff.

She thought of the City of Brass, and Nafara realized she might never connect because they had no way of picturing the city as it could be now. Tanya pushed the thought aside and created an image of the ancient city, as Nafara had described it, floating on a sea of dunes. She imagined how the city might have developed over the years, like a time-lapse video. Tanya tried to release her biases about human nature, design, and feelings. Locked outside a world once their own, she pictured the Jinn's loneliness. The image shimmered, growing upward, and expanding. As people built higher domes, the city transformed into shining beacons. A magnificent city took form, with tall gleaming arches glowing in the sun. The buildings sparkled, and lightning seemed to jump from building to building in a neutral, flowing manner. The city expanded in all directions.

Tanya played, picking up the pace of the song and adding an underlying melody she had learned from the recital song. The sand swirled around the outer limits of the city, giving the appearance of floating among golden clouds. She continued playing, moving closer to a point in the city. The building stood tall above her. They were just like any other city, only more vibrant, and made of a glittering crystalline substance. She continued the tune and imagined herself standing at the base of a tall, domed structure. Tanya found a point in the city that seemed to hold the essence of loneliness like an anchor and focused on it, moving closer, the buildings growing around her.

She resisted the elation she felt at finding the city. The emotions at the anchor changed. A presence grabbed her attention — strong, defiant, chaotic. She wove a beckoning tune into the song and reinforced it with the smells of the flowers surrounding her. The feeling grew stronger, creeping from behind her. She turned, continuing to weave the song, smells, emotion, and sights together. A dark shape stepped from around the edge of the tower, out of her view. He was much taller than her, his hair black as night, his skin the shade of dark worn boots. His yellow eyes watched her. She sensed curiosity and a hint of desire and tried to add their essence to the song.

A connection formed. She felt the presence nearby and reached out, beckoning it closer. The mood shifted in an instant as the being's mind snapped to chaos and rage. She fumbled with the melody, and the image vanished.

Tanya stood in the underground grotto, covered in sweat. Would they have killed her? She didn't know. The rage was intense. She felt it take hold of the thread she had drawn inward, changing its place in the weave. She felt fear and exhilaration fighting for supremacy. In sorting through her thoughts, one word stuck in her mind.

Krazack.

Chapter 15

"Tanya, I have a gift for you. I'd like you to wear it for dinner tonight." Nafara handed her the box.

Tanya took the smooth, dark blue velvet jewelry box and opened it. Inside was a necklace of swirling blue stones polished into round orbs, capped and connected on each end with gold. A larger, inch-wide oval, made of the same material, hung from the bottom of the necklace, surrounded by a gold border.

"It's beautiful! It looks like a deep blue pearl necklace. Are they pearls? What are the stones? I haven't seen them before?"

"Lapis Lazuli. Do you like it?"

"I love it." She took the necklace out of the box and fastened it around her neck.

"That looks good. I think the design and color accentuate your dress."

Tanya turned to each side, examining herself in the mirror. She had chosen a navy-blue dress that mixed the businesswoman look with formal dinner wear. The necklace complemented the outfit. *Could Nafara read minds?* She had picked up the dress only yesterday. She looked to the Jinn for a response to the thought and saw nothing.

"That necklace is ancient. I don't know if a hakim of old wore it, though the stones are from that era, cleaned up with new settings."

"It's beautiful," she remarked, admiring the necklace in the mirror. "I'll be careful to return it intact."

"That's not what I meant. The necklace belongs to you. You can detach the pendant from the necklace and wear it alone. I believe those stones can enhance spiritual vision, wisdom, and truth. I would like you to wear one version or the other."

Tanya didn't feel any different and had yet to see a talisman, trinket, or anything that could affect her connection to the weave or affect Nafara.

Tanya whirled and hugged Nafara. "Thank you."

Her vision clouded in darkness for a moment, clearing to reveal an image of Nafara standing over several dead bodies, all in military fatigues, blood-soaked. Clasping the image in her mind, she refused to let it go. She turned her head, taking in the scene around her. She felt as if she were in a 3-D stop-motion image, where everything froze in time. The screens held camera feeds showing rooms, halls, and the exterior of wherever the room was. Bodies lay scattered everywhere. Her stomach turned. She wanted to understand what had happened. A melody entered her mind. She felt the music. It was a quick tune, not complicated. After it played twice, she was sure she knew the notes. The scene faded.

"Tanya, are you alright?"

Her vision came back into focus. She was sitting in a chair, with Nafara kneeling beside her.

"I had another vision." The image didn't fade from memory as dreams often did. It remained vivid, but unlike her efforts the night before when trying to connect to the City of Brass. She hadn't told Nafara, hoping to understand everything she felt, before broaching the subject.

"What did you see?"

Tanya hesitated. Should she tell Nafara? Would she be upset? Was she surprised at the content of the visions? *Not at all. Nafara was who she revealed herself to be.*

"I saw you standing in a room. It looked like a military building, American. You had blood covering your hands and arms, and your nails were out. Bodies surrounded you." Tanya looked to Nafara, hoping for some reassurance that she didn't see this as a possibility, or that she would try to avoid killing, but the Jinn remained silent.

"Do you know where this will occur?"

"I didn't recognize it." She didn't doubt it would occur. She accepted it as her fate. Many people were going to die. Could she stop it? Would Nafara allow her the freedom to look for alternatives? Am I even there? Maybe she was retaliating for their killing me? The sheer number of variables was overwhelming. She wanted to add the image to the journal she kept. Even if Nafara knew everything that went on in their lives, Tanya wanted to believe they were friends, and that Nafara would look out for her no matter what.

Nafara looked up at Tanya, her eyes on the necklace she wore, a smile showing her approval, unfazed by the graphic vision. "It doesn't matter. It won't be tonight. I need you to get ready for dinner," Nafara's voice trailed off as she looked past her. "Tanya, the path we are on won't be easy. I have shielded you from many of the things I do. With the increasing frequency of your visions, and your growing understanding, I feel it may be time that I stopped protecting you from what you don't know. If you are to rise to your full potential as a hakim, wise one, in this new age, I need you to be steeled against whatever we may face. Do you agree?"

Tanya stood and took the hand of her friend and pictured her as Yasmin. "I promised you my full support, and by the song, we're bound together. Nothing will change that."

Nafara looked at Tanya, her expression hardening. She squeezed Tanya's hand. "I will protect you with all my power. Others of your species may not be so fortunate."

Tanya's doubt yielded to the despair she felt the night her father died. She accepted her place and her love for her friend. "I understand."

"Let's get downstairs. Our guests will arrive soon."

"Wait!" She lunged for Nafara's arm, pulling her back, the Jinn turning in surprise.

"What?"

"I saw the city."

Nafara faced her. "Are you sure? What did you see?"

"It had elements of the stories you told me, the ornate domes and spires reminiscent of the most beautiful buildings of ancient Persia, their brass surfaces glowing in the sunlight. The sand swirled around the city, giving the appearance that it floated on golden clouds."

Nafara pulled her down onto the two chairs. "I only know the stories of what it was like. It sounds beautiful."

"It is. The brass spires of old were there, but among them were more modern versions, made of crystal, blue, gold and ornate, decorated with sparkling stars. There were several tall buildings with grand arcs between them, lightning dancing among their highest spires. I'm not sure of everything I saw, but your people have expanded the city until it extended to the horizon in all directions."

Nafara sat quietly, her eyes filled with wonder. "I knew it! Why would they be stuck in time? As much as humans have advanced here, why wouldn't my people continue to advance? Oh, the wonders that must exist. It's beyond comprehension. Did you see any of my people?"

"I didn't see anyone, but I felt a presence. I lost it before I could find them."

"This is very promising. If you can picture the location, you're one step closer to opening a path between their city and ours."

Chapter 16

Krazack wandered the streets of the abandoned old quarter of the city. His cackling laugh echoed off the metal, stone, and crystalline walls. He ran haltingly down the street in what looked like a speed shuffle. He stumbled, closing his eyes as a piercing pain erupted within his head. His scream pierced the afternoon air. At least the voices were silent. Were they plotting against him? He paused, placing his hand on the wall at the base of a tall parapet. His legs shook with the effort to keep him upright as the pain intensified.

A sweet smell wafted through the air. Krazack snapped his head around, searching for the source. He felt the air moving between the buildings and turned, shuffling into the slight breeze. The smell was something he had not smelled in centuries. It contained fruits, and some others he didn't recognize. He started forward again, his pace shuffled as his body reacted to the pain in his head.

Concentrating on the scent, instinct took over. He pressed forward, attempting to ignore the pain. His posture shifted, his muscles acting on instinct, becoming more feline. The pain lessened as the scent grew in power and his body adjusted to the hunt. *What is this unfamiliar smell?*

He slowed as he approached another turn in the streets as the sound of foreign music reached him. It surpassed anything he'd ever heard, filled with a gentle melody, and the musician's vulnerability. The traits of prey. He crept around the corner. His tense muscles relaxed as he approached the woman from behind. *Was she prey?* He felt something foreign, soft. Krazack paused, confused. The air moved about her, encompassing the harsh foreign smells and sweet fruit. Her scent was stronger, and her appearance otherworldly. *Who is this woman? She is not Jinn. Could she be human?* He observed her as he would a flower. Admiring her beauty, careful not to chase her away.

Mine!

The voices inside him warred. One whispering in reason, another shrieking for blood. Pain erupted in his head, and he reached for the woman as her image shimmered and faded from sight, her scent the only remaining proof that she was real.

[No!]

Mine!

Pain shot down his spine as a cacophony of voices erupted in his head, each claiming dominion over the woman who was no longer present. He took a deep breath, sniffing the air to capture her scent. He ran from side to side in the street, trying to absorb everything left behind.

-No! Mine!-

Convinced there was nothing remaining, he sat down and stared at the spot on the road where the woman had been before she disappeared.

Was this an additional punishment? Torture? Where did she go? He closed his eyes, recalling her scent, the music, and her appearance.

I will have her.

Krazack remained motionless, the pain subsiding as he focused on the ghost of the woman who had entered his world. He felt hunger grow in his stomach but pushed it aside. Nothing would distract him from finding this woman. She will see in me all that she desires. I will become the person I used to be.

She will join me at my side.

She will love me, as I love her. I brought this beauty into my world.

-She is a gift provided to me alone to ease my suffering.-

-Yes! She will end my suffering.-

-She will comfort me and keep the pain away.-

My redemption is at hand. The fire that burns in me will burn for her!

He didn't notice the shift of wind from above. A figure dressed in the maroon uniform of the dātabara, the givers of law, enforcers of justice. The figure observed until the sun set. The behavior was uncharacteristic.

Krazack sensed the dātabara behind and above him. He detected the familiar scent of his watcher. She was no threat to him as he sat in the street.

What if she was here because of the woman?

[She is going to steal her!]

She wants to deny your love!

[She is a threat to you.]

-It's forbidden. There are laws.-

What laws?

-There is nothing above love.-

We must heed the heart.

The dātabara will steal her from you.

-The pain will come back.-

[You will suffer pain and loss.]

-You must not!-

Watch.

The voices went silent. Krazack wailed into the night air.

Why have I been forsaken? Tears flowed from his eyes. He lay in the street on his side, body shaking from grief. Though overwhelmed, he felt the dātabara approach. He increased his wailing and projected his pain. He adjusted, setting his legs underneath. *She is curious, too much so.* He pounced, his muscles exploding, covering the distance between them in an instant. He grabbed her arm above the elbow and held his other hand over her mouth. Her mighty blows pounded his ribs, fueling his anger.

His eyes flared with hot intensity. Her uniform and skin below his grip blackened in the heat of his focused touch. He saw the pain in her eyes and welcomed it, intensifying the fire.

-You will not take her from me. She will be mine.-

He felt her muffled screams of agony in his hand.

[Kill her!]

Fire, feed the fire!

Ha, ha, ha, ha! The voices echoed in his head. The fire intensified, spreading through her body. As the spark of life left her eyes, he let go, letting the burned body fall to the ground. He looked at her for a moment before sitting and staring at the spot the woman had been. Thoughts of the dātabara were already gone from him. He focused on the memory of the woman, the music, and her scent.

Chapter 17

"What were the results of the latest tests?" Nafara stood over the researchers huddled around a screen looking at a detailed 3-D map of a brain. She could see the Eunoia device and its transmissions.

"Eight of the ten subjects are showing progress in remapping the neural pathways," Dr. Gutierrez said, his gaze focused on the data.

"What is going on with the other two?" Nafara asked.

Dr. Gutierrez adjusted the image, swiping across and selecting another of the patient profiles. He enhanced the image on the screen. "I believe it's in the nature of their trauma. All test subjects are veterans with similar mental traits in how their minds have adapted to the traumatic memories. These two individuals are resisting the remapping of the pathways. They were injured in IED attacks, both were in comas."

Nafara examined the image. "What is going on here? What are the yellow regions?" She pointed to the image on the screen.

"Those areas are signaling the amygdalae, amplifying the emotional response, instead of helping regulate it."

"I want to see them. One at a time."

"Of course." The doctor nodded to an assistant, who typed something into a tablet.

He scrolled back to the main screen and showed her the results of the other test subjects. She nodded along as he described each patient. It was his research that had led to this breakthrough, but he didn't remember it that way. She had met Hector after an extensive search for breakthroughs in emotional and psychological influencing technologies. It hadn't taken long to understand the implications of Hector's theories, and to find an engineer capable of building the Eunoia device.

After she observed the other seven subjects, the researcher returned. "Doctors, the two subjects are standing by."

Nafara followed the young woman into the first room, letting Dr. Gutierrez enter first.

"Hello Jacob, how are you feeling?" Hector said as he sat down across from the man.

The large man's left leg was missing, and burns had left scars on the dark skin of his left arm and the left side of his face. He wore army-green shorts and a black T-shirt.

"I feel like shit, Doc. I still can't sleep while all the other motherfuckers are bragging about how good they have it." Nafara smelled his pheromones. He was going to be difficult; his defensive instincts were active.

"I'm sorry to hear that. This is Dr. Nafara Kavioni, the founder of this company. She is concerned about your resistance to the treatment and would like to ask you a few questions."

"Sure, why not?" Jabob sat back, crossing his arms.

Nafara stepped closer. "Jacob, what are you feeling at this moment?"

Jacob looked at her and didn't hide his gaze as it wandered from her eyes, down her body. "I can't get sleep. I hear a buzz in my head. Not my ears, but in my head." He tapped the side of his head, emphasizing each word.

"When did it start?"

"Right after I got the device. I had insomnia before, but the buzzing is driving me bat-shit."

"Okay, we're going to adjust the setting."

He winced and closed his eyes for a moment. "Yeah, whatever, I'm gonna drop out if you can't help. This is too much."

Nafara nodded to Dr. Gutierrez, who adjusted the setting on his tablet. "I'm going to place my hand on the side of your head."

Jacob gritted his teeth and nodded. Nafara placed her hand above the small device. She felt the energy of the device flowing into his mind. She shifted the illusion over her eyes to reflect a look of concern. Behind the illusion, she closed her eyes and reached into his mind. She couldn't read his thoughts, but she could feel his emotions. "Reduce the frequency in all zones, disable zones one and six." By adding her strength to it, she guided the energy. She saw the pathways regenerating. She felt her strength fade. This was something she didn't do often enough as it exhausted her. She took her hand away and shifted her illusion back to normal.

"How do you feel?"

"Better. The buzzing is still there, but it is maybe a third of what it was."

"Doctor, what do the readings show?"

"His brain is responding. You did it again. Your insight is amazing. Rerouting away from those two zones shielded him from the emotional response associated with the trauma."

"Not insight. I saw the problem areas on the model of his brain we looked at."

"It's still an interesting approach. I think we can improve the effectiveness of the treatment by blocking emotional responses. If we can inject a sense of calm instead of their normal response to the trauma, it would be a significant breakthrough."

"If we can do that, we can get this out to everyone and keep them calm all the time," Nafara said.

Dr. Gutierrez chuckled nervously. "I don't think the FDA would approve that. We already have two investigations going on regarding the potential for manipulation or control."

Nafara looked down at Jacob, who they had almost forgotten was in the room. He lay back in his chair, a stuttering snore escaping his open mouth.

"That should keep him in the program for now, watch his settings, and let him sleep through the night."

Dr. Gutierrez nodded and motioned for the junior assistants to help Jacob.

"I don't have time to get to the last patient. Look for the blockages like what Jacob's model showed and apply a similar change. I've got to get home. We've got our first rally tonight."

"Dr. Kavioni, good luck. I'll call you later if we run into any difficulties."

"Thank you, Hector."

Nafara left the lab and got into the back of the extended car. "Did you retrieve the route Tanya took home the other night?"

"Yes, ma'am. I pulled it off her GPS," her driver replied.

"Take me to the field she stopped at." Was there something else at work here, and it was sending two messages, the vision of a shaman, teaching her knowledge she sought, and the attack from the wolves? Although unrelated, their mysterious connection is perplexing.

"Yes, ma'am."

Forty minutes later, the car pulled off the side of the road. A car passed them. It was one of only a handful they had seen since leaving the lab. Nafara got out of the car, looking across the field of yellow flowers.

Why would you stop here?

She walked into the field, toward the small open area further into the field, toward the tree line. As she stepped into the circular open area, she looked around for anything out of the ordinary. She sniffed the air, wrinkling her nose at the smell of wolves.

"Filthy beasts," she snarled. *They wouldn't dare challenge me.*

Nafara kneeled, placing her hand in the dirt. Nothing here. There were no signs of anyone else. Was it possible that Tanya wasn't telling her the truth? No, despite all that had happened, she was loyal. She stood and looked around one more time before heading back to the car.

"Take me home." While it was strange, the hakimah had survived and learned from the encounters. It was a satisfactory outcome. Still, she felt an urge to hunt the wolf pack down. The small pack yielded only eight distinct scents. Maybe she would come back to hunt when she had more time.

"Yes, ma'am."

Chapter 18

Yusuf turned the page and read the passage again. He took his time going over each word, making sure he understood the author's meaning. The transliteration notes helped fill in the reasoning and allowed him to make his own conclusions. He refilled his teacup from a nearby pot to prevent any accidental spills on the ancient texts. He closed the testament of the Prophet Sulaiman. The Quran and the ancient texts he had read provided a better picture of the Prophet Sulaiman and his control of the Jinn.

He stood, stretched, and started his walk around the room. In awe, he marveled at the potential knowledge hidden away from the rest of the world. Countless unknown texts and scrolls filled the shelves. Reza had provided him with access to everything in the room. He had spent the last two days poring over the Book of Solomon, which described each engagement of the prophet with a demon. The records documented over one hundred instances. Following each encounter, the Prophet ordered the Jinn to help build Jerusalem and then questioned others. It must have been an exciting time.

As he shuffled back to his desk, he caught sight of Reza. The dim light from the lamps cast a serene glow throughout the room. Reza's smile expanded as he approached.

"Greetings, Yusuf. Peace be with you," Reza offered, his voice calm and respectful.

Yusuf paused, returning the smile. "And with you, Reza. How are you this morning?"

"I am well," he stated as he approached the desk. Reza looked at the tome that sat open on the table. "Ah, the judgments. It is interesting, is it not? How methodical the prophet was."

"Yes, with all due reverence, it feels like a recollection of job interviews."

Reza laughed, his voice carrying through the room. "I hadn't thought of it that way. But you are correct."

"There were far more than I expected. One led to another down the line. If this is true, it explains the rapid growth of the city."

"I believe it to be true. The accounts don't clarify the difference between demons and Jinn. To the people in that time, they wouldn't understand the difference between the two."

Yusuf cocked his head slightly, nodding.

"What are you thinking?"

"Demons retreat to hell, only to return later to cause problems for us. I wonder whether the Jinn have the opportunity for redemption, or were they locked away by the prophet Sulaiman as the final judgment? There is no redemption for demons, but for Jinn, there is. The Prophet described the opportunity to convert to Islam, and by some accounts, many did."

"I follow your reasoning. What has your attention?"

"Why did this Jinn, this Ghul, choose that time and place to reveal herself?"

"But did she reveal herself?"

Yusuf thought for a moment. "No. I was supposed to die."

"But you don't know what happened. Your report states that the sun broke through the clouds and blinded you. The toxin in your system overwhelmed you. Later, you wake up in the hospital and the Ghul was gone." Reza held his gaze, his lips pressed together. "I would like to help you remember, if you are up to it."

A pit formed in his stomach. Thinking about the incident still filled him with fear. He knew in his heart that Allah had saved him, somehow. Did he need to know how? No, but something scratched at his interest, a feeling that someone had helped him get away and hide him from the Jinn.

Yusuf sat up straight. "I would like to know what happened."

Reza nodded and indicated one of the more comfortable chairs. "Sit here."

Yusuf sat in the chair. The cushions were soft, and the back reclined. It wasn't fully a recliner but was comfortable in its similar design.

Reza's tone became more monotone, with emphasis on certain words, creating a rhythmic beat. "Relax and close your eyes. Let me know when you are ready, then listen to my voice."

Yusuf closed his eyes and took a series of deep breaths. He relaxed his muscles as if he were trying to fall asleep. "I'm ready, Reza."

Yusuf slowed his breathing to match the counting and relaxed as Reza walked him through focusing on each area of his body.

"Focus on my voice." The rest of the sounds of the room—air conditioning, dehumidifiers, and the slight buzz from the desk lights—all faded. Yusuf couldn't help but listen. All other sounds faded into the background.

"Yusuf, think back to your encounter with the Ghul. You will not feel fear. When the image is clear in your mind, tell me what happened."

Yusuf described the scene as he followed the sound in the house to a room upstairs. He described Nafara, her appearance, smell, and her voice. Her mocking tone throughout the conversation, and her last words as she positioned him in the backyard, looking up at the gathering of vultures.

He prayed, "Allah is with me. I am his faithful servant. Have mercy on my soul. Grant me strength, oh Lord." He repeated the prayer as the vultures watched. The sun broke through the clouds, burning his eyes, blocking out everything he saw.

"What do you see?"

"The sun. It's burning my eyes. I can't turn my head. I know the vultures will come for me soon." His body tensed, reacting to the memory.

"You are protected. Allah watches over the faithful. Look through the light. What do you see?"

Yusuf's breathing increased. He tried to focus, but the sun was too bright. "I can't."

Reza commanded him. "Yusuf Ahmed Al-Fortwani. You will open your eyes and tell me what you see."

Yusuf felt obligated to do what he was told. He looked into the light, and it evolved into the shape of a person. The bright light was emanating from them. "Someone is standing over me. I cannot see who it is. The light is not from the sun, it is radiating from the person standing over me. I cannot make out any features. They are kneeling beside me, and I feel their hands on my skin. It is wonderful, calming, peaceful. I feel myself being picked up and carried."

Yusuf's eyes flew open. "It can't be. Praise be to Allah."

Reza held his gaze when he turned to the older scholar. "Allah, praise be upon Him, sent an angel in answer to your prayers."

Yusuf wept. Praising God for saving his life. Why? He wasn't worthy of such attention.

"This has been a traumatic experience for you. I think you should rest. Now, we have a better understanding of what is happening. I need to think on this revelation. I will send for you once you've rested, and I've gathered what I need."

"Thank you, Reza. I will take my leave. I feel drained and unworthy of this blessing."

Both men stood, silence hanging in the air between them as each considered what they now knew.

Chapter 19

Tanya sat on a shaded bench overlooking one of the koi ponds. Families crowded the Japanese garden, visiting while school was out for the summer. The cool feel of the shaded stone was comforting in the warm summer air. Someone had placed it with care to ensure it remained in the shade. She could see the large koi swimming along, hoping for someone to drop a treat for them.

She envied the fish. Their simple lives. Search for food, stay cool, avoid danger. She wanted to reach out, to sense their contribution to the weave. No, she was pushing herself too hard, which is why she was here, searching for calm tranquility. She had bags under her eyes from restless nights haunted by visions. Images of the ancient city were always nearby. Did it have something to do with Nafara? A splash near the shore distracted her from her thoughts.

She dreamed about the city she had seen with its smooth, spiraling towers. In her dream, there was a presence, a dark figure just out of sight, watching her, waiting to see what she would do next. The dream changed, but the presence was always there. Did it have something to do with the visions she had of Nafara? She didn't know.

Tanya understood Nafara had her plans and she wouldn't let anything get in the way. Were her visions likely or absolute? Could she change her visions? How was she supposed to know whether she was doing the right thing? Nothing in the documents Nafara provided gave much insight into the role or potential of a hakimah. Google offered a few sentences about the Persian origin of the word and their ties to the priest caste responsible for interpreting omens, dreams, and performing rituals, but that was it, unless you wanted to travel down conspiracy theorist rabbit holes on the age of enlightenment and spiritual attunement.

Should she take them more seriously? What would they think of her? She was supposed to interpret signs and portents from astrology, which was more difficult to accept. She understood science, math, and music. Formulas produced clear results. Accepting a celestial body's movement in connection with a terrestrial event proved challenging. She wasn't willing to go that far in all of this. Jinn exist, which until five years before she would never have believed, but she had proof. She had asked about other supernatural beings, but Nafara deflected at every opportunity. Modern texts from fringe scientists talked about Jinn being responsible for all of humanity's fables and tales of fairies, elves, ghosts, goblins, vampires, and every other thing that went bump in the night.

If we could attribute all the tales throughout history to the Jinn in various forms, there would be a wealth of information. In that case, it was too much. If true, would she unleash our worst nightmares on Earth? She couldn't. She wouldn't be responsible for that level of chaos. Nafara insisted her goal was to free her imprisoned people. In truth, Tanya hadn't found a credible apocalyptic story that talks about the monsters from our nightmares being unleashed.

Nafara's presence loomed in her visions of the civilian and military carnage. It still may not have been her. She had never seen her friend conduct a mass act of violence. She heard Sheri's voice in her head. *Well, except for the massacre in the church meeting room.* Tanya felt guilt creep in. It had all been part of the plan to 'save' her. It was necessary. Just like her current obsession with politics.

She rose and walked down the path to a small, wooden, arched bridge over the water. She paused at the top and looked down at the koi. What are they thinking? Her curiosity overcame her hesitancy. Upon opening her mind, she witnessed the filaments materialize around everything. She had gained more control, at least in her perception of what the filaments looked like. She concentrated on the filaments, decreasing their intensity. The amount of associated glow made the intricate pattern of filaments look like threads. The image of the woman in the field flashed in her mind. It made sense and reminded her of creating braids and weaves at summer camp when she was little.

She reached for the filaments of a white koi, adjusting its glow. The fish swam towards the lily pads. Tanya wove its threads with those of the plants, trying to replicate the woman in her vision. The filaments resisted at first, then joined into a thicker thread. But the weave was wrong. The fish thrashed, struggling for air. She tried to undo the joining, but was too late. It ballooned, then burst. Blood spread through the water. People gasped, phones raised. The red color's spread was more rapid and expansive than expected. A bloody thickness coated the pond. Frightened, the other fish sensed something foreign nearby. They swam away toward the open area of the large pond, with the red liquid following them.

More people were gathering along the path, watching the red path spread. Several of them had their phones out, recording the incident. The red stain in the water continued to spread in both directions, moving into an adjoining larger pond, and back up the small connecting waterway under the bridge. It took less than half-an-hour for all the water to turn red.

A park attendant approached, her eyes wide. "What happened here?"

"Red fungal bloom," she heard one say. "But I've never seen it happen this fast." It wasn't a fungus. They would soon figure out it was blood.

The attendants tried to call for help from their environmental group to save the fish, but there wasn't enough time. Tanya looked out at the gruesome scene of a pond filled with blood, topped by several dozen dead fish.

She fled the park, weighed down by guilt. She had killed them all, the fish. Although she tried to help, she was unsuccessful. The terror they must have felt as they suffocated in blood haunted her thoughts.

That's not true. I didn't mean to.

To what? Kill them all. Is that what Nafara will tell you when she kills all the people in that military facility?

Chapter 20

"I don't understand why you are upset. They're fish." Nafara waved away the comment.

"I killed them. They were living creatures. I did something and killed them. Look!" Tanya pointed to the news. A commentator was talking about the bizarre fungal bloom at the Zilker Botanical Garden that resulted in killing all the fish in the Japanese Garden. The video from a drone showed the park attendants working to collect the fish.

Tanya turned up the volume.

They expect the cleanup to take weeks. The exhibit will be closed while officials investigate the event.

The image shifted to the reporter, who was in a cordoned-off area with a large gathering of people behind him. One held up a sign with Revelations 16:4 written in red marker. Nafara turned to the screen. "That we can't have!"

"What?"

She went to the screen and tapped the man holding the sign. "That! I don't need people getting it into their heads that the end times are coming. We don't need the additional attention."

"That's normal. There's always someone with a sign quoting a Bible verse, prophesying the end of times."

"I understand that. But we do not need 'end of times' talk to draw unwanted attention to what we're doing."

Tanya wasn't sure what Nafara was getting worked up about, but she didn't offer an explanation, either. It wasn't a big deal because most people would ignore it and move on with their lives. What bothered her was that Nafara didn't care that she had killed everything in the water.

Nafara turned away and began pacing. Tanya watched her, waiting for Nafara to share her thoughts.

She stopped, looking out the window at the open lawn below. "I think you should limit your practice to controlled environments."

Tanya's sadness about the fish changed to anger. She held her tongue, not wanting to anger Nafara, but she needed to speak her mind. She thought about what she wanted to say before speaking. "I know you're mad, but I don't have much to go on here. I'm piecing things together from YouTube videos, trial and error, and very little from the texts you've provided me. Besides visions of the golden lady, and instinct, I'd say I'm doing pretty good. Yes, I'm sad for the fish, but I am trying."

"Tanya, I am doing what I can to help you. Your instincts have been amazing. You learn with every advance you make. These things will happen. I'm not chastising you, or upset. I'm trying to keep you from becoming YouTube famous. Am I holding you back?"

Her anger subsided a little. "No, you aren't, but I think it would help if I knew what you wanted me to do and what my role is in whatever your plans are. I know I'm a hakimah, Magus, or whatever, but what the hell does that even mean?"

Nafara's gaze was intense but not threatening. "You have a basic understanding of the weave. As you've seen, everything is connected. From what my elders taught me, there were more people connected in the past, but your kind has lost it, or more accurately, abandoned it. Because of our inherent link, my people can do things that appear supernatural to you, such as flying, shadow-walking, and even how I feed. Those are instinctual. When humans were created, I believe your connection to the weave was weakened. I am sure there are things written to explain all of that, but it is ancient history. Your people loved to burn libraries and destroy knowledge that was counter to their beliefs."

"What am I doing? Why did you need me?"

"We don't manipulate the weave. We understand it as much as you know how and why you breathe. Your link to the weave allows for manipulation of the weave. You are familiar with King Solomon?"

"Yes, from Sunday school when I was little. He was wise."

"What your religion doesn't teach anymore is that he was a magus. Humans think of the weave as magic, some mystical force. How would you explain filaments and threads to another person? They think it's magic. You are learning to manipulate the weave, which is the essence of what things are. You are the first legitimate hakimah, I have found in over a thousand years. I need you because it was another hakim like you who sealed my people in their city. He used the weave to block the pathway. I have searched for his seal, and it must be lost. Only you can open a portal."

Tanya thought about the explanation. It made sense, despite everything she had known of her world until she had met Nafara in her Yasmin persona. "I think I understand the problem, and I'm learning the basics of the filaments themselves. What I don't know is how to combine or manipulate them. Where is that knowledge?"

"I suspect there is a repository of ancient texts and knowledge, but it is impenetrable."

"Even for you?"

"Specifically, for me."

"Where is it?"

"The Vatican. Christianity takes a harsh view of magic. Look up Deuteronomy 18. Everything you talked about in trying to figure out your role as a wise one is forbidden."

"What about other religions?"

"That's where I am focusing my efforts. There is another place, but I would need to return home, and I haven't been back in a very long time." She looked out the window again.

"Then we need to go there."

"No, I have a contact. I haven't written in decades, but he may be able to help."

"That's it? If it were that easy, why didn't you ask sooner?"

"There are complications."

Tanya held her hands up, waiting for her to continue.

"I am not the only one of my kind that didn't get locked away. The Prophet Muhammad presented my kind with the chance to convert to Islam when he received the teachings of the Quran. We are like your people. We have free will to choose the path of our lives, our beliefs, and what the consequences may be. I'm telling you this because the person I need to talk to converted to Islam."

"Wouldn't his long life make it obvious?" She knew the answer as the words left her lips. "Shapeshifting and illusion. I got it. Will he help you?"

"I don't know. We need to get ready. The car will be out front in an hour. I didn't expect to tell you this much this soon. I'm not hiding information for any reason other than not wanting to overwhelm you."

"Taking care of me?"

"The knowledge of my existence alone has driven some to insanity."

"I've learned from you. I can take it."

Nafara stopped at the doorway and looked back over her shoulder. "We'll see. The path ahead is dangerous. I can't promise people won't get hurt or killed."

Tanya crossed the room. "You have my loyalty, but I don't want to hurt anyone we don't have to."

Nafara took her hand and squeezed. "I know."

Chapter 21

Yusuf turned his head to the right. "Peace and mercy of Allah be upon you." He turned his head to the left and repeated the phrase. He got up, gathered his items, returning them to their places. The room was pleasant, plain, and quiet. He chuckled to himself at the thought of returning to his office. Farid would occasionally chide him, more so now as they were closer. He knew where everything was and had taken some gratification in sending Farid in to find a manuscript, or item he wanted, knowing it would take him some time to find it.

He opened his laptop and saw the airport notification, which stated the reservations were set for two days from then. The information and knowledge he had gained provided some insight, but since their discussion of the Prophet Sulaiman, Reza had been unavailable. Yusuf had received two notes from the Ayatollah recommending he study a pair of books, one on the chronology of Jinn, and another discussing the fallen families, which included the Al-Hiyal family, which had been quite prominent, despite their lack of engagement with the politics of the time. He recalled the shock he felt at seeing the symbol for the Al-Hiyal family on the page while recalling the grisly scene at the Qadir family home.

Knock-knock-knock.

"Come in."

He waited for the door to open. When it didn't, he shuffled across the room and opened the door. An envelope was taped to his door. Removing it, he found it blank. He looked down the hall in both directions. It was quiet. Everyone should have been completing their prayers. Closing the door behind him, he opened the envelope. A smaller square envelope was inside with a blue wax seal.

He didn't recognize the symbol pressed into the wax. He turned the envelope over, not seeing any other marks or script. Breaking the seal, he opened the envelope and retrieved a card. He paused as a bitter, pungent, smoky smell wafted up. He looked in the envelope and saw nothing else inside.

Sayyid Yusuf Ahmed Al-Fortwani

May the blessings of Allah be upon you.

We invite you to join the Society of Al-Batin

9:00, 42 Al-Mustafa Street,

Darvazeh Qal'eh Neighborhood

Yusuf examined the card, bringing it close to his reading lamp. He looked at his watch. In order to make it on time, he would need to hurry. He threw on his cloak and turban, checking himself out in the mirror before heading out. He didn't know what it was about, but he had a sneaking suspicion it had something to do with his research and Reza's absence.

Yusuf arrived just before the top of the hour, sweating from the rushed pace. The address led to a door like all the others in this row. To both sides, they were identical. The neighborhood was quiet and empty. It was as if the living portions of the city had left this one locale to itself. He reached for the door and hesitated, the memory of entering the cursed house haunted him. Could this be a trick of the Jinn to get him away from the seminary? Perhaps they thought he knew too much about their presence. He pulled his hand back from the handle and knocked. Was this a trap? Unease encroached on his mind. *Let them come to me.*

He heard a bolt slide, and then another. The door opened, and a young man with a commanding, militaristic look about him stood in the opening. Yusuf and the man stood looking at each other. The younger man held his gaze, unwavering. Was he waiting for something?

Yusuf reached into his cloak, retrieved the invitation, and passed it to the man. The man held his hand out, stopping him.

"Take a deep breath from the invitation." The man's stoic expression remained.

Yusuf did as instructed, trying not to make too much of a face at the pungent smell. The younger man nodded and stepped aside to let him in.

It was a home, decorated as any typical Iranian home in the city would be, modest and neat. A Quran sat next to the couch in the living room. If it weren't for the strange entrance ritual and the military man, he would have thought he was in the wrong place. He followed the man through the house and out what looked like the back door. It instead led to a hallway that went for another fifteen feet before reaching a set of stairs leading down to a larger room that must be underground. It resembled the seminary's occult library.

Reza and a few other men sat around an octagonal black wood table inlaid with the symbol from the wax. The men sat on large cushions.

"As-salamu alaykum, you are among friends. Please join us." Reza indicated an empty chair at the table.

Yusuf sat, taking in the men around the table.

"Yusuf, I apologize for the caution. Let me explain. We are members of The Society of Al-Batin. Our order has existed for over a hundred generations. The Prophet Sulaiman (peace be upon him) created us after he regained his throne. Strengthened by his faith, he understood the solemn duty to protect his people from the evil Jinn. He gathered the Jinn in the City of Brass and closed the doorway between our worlds, locking them away. It is our responsibility to ensure that the doorway between their realm and ours is never opened."

Yusuf sat in wonder at this revelation. Were it not for his encounter with the Ghul, he would not have believed the story. He cleared his throat and took a sip from the glass of water before him. "I admit my reluctance to accept this story. If it weren't for my encounter, I certainly would not. What evidence do you have that would lead you to believe that this threat still exists today, thousands of years later? From the time of the Prophet Muhammad (peace be upon him), there have been no indications within Islam that what you describe is a possibility."

Reza nodded as he spoke. "We have all been where you are now, though I admit you are the only one of us to encounter a living Jinn. Others in our society have discovered or identified potential people who may be Jinn, only to have all traces of their existence disappear. Our concern is that the one you encountered was in the open, and chanced discovery. We believe something must have changed for one of them to have revealed themselves."

Yusuf shook his head. "As far as I know, she thinks I am dead. I don't believe she revealed herself. I believe there is a person, a girl, that may still have contact with the Jinn, but we have seen nothing like what happened in the other city, no killings."

The man next to Reza leaned in, whispering to Reza, who nodded. "Yusuf, this is Mullah Hassan al-Kazemi."

"Ayatollah Al-Fortwani, I know this information stretches the imagination. All of us around the table at one time in our lives believed the stories to be myths, tales to scare wayward children. Reza speaks the truth. While your tale is the only validated proof of their existence, sightings have significantly increased over the past decade."

"Esteemed colleagues, I don't doubt your sincerity. The attendance of Reza alone lends enough credibility for me to believe. Do you believe someone is actively seeking to open the portal?" He shuddered at the thought of a thousand Ghul released on the world, not to mention all the other species.

Reza held his hand up to reclaim the conversation. The others deferred to him. "The Prophet Sulaiman believed the Jinn were a threat to humanity. They possessed abilities that gave them an advantage in most things. An enraged Jinn could tear through an

96

army without the proper weapons to stop them. Imagine a world with two species vying for dominance."

Yusuf thought of the stories he had read, of Sulaiman enslaving the Jinn to build Jerusalem faster and grander than men were capable. He didn't want to know that even one more Ghul was alive. "What do you require of me?"

Reza smiled. "We would like you to be the representative of the order in America. Search for evidence of the Ghul and recruit local members that you trust to keep our secret."

Yusuf thought about it. He would ask Farid to join and would need to press for contact with Tanya. "I accept."

"Excellent. We plan to delay your return. I will draft a letter to your school, the Institute, about the necessity for you to remain for a while longer." He motioned to the shelves around the room. "You should begin your indoctrination immediately. Get to know all the other council members and begin your studies."

"It is like being back in seminary."

"I expect this will not test your faith as much as increase the understanding of the power of Allah."

Chapter 22

Tanya pulled the white Rice University T-shirt over her head and down, letting it hang over her faded blue jeans. She grabbed perfume from the counter, spraying two times in the air and leaning in. She didn't need it, but she had developed the habit since she had been invited to several no-notice lunches with potential donors. Nafara wanted her involved in the campaign but recognized the necessity of her continuing to learn her craft. It was just past eight in the morning, which meant she had time to try something new. She had watched *The Fifth Element* last night and decided to try using the four 'prime elements.' She laughed at herself. The slight doubt compelled her to try it, despite its absurdity.

She headed downstairs, stopping to start the garden sprinklers on her way to the garage. She gathered everything she needed and set it outside. The familiar scent of cinnamon greeted her as she entered. Nafara left a note that their newest partner, the CEO of a large natural gas company, had delivered the cinnamon rolls this morning. In parentheses, she wrote, 'They're safe, enjoy.'

Tanya took one of the large rolls and made a cup of tea. The bitter tea contrasted with the sweetness of the pastry, making a pleasant breakfast. She acknowledged that Nafara's tea might be growing on her.

As she sat enjoying her meal, her thoughts drifted back to the presence she had felt in the City of Brass. The source eluded her, but its power was undeniable. She felt she was on the right path. Switching to view the weave was becoming easier. With a thought, she could turn it on and off, bringing the bright filaments into view. She looked at the cinnamon roll in her hand and saw the intertwined sensory essences woven together. She thought of intensifying the taste but didn't understand the ratios of each variable that created the resulting flavor. Her mind flashed to the fish from the previous week, and she let the weave fade from view. Later. For now, she needed to work on the portal. She finished her meal and went to the garden.

Tanya stood at the edge of the circle, letting the mist from the sprinklers drift around her, evaporating in the warm air as it touched her skin. She pushed the tiki torch into the ground, on the north point of the circle. She adjusted the tall torch flame to be at eye height. Stepping back, she verified its alignment. Satisfied, she repeated the process three more times, marking the four cardinal points on the circle. The flames writhed in the mist, as if trying to avoid the moisture. She pulled a remote control from her pocket and started the fans blowing toward the circle, creating a counter-clockwise flow of air. That was it, all four.

Tanya retrieved her flute from a small table outside the circle and closed her eyes. With her mind open, she saw the filaments extending around her. The music guided her movements. As the music played, she commanded the sand to flow with majestic power, creating two pillars of shifting sands that rose from the ground. She wove in a flowing melody that twisted and turned like the eddies of a river, moving the mist between the grains of sand. She launched into a fast pace, almost out-of-control countermelody that threatened to consume the other melodies. The flames extended from the torches and flowed around the sand columns, playing a cat-and-mouse game with the water, which shifted to allow it to flow while countering another. She once more changed the melody, keeping the three going, adding the airy, ethereal tones of a whispering breeze.

She opened her eyes and saw the pillars of sand, strengthened from within by the water, and on the outside from the fire, creating a glass coating to the columns. The air swirled in an oval between the pillars. The entire structure was a lattice of intertwined filaments, not connected, but building on the strength of the others. Driven by a need for confirmation, she explored her bond with the being. She reached out, seeking the chaotic spirit. She pushed aside her fear and embraced the feeling of desire she had felt. A small flame appeared in the center of the vortex, swirling between the pillars.

Something pulled her forward. Continuing to play the melody, she allowed the four melodies to intertwine, her fingers moving with purpose across the flute. She focused on maintaining the portal and allowed a brief distraction to loop the filaments of sand around her feet. As she reinforced her body against the pull, she stood tall, letting her thoughts flow down the filament she now saw, reaching through the vortex, wrapping around her. She loosened its hold but didn't let it go. Taking control, she concentrated on uncovering where it would lead. She saw the scene from within the City of Brass take shape as the swirling air shimmered.

The polished buildings, domes, and spires gleamed as the sun shone upon them. A radiant glow filled the garden as the bright light streamed through the portal. She felt something slip. The balance shifted. She could feel control of the four elements slipping. Tanya willed the portal to open, attempting to hold the shape before her. Her throat dried, and she knew she wouldn't be able to continue playing, losing this moment. She expected to feel it slip away, but it didn't. The elements seemed to rebel against her manipulation and fought against being near their opposites. She closed her eyes at the flash from the portal, raising her arm to shield her face. Heat washed over her. Tanya dropped to her knees. The song ceased, and a force knocked her to the ground. As she fell, she felt the blast of sand on her exposed skin.

The air was scorching. Spots filled her eyes as she heard the sizzle of the mist hitting flame.

Chapter 23

Krazack felt the hair on the back of his neck stand as the electricity in the air became palpable. His muscles tensed, his eyes focused on the spot the portal had appeared days before. He felt a connection with the woman on the other side. She was looking for him. Who was she? There was no hakim with the Jinn.

He felt the pull again and returned a feeling of resistance. The air shimmered again but remained turbulent. Fresh scents reached him. Krazack leaped, hitting the horizon of the portal before it collapsed upon itself.

He landed in front of the woman, who lay on her side in the red sand. Fire flared around him. Sweet smells mixed with a harsh, acidic tone greeted him. The sound of flames crackled in the swirling mist in the air. Around him, smoke and sand swirled in the air. The woman was down. She was small, unlike the denizens of the city. The heat from his hand dissipated, returning its natural black color. He hesitated before running his finger along her cheek. She was injured. Blood was seeping through the cloth wrap.

He took a deep breath, filling his nose with a cacophony of foreign scents. Hissing enveloped him as the mist touched his skin. He kneeled, reaching out to see if she was alright.

No!

[She stole us away!]

[Destroy the hakimah before she sends us back.]

-She is beautiful.-

-What if she it hurt?-

Finish her!

A smell he recognized broke through the other smells, Ghul.

He jumped back, eyes searching for his kin. If the hakimah had a connection to the Ghul, he must get away from this place. Was he pulled through to become a thrall to his powerful cousin?

The woman coughed, trying to get up. She looked up into his eyes, and he felt something foreign. An irresistible pull drew him closer. He wanted to pick her up and take her away from this place.

[Run!]

It's a spell. She will bind you.

[Kill her.]

-No, the Ghul will hunt us.-

Get away from here.

-I don't want to die!-

He shook himself free from the enticing thoughts and jumped toward the glass doors ahead of him, clearing the distance with ease. He reached out and released a burst of flame. The stucco walls caught fire, causing plants in a wide radius from the doorway to burn away.

Before dashing into the foreign structure, he glanced back at the woman. Would she survive? Shaking off the thought, he continued straight to a set of wooden doors, reaching out and releasing heat from his hands. He looked over his shoulder. Smoke and flames now obscured his line of sight to the woman.

You know what you must do.

[Do it! Do it! Do it! Burn it all!]

Krazack reached to either side of the doorway and grabbed the frame. He fed his energy into his grip, the veins in his arms lit up like molten lava. The energy flowed through his hands, setting the doorway ablaze. Satisfied with the spreading flames, he ran across the lawn, leaving smoldering grass in his wake. At the wall, he jumped, appearing atop it in an orange blur. Without turning around, he knew the fire was consuming the area. He could feel the waves of heat extending outward.

The sun's heat was much brighter than he was used to. It was glorious, refreshing the energy he had used to set the building ablaze. Foreign smells continued to assault him. There were so many. Had he escaped their prison? Returned to the birthplace of his people? This place looked nothing like his home. The buildings were spread apart, not built on top of one another, and plants grew everywhere. Several of the small fields were being fed with spraying water from whatever devices sent it to wet the entire area.

He slowed as he moved toward what looked like a sprawling city in the distance.

Honk! The sound continued to assault his ears as the driver kept the horn pressed as they passed him. Thoughts and snippets of language appearing in his thoughts.

A screeching sound filled his ears as he turned in time to see a chariot of some kind was trying to slow before getting to him. It was on the verge of striking him. Krazack whirled and slammed his fists down into the front of the chariot, releasing heat and fire from his hands. He could sense fire inside the vehicle, and reached out to it, intensifying its energy. The vehicle exploded, bathing him in fire. Debris shredded his clothes, dark shirt and pants, nearly as black as his skin, from the explosion. The pieces bounced off him, leaving him unharmed. He heard the screaming of two people inside and moved to look at them.

He smelled burning flesh. The smells differed from those haunting him from the war. The screams filled his ears as the people were pinned inside. He placed his hands on the large pane of glass and held it as it melted away. He reached inside and pulled the two screaming figures out, holding them up, examining them. They were soft, vulnerable.

They exiled us.

-We are free!-

Make them pay!

[Burn it all down!]

Krazack narrowed his eyes, clenching his teeth. He let the fire flow into these squishy beings. Their screams intensified, then died as life left the charred corpses.

A scream sounded from the side. Several people approached from the buildings, some holding up small devices. *Phones? Communication devices.* He recoiled, expecting punishment from the foreign artifacts. When nothing came, he became a hot-burning wind, moving faster than they could perceive, appearing before each of them, grabbing them and releasing the fire. Each burst into flames, their screams filled the day.

Ha ha ha!

[Weak! They are weak.]

Make them pay for our banishment.

-Not her.-

Ha ha ha. Not her. She freed us.

-The Ghul will come for us.-

[Let her come, everything burns!]

[It's glorious.]

Krazack opened himself to the heat from the sun and moved with blinding speed down the hill toward the city. The voices subsided, murmuring in the back of his mind. He needed to find a place to hide and to eat. Trying to make sense of the scents assaulting him, he shook his head. There were no familiar ones he could find. He would reshape this place with fire.

Chapter 24

Tanya felt the heat around her. She struggled to get up, standing on her good leg, the other weak and bleeding from the portal's collapse. She tested her leg, feeling pain. It wouldn't support her weight. The intensity was significant, yet tolerable. She hobbled toward the glass doors at the back end of the house. Smoke filled the house's interior rooms, pouring into the garden from the damaged area behind her. She coughed. In the garden, she could breathe, but it wouldn't be long before she found herself surrounded by a ring of fire. Quick math told her she wouldn't survive the heat transfer despite the open area barring a torrential downpour. There were no visible flames on this side of the house. Looking back, she saw the raging inferno burning the walls and through the ceiling to the second floor.

She paused at the door. She needed only to get through the open area and down the wide entryway to the back door. The thick gray smoke prevented her from seeing anything. Taking a deep breath, she opened the door and crept through the room. Tanya tried to remember where everything was. Crawling out, staying low, wasn't an option. Hurriedly, she moved as fast as possible with her injured leg, squinting her eyes to reduce the irritation caused by the smoke. She heard approaching sirens. Colliding with a table, she fell to the ground, gasping in agony.

She inhaled, then coughed, fighting for breath. Unsure of where the door was, she panicked. She found the table and tried to recall the alignment. She was on the side, just go straight. Her coughing increased. Her head hurt, and her throat was burning. She pulled herself forward. She thought she heard a helicopter outside and adjusted to the direction of the sound. Breathing was difficult. She was tired, and just needed to rest for a quick moment. She laid her head down on the cool stone floor. It felt comforting.

As she lay still, her vision faded. The burning in her throat was gone, and her pain faded away. She embraced the feeling, slipping into the darkness. She felt someone grab her and lift her. Strong arms around her shoulder and under her legs. She smelled hyacinth and smiled, slipping back toward sleep.

"Tanya!"

She could breathe. The air was cool, but the burning sensation returned to her throat. Tanya opened her eyes. The sun blazed. She was in the fire! She tried to roll quickly to get away. Pairs of hands held her in place.

"Tanya! You're safe. Relax. You're outside."

She looked around. She was on a gurney outside an ambulance. Nafara stood at her side while two EMTs were working to get an IV in her arm.

"Ma'am, please hold still so we can get this in." The blonde young male paramedic directed while the older black-haired Hispanic paramedic held her arm steady, piercing her skin with the needle. She felt the pinch and held still.

"Do you know where you are?"

She coughed and spoke hoarsely. "I'm at home."

"Do you know what happened?"

Her eyes shifted to Nafara, wondering if her aunt could tell what she did before she shifted her focus back to the paramedic. "I don't know. I was relaxing in the garden and woke up to find the house on fire."

"Do you remember an explosion?"

"I don't know. My leg was injured previously because of a dog bite. It feels worse now."

"You have several lacerations. We have them bandaged, but you'll need to go to the hospital."

"Yeah, of course."

A commotion on the side caught her attention. A woman with a microphone and a cameraman were arguing with police officers.

"Ms. Kavioni, can we get a statement?"

Nafara patted her hand and directed her attention to the EMT. "Do what you need to do. I'll follow you to the hospital."

Tanya watched as Nafara approached the reporters. "Is it true that you rushed into your burning house to save your niece?"

Tanya sat back in her hospital bed, which was in the sitting position. The medical staff had finished their second round of tests. She held her phone, watching Nafara's interview.

The background video changed to the perspective of the helicopter showing their car pulling around the house into the back, the tires shredding the lawn. Her aunt jumped out of the car and ran into the house. Minutes later, she emerged with Tanya in her arms. Carrying her to safety, laying her in the grass.

"Yes. When I saw the house was on fire, all I could think about was my niece. Tanya is the only family I have left. I couldn't imagine life without her." A tear rolled down her face as she turned to the camera. "Given this tragic event, I may need to suspend my campaign for governor temporarily while I make sure my niece is taken care of. Texans know that family comes first. We take care of our own." She wiped away a tear and forced a smile.

"Are you announcing that you are suspending your campaign?"

Nafara looked down, and then back toward Tanya's ambulance as it drove away in the background. "I'll decide in the next few days based on the wishes of my niece. If she needs me, I want to be here for her." She turned back toward the camera. "I'd ask one thing of the great people of Texas. Please pray for my niece. Thank you, and God bless Texas."

It was a masterful performance, Tanya almost believed it. She knew Nafara cared about her, but the rest was political. She wouldn't suspend her campaign. This incident would strengthen her in the polls, bringing her closer to the two candidates from the other parties.

The door opened, and her aunt walked in, dressed in the same outfit, the smoke-stained white blouse now tucked in again to the black knee-length skirt.

"Are you okay?" Nafara asked while walking to the side of her bed.

"I feel better. The doctor gave me something for the pain and my throat. She said it would be a few days before it would feel better, but there wasn't any permanent damage. My leg hurts like hell, though."

"What happened?"

Tanya looked past her aunt and lowered her voice to a whisper. "I opened a portal, but it was unstable. I didn't have full control of the elements."

"What did you see?"

Tanya described the City of Brass and everything she remembered.

"Did anything come through?"

Tanya tried to remember. "I don't know. I felt a presence, but I don't know if it was on our side of the portal or the other."

Nafara considered her words, keeping her gaze on hers. "We have to be careful. Next time you attempt it, make sure I am by your side."

"I'm sorry. I was close, I know it," Tanya pleaded.

"When I went into the house, there was a scent, brimstone. Without seeing what happened, I don't know if it was your spell, or an attack from the other side. It could also be an effect of the sealing spell used by Solomon. Once you recover, we can try again, with more precautions."

Tanya felt a tickle on her cheek. "There was something else."

She raised her hand, caressing her cheek. "I could swear I felt someone caress my face. Was that you?"

Nafara's expression changed, becoming serious. "No."

GHUL

The Ghul wears beauty as a mask, feeding not on corpses alone but on the living soul. In the old tales, they haunted graveyards. In the new tales, they haunt us still, in the shadows, in power, and in love.

Chapter 25

Tanya lifted herself out of the wheelchair in front of the hospital and climbed into their car. Nafara was sitting inside, Lucy was across from them in the back-facing seats. Her phone was in hand, but she wasn't on a call or social media like normal.

"Tanya, I'm glad you are okay," Lucy greeted her.

"Thanks. I'm sorry I haven't been much help lately. You must think I'm the most accident-prone person you've ever met," Tanya said.

She laughed. It resonated like the sound of a bird's call. Not annoying, more cute, of course. She was the complete package, which was why Nafara had hired her away from her opponents. "Not at all. This is a dangerous business. With all the attention on your aunt, things can get a little crazy."

Tanya nodded. She sounded reserved, not the "in your face and make things happen" campaign manager she was. She looked at Nafara, who seemed to ignore the entire conversation. "Did the fire at the house hurt the campaign?"

She laughed again. "Don't take this the wrong way," Lucy looked nervously at Nafara, "but if we can have something happen like this every week, we'll be competitive in the fall."

"You don't think we'll be competitive?" That had gotten Nafara's attention.

"I do. Of course, but I think it's going to be a battle the whole way. There's precedent for third-party success in the state, but it's rare. Most Texans are comfortable with the two-party system. Think of it as a gunfight, or a duel."

Nafara waved her hand, dismissing the comments. "We're going to change that. Three parties first, then one."

Lucy smiled, but it looked forced, not her normal fake smile that could pass for genuine. Something was bothering her. Nafara didn't seem to notice or care.

Tanya tried to break the chill in the air. "What are the numbers at?"

Lucy's expression became focused. "Well, it's been a fight, but we've made good progress, climbing fourteen percent this week, which is fantastic. That's a ten-point jump in the polls, bringing you to twenty-four points. The video of your running into the burning house to save Tanya resonated with voters. Your interview afterwards, talking about family and doing anything to save them, gave you a twenty percent boost with women and older men."

"What about my opponents?"

"Governor Baker is polling strong as the incumbent at thirty-five percent, and the Democrat, Marcia Garcia-Fernandez, is sitting just ahead of you at twenty-eight percent. You are affecting the governor's numbers, pulling him down but not enough to be in danger yet. The rest are undecided, which is an increase, and bodes well for us."

Nafara turned her head to look at Lucy. "I'm not worried about Marcia. I don't think she's going to make it to the election."

Lucy's face paled at the comment. "What do you mean?"

Nafara chuckled. "I mean that I have received information that her happy family is not so happy behind the scenes. Not everyone wants her to run. If there were to be a distraction, or a change in their situation, she might drop out of the race."

Lucy let out a breath. "If you're talking about her brother, she's already weathered the storm on that one during her house run. Her opponent brought his drug problems up during a debate, and she was ready. It hurt him in the polls. She's sharp."

"Attacking family members is a losing strategy. Maybe we can offer her something to drop out of the race. An incentive to hold on to her seat in the house," Tanya offered.

"She won't do it. It'd be political suicide. She'd lose the backing of her party, which she needs if she wants to make a legitimate run at the White House. She thinks the governor's office is the last step she needs."

Tanya shrugged, sitting back in her seat.

"I'm not dismissing your idea. It would be a less messy solution. But she likes to get messy," Lucy said.

Lucy checked her phone. "Your release picture is doing well on Instagram and TikTok. We've secured the rights to the song *Unstoppable* by Sia to use for the campaign."

"Wow, how much was that?"

"Not as much as we thought it would be. Your aunt met with the artists and outlined her campaign stances. It turns out they are in favor of several of Nafara's initiatives — education, drugs, and leveling the playing field."

Nafara reached over and squeezed her hand. Her vision faded to black. She was in a shadowy room. She couldn't see the walls. Water was raining down on the pair. She was sitting on the ground, holding someone. She was sad, crying. Nafara lay in her lap. Several wounds caused her black skin to crack and bleed across her torso and both arms. Tanya held her head in one hand, and her hand in the other. She looked down at her friend's wounds. She was in pain, and Tanya's heart ached in response.

"Help! Please, she's hurt bad!" her voice echoed in the large room, but no help came.

The fire in Nafara's eyes was dim, lacking the blazing intensity she knew. She was going to lose her, and there was nothing she could do. Tears fell from her eyes.

"No! Please don't leave me," her voice broke, trailing off.

She sensed a presence in front of her. The dark man stepped from the shadows. His eyes blazing, and the veins on his bare arms glowing as if filled with molten rock. His face displayed a mixed expression, balancing malice towards Nafara and concern for her.

"You did this!" Tanya screamed.

"Yes, I did."

"No!" she screamed as the vision faded away. She felt sweat on her brow. She struggled to figure out where she was, her eyes filled with panic. The leg hurt as she twisted in her seat.

"Tanya, it's okay. You're safe."

She calmed down at the sound of Nafara's voice. "I, I had a vision."

Nafara gave Lucy a look before giving her full attention to Tanya. "Tell me what you saw."

Tanya described her vision, reliving the emotions. Tears were running down her cheeks.

Nafara listened in silence. Caressing her hand.

Nafara hit a button, lowering the divider to the driver.

"Take us to River Oaks."

"Yes, ma'am."

"We have a few hours ahead of us. I think it's time to fill you in on a few things. Both of you."

Chapter 26

Krazack pushed the truck, sliding it sideways and allowing him to escape from the metal fortress he had made from abandoned vehicles.

Argh! The smell is noxious!

[It asks for heat. Incinerate it!]

-No, we are safe here!-

They are pathetic!

We are safe anywhere among them.

-We need to eat.-

"Hey! You're not supposed to be in here," a voice said from his left.

Krazack turned to the voice. The man stood at the end of a row of stacked vehicles. He held something in his hand. He looked soft, balding, with a large, round belly, and dirty clothes.

"Gray!" the man called.

A dog stood beside him, lean, pointed ears, and fierce eyes. Krazack approached the man.

"Stay back, I mean it." The man raised the device in his hands. It looked like a piece of bent metal. He detected the smell of brimstone.

Grrrr! The dog beside the man showed its teeth as a deep growl rose.

He was ten feet from the man when he heard him say, "Attack!" The dog, quivering with restraint, bolted forward, and leaped at him. The Jinn caught the animal in his right hand and moved as a blur to the man. The veins in his arm glowed. The dog lost all sense of fierceness as the skin around Krazack's grip bubbled and cracked, smoke rising.

Bang!

Bang! Bang! Bang!

He stumbled backwards, feeling as if a Marid had punched him in the shoulder and chest. His shoulder ached. A few of the rounds had penetrated his skin. He extracted the information from the man's mind. A gun, a projectile weapon, shot him. His left hand flew out and grabbed the man by the throat, lifting him off the ground.

[Yes! Kill them!]

-What is this weapon?-

[Kill them both!]

Hahaha hah!

The heat intensified until both the man and dog stopped moving. The smell of burnt flesh filled the air. He listened and looked around for anyone else. There had to be dātabara here, lawgivers who kept order. Where were they?

He leapt to the top of the stack of cars and stuffed the two corpses through a broken window before jumping back to the ground. He went to the opening in the fence he used to get in, listening for others. Hearing nothing, he stepped through the opening and walked down the road toward the tall, ugly buildings.

Metal poles lined the streets, some with lights shining down on the road. These were like the floating lights found throughout the City of Brass. Pain shot down his spine. He dropped to his knees, his muscles wracked with spasms.

Primitives, they will worship us!

[Hahaha! Banished at home, but a god here.]

As the pain subsided, he examined the bullet wounds on his shoulder. They were healing, the skin already closed over the holes. The weapon didn't use iron.

-Weak metals. We must study the weapon.-

Study it? It is useless. Beneath us.

He stood, rolling his shoulders, cracks coming from his joints. He caught the scent of people.

[Set them on fire! Establish your domain!]

-No. We must study them.-

Krazack heard voices before they were in sight. Rounding the corner, he saw dozens of people sitting, standing, and moving about between tents, trash, and other debris. They were dirty, and their smell was foul.

They are the abandoned.

-These would be food for the Ghul, the lost.-

He sniffed the air, searching for any scent of the Ghul. Nothing, only these wretches. He continued toward them, catching the attention of several men who approached him.

"Hey. Whaddya want?" a tall man with a long gray beard asked.

Krazack ignored the group, sniffing the air, searching for food. Pain coursed down his neck to his spine. Food would help. His body needed sustenance. He pushed forward, resisting the urge to drop again, the pain in his neck creeping up.

One man, almost as tall as Krazack, with skin darkened from time in the sun and tangled black hair, grabbed his arm and pulled. "Hey motherfucker, I'm talking to you."

Krazack turned his head to glare at the man holding his arm. The meaning of the insult became clear. Six men encircled him. Many smells filled the air, yet none hinted of iron. He smiled, showing his pointed white teeth.

"I'm not scared of you. You know what I'm gonna do? I'm gonna help lighten your load, man. You hand over some of those bracelets and we might let you walk outta here."

They dare?

[Thieves, they would rob us. Punish them!]

Leave a message. They are filth!

In the blink of an eye , Krazack faded from sight, becoming one with the wind. Nobody noticed the two pieces of metal that fell to the ground where he had been. He became the essence of creation. Fire roared as he moved in and around the people, igniting the people and their shelters. The flames engulfed the tents, debris, boxes, and carts of junk, leaving nothing untouched.

Krazack reappeared among the frightened men, his shoulder ache barely noticeable. He grabbed a short, red-haired man by the face, sending fire from his palm to wrap around his head, burning skin, hair, and muscles away from the bone. The others screamed and tried to run. He shot forward, grabbing two of the men by their arms, throwing them down, their heads bouncing on the ground, lifeless. Transforming into the wind once more, he dispatched two additional enemies with fire, leaving only the large man who had seized him. Appearing in the man's path, he swirled forward, returned to his physical form, and seized him by the dirty, thick jacket he was wearing. The veins in his arm glowed, smoke billowed up from the cloth.

"Please! Please don't kill me."

"You are pathetic, thief!" Krazack's deep bass voice rang out.

"I am the lowest. I am nothing, please have mercy."

Krazack smelled urine and saw that the man had soiled himself. The man whimpered as the heat of his grasp burned the man's chest.

"What land is this?" Krazack growled.

"It's Austin, Texas," the man whimpered.

> *[Lies! There is no such place. He is trying to deceive us!]*

"What are you?"

"I'm just a man. A veteran. I was in the Army."

Krazack sniffed the air, a sweet smell wafted through the air. Fruits!

The man was crying, his jacket now burning, his skin across his chest beginning to blister. Krazack dropped him and turned to follow the scent. He didn't look back. Heading up the road, between buildings, following the smell on the wind. At the next intersection, he observed a woman holding a box of fruit. He looked past her. Her vehicle was overflowing with food.

She must have sensed movement as he got near, because she dropped the box and let out a scream. She ran toward the building, dropping the box of fruit. Peaches, pears, apricots, and oranges. He ignored the women, kneeling and eating the fruits. The juice dripped down his chin and onto his loose black shirt. As fast as he finished one, he took another. He hadn't eaten fresh fruit since his banishment. He took two large crates of fruit from the vehicle and began walking down the road toward the taller buildings lit up in the distance. These would feed him for a few days.

What other wonders does this world hold?

Chapter 27

Yusuf stood again in the shell of a house that was the Society's headquarters. The other council members formed a semicircle around him. In the middle was a black stone column attached to a wide base. The top of the column was waist height, with two sets of dark leather straps.

Reza stepped forward. His desert tan robes complemented his scholar's garb. "Yusuf Ahmed Al-Fortwani, you have been called to join the Society of Al-Batin. We will offer you three options to demonstrate your faith. If you refuse one, we will not offer it again. Do you understand?"

Yusuf stepped forward. "I understand."

"Pull up your sleeves and place your right arm on the column, across the straps."

One council member stepped forward from either side and secured the buckle, holding his arm in place.

Sheikh Ali al-Ridha stepped forward with a wooden box. He opened the box, revealing a vial of dark ink and a needle. "Will you accept the permanent mark of the Society?"

Yusuf's heart sank. It was forbidden. "As is known, the Prophet (peace be upon him) taught that we should not alter what Allah has created. The Hadiths confirm this teaching. Therefore, I cannot accept a permanent mark on my skin except as commanded by Allah."

The sheikh stepped back to his place in the semicircle.

Mullah Hassan al-Kazemi stepped forward from his right. He pulled a brand from within his cloak and set a stone bowl in front, pouring contents into the bowl, which glowed. He felt the heat of the bowl on his arm. The mullah dipped the brand into the hot liquid until the brand glowed. Pulling it out, he held it above his arm. "Will you accept the brand of the society to demonstrate your commitment?"

Yusuf raised his chin. "As a follower of Islamic teachings, I believe in preserving the natural state in which Allah created us. The Hadiths guide us to avoid altering our bodies with permanent marks. Thus, I must respectfully decline to receive a brand."

The mullah stepped back, laying the brand on a stone table to the side.

Sayyid Mahdi al-Jaberi stepped in from the right side of Reza. He stopped in front of him, staring into his eyes. "You have denied the mark twice. Will you accept the unknown? If you deny the third offer, we will excuse you to return to your life with no further contact."

Yusuf glanced down, seeing the small ceremonial blade in his hands. Yusuf looked into the eyes of Mahdi. He looked at his exposed arm. He would not deny his faith but felt he was being called to a greater purpose. All of those present accepted one test. He trusted Reza, the leader of the group. They would not violate the Word of God. He had to have faith in those offering this responsibility.

I place my trust in Allah, and there is no power and no strength except through Allah. At the completion of the prayer, he was sure this was his path. He nodded. "I accept."

Mahdi raised the blade and cut the leather restraints. He placed a necklace in Yusuf's open hand, suppressing a smile. He stepped back into the semicircle.

Reza stepped forward, as did the initial two, who strapped his arm down. "Well done, Yusuf. It's important for all our members to demonstrate their faith with clarity. If you had accepted one of the other tests, we would have sent you home. Welcome to the Society."

The other members stepped forward, laying their hands on him.

"Allah guides our actions. We must ensure the Jinn remain locked in the City of Brass."

Afterward, Reza pulled him aside and led him to a side room. "Yusuf, you need to get home. I've discussed it with the others. If you believe that the girl you told me about, Tanya, may be in contact with the Ghul, she is in danger."

"I am convinced of it."

"Then you need to persuade her that her life is in danger. I am going to provide you with a tool, a last resort defense against the Jinn."

"A ward or weapon?"

"It is a weapon. Their kind are susceptible to iron and some forms of steel. Maybe modern armor-piercing rounds will wound them, but we don't know. There aren't any other Jinn to test the theory on. Just like a human can survive, a Jinn can as well. It's the iron that interferes with their supernatural essence."

Reza slid a key from his pocket and unlocked a drawer in the wall. He pulled out a box and handed it to Yusuf. As he did, he opened it to show the dark gray simple blade etched with the seal of Solomon at the base of the blade. "This blade is an important artifact. Our team has confirmed the authenticity of the blade."

"You want this girl to kill the Jinn? I don't see how she can pull it off. Let me find someone of faith, built like a warrior."

"If the Jinn has formed a bond with the girl, she is the only one who could get close enough. The Jinn must still be wary. She would see an assassin coming."

"I'll try. I am supposed to meet her when I return. How soon can you get this to me in the United States?"

"You will take it with you."

"I think security might take issue with this."

"We will take care of it. Ayatollah al-Hussaini will approve your application for diplomatic status. You will breeze through. All official notifications are being made."

"What is the timeline for all of this? How much time do I have?"

"There is a prophecy regarding the Jinn's return to Earth. It is passed down through word of mouth, and no written record exists to confirm its legitimacy. It could occur tomorrow, or within the next few years, or far into the future. If she is trying to open the gateway between their realm and ours, it will be difficult without the Seal of Sulaiman."

"Do we have it?" Yusuf questioned.

Reza laughed. "No. The Society destroyed it shortly after our founding. Releasing the Jinn would have been easier with the seal. Without it, she will have a much more difficult time locating the city, understanding the link between our realms, and how to open a portal between the two. Could they do it with science? I don't know. People nowadays don't believe, let alone understand reality."

Reza closed the box.

Yusuf took the box from Reza. Its weight felt more significant. He couldn't tell if it was the physical weight or the added responsibility that added to the load. "I will do my best. May I tell her whatever I need to get her to agree?"

"Yes," Reza answered immediately.

Chapter 28

"The mayor has postponed his meeting with us. Apparently, there was an incident in an area known for its homeless population with a few dozen casualties, as well as fires in the surrounding buildings."

"Is the information in the governor's briefing package?"

"Not yet. I don't believe the mayor has contacted the governor's office."

Nafara flipped through the binder. "We have rallies scheduled in El Paso, Fort Worth, San Antonio, and Austin over the next six weeks. Have you been able to review the drive-by stops through the state?"

"Yes, those are all good," Lucy replied, her eyes on the schedule in her hand.

Nafara dropped the binder onto the seat to her side. "We need to look for other areas to take advantage of failures or missteps by my opponents. I want to pull ahead and not look back."

Lucy shifted in her seat. "We should get the next set of polls in a few days. One positive thing I am hearing is that your focus on family and communities is playing well. It's something voters from all sides appreciate."

"Good. I think we can continue to push the Texas-first agenda to show how we will make their lives better."

"That's the goal of the Republic Unity Party, isn't it? To bring everyone together within a unified vision of the future."

"It is."

Lucy's phone buzzed. "Hello, Kavioni Campaign, this is Lucy." She hung on the caller's every word. "Okay, send the pictures to this number. I'll pass them to Ms. Kavioni. Thank you."

"What was that?"

"That was Mayor McWilliams, wanting to pass information to you. They have retrieved images from the security cameras at your home. While the smoke obscured them, and there were system failures from the fire, they were able to retrieve a partial image of a person leaving your home. It was arson. Someone intentionally started the fire."

Nafara clenched her jaw. How much did they know? Certainly not enough about the person she suspected to be a Jinn, more specifically, an Ifrit. "Do they know where this person is?"

"No, but they have matched his image to a cell phone video sent by someone linked to the building fires, and it looks like the same person."

"A random arsonist?"

"Maybe, but I may leak hints we received threatening messages from a group or party that supports the governor. If we imply this arsonist is attacking you and the homeless, we can imply that the governor's policies may have resulted in a person taking matters into their own hands or something more nefarious. With the right wording, the public will fill in the blanks, and we can't be tied to misinformation."

Nafara smiled. "Now that is more in line with what I expect of you. I like it, but we need to make sure it's timed correctly."

"I think we should release it now. If anything else happens, we continue to push for answers and put it in the people's minds that he's to blame."

Lucy's phone buzzed again.

132

Nafara tapped a finger on her chin. "I'm tempted, but let's see what he does next. I don't want to publish anything that can be traced back to us."

"You got it." Lucy held the phone up, checking with Nafara.

She nodded. Looking out the window, she was hungry.

"It's for you."

Nafara eyed the phone suspiciously. She didn't carry a phone. There was something with the signals from the newer phones that gave her a headache if she had one on her person for too long. Only Hector knew the pain it caused her. When they were developing Eunoia, she had become prone to migraines, which had led to several members of their team going missing. She chuckled to herself. *Wrong place and time.*

"Hello?"

"Sister, you do not know me. But I know of you."

The hair on the back of her neck stood up as she became very aware of her surroundings. "I'm not sure what you are talking about."

"I read the news. It's a tragedy, what happened in Cedar Ridge. I guess they're lucky someone killed the counselor."

She relaxed, realizing it was probably a reporter or someone looking for a story to tell on social media. "It sounds like you know everything that happened. I'm just thankful that I could get there in time to help my niece. Who is this? Your number isn't on my phone. Who are you with?"

"I'm not anyone you know yet, but you will in time. Don't worry, Sister, your secret is safe with me."

"I'm not sure what you're talking about, but if you would like to meet, you can coordinate it with my campaign manager."

She heard the laugh on the other end. "No, it's quite alright. We will meet in due time. All our kind make their way to me, eventually. I've lingered long enough. We'll talk soon."

She tossed the phone to Lucy, feeling the onset of a headache. The call was going to bother her. He implied he knew who she was, but not threateningly. She didn't like the unknown.

"Who was that? You look bothered." Lucy looked at her with curiosity.

"I don't know, probably an annoyance."

"There's nothing I need to know, is there? I'd like to get ahead of any issues."

"I'm sure it's nothing. They were asking about Cedar Ridge." She pressed a button, lowering the divider to the front of the car. "Let me out here. I'm going to walk back. I need to stretch my legs and get something to eat."

The driver nodded, accustomed to such requests. He, like Lucy, knew that she held their lives in her hands. She paid them well, just in case, but they had seen what she could do to someone. It bought loyalty.

Lucy looked around. "Here? This isn't a bad part of town, but it certainly isn't the best."

"I'll be fine. I need some air, and I'm feeling cramped. We've been running between meetings all day. I'm tired of being in the car, and I'm starving. Let Tanya know I'll be in late."

"Will do, boss."

Nafara took off her jacket, skirt, and blouse, and kicked her heels to the side. Lucy watched as Nafara became Yasmin. Her body shifted, transforming into a black-haired high school girl from Iran. She noticed Lucy's eyes wander as she changed shape, still in her underwear. *Interesting.* Yasmin dressed herself in black jeans, a dark brown T-shirt, and matching sneakers, taking a little more time than she needed, observing Lucy's reaction.

"That must be so liberating." Lucy's eyes sparkled.

"You have no idea." Yasmin flashed a devilish grin and stepped out of the car.

Chapter 29

> Yusuf: Ms. Janessy, I have returned from my trip. I feel it is important for us to talk as soon as possible.

Tanya read the text message. It mirrored the email she had received an hour before. She was uneasy about meeting with the imam. As far as anyone was concerned, she had moved on with her life, leaving all the bad memories behind. He had been there for her beforehand, and she presumed he was dead. When he reached out to her, she began to worry that Nafara would be uncovered. It wouldn't hurt to find out what was so urgent. Nafara had been very careful in creating her persona.

> Tanya: I am not in Cedar Ridge anymore. We could video call if you need, but I am in Houston for the time being.

> Yusuf: I am in Houston as well. I am teaching at the Darul Hikmah Institute.

> Tanya: I'm not sure how far that is from downtown, but I'm sure I can make my way there.

Tanya looked at the calendar on her laptop and didn't see any conflicts. Nafara was at the Eunoia Research Facility for the day. She wasn't supposed to return until later.

Tanya set her phone down and walked to the window of the penthouse. The main buildings of the city, which were big for Texas, surrounded her, but were small compared to New York City.

The streets were busy with people going about their normal business. What would it look like once she opened the portal? Had someone come through? She could still feel the warm, lingering touch on her cheek. Nafara had brushed it off, but her behavior of late seemed more on edge. She was sure Lucy didn't notice.

On the muted television behind them, a news segment flashed grainy footage of a religious procession in Shiraz. A deep male voice translated over the chant: *"...the Flame shall walk in flesh..."*

She stepped onto the balcony, smiling as the heat hit her. If she came from a cool room, no matter how hot it was, she enjoyed being surrounded by a wave of warmth. She took off the bandage on her leg to give it some air. She didn't know if it helped, but she remembered her mom telling her to do it when she was little. The muscle was sore where the wolf bite had partially torn her calf. Because of the blast from the collapsing portal, the wound had partially reopened. The skin around the wound showed signs of bruising. Thankfully, it didn't look red from infection. She sat in a patio chair, leaned back, letting the sun warm her body.

She heard the flapping of wings, and a shadow blocked the sun. A raspy hiss made her jump out of the chair and hop to the door. The large vulture clung to the rail of the balcony and watched her. She stopped in the doorway, ready to slide the large glass door shut. She kept her injured leg bent, all her weight on her good one. The vulture was huge, almost three feet tall.

"What do you want?" She waited, half expecting the bird to answer. There were two others flying above them. If they all start roosting here like they did at home, the building manager is going to be freaked out. Nafara explained they would not harm her, but there was something about their dark black eyes that seemed to stare at her.

"Bet you don't understand a word I'm saying, huh?" Tanya muttered, gazing at the bird perched on the railing. Nafara had explained that their communication was akin to telepathy, not through words but through feelings, wants, and desires. She considered using the weave to communicate with animals like some Jinn, but memories of the koi squashed the thought. The vultures roosted in the trees around the house, in symbiosis with the Jinn. They acted as sentinels, alerting them to any disturbances. She suspected the Jinn had provided them with some sustenance in return. Could she replicate this connection using her understanding of the weave? Dr. Gutierrez might hold the key. His research into neural pathways and their capacity to repair and reroute after traumatic injuries, both physical and mental, could offer valuable insights. If neural pathways could be rerouted, perhaps they could bridge the gap between human and animal minds. She needed to delve into the science of the brain and combine it with her growing knowledge of the weave to forge a new communication.

The matter required reflection, though she doubted the merit of consulting the vultures. Dolphins might be cool, or whales. They were supposed to be self-aware. Apes had learned sign language and had proven they could reason. Maybe she should borrow one of the Eunoia devices and visit the zoo or Sea World.

Another loud, raspy hiss interrupted her. The sound reminded her of pebbles scraping across a thin sheet of metal. "What?" She and the bird stared at each other. She felt the hair on her arms stand up. Yep, they still affected her.

"I'm going inside. The balcony is all yours." She looked up and saw that three more vultures had joined the group. *Great.*

Tanya closed the sliding glass door. There were a few hours left before she had to meet the imam. She was curious about why he had

137

waited so long to contact her. She and Nafara had never mentioned him. If she were being honest, she thought he had been killed. He hadn't been at their last scheduled meeting, and his assistant had reached out to her. What had happened? Maybe he discovered Jinn were real, and it frightened him. She didn't blame him. There wasn't anything he could have done to prevent Yasmin from getting what she wanted. Thinking back on those last few days, Tanya wasn't sure she wanted anything different. Her life now was good. The friendship she developed with Yasmin was still present. At least she believed so, but she still had doubts about whether it would have been the same if things were different. Would she have been just another sheep slaughtered in Nafara's quest to find a wise one?

The look in Nafara's eyes when she killed a human wasn't one of pity or sorrow, it was a blissful indulgence of their pain and fear as she drained and consumed them. The question she didn't want to ask was whether Nafara could turn on her. She shuddered, a chill running up her spine. In all her visions, none had threatened her. She didn't want to continue the train of thought and turned on the news.

Chapter 30

Krazack pushed the truck aside, and stepped out from the shelter he had set up within the pile of abandoned vehicles. The sun was low on the horizon, and the air was hot. He spread his arms to the side, letting the sun bathe his exposed arms in its light. The room behind him looked like a spacious cave with walls made of dripping molten metal. He pushed the car back into place. Changing into fiery wind, he flew to the top of the pile of cars and resumed his natural form as he settled on a flattened yellow vehicle. He removed the brown sleeveless shirt and sat bare-chested, absorbing the heat from the sun. It differed from home. The sun here was more vibrant and brighter.

This graveyard of vehicles was on the outer edge of the city.

How do they put up with the smell?.

-Squares and points, no imagination.-

They have developed since we were separated.

-Their world is ugly. Perhaps we could teach them.-

[Ha ha ha! No!]

No, subservient clay beings. They are soft.

[Like the peaches we consumed.]

Hunger. We hunger.

       -What of the Ghul? Where are they?-

Not our concern. We must stay away from them.

       -But the woman.-

Yes, the woman.

       -She glows brightly. She could help us.-

[No! No, no, no!]

Still...

His mind calmed as he recalled touching her cheek with his hand. The voices were quiet for a moment. His stomach reminded him of his hunger.

       -We must explore and find a source of food.-

Yes.

[Yes.]

Krazack shifted again, darting to the ground before taking shape outside the perimeter fence. His body had a slight hunch. When he tried to stand tall, his lower back rippled with waves of pain. He let himself slouch and walked up toward the city. He had seen the human police, the dātabara, searching for him. While they searched the area, he stayed hidden. Krazack smiled at the thought of these weak humans trying to calm him. None had shown the dominating abilities of the marid dātabara. He winced at the thought of their assault on his mind. But he had resisted, hidden away as one of the others bore the burden of pain.

Nearing the city, the pathways along the roads filled with people. Their language was unfamiliar, but his mind picked up their words, while images filling in the things he didn't understand. He was thankful that they hadn't lost the trait after thousands of years of separation.

As he approached a group of humans, their language entered his mind, filling it with foreign images.

How could they live like this?

-It's chaos.-

We will make it right.

-How?-

Once we understand this land, we will conquer it.

Two females in a group with three males turned to look at him. He could feel their intent, and smiled at them, letting thoughts of pleasure fill him.

It has been so long.

-They are so frail.-

[They do not fear us.]

"Hey asshole, why are you looking at my girl?"

141

Krazack stopped. The man speaking was tall, with a strong build.

How dare this human speak to us this way?

[Kill him where he stands.]

Krazack punched the man, his arm a blur. The man didn't have time to react, taking the full brunt of the attack on his chest. He flew off the sidewalk, into oncoming traffic, hitting the front of a passing utility truck, before falling off and getting run over. Krazack looked at the man, his body twitching in the street. He stepped off the sidewalk, and a blue car swerved around, blaring its horn. The rest of the group was stunned. The women screamed.

Ignoring them all, he leaned over the man whose eyes were filled with pain, his body twitching. Krazack stared into the man's eyes as he tried to speak, blood dripping from his mouth. He could burn him, filling him with agony, and end his misery.

-No, leave him.-

We are hungry.

Krazack grinned at the man. "Asshole."

The vehicles, *cars*, stopped, people getting out to see what happened. He recognized the siren of the police in the distance. Images and words flooded his thoughts. He felt pain at the base of his skull, and he dropped to a knee, reaching back.

Too much.

-There are too many.-

[Kill them all! We need silence!]

He forced himself to his feet and started walking his original path toward the city, picking up a scent of fruits. *Grocery store*, that is where food would be. Images of rows of fruit threatened to overwhelm him. He saw a large building ahead and across the street. He could wisp across, but it would tell them what he was. The people behind him were watching, holding up devices and phones to capture images of him. They thought he was one of them.

-It is a tactical advantage.-

Let them underestimate us.

[Stupid creatures. Ha ha ha, God's chosen indeed.]

He didn't wait for the traffic to clear before running across toward the store. Cars swerved around him. In the lot in front of the market were neat rows of cars extending from one side of the building to the other. People were going in, and coming out with food, their groceries. He grabbed a cart being pushed past him with bags of food. It smelled odd.

This is not food.

"Excuse me!" The woman challenged him.

He pushed down on the cart, bending the metal frame. He ignored her and went toward the main doors. The woman continued to yell at him. He tuned her out, ignoring her crazed rant. He stepped through the doors into a spacious rectangular open area that looked like a great bazaar, except no one was selling anything. Home markets roared in contrast to this quiet. The disgusting smell of oils, foul wheat, and other things he didn't recognize turned his stomach. To his right, though, he smelled fruits, apples, grapes, familiar scents.

He pushed his way past a line of people waiting to pay, their carts full. He ignored their exclamations, and that of the cashier telling him he was going the wrong way, moving with purpose to the stacked fruits. His stomach grumbled at the sight. It was a buffet. With a large apple in hand, he took a bite of the sweet fruit. He strolled, looking at the many options. He tossed the apple core aside and pulled a bunch of grapes and began eating them.

"Sir, you're going to have to pay for that."

Krazack turned and looked at the man. He wore dark pants and a short-sleeved blue shirt. Gold embroidery adorned his chest. Security. Not police.

"No."

A garbled sound came from something on the man's belt, a radio. "The police are on their way. It would be easier if you cooperated."

[Kill him.]

He is interrupting our meal.

-The police are coming.-

So hungry!

Krazack grabbed the man by the arm and took a bite from the bunch of grapes he held in his other hand. The veins in his arm glowed, and the man's arm caught fire. The security man screamed, pulling to get away. The veins glowed brighter as the fire spread up his arm and onto his torso, his lower arm charred. Screams erupted around him. As the man's screams died, Krazack released him and headed toward the peaches.

Bang! A shot rang out, hitting him in the leg. It stung. More shots followed. These weren't police, they were ordinary people. Was everyone armed? The pain in his leg burned. His rage took over as fire flared around him.

Chapter 31

Tanya sat at a table outside on a large patio shaded by palms and a large awning that adjusted to keep the patio cool. She didn't know what the imam wanted to talk about. She was a little early but was tired of waiting in the hotel room. It provided comfort and necessities but lacked the feel of home. She admired the patio setting. Several other parties occupied tables throughout the area, but the noise level was comfortable. She sipped her sweet tea and checked the time on her phone again.

It was cooler than she expected on the large deck. She felt the breeze coming from outside the restaurant. Cool may have been stretching it, but it kept the guests from sweating, and Tanya thought it felt good. Shifting in her seat, she felt a twinge of pain along her calf. She took two pills from her handbag and washed them down with tea.

She spotted Yusuf as he came through the door, right on time. He wore khaki pants, a white shirt, and a black skullcap. He looked aged, his eyes tired, and with a few more wrinkles than she remembered from years before, his white beard was well trimmed. Tanya rose. "Yusuf, you look well."

"Ms. Janessy, you look healthy as well. I am pleased to say."

She waited for him to sit before sitting. "I'm sorry I didn't answer your request sooner." She averted her gaze before continuing, "I've tried to move past everything that happened, but it's difficult."

"I understand. What you went through is unimaginable."

Tanya nodded, her heart heavy with memories of Sheri, Amara, and her mom.

"I can only imagine what you've thought of me all these years. We were supposed to meet, and I wasn't there. I'd like to share my story if you're interested."

"I feared the worst. I was certain the killer also targeted you." As she sat, she offered, "Would it be alright if we order? I looked at the menu. There should be a good selection for your diet." Her eyes drifted to his left arm, held close to his body, his hand curled. Was it age, or Nafara?

"Thank you, that's considerate," he said.

They ordered and made small talk while they waited for their drinks to arrive. Both selected water and tea. The outdoor lights came on and dimmed, adding to the cozy ambiance. A selection of herbs and olive oil accompanied a serving of fresh flatbread. The remaining tables filled with patrons, whose conversations created a dull roar throughout, making it more difficult to hear.

Yusuf described the events of the day, from seeing Amara entering the house, through the encounter with the Jinn. He took a deep drink of his iced water at the end.

"I thought I would die behind that house, but my prayers were answered, and I escaped to a hospital, where I fell into a coma."

"That's horrible." She hadn't known about the encounter with Nafara. His recollection stirred her own memories from that day. He didn't say her name.

Tanya watched his eyes as he awaited her continuation of the story. She set a piece of bread down and fidgeted. "I went to the library looking for you. While I was there, my father returned to my house." Tears filled her eyes as she remembered her mother, bloody, lying in bed. "He killed my mother. I couldn't get her out of the house before

146

the fire became too much. I saw him on the street and took off after him, following him to the Vulture House. Inside, I discovered him and Diane, the counselor, arguing, but I don't know why he was there. The fight escalated, and they attacked each other. I saw Diane stab my father with a large kitchen knife. There was so much blood, she must have hit an artery. By chance or divine intervention, Diane slipped in the blood and struck her head on the counter. I called the police. They said she died shortly after impact. Afterwards, my aunt drove up from Austin and took me in."

"Ms. Kavioni?"

"Yes, Aunt Nafara has been a blessing." Something flashed in his eyes at the mention of Nafara's name. Did he suspect? "It's been quiet since then. Four years at Rice, and now she is fulfilling a dream and running for office."

"Kavioni is a Persian name. Is your aunt from Iran?"

Tanya smiled. "Her family is, she's second generation American. She married my mother's only brother." She recited the story they had rehearsed. Nafara insisted that any search for documentation to support the claims would be foolproof.

Their food arrived. Tanya accepted her Grilled Chicken Greek Salad, though Yusuf's Falafel and Quinoa Tabbouleh looked good as well, and the lemon smelled fresh. They thanked the waitstaff and prepared to eat, making sure he was out of earshot before continuing.

"Tanya, I am worried about you. How well do you know your aunt?"

"I've known her my whole life. We used to visit every few months." She fought to remain calm, her instincts screaming at her to get away.

"If something was off with her, would you be able to tell the difference?"

"I am pretty sure. Why? You're scaring me." He's fishing for information, but he seems sincere.

He leaned closer. "I am worried about you. I believe we encountered a type of Jinn, a Ghul. In all my research, Ghuls don't let their prey escape. I don't mean to alarm you, but they are incredible shapeshifters. I was worried that it was too convenient that your aunt arrived in time to save you."

Tanya stared at him, trying to act worried. "I would know if there were something off with my aunt. I know her. Besides, there have been plenty of opportunities to hurt me. I was in college, not locked up in protective custody."

Yusuf shook his head. "I'm sure you're right, Tanya, but I'm afraid something bad is happening."

"What do you think it is?"

"I can't say yet. I need to gather more information. If what I believe is true, a Jinn attacked me and was hunting you, which means you're still in danger. There is a possibility that this is much bigger than me and you."

Could he know she was trying to help free the Jinn? He couldn't. Maybe he saw the story about the fire and somehow put the pieces together. No, that couldn't be it. He had no way of knowing. Should she tell Nafara? Would her aunt go after him again? She hoped not. She didn't know Yusuf that well, but he was a link to Amara and Sheri.

"Well, well, Tanya. What have you been up to, and who is this handsome man?" Tanya's blood ran cold, and her breath caught.

Nafara walked to their table, looking down at the pair. If she recognized Yusuf, she didn't give any sign.

"Aunt Nafara. We were just talking about you. This is Imam Yusuf Ahmed Al-Fortwani." She hoped she got his name right.

Yusuf stood, inclining his head. "It's Ayatollah. I am a scholar and teacher at the Darul Hikmah Institute."

She held his eyes for a moment before breaking into a smile. "I've heard of it. It is the largest Islamic institution of learning in the state of Texas."

Lucy rushed through the door, a tablet in hand. "Excuse me, Ms. Kavioni, you need to see this." She placed the tablet on the table. The video showed a live news feed from Austin. Several buildings were on fire, smoke billowing into the air. The scene shifted to a newscaster.

"...I have to warn our viewers that this next part will be difficult to watch. We have video from witnesses in the Kooper's Super-Grocery, who say a man used pyrotechnics to burn another man alive, kicking off the chain of events leading to this blaze."

The screen split, with the reporter on the left and the camera video on the right. Her face was stoic until the man seemed to burst into flames in the man's grasp, where it changed to a look of horror.

"Ifrit," Yusuf said under his breath, but loud enough to be heard.

"Excuse me?" Nafara asked.

"That is an Ifrit." His face had hardened with worry.

Nafara laughed. "Ayatollah Al-Fortwani, you can't be serious. The Jinn are stories made up to scare children. My mother terrified me with tales of Jinn punishing children who misbehaved."

Tanya recognized Nafara's expression. She was laughing off the idea while measuring his understanding of her people.

"I assure you, Ms. Kavioni, the Jinn exist."

Her aunt waved off the comment. "It looks like Hollywood special effects."

Lucy inserted herself between the two. "Ma'am, we're going to need to make a statement."

"You're right, of course. Tanya, Ayatollah, I'll leave you to your meal. I had hoped to join you, but work calls." She bent and kissed Tanya on the head. She addressed Yusuf as she turned to depart. "It was nice meeting you. Maybe I'll stop by the institute to discuss how we can strengthen the relationships within the community."

Yusuf nodded. "I look forward to it." Tanya didn't believe him for a moment, which meant that Nafara didn't either. She would need to talk to her aunt. He was a link to Amara, and she had enjoyed their dinner, despite having to lie to him. She worried Nafara would kill him to tie up a loose end.

"We're almost done. I'll be right up."

"Take your time. It's always good catching up with old friends."
She locked eyes with Yusuf, and the two seemed to size up the other.

Great, Tanya thought.

Chapter 32

Tanya closed the door behind her and heard a newscaster reporting on the chaos in Austin. Nafara was standing while Lucy sat on the couch, her tablet in her lap.

"Well, are we done conspiring with the enemy?" Her smile implied jest, while her gaze was serious.

"Nafara, I am completely loyal to you, and I always will be. You know he was a brief anchor, keeping me grounded during that time. But you saved me. I'll never forget that."

"I was surprised to see him."

"He told me the story of your encounter. I told him my story, unchanged since that day." She knew Nafara would understand the meaning. Lucy, while loyal to Nafara, didn't need to know everything.

"What else did he tell you?"

"I think he was holding back, testing me."

"Does he suspect me?"

"Maybe at first, but after meeting you and seeing the news from Austin, I think he's unsure."

"He bought my act, then?"

Tanya shook her head. "I wouldn't go that far. He believes a Ghul was hunting me, and that if it were true, they wouldn't give up."

Nafara walked to the large windows, looking over the city. "True, but why would he care? I understand his personal concern for you. You were friends with one of his followers, but why now, after all these years, would he be concerned about all of that?"

"You know what they say, 'for every action...' Maybe there is someone out there who is working to make sure the Jinn don't succeed," Lucy added.

"I'll remove the threat. I can go to his institute tonight," Nafara declared.

"No. We can use him to get more information. He had suspicions when we were in Cedar Ridge, but he didn't have proof. If he is more focused now, Lucy is probably correct that there is a group working to prevent you from succeeding." She needed Yusuf to be safe. She just did.

"I understand your reasoning. But are your feelings for him clear?"

Tanya crossed the room to Nafara and hugged her. "I feel a connection to him because of what he did for me and my friends. Believe me, though, I'm loyal to you."

Nafara reached out and stroked her face. "You'll keep me informed."

"Always." Nafara held her gaze for a moment.

"Okay then, until he gets in my way, I will leave him alone," she paused before walking back to watch the unfolding events on the TV, "as a favor to you."

"Thank you. What is going on in Austin?"

Nafara sat in a large chair on the side of the room. "I hate to admit it, but the holy man is probably on the right track. Are you sure you remember everything about the fire at our home?"

"I think so. like I said, I remember feeling a presence, but not seeing anyone."

Nafara pointed to the images of fire and destruction. "That looks like the work of an Ifrit."

"Can you talk to them?"

"I believe so. What I don't understand is why they are drawing attention to themselves."

"If they came through the portal, maybe it affected him somehow. They could be angry about being pulled into our world, somewhere completely foreign to them."

Nafara didn't seem convinced. Did the Jinn know something she wasn't willing to share? What if she was correct in her reasoning? The destruction in Austin was her fault. Tanya felt like she had been punched in the gut. She eased herself onto the long couch, hand outstretched. She had accepted Nafara's nature, and her need to feed. Her love for her friend led her to reason herself into a comfortable position. She looked up at the TV, seeing the raging fires burning across the strip mall and surrounding buildings. This was her fault. Those deaths were on her.

"Tanya, what's wrong?" Lucy asked. Nafara turned to look at her as well.

She pointed at the screen. "This is my fault. If I let someone through, and they're on a rampage, then all of this is on me. All those deaths are on my hands."

"Don't be weak," Nafara commanded.

The words were a slap to her face. Nafara rarely spoke to her in this manner, but she felt the intensity of her gaze. "They are acting within their nature. There is a reason, and it has nothing to do with you."

Tanya nodded, shaken by the rebuke.

"You have your role. I need you focused on your task. The same applies to Lucy," she talked past her campaign manager.

"Our goal is clear and noble. Free my people from an unjust imprisonment. Don't think that it won't get messy." Nafara kept her expression neutral, but Tanya felt the disappointment in her words. She was right. If an Ifrit traversed the portal, it chose to. Its actions were also of its will. She swallowed her emotions, locking them deep inside. Nafara's words were true. She could not take the burden of their actions onto herself. When she opened the portal, there would be many of her people freed to make their own decisions. The Jinn, like humans, had free will.

"You're right, of course. I'll find out what Yusuf knows and continue to work on understanding the weave."

"Focus and use your music. You've shifted too far into the mathematics, treating it like a problem to be solved. Embrace your feelings, and the sight to gain a better understanding."

"I will. I'm sorry."

Nafara crossed the room and helped her up. She shifted to her Yasmin persona, holding both of Tanya's hands. "You don't have to apologize to me."

Tanya hugged her. Doubts about whether she would have been a victim if Nafara had chosen someone else crept in, and she felt like she was embracing her own doom.

"Nafara, if you don't need me, I'm going to go back to my room. I'll have your press release ready in the morning."

Nafara shifted back to her current persona and reached out to take Lucy's hand. "I hope you two know that we're going to change the world."

Tanya smiled, wondering if Lucy felt the same way she did.

Chapter 33

As Tanya stepped out of the car, a small group of bystanders clapped to greet her. She waved, smiled, and shook hands. Nafara, the candidate, took control of the scene, bringing the attention of the on-scene commander and representatives of the fire departments and police.

"Ms. Kavioni, I'd say it is a pleasant surprise. However, under the circumstances, I'll drop the pleasantries."

"Mrs. Bradlow, how is the recovery going?"

"Slow. I think we were fortunate that this occurred during the late evening, and most people had the good sense to get and stay away."

"The economic impact will be catastrophic for the community."

The fire chief nodded.

"What happened to the man who caused this?"

"We're still looking for his body. I don't think anyone could have survived this. He was spotted inside the supermarket after the police had set up a perimeter to let us do our work."

Nafara looked toward the wreckage. "He hasn't been identified?"

"No, we've had dozens of call-ins, but nothing has panned out yet."

"Has the governor been here?"

She shook her head. "I saw his press release. With the low death count, I wouldn't expect him to show up."

Lucy approached the pair, a cameraman, and a reporter in tow. When they got close, her assistant maneuvered the pair to place the wreckage in the background and helped set up the shot. Lucy introduced the pair and stepped out of the way.

"Ms. Kavioni, would you like to make a statement about the tragic events that unfolded last night?"

Tanya walked away from the group as her aunt engaged in the spontaneous interview. Lucy and Nafara had gone over the specifics earlier in the morning, with Lucy arranging for the interview. As a result, she and her aunt were having dinner with Camila Navarro. The host of Good Morning Texas had become a fan of Nafara and was ready to take the next step of endorsing her campaign.

She walked toward the yellow tape. Lifting it enough to pass, she stepped under and walked across the open space toward the collapsed strip mall. Taking a quick glance around, she made sure no one was watching her. Kneeling down, she opened her eyes to feel the weave. She saw the strands filling the space above the wreckage. As she reached out, she touched each one to identify what it was. There were so many flavors of smell wafting upward. Each of the foods, the construction materials, and one she recognized from her garden — death. The visual filaments didn't appear damaged. They were instead of color from the materials that had burned. She didn't understand the discoloration, as some were brighter and others dull.

To avoid being seen, she ducked behind a large pile of debris, venturing further into the wreckage. Nafara might get angry, but she wanted to know if the Ifrit had died. Would she recognize him? She didn't know.

She felt an urge to touch the filaments. Checking her surroundings and finding herself alone, she acted. She looked at the filaments extending upward from the rubble. She inspected each one, their essence giving a hint toward the original form. When she found one that might be easy, she took hold and sang. The notes felt counter to the wreckage. They brought a sense of joy. Her focus was on the happiness her friends and mother brought her, as she brought up images of them, not allowing the tune to shift toward sadness. With her emotions as her guide, she strengthened the filament of the music and wove it with the one she held. She became aware of the connection between the three and sensed the necessity for others. She reached out, shifting her song to add longing to attract the filaments she sought. One raised up from below, and another flowed through the others under the rubble. She could see all the filaments, and worked a more complex weave, balancing how much of each source filament fed into the whole. She felt something new. It rose from beneath her. She could see the rubble shifting as the source pushed upward. She moved back, continuing to sing and guide the plant. A small growth broke through, pushing upward.

She felt the plant grow. The potential had always been there. It was her guidance that brought together the elements. As she sang, the small growth continued upward, becoming a small sapling. She sensed the positivity of the growth as the small apple tree continued to rise. She glanced past the sapling to the rubble she was behind and saw yellow eyes staring at her. Startled, she stopped singing and screamed. The high-pitched sound cut through the late morning air.

* * *

Krazack heard the surrounding movement, water flowing between pieces of rubble, and something pressing through the surrounding stones. He shifted his form, drifting between the large pieces of wreckage until finding a space that could hold his physical form. He took shape, lying between the collapsed portion of the wall. She was here! The woman who had released him. Her face held an exotic beauty not found in the City. Her thoughts were quiet, but her presence gave off a feeling of power. She was frail and needed protection from the harshness of the world. He listened to her song. Her voice was soft, comforting. He didn't notice that the voices were quiet, his thoughts clearer and less conflicted. Her eyes found his, and she screamed, the piercing sound wrenching at his heart. He recoiled back into the darkness, seeing other people come to her aid. Krazack sensed the Jinn before she appeared. The Ghul was here.

He felt a powerful pull toward the human woman, despite his urge to flee. He watched the Ghul move with ease across the broken ground. This is where she would set up, a broken place to attract unwary travelers.

Nafara bounded past the tape, careful to make her movements appear human as she neared Tanya. The woman she had been talking to, the person in charge, trailed behind.

"What is it? What are you doing out here?"

Tanya felt relieved in Nafara's presence. "I thought I saw something." Conscious of the eyes on her, she tried to signal Nafara. Seeing her aunt look toward the opening, she pointed to the area she had sensed the dead person. Two of the firefighters moved to where she was pointing and began sifting through the rubble. After a few moments of digging, they called out that they had found someone. Nafara helped Tanya out of the field, getting her to the car.

"He was here. I saw his eyes watching me," she whispered.

"I can smell him."

"Are you going to warn them?"

"No."

"Is that what we want?" Tanya asked.

"Were you threatened?"

"I don't know. His eyes burned like yours, but yellower. I was startled, but not afraid."

"That confirms he's an Ifrit. What concerns me is his response to you."

Nafara's comment didn't comfort her. What did she mean by it? She noticed the fire chief and some rescue personnel standing around an apple sapling with a few large apples.

The fire commander was kneeling by the small apple tree. "How the hell did this thing survive the fire?"

Nafara looked at her niece.

Tanya turned away, heart pounding. She could still feel the song thrumming in her bones, alive in the air.

Chapter 34

Tanya got into the car, followed by Nafara. Lucy got in from the opposite side and sat facing the pair in her usual position.

"Something's up. I can see it in your expression," Lucy stated.

"I saw him, at least his eyes. He's right underneath them. They're going to find him."

Nafara waved the comment off. "He's safe for the time being. The humans won't find him. Did you distract them on purpose?" Nafara looked at her.

"Yes. I was trying to signal where he was to you and needed them to focus somewhere else."

"How did you know there was a body there?"

"I was trying to use the weave, and I could sense it, like in our garden, before you cleaned it up."

"Wait! There were *bodies* at the house?"

"Don't worry, Lucy, I took care of everything before the fire," Nafara said, shaking her head.

"Everywhere? If there is anything there, the construction could reveal it. I don't think I could deflect that kind of heat."

"I said I took care of it. I've been doing this for a long time. And the bodies in the garden were a test."

"You put them there on purpose?"

Nafara shrugged. "I was testing your progress without pestering you about it."

Tanya remained unconvinced. One would have been good for a test. There had been two bodies buried in different areas of the garden. "Who were they?"

Nafara smiled. "Nobody significant."

The answer didn't make her feel any better, but she let it drop. "What construction? Are they fixing the house?"

"No, the house is a total loss. I purchased the home in the next lot over to the right."

"The white stucco ranch with the red shingles?"

"Yes, that's the one."

"Thank goodness. I was worried it was the boxy modern one on the other side."

"No, too many windows. Ours has windows that provide plenty of natural light with the vaulted ceilings, but plenty of cover from wandering eyes with the landscaping and tall palms."

Tanya had visited the couple who lived in the house. They had been pretentious but appreciated Nafara's business acumen in developing Eunoia. She wondered how her aunt had convinced them to sell but stopped herself. They were dead, buried on the property, or consumed after signing the bill of sale. *Focus on the goal.* She planned to bring the Jinn back to her world and have them help create a new renaissance, an era of enlightenment.

The car passed through the formidable gates to their community. She chuckled, *Ash Creek Estates*. It was a fitting name. She was happy to be back. Residents remained unaware of the unnoticed security presence. They passed over the small bridge and waterway, turning toward Ashton Hill. She was struck by the amount of work going on around the open lot their home had been in. The remaining debris was in two moderate-sized piles near the street.

"What are they doing?"

"Putting in a private park."

"I guess that's better than putting up a new home. Most of our neighbors wouldn't be happy with the construction and all the noise."

"It's not for them. I'm connecting the two lots. Your garden will be at the center of the plot."

It made sense. Her portal opening proved its possibility. With the surrounding landscape, she could continue her studies. She recalled the spell she had tried, unaware of her mind blocking everything else to focus on the replay. The balance of base elements woven into a stable, non-attractive event horizon. She pictured the swirling portal she had created for the briefest moment, and it hit her. She needed to use the Kerr metric, which accounts for a moving event horizon, a portal not fixed in space, but spinning and shifting like a whirlpool. Stability was the issue. The portal she had opened could not stay open, which is why they needed to move the Jinn from the City realm to Earth.

She had the math locked in her memory and visualized the concepts as a 3D model. Music was the key. In order to stabilize the field, she needed to determine the frequency on the Earth's side while incorporating the elements into the design. Figuring out how to stabilize the frequency on the other side without knowing the harmonic resonance would then be her next challenge. She reached up and massaged her neck as she ran through the calculations again.

As they drove through the gate to their new home, Tanya's vision faded to darkness before resuming focus. It was a dark morning or evening, the sun not poking through the thick clouds with any intensity. She was inside an unfamiliar home, being pushed back to a small door in the center of the house. As she entered, the lights came on, neon red, lighting the way down the cement steps. At the bottom was a large yellow-silver door. On either side were a pair of very fit, blue-skinned people in uniforms made of a cloth that seemed thin and soft. As she passed through, they snapped to attention, and she entered the large room beyond the door. Another blue-skinned Jinn was in discussions with a grizzled older man. She moved closer, seeing the black globe and anchor on his gray digital camouflage uniform. She saw he wore a device above his ear that looked like an Eunoia module, but unlike any she recognized. The room contained unfamiliar devices, although they had a basic design similar to computers, but smaller and sleeker.

Tanya's heart raced. The future was forming itself without her consent, and she was being dragged toward it. Opening her eyes, she inhaled a deep breath, as if she were starved for air. Nafara kneeled over her on the lawn of the home. "What happened?"

"A vision."

"When?"

"Not for a while, and not here."

That seemed to satisfy Nafara. "I hope you're writing them down."

Lucy offered her a water bottle. "Are you okay with walking? We should get you inside out of this heat."

"I'm fine, and yes, I am recording them when I get a chance."

Lucy and Nafara helped her up and guided her toward the tall, light-wood arched doors.

Chapter 35

Yusuf set his satchel down on his desk, retrieving his phone and today's copy of the *Houston Chronicle*. He latched it closed and set it in its place next to his coatrack, between two bookshelves. He sat down to start his day. Moving his large black spiced tea to the side, he opened the paper. On the front page was an image of firefighters pulling a victim from the wreckage, all three covered in ash. Smoke billowed up from the ruins in the background.

"City on Edge: Arsonist Behind Devastating Blaze Remains Uncaught"

He read through the article, which described what he had seen. Police had several images of the man, describing him as calm and comfortable handling pyrotechnics. Several videos surfaced, showing the man setting the fires and burning at least one man alive. Experts suspect that he has experience in movie special effects and that he applied a fire-resistant gel to himself.

There wasn't anything else that changed his mind. This was a Jinn. An Ifrit, a race associated with pyromancy. Were there two now? Or was their understanding of Jinn outdated and inaccurate?

"Good morning, Sayyidi," Farid greeted him from the doorway.

"Good morning, Ibni. Have you been watching the news?"

"I have. Last night, the Austin fire made national news as a quick mention before they shifted to politics and the unprecedented three-way race here."

"I met her, the candidate Ms. Kavioni, a few nights ago."

"And…" The word hung in the air.

"I don't know. Did you know Tanya's aunt is Persian? Married into the family."

"I didn't investigate that specifically. There was a photo of her with Tanya at her graduation, and then, of course, articles about her doctoral work and the technological breakthrough that allowed her to create the company named after the device they're working on. It just received permission from the FDA for testing with the VA, by the way."

Yusuf shook his head. "I worry about her. She still feels the pain of that time, but I think she is hiding something."

"Good or bad?"

"I don't know yet. When her aunt showed up, her body language changed, but it didn't feel like she was under pressure or coerced. The woman was intense. It felt like she was sizing me up, but it doesn't align with anything I've read about Ghuls. And now this." He put his finger on the picture from Austin. "I don't know what to think."

"Do you think there is a link between them? The police think they have a serial arsonist. There was a homeless camp that was attacked, also with fire, and a man matching his description stole a crate of peaches from a woman nearby. Oh, and a fire burned down the home of Ms. Kavioni."

"I do. You've seen the news. You know our beliefs. What do you think it could be?"

Farid was quiet. He looked to be struggling to find the words. "I will start my answer by stating that I do not fully believe in the Jinn, but given the circumstances, it could be an Ifrit."

Yusuf stood up and clapped his hands together. A smile spread across his face.

"Sayyidi, I believe you and what happened to you. I thank Allah, praise be upon Him, for your survival through it all, but why would Jinn choose to reveal themselves now, after all these years?"

"Close the door, Ibni Farid. Sit with me."

As instructed, Farid took the seat across from his teacher.

"I haven't told you all that occurred in Qom."

Over the next half hour, he recounted the events in Qom, leaving nothing out except the identities of the council members. Farid listened, his face revealing his conflicted emotions.

"Again, Sayyidi, if I didn't know you, I'd say you were delusional or writing a dark fantasy story."

Yusuf pulled the necklace from beneath his shirt, revealing the coin with the seal.

"The Society of Al-Batin."

"The hidden? To whom does it refer? The Jinn or the secret society?"

"I believe it refers to both, a dual meaning given by the Prophet Sulaiman."

"What are you expected to do? If the Jinn are now moving to open the way to the City of Brass, what can this group do against them? I've studied the Qur'an, and I know the passages from Surah Al-Falaq and Surah An-Nas. The Lord will provide us protection, as He did you, but what about everyone else? How many Jinn are here on Earth? Two in Texas at least. How many are on the other side?" Farid was sweating, and he couldn't find anywhere to put his fidgeting hands.

"Ibni Farid, we need to remain calm. If we let our fears overwhelm us, we cannot do what we are called to do. I need your help. I want you to join me."

Farid stood and began pacing. He gave a weak laugh. "How do you turn that down? I know you're telling me the truth. It's a lot to take in. The Qur'an does not include this."

"Allah does not give us tests He believes we cannot succeed."

Farid calmed his breathing, clenching his hands to stop his fidgeting. "Sayyidi, I will follow you. But I am afraid."

Yusuf walked around his desk and put his hand on his student's shoulder. "Allah is with us." He reached into his pocket and pulled out a coin and handed it to him. "Welcome to the Society of Al-Batin."

Farid turned the coin between his fingers, studying the seal. Yusuf returned to his seat, already planning their next move. The room seemed smaller now, bound tighter by the oath they had just shared.

"Now that we have that out of the way, we have work to do. We need to dig up everything we have on anything involving fires in Austin. Next, we should thoroughly investigate and collect all relevant information from the events in Cedar Ridge, specifically aiming to find any evidence linking it to a Ghul."

"I'll take those tasks," Farid offered.

"Good. I am going to talk to Tanya again. There is more to her and all of this. It's too much of a coincidence that two Jinn have appeared near her."

"What about the Society?"

"I'll keep them informed, just in case anything happens to us."

Farid looked at him, his face revealed a mixture of fear and resolve.

Chapter 36

Tanya stepped onto the large deck, which included an oversized wrap around a pool with a beautiful stone waterfall, highlighted by a colorful display of tropical plants. She hadn't had time to explore or try everything out, but looked forward to relaxing evenings by the pool. There was a full kitchen, a pizza oven, and a barbecue large enough to grill for dozens of people. Everything looked new or unused. She understood that the previous house staff was larger than what Nafara had brought onboard, which included the personnel from the previous home, minus the chef and housekeeper, who had both perished in the fire.

She followed the pathway to the left of the pool to a wooden gate that also looked new and displayed an ornate black wrought iron K. Her foot sank into the new cedar pathway as she stepped off the stone deck. Saplings spotted the large open lawn behind the house, filling in the fully open appearance. Nafara told her she had become fond of forests and trees. Open spaces, whether grass, concrete, or sand, reminded her of her early life in the barren areas of Iran.

The path continued beyond the gate, crossing the area that had once held their previous home. The large piles of debris were still near the street but were not visible behind the walls of hedges encircling the much larger garden area that occupied the house's footprint.

Bzzzt!

Yusuf: I saw you on the news. Have you moved
back to Austin?

She was relieved by his gesture. His attentiveness reassured her,
although she brushed aside his worries. Tanya suspected he was
holding something back, but weren't they all? She had to be careful
to keep his focus away from Nafara. Keeping them apart was an
option, but hiding in plain sight often proved to be the better option.
Nafara, despite her nature, was careful to disguise her efforts. Those
unlucky enough to see her true nature or form weren't often around
to say anything. She should respond to his text, or he'd worry, and
she didn't want him digging more than he already had.

Tanya: Yes. It's better for the campaign.
Are you doing well?

Yusuf: I am. My arm bothers me. I don't think I'll
ever get used to it.

Tanya: I hope you feel better. I'm sure
it doesn't help moving into hurricane
season.

Yusuf: I hadn't thought of that. The reason I'm
contacting you is that I have some business in
Austin next week, and I'd like to meet with you.

Tanya: Sure, that would be great. Let me
know when.

Yusuf: I will notify you once I have completed
my schedule. May Allah's blessings be upon
you.

Tanya: Thank you!

She always wondered if she should answer with the phrase "and with you," but it felt too close to what she remembered the adults saying in church, and it wasn't the same religion.

Tanya followed the path around to the central circle of the new garden. The grass had been replaced with sod that was not quite set. Most of the flowers had been replaced with similar ones from before, all held in place or anchored to tall dowels stuck in the ground. She set her phone down on the stone outside the sand circle and kicked off her shoes. Temperatures soared, exceeding eighty degrees and climbing toward one hundred.

Tanya slipped her T-shirt over her head and kicked her sandals off. She wore a sports bra and short spandex shorts. If it weren't for the tall hedges around her, she wouldn't have exposed so much of her skin, but Nafara assured her that the garden was safe. Within a few minutes of feeling the sun on her skin, sweat beads formed. She opened the little case she had brought and took out the wooden flute. She wet her lips, raised the instrument, and went through a brief series of drills and scales to re-familiarize herself with the instrument. When she felt comfortable, she took one dowel and pulled it from supporting a hyacinth plant. Reaching the circle's center, she planted the wooden rod vertically.

Tanya looked around to get her bearings and took her position, sitting on the ground. She took herself through a series of breathing exercises before opening her eyes to the weave. She concentrated on the heat from the sun, seeing the multitude of filaments surrounding her. With the flute raised, she played, drawing inspiration from the flowing and flickering filaments of heat as the tune was quick-paced and chaotic. To gain control of the filaments, she adjusted the tune several times. She understood she didn't need to reach out to manipulate the filaments, the music would guide her.

When she found the melody that gave her the best control, she repeated the process, projecting her will into the music. Focusing on the five filaments closest to the dowel, she guided them together at the tip. She added a swirl, imagining an eddy in a stream within the wooden stick, feeling the atoms move faster, gaining momentum from the music. The end burst into a brilliant flame. She felt the speed at which the wood was being consumed and slowed the tune to slow the burn.

Tanya played the melody, releasing the filaments from the sun, and focused on the flame on the dowel. With effort, she could influence the flame to sway to either side, and to grow in brightness, or dim to a low glow. Sweat dripped from her body. She stopped playing and relinquished control of the flame. Drained and tired, she felt the effects of her efforts. Fire was more difficult than the other elements. Tanya thought about the portal she had opened and worked on the core elements. She chuckled at the word *elements*. The ancients didn't understand or have a concept of the periodic table. What would happen if she focused on individual elements? Could she change elements? It had to be possible. There was a reason that the concept of alchemy exists.

She thought again about the fire, understanding the energy necessary to pull an electron away, or add one in, gave her pause. Modern-day magic, manipulating modern-day science, made things much more complex. She looked up at the filaments surrounding her in the sunlight. She took one and hummed a tune, focusing on reaching the resonance of the energy. The energy increased, and the filament seared her eyes. She felt a rapid buildup of heat across her skin. She released the filament and watched as it retracted into the sky, wavering about, casting a rainbow, highlighting several clouds in color.

A moment later, the effect faded. She wondered if anyone had noticed. At least it wasn't as bad as killing all the fish in the park. She chuckled. *No birds were harmed in creating this rainbow effect.* She gathered her things and headed back to her new home. It was a good session. Fire was more chaotic. It would take more practice.

Chapter 37

Krazack lay atop the pile of cars in the junkyard, staring upward. The sun's heat caressed his body. He lay on the hot metal, stripped down to his undergarments, the heat bathing his body. The sky wasn't cloudless, and several groups made their way across the sky.

This is a strange world.

-They do not believe anymore.-

Too many. There are too many of them.

No one can control them.

[If they fear us, they will kneel.]

[Make an example of this city.]

It is fragile. They are weak.

-Where is the woman?-

Krazack looked down at where the scars had almost disappeared. Running his hand over his exposed stomach, he sensed the bullets' impact.

We were unprepared.

[Burn this city to the ground, and all its people and others will fear us.]

A flickering light caught his attention in the distance. The light flared wildly, dancing in the sky.

A hakimah?

-Is it the woman or are there others?-

Krazack was drawn to her. He didn't understand why. She calmed his mind. Allowed him to focus. She couldn't be a hakimah, could she? Legends spoke of wise ones summoning and compelling Jinn, some with offerings, others through force. She hadn't compelled him to come forth. It was his choice.

What if she works for the banisher?

-Sulaiman.-

[Argh, the accursed jailor.]

Curses be upon him.

-We must find out.-

If we can seduce her, she may help us.

[We will be unstoppable.]

Krazack stepped off the pile of cars, kicking dust from where he landed. He shifted into a whirlwind of hot air, flames flickering in a vortex that had spawned the name dust devil several millennia ago. He didn't stroll up the roadways as he had before. The humans were looking for him. They were irrelevant. All that mattered was finding the woman.

What of her protector?

-The Ghul?-

-She was different.-

What if they are bound?

Krazack shook off the building pain at the base of his skull. What had he been taught about hakim? A bonded pair had a symbiotic relationship. Each influenced the other, sharing their power. Willing bonds were rare, one of the two often wanted more power and ended up sacrificing the other to gain it.

[If they are bonded, we must break it.]

-Kill a sister?-

[We have done it before.]

Silence took over his thoughts. Memories of his banishment within the old city still haunted him. After the War of Seven, the council of kings enacted a law forbidding the killing of another Jinn without a trial, and only the lawgivers would mete out punishments. He broke that law, and the council punished him. His anger rose. He was innocent but didn't remember how. He felt no remorse.

His path was clear. He would kill the Ghul, and the hakimah would come to him. Did she feel what he felt? She had to. The woman would help him claim this world as his own. The legends are true, humans are soft. They had forgotten to fear the Jinn. That would change.

He flowed around the buildings and homes toward the flare. The intermittent sparks leapt out, starting fires in his wake. Krazack believed his path would remain undetected unless someone watched from above, and there was no Marid here.

Any trace of the flared rainbow effect was gone. He shifted forms to his natural state, walking among the homes spaced on either side of the road. He had crossed a wide roadway comprising many overpasses. There were so many people driving their vehicles, cars and trucks. The world wasn't quiet anymore, and the air was repugnant. These people scurried about like ants. They didn't understand what they were doing to the Earth, poisoning it. His people would never defile the Earth.

As the sun neared the horizon, the air remained warm. He couldn't see the stars despite the clear sky. It didn't matter. He had spent nights lying on top of the cars looking up, not recognizing the patterns in the sky. He passed people as he made his way through the suburbs, communities, and villages on the outskirts of the large cities.

Whoop! Whoop!

The sound turned his attention to an approaching police car. He stood waiting as the vehicle stopped. The intensity of the lights didn't affect his sight.

Dātabara!

-Police!-

[Kill them now.]

-No. We must get to the hakimah.-

[We can do both.]

Krazack watched as a man, and a woman in similar garb got out of the vehicle. The policewoman further away had her weapon in hand, pointed at him. The closer officer stepped onto the sidewalk; his weapon also pointed at the Ifrit.

[Now!]

-No, patience.-

"Turn away from me and get down on your knees. Place your hands on the back of your head."

Krazack glared at the man, not moving. His muscles were tense, ready to leap. The officer repeated the command. A smile crept across his face as he turned and did as the officer instructed.

"You should let me go," his voice croaked from lack of use.

"You're under arrest. We're going to take you in for questioning. Don't move unless directed to do so."

[Insolence. Kill him!]

"You think you can command me?" Krazack stood, turning back toward the officer, now a few feet away, his weapon pointed at Krazack's chest.

"Get on your knees now!" the officer yelled.

He shifted his eyes for a moment to the woman, sensing her surprise as his yellow eyes flared with intensity. Krazack shifted into a fiery wind, swirling around the man. His screams filled the night as the fire burned his clothing, and then his skin, from his body. Krazack stopped short of killing the man outright, shooting across the front of the car to reform in front of the woman. The burnt, skinless man continued to whimper in pain. The female officer's eyes locked on him. As she realized the threat was near, she fumbled with her weapon, attempting to bring it around. Krazack grabbed her wrist, his veins incandescent on his arm as heat flowered through his hands. His grasp reduced her arm at the wrist to ash, eliciting a scream of pain from her.

As she fell to her knees, he reached forward, catching her at the top of a thick protective vest by her neck.

"How did you find me?"

Her arm caused anguish to fill her face. She looked up at him.

"Answer me, Dātabara."

"I, I don't know what that is. There is a warrant for your arrest."

He sent heat through his hand, smelling her skin burn under his knuckles.

She screamed again.

"How did you find me here?"

"Someone recognized you. They called us. Please, I have a daughter and a family."

"How did they call you?"

She squirmed in his grasp, crying as smoke rose from her chest. "On their phone."

Images filled his head, filling in the meaning of her words.

"Muéstrame quién te llamó." *Show me who called you.* He shifted to her prominent language.

"*I can't, I don't know,*" she answered in Spanish.

"Then they'll all burn." Heat flared from his hand, charring her through to her heart.

He looked around at the people, some gathered on their lawns, others looking out their windows. They held up their phones, sharing what they saw.

Now the world will see!

[Hahaha.]

-But the woman.-

She can wait, they must learn their place.

Krazack shifted to the fiery wind and flew forward, swirling among the people outside, setting each on fire. He smiled as he watched others get away to where they thought they were safe, their homes. Flying between homes and setting them on fire, he moved without patterns, his rage growing with each blaze he set. He lost himself in creating the inferno, spreading from this street to the surrounding streets, expanding the area of destruction.

Chapter 38

The fires in the suburbs were on every news channel. Every fire department in the area had been called in to respond to the massive blaze that had broken out in the Oak Hill community. Firefighters were trying to get control of the conflagration, which was spreading in an unusual pattern, against the wind. Over two hundred homes were burning or had been destroyed, resulting in hundreds of casualties. Local social media was abuzz with news from inside the area. Several witnesses described a hot wind moving through, carrying the flames between homes. It was the largest suburban fire since the Bastrop County Complex fire of 2011. Dry heat and drought-like conditions were making containment difficult.

Tanya sat on the edge of the couch, searching the people's faces for anything.

The sound of a ney flute playing grabbed her attention, and she reached for her phone on the nearby end table.

"Hello?"

"Ah, good, I was worried. It seems checking on you has become a habit. Are you okay?"

She looked down at the caller ID. "Yusuf, yes, I'm fine. The fires are not in our immediate area."

"Well, that is good news. Have the authorities identified a cause?"

"No, they said they won't know for a few days. It is spreading fast, jumping from home to home, and against the wind. It seems to have a mind of its own."

"It has to be the Ifrit."

"But why would it do this? The only thing I know about Jinn is what you told me about Ghuls. Are the Ifrit as dangerous?"

She heard a sigh on the other side. "I will send you the information that I have on the Jinn. Like us, there are different races. But in essence, they are like us in temperament. They have control of their lives and can choose between good and evil. The Ghul are cunning and stealthy, while the Ifrit relies on strength and speed to create chaos and destruction. In legend, they have the attributes of pyrokinesis, control of fire."

"And that's why you believe this is an Ifrit?"

"This, and what happened with the homeless camp up there. From the images of the bodies and the surrounding area, it looks like some victims burst into flames with no heat source. Spontaneous combustion."

"It still could be coincidence, though, right?"

"Tanya, I'm going to be open and honest with you. I suspect you are the common factor in both encounters. The Ghul revealed itself near you, and now an Ifrit has done the same. That is not a coincidence. Nothing like this has happened in over a thousand years."

He confirmed what Nafara had told her. Did the Ifrit know she was a wise one, as Nafara identified her? Was she attracting him, and if so, would others come for her as well? Did Nafara tell her everything? She believed the Jinn cared for her and didn't want her harmed.

"Are you there?" he asked.

"Yes, it's a lot to take in."

"Tanya, do you know what happened to the Ghul that was after you?"

She thought of telling the truth for the briefest of moments before answering. "No. As far as I know, it was Diane who manipulated my

182

father. I believed it was her." Which was the truth. She had believed right until Yasmin revealed herself.

"I don't believe that she was the Ghul. It's too easy, and what you described as happening would not even phase a Ghul."

"Do you know how to kill a Jinn?"

"There are tales of prayers keeping them in check, and of weapons with certain properties, like iron. When I encountered the Ghul in Cedar Ridge, I didn't know what I was doing."

"Do you now?"

"I'm better prepared. What I know is that you are in danger. However you escaped the Ghul, it won't work with the Ifrit. If it's focused on finding you, then you and your aunt should get as far away as possible."

"That won't happen. She's at a campaign rally right now. She won't give up the race."

"You need to be careful, then. If the Ifrit gets close, it could quickly unleash its fiery fury on you both."

"I will. My question pertains to the lore surrounding Jinn. I read something online about the hakim. Do you know anything about them?"

"Sulaiman, peace be upon him, was hakim, a wise one. The Prophet possessed control over the natural and supernatural and was rumored to possess amazing abilities including communication with animals."

"That sounds handy if you are looking to have an early warning."

"As far as I know, there have been no hakim since Sulaiman, at least none that have had anything written about them."

"I was just curious."

"No, it is a good point. I don't know much about them or how they were selected, but there may be something in the old texts that could help."

"If this is in fact an Ifrit, and there was a Ghul up north, perhaps there is more to it."

Had she thrown him off enough not to ask questions? She didn't know. She would talk to Nafara. The Jinn might head out to search for the Ifrit. She felt annoyed that they were diverting attention from the race for governor. Maybe Yusuf would find something that would help her understand her ability to see and manipulate the weave. Should she mention the weave? No, it would tell him she knew things she shouldn't.

"I believe they are Jinn, and that worries me. They have shown themselves after being gone from our history. The stories talk of Jinn interfering with human progress to slow our advancement, or just to be malicious. I am going to reach out to a few scholars on the matter. I would like to discuss your circumstances if you are okay with that."

Was she? "Sure, that would be fine." She watched the continuing coverage of the fires. "If it is an Ifrit, I'd like to keep my distance."

"If anything comes up, please call me. I hope to get up there in the next week."

"I will. Thank you, Yusuf."

Chapter 39

"I will not sit and wait for that idiot to ruin my plans," Nafara fumed.

"Yusuf agrees with you. He's convinced it's an Ifrit."

Nafara whirled. "What else does the holy man say?"

Tanya felt the Jinn watching her for the slightest reaction. "I can tell you every day until we release your people that you have my loyalty. Why don't you believe me?" Tanya stood defiantly. She hoped her friendship was enough to spare her from the Jinn's wrath.

Anger flared in her aunt's expression for the briefest moment before she smiled. "It's not you that I don't trust. It's him. To him and others like him, I'm not just Jinn. I am Ghul, a creature that lives in graveyards, feasting on the rotting corpses. Beggars and thieves, malicious spirits intending only to hunt your kind."

"But you aren't like that. Even as a cover, the Eunoia treatment will help people. As governor, you can help people. You're not luring unsuspecting caravans into a deadly ambush." Tanya recalled the death of the billionaire over a month before and Nafara's manipulation of those she needed, gaining their trust and bringing them onto her team. She had evolved, maybe more deadly, to those who opposed her.

Nafara calmed. "I don't trust him. He knows too much about my kind, and his insight is surprisingly accurate. He made the jump from the Ifrit, Ghul, and you. My kind has been absent from your world for a long time. Died off or hidden as I was until it was the right time to come forward."

Tanya perked up. "Yes, he said that. He didn't understand the timing, and that both of you being here has to mean something."

"I need to find the Ifrit. Lucy is working on stories and diversions to spin, placing blame on the governor. We haven't moved up in the polls in the last week. We're at a wall."

"You could kill him."

Nafara smiled. "I said the same thing. Lucy said that the lieutenant governor is too popular, and his positions are more centrist than the governor, which brings him closer to our positions, leaving him the advantage in a head-to-head race."

"I wasn't serious."

"I know, but I considered it."

"That would get the attention of the Ayatollah, and whoever else he may work with."

The lighting in the room dimmed. Nafara shed her clothing, shifting to her proper form—black skin with burning cat-like eyes. Shadows swirled around her, wrapping like a billowing dark cloth in the wind. She was going to hunt.

"What will you do if you find him?"

"We'll chat about what he thinks he's doing to my city." She felt a predatory threat implied in the words.

Nafara flowed, shifting and moving between the shadows of the night. She moved through the large houses toward the fires. She could feel the people in the homes she moved around. Some were frightened, others indifferent. She continued outward toward Oak Hill. The darkness was her ally. The Ifrit was stronger in the day, and the Ghul was stronger at night. As she neared the fires, she smelled the Ifrit's essence in the smoke. She paused, shifting her form in the shadows, free of smoke and ash. She stepped out of the shadows, dressed in a gray button-down shirt, rolled sleeves, and jeans with boots. Emergency personnel were helping the residents. She rushed forward to help support a woman who was about to fall out. Her face was gray with ash, and she wore shorts and a T-shirt. Her eyes were glazed with shock. Nafara supported the weight of the woman, moving her to another ambulance.

"She's about to collapse." After holding the woman, Nafara waited for the EMT to help, offering water and a seat.

She was aware of the looks she was getting from the residents and the emergency personnel. Perfect, as she hoped, they recognized her. While continuing to help people, she nodded to them. She passed out bottled water and assisted others by guiding them toward the volunteers. She went from person to person, moving deeper into the cordoned-off area. Waiting for an opportunity, she moved between shadows and took shape within the conflagration area. Firefighters hadn't made it this deep into the affected area. The smoke was heavy, hanging in the still air. Movement caught her eye. A man was carrying an older woman. He stumbled forward, tripping on an uneven sidewalk and falling into the grass.

She stepped into his view.

"Help, please. My mother can't walk."

She walked toward him, concern on her face. "Let me help you." She kneeled next to the woman to help him pick her up. The woman broke into a coughing fit. She twisted into a problematic position for the man to get his arms under her. Nafara placed a hand on the woman, holding the side of her face. A quick flick of a fingernail left a scratch on her cheek. The woman convulsed.

"Mom! Hold on, we'll get you out. Grab her arm. We can carry her."

Nafara looked at the man, who was so noble in his desire to help his mother escape this hell. But the fires were the least of his worries. She stood and moved around the convulsing woman, kneeling again by the man. She was hungry. Keeping up appearances and shifting forms took their toll on her. She touched the man's hand, scratching him with the same toxin that was now in his mother. The man collapsed onto his mother, his body shaking, drool dripping from his mouth. She scanned her surroundings, not sensing humans. She placed her hand on the man's back. After a moment, blood flowed from him. After he was drained, she consumed him. She repeated the process with the woman. Satiated, she again reached out, searching for the Ifrit. She sensed someone nearby. She spun toward the area she felt the presence. Flames engulfed homes, trees, and vehicles in all directions. He was nearby, but cautious. He was watching her.

This is not your place, Ifrit!

Leave this city. Go into hiding, and I won't have to hunt you down. If you interfere with my plans, I will kill you!

She turned, searching for her kin. She wouldn't be able to find him if he were hiding in the flames.

I won't warn you again. She let the warning hang in the air, not expecting a response.

Chapter 40

Tanya opened her eyes, tossing the thin summer comforter aside. She knew Nafara was close, despite the Jinn's efforts to be quiet. She opened her sight to the weave. The connection became easier the more she practiced. Focusing her thoughts and adjusting her sight allowed her to minimize the glow of filaments to just above sewing threads. With practice, she imagined moving about open to the weave, noticing only those things she was interested in. Like how humans saw the world around them.

From her bedroom, she went down the hall to the living room. She didn't see anyone, but the large sliding glass doors were open. She felt guilty about the comforts of wealth that surrounded her, as so many suffered nearby from the fires. This was the first time she had seen the wall of glass open, the back deck and wrap-around pool becoming an extension of the expansive room. The city wasn't visible, hidden behind a wall of privacy trees. A dark cloud hovered above the tree line, with several hundred fires still burning below.

Tanya again focused on the weave, sensing the Jinn across the pool, in the yard, near the line of cypress trees. She walked barefoot through the grass toward Nafara.

"You can't sleep?"

"I heard you return."

Nafara looked over her shoulder with a look of disbelief. "I love you but find that hard to believe."

Nafara wore her natural form of a tall, beautiful, dark woman in a royal blue wrap-around gown. She turned and held out her hand. Tanya took it, feeling the cool touch of the Ghul.

"Did you find him?"

"He was close. I could smell him."

"Is that an innate ability?"

"Yes, we can usually detect one another, though with work, it's possible to stay hidden. If you didn't know, we invented assassination, much to the dismay of the Creator."

"God?"

"That's what you call Him. We had another name for Him." Tanya felt her friend's grip tighten before loosening again.

There were always more questions she wanted to ask. Nafara offered some information, but she deflected or avoided much more. "What does the essence of an Ifrit smell like?"

"Hot wind that has traveled the expanse of the Rub' al-Khali. It's distinct. Dry and earthy, with hints of sulfur and salt. You never forget it once you've smelled it. The wind moves and shapes the expanse of the desert. If you were to feel it blowing around you, you would swear there is a presence surrounding you." Nafara looked past her, imagining the scene.

Tanya held Nafara's hand and again connected to the weave. The trees, the backyard, and Nafara all became more vivid. Pushing aside thoughts of other filaments, she focused on Nafara. She discarded the filaments clinging to her, as if she were picking dog hair off a dark jacket. She found it took less effort to find what she was looking for—the essence of the Ifrit. Focusing on the filament, she found the elements that were woven together, their smell, touch, blended.

Her vision of the weave snapped shut and shifted to a large room lit by emergency lighting. It was dark, but she could make out the rough green carpets, the rows of dark leather, and oak furniture, facing a raised dark wood desk. It was the Texas House of Representatives.

She saw Nafara lying on the floor, battered and bleeding, glaring up at her, supporting herself on one arm, the other dangling at her side. "You don't know what you've done!"

"It doesn't matter, Ghul. Soon, you'll join all the others that escaped banishment."

"She'll never—"

The vision faded. She turned and hugged Nafara.

"I'm worried about your conflict with the Ifrit. My visions show the Ifrit standing over your injured body, gloating. I'm scared."

"It's okay. Visions only show likely outcomes. I'll be ready."

"But you don't know for sure. What if it comes true?"

Nafara turned to face her. Placing a hand on each shoulder. "I don't intend to die until long after my people are free. You and I were chosen." She let the word hang in the air.

Nafara pulled a small, rolled scroll from somewhere. She opened it, holding the edges to keep it from rolling up. The paper looked ancient but had no signs of brittleness. "My grandmother passed this to me. It's a fragment from the Al-Hiyal Lineage."

"What does it say?"

"The flame shall walk in flesh. Through her, the gate shall open, and the world shall burn clean."

"Do you think this is what's happening now?"

"Yes, and it was written over three thousand years ago, just after the banishing. I believe this describes my impending encounter with the Ifrit. I need something from you." Nafara's expression became serious. "If anything happens to me, I need you to promise to open the portal."

"I promise." Tanya was afraid and worried about her friend.

"Good. Then I have nothing to be concerned about."

They walked back to the house, holding hands. The grass felt pleasant under her feet. As they walked, Tanya detected a familiar filament. They weren't of death themselves, but more a byproduct of Nafara's feeding. Tanya wondered if something were wrong with her, that she could accept death so easily, walking hand in hand, devoted to someone others would consider a monster? Was this a trick of psychology that occurs between kidnappers and their victims, Stockholm Syndrome? She didn't care. Nafara was her friend, her family. She would protect her with all she could. Her mind jumped to Yusuf, the protective figure that wanted to shield her.

She laughed.

"What is it?"

"Nothing, just a realization." A realization that she was in the same situation as she had been with her parents, minus the abuse. Both cared for her but would kill each other if she didn't stop them. There had to be a way to prevent that from happening. Maybe the Ifrit would provide an opportunity for all of them to work together. She wasn't sure if it could be done, but she would worry about it in the morning. It was after midnight, and they had a fundraising luncheon across town.

Chapter 41

Krazack swirled through another home, setting it ablaze. It had been a long time since he had released his full fury on anything. The City's laws prevented any race from exerting its power over the others. Except for Marid. "The good of the people" was justification enough for laws to be enforced without mercy.

But those laws don't apply here.

-Don't lose her! She will lead us to the hakimah.-

[These pathetic humans cannot defeat the flames.]

Krazack shifted to his normal form past the line of firefighters, attempting to control the blaze. Moving past a pair of larger fire engines, he resisted the urge to consume them in flames.

-Stay focused!-

He sniffed the air, searching for the scent of the Ghul. She would be more difficult to track if she were walking between shadows. He began jogging in a back-and-forth pattern, searching for her scent.

He was sure she had passed this way. She was brave and foolish to have searched for him.

Distractions fill your thoughts.

-Enough, concentrate!-

He caught her scent. A fresh garden blooming in the spring, a hint of earth mixed with the fresh blooms of many flowers. He recalled the stories of his youth about the beauty of Babylon and the Hanging Gardens. Before people knew them as such, the Ghul had a different name then. He grinned, thinking about how humans were made from clay or earth and God's divine breath, both of which make humans the best fertilizer. Thus, the Ghul, cultivators of nature, killed this young species to bring their elaborate gardens to life. He hastened to follow the scent, staying out of sight. He had to avoid another human recognizing him.

The Ghul hadn't done a good job of hiding her scent.

She is not of the City.

-A lucky one who escaped imprisonment.-

[Curses be upon Sulaiman the jailer!]

Her scent led him to the base of the cliff. He stayed hidden as several cars drove past. Waiting for an opening, with no one in sight, he transformed and flew up the cliff wall, reforming at the top. Krazack kneeled beyond the line of cypress trees, seeing only a few lights in the house the scent led to. He rubbed the back of his neck, and a sharp stinging shot up into his head and down his spine. Harsh, but not debilitating.

Find the hakimah!

[The pain!]

She can take away the pain.

Krazack fell to the side, curling into a fetal position, as the pain continued to lance upward into his mind. Each spike makes the voices scream in agony. He bit down hard, tears forming in his eyes. He squeezed his eyes shut, hoping the pain would stop.

-Move back. It's in the trees!-

Krazack crawled away from the tree line, along the cliffside, away from their home. As he moved away, the pain lessened, becoming tolerable. He sniffed the air: cedar, rose, and rue.

Clever. She knows the ancient wards.

He crawled along, staying outside the property line. The Ghul had surrounded their land with flowers and plants to ward against all Jinn except her race. Brilliant indeed, but she had made a mistake.

Does she lead these humans?

[Maybe the hakimah controls her.]

-No. She is in control.-

The hakimah follows her.

As he thought of the woman who had opened the portal, the pain in his head lessened. He inched closer to the tree line, and the pain returned, but not as strong as before. What was it about the woman that took away the pain?

We need her.

-She is not like the wise ones of legend.-

There was something about the hakimah that drew him to her. The voices were mistaken. She didn't want to hurt or control him. As the old stories described, she didn't call him to serve her. She had opened the gateway. He imagined her sitting in the circle outside the portal. Her soft brown hair hanging past her shoulders relaxed. There was no malice, worry, or ill intent, only focus. She was curious. Innocent. She was beautiful, the first beauty he had seen in this world.

He shook himself from the thoughts, realizing his body was exposed. Why did she distract him?

Krazack moved through tall hedges. He was in an open expanse covered in grass behind another large home. He shook his head.

-These people have no imagination.-

[Boxy, ugly places.]

They have no appreciation of the beauty of flowing with the environment. He walked toward the home, his eyes fixated on the house next door. Lights flared around him. He stopped, ready for an attack, bathed in light.

"What the hell are you doing in my yard?"

Krazack turned toward the man who addressed him. He held a long weapon in his hands, pointed toward the ground between them. A rifle. Another projectile weapon.

"Did you hear me? Get the fuck out of here!"

The lights!

-She will see us!-

He will give our position away!

Krazack leaped forward at inhuman speed, closing the distance between them in a blink. He grabbed the man's wrists, preventing him from raising the weapon. He let the heat flow, charring the man's arms. Screams filled the air.

Boom! Boom!

The weapon fired into the ground beside him before falling to the ground among the charred ash of what had been the man's lower arms.

A scream pierced the night, and Krazack looked toward the back of the house. A woman was holding a phone to her ear.

Stealth is lost.

-The police will be coming.-

[Kill her. Maybe it's not too late!]

He shifted to the fiery wind and swept across the distance to her, setting her aflame. He moved into the home and swirled through, igniting flames throughout the structure.

The Ghul would notice his presence. He flew outside, stopping by the whimpering man in a heap on the ground, his arms gone. He kneeled beside the man, lowering his face to the crying man's. The man was in shock and didn't recoil as the Ifrit's face closed with his. Krazack sneered at him. "There are legends of your warriors hunting my people down. Your people are weak. I am going to burn this world to cinders and begin anew." He leaned closer to whisper in his ear. "Let them know."

Krazack glimpsed the Ghul's home before disappearing across the backyard and over the cliff. Flames engulfed the home behind him.

She will be angry.

-This will bring her wrath.-

[Let her come.]

A proper Jinn would not have allowed a threat so close.

-Maybe she doesn't fear us.-

She will.

Chapter 42

Tanya bolted out of bed at the sound of gunshots. She ran to the back door. Nafara was ahead of her, in her natural form. The inferno burning next door illuminated the sky. Flames engulfed the entire structure. The sound of distant sirens was moving closer.

Nafara rushed back to her. "Get inside." Her eyes flared, burning like hot coals. Tanya didn't question the order, suddenly feeling vulnerable outside in her pajama shorts and shirt. She probed the shadows, looking for anything.

"Tanya, now!" Nafara commanded.

She turned and ran inside the home, going to the kitchen and taking the largest knife they had. Looking back through the large glass doors, Nafara was gone, moving in the shadows, searching. Tanya felt conflicted. She wanted to go outside, but Nafara had been clear. She went to the panel by the glass doors and turned on every light in the back. The expansive yard lit up, with shadows from the cypress trees providing lines of cover. Despite her uncertainty about the Ifrit, she was confident in Nafara's ability to move undetected between the shadows.

Her lack of understanding of the Jinn worried her. He could come in through the front, or the side for that matter, burning his way in as he had done to their old home. She shuddered at the thought of the victims she had already seen, some charred over their entire bodies, and others only in limited areas.

Her eyes darted back and forth. She felt vulnerable with Nafara gone. Pulling her phone out, she called Yusuf.

"Hello?" His voice was weak, as if he was waking from sleep.

"Yusuf, it's Tanya. I need help."

"What's happened? Are you alright?" His voice became clearer.

"Yeah, I'm okay right now. The Ifrit has gone on a rampage, and somehow, found me. I don't know if our neighbors are alive, but their house is fully engulfed in flames."

"I was afraid of this. There *is* something about you that is attracting these beings. Have you noticed anything out of the ordinary?"

Tanya wanted to tell him the truth, that she was hakimah and all that it entailed, but she couldn't betray Nafara's trust. She was doing bad things, but with a good purpose. Freeing the Jinn from eternal imprisonment was a noble cause, wasn't it?

"I don't know, maybe. When I play my music, I get carried away sometimes. It's like I'm transported somewhere else, and it's all so real. I can see, hear, and feel everything around me. But it can't be more than just getting lost in the music, can it?"

"It's possible. I'm coming up there. I was going to wait until next week, but I think I need to be near you. There are talismans of protection, like the ones I was bringing to Amara's family. I'll bring one for you."

He sounded as if he were going to say something else. Silence hung in the air.

"I'll be honest. I'm afraid for myself and my aunt. What can we do against an Ifrit? If that's what it is?"

"The most potent recommendations would be to go to a mosque, perform a purification ritual, and learn protective prayers. However, that's not an option. The best choices would be protective talismans, salt, and iron."

"I'll be there tomorrow. I'm going to bring you a talisman. For now, look for salt and anything around the house made of iron."

Tanya didn't feel any better. Now that she thought about it, she didn't recall there being salt in the kitchen. She rarely used it when she cooked, and the staff prepared their meals. It had to be at Nafara's direction.

"What will the salt do? I thought that was vampires."

"Many cultures have used it in the occult. The belief is that salt is associated with purity and cleansing. I offer it only as a suggestion as there are no current recorded cases of Jinn except ours, and salt wasn't involved."

Should she chance it? Sneak out while the police and firefighters were nearby? No, Nafara would be furious with her. She'd be too vulnerable. She needed anything Yusuf had on the hakim, but she needed to bring it up without feeling like she was fishing for information. Before they left for the rally, she would fetch salt in the morning.

"How long will it take you to get here?"

"I'll leave early to avoid traffic."

"Ok, we'll be at the Auditorium Shores. It's at Town Lake Metropolitan Park. I'll let security know you're coming. The rally starts at 10 AM. But she will probably be on closer to 10:30. It's not too far, and we won't know until the morning if the fires will affect it."

"Are you sure you should go out? These are two close calls. It's obvious he wants to get to you."

"I'm pretty sure my aunt will want me near. There will be security at the rally in case anything happens."

"Unless they are using iron bullets, they'll be useless. Modern firearms might slow them down. This is all new ground. I've been in contact with people who are more experienced than I am in this field. I told them my story. They can help us."

"I'm open to anything, but you heard my aunt. She doesn't believe in the Jinn, so we should keep what we discuss between us."

"That's probably for the best. You can't rule out that there is someone on your team who is feeding information to the Ifrit."

Tanya hadn't considered that. She would have to bring it up with Nafara. Their inner circle was small, though. Lucy, herself, and Nafara. They vetted the staff. Maybe it was one donor who knew her true self. The list of people wanting revenge was getting larger. Maybe one of them stumbled on the being after she let it into their world.

"I hadn't thought of that."

"Be very careful who you trust."

"I will." She trusted Nafara and believed Yusuf had good intentions, but she wouldn't let him harm her friend.

"I need to check on my aunt."

"Be careful, Tanya. I'll see you tomorrow. May God grant you a peaceful night and protect you."

"Thank you." She hung up. *I hope we make it through the night.* The glow from the fire next door caused shadows to dance in their yard.

Chapter 43

"Good call last night getting out and assisting during the fires!" Lucy exclaimed excitedly. "The media are asking hard questions of the other candidates. Now you have been present at the scene of two major incidents, and conspiracy reports are circulating that one of the other candidates is linked to the attacks on you and your niece."

Nafara smiled. The top three union leaders were on stage, exclaiming their enthusiastic support for her campaign. Tanya suspected that, like many of her high-profile supporters, someone might have forced them. Nafara was a mastermind at determining what the most powerful influencer is on a person. In the end, fear of being consumed ranked at the top of the list.

Lucy showed her the headlines on several websites, scrolling through. The message was that she cared for the people and would get dirty to help them.

They stood behind an awning, blocked from the crowd, waiting for the union leaders to introduce her. Nafara looked like she was searching for someone, her eyes held a moment on an old woman near the stage.

"…and when the day comes, the world will burn clean," the old woman said, voice quivering. "My grandmother told me. The ancients wrote it so."

Nafara smiled faintly.

"Do you think he's here?" Tanya asked, with a sense of unease growing in her stomach.

"I would be," the Jinn stated, stepping back from the opening.

Tanya stepped further back into the covered room.

Nafara turned, a flicker of her orange-yellow natural form flashing in her eyes. "Do you sense him here?"

"There are too many people," Tanya replied.

"You need to try because there are only so many opportunities where you'll have the chance to be covered in a crowd like this."

Tanya nodded and took a deep breath, opening her eyes to the surrounding energy. She gasped at the overwhelming volume. She relaxed, feeling her muscles release their tension, starting at her feet and working her way upward. The filaments faded and shrank in size, becoming thin threads, linked to everything from the grass and sun, to each person. She thought about the characteristics of fire. A surging, chaotic wave of energy. But that wasn't accurate. Flame needed fuel, heat, and air. When she had focused on the filament, she could see the attraction of the flame, seeking the best source of each.

She reached out through the crowd, onto the stage, and around the event, not sensing fire. As she moved through, she felt excitement, curiosity, appreciation, and apprehension and doubt. She pulled back into herself, looking at Lucy and Nafara. She purposely avoided the Jinn, unsure if she would be detected. Lucy showed excitement as she watched on her phone, scrolling through it. Her attention centered entirely on Nafara, a genuine believer. There was no malice or lingering effect of coercion. Lucy wanted Nafara to succeed. The revelation was reassuring and frightening. She could become a zealot, blinded by loyalty.

"I don't sense him. The crowd is overwhelmingly supportive, though there is doubt among some."

Nafara nodded to her, then shifted her gaze to Lucy. "I think it's about time a candidate dropped out."

"You're gaining support from the Democrats, which is cutting into the Garcia-Fernandez base. It'll be more difficult to explain why the incumbent would drop out in a state his party controls."

"Maybe we should engage her brother," Nafara Mused

"She has disavowed her brother. He's sitting in a Mexican prison with no expectation of release," Lucy countered.

"Yes, I know. Addicted to the product he was moving, he's wasting away down there." She looked up as she heard her name announced. Looking back, she winked. "Make sure you get this up quickly."

"Of course," Lucy assured her.

Nafara glided up the steps and across the stage. She wore her favorite blue business suit and skirt with a white shirt. The new party pin, a star with the Texas state flag on top with background graphics, tested to attract younger voters. The logo was also the center of the enormous banner behind the stage, positioned for the crowd to see it, but not lose sight of the buildings of Austin in the background. She waved to the crowd, a wide smile on her face the whole time.

"Hello Austin!" She paused for the crowd to respond, which they did with a roar. "First, I'd like to thank Martin, Laura, and Jorge for their enthusiastic endorsement." The applause continued.

"We love you, Nafara!" a voice yelled from the crowd.

"Well, I love you all, too. I want to talk to you about the problem we are having here in Austin." The screens on either side shifted to show images and aerial video taken from the two major fires. "I don't know that I'll be able to get away from the smell of smoke. It's in the air, with portions of Oak Hill still burning. I have to wonder what the governor is doing? I saw him on the news last night at a gala in Washington, D.C., rubbing elbows with politicians who couldn't care less about the fires burning in our capital."

Tanya stood in the open doorway of the tent near the stage. She watched Nafara work the crowd. The Jinn accused the governor of shirking his responsibilities but shied away from calling out her Democratic opponent.

"I have an announcement to make. Last night, after wading into the trenches with our brave first responders, I received a call from my associate at Eunoia. Initial tests have been successful, and the FDA has approved expansion of our non-invasive testing to a larger group. I would like to open the opportunity for anyone affected by the string of fires to sign up to test the device and procedure that is taking trauma recovery to a whole new level. I want to assure you all that this is free for any residents of Oak Hill or Montopolis. While there are no guarantees, we are seeing success with our veterans who have suffered overseas in combat, even in the most extreme cases. I, along with my team at Eunoia, am confident that we can change the course of our culture and help us escape from the mental health pandemic." The crowd cheered.

"As we continue to understand trauma and the brain, we gain an insight into how each of us deals with the stresses of life. Breakthroughs in research by Dr. Hector Gutierrez may lead to treatment of addiction. Preliminary results have been positive. Although this was not our original focus, it's a welcome step.

"I want to assure you that this is not an advertising campaign for my company, but another example of what I am doing for you. Whether it's working with the leading scientists to address some of the most significant threats to society today or working alongside our brave first responders. I am focused on what is best for Texas and its residents."

The applause was deafening.

Chapter 44

Krazack stood on the shore of the waterway near the gathering of the Ghul and her followers. He didn't sense any other of his kin nearby except her.

-She practices the old ways.-

[The forbidden practices.]

Forbidden? Those rules don't apply here.

-True. We can make our own rules.-

[Kill the Jinn and make her followers ours.]

Would they respect power?

-They have seen what we can do.-

[We must kill their deity in front of them.]

-She will be prepared.-

Krazack walked from the tree near the water's edge to a narrow footbridge crossing the flowing water. Others of his kind would have balked at crossing over the source of power for the Marid. He disregarded it. The urge to kill the Ghul drove him towards her. He must free the hakimah from her grasp. His feelings changed to anger at the thought of his beautiful rescuer suffering under the control of a Ghul. Her people should worship her. She would be placed on a dais and praised. Yes, that is what he would do. They will worship her, with him at her side to protect her and bring justice to any that opposed her.

[Justice? Remember our pain!]

-It's not her fault.-

If you kill her, there can be no more doorways to the city.

Krazack faltered, slowing his approach to the gathering. Without her, he would be free to do what he wished. Why did the hakimah open the doorway in the first place?

-Because she sensed us. We felt it for the first time.-

She needs us.

[No! We will be a god among these people.]

"Silence!" he said, startling a couple walking in the opposite direction. He rarely spoke out loud to the voices, but their distraction made his approach messy. "We hunt."

The voices went quiet as he focused on the gathering before him. Many people gathered to listen to the Ghul speak on stage. He moved closer to the group approaching her and remained out of her direct line of sight. He ignored her words, steeling himself against the attraction used by the Ghul to lure unsuspecting travelers. His eyes

208

focused on the raised platform. Her voice was powerful, reaching him in the way a Jann manipulated the air to carry the voices of the Marid leaders.

Their…he searched for the word, concentrating on the things he saw around the crowd, reaching toward the humans to gather the proper words. *Their technology is impressive. These powerless beings have conquered this place. It has still proven useless against us.*

As he approached, he slowed, staying near the back of the crowd. He tried to block out her words, but his head hurt like before. Was it the proximity to the Ghul? Had the Marid done something to him, driving him away from their kind? That had to be it. Enacting an undisclosed punishment was illegal. His anger surged. While turning to get a better view, he collided with an older human wearing robes and a black turban, whose smell set them apart from the rest of the crowd. He dressed differently, resembling the descriptions he remembered from the tales of the time before they banished the Jinn. A younger man grabbed the older man's arm, steadying him. The turbaned man looked up, and his eyes went wide. He turned away and fell to the ground, his hands reaching into his robes. He pulled out a small talisman.

Iron!

-It's a holy talisman.-

We are discovered.

[Kill him.]

-It's too late.-

[Attack! Kill the Ghul!]

Krazack leaped away from the man holding the iron talisman, knocking over several participants. He opened himself to the fire, feeling the heat build inside. Gasps from the crowd, along with several shouts, rang out. He stood tall and gathered the flames in both hands, forcing a ball of fire to form between his hands. Continuing, he fed energy into a basketball-sized sphere of flame. Releasing the energy, he pushed his arms forward toward the stage and guided it toward the Ghul. She looked to her right as the woman, the hakimah, stepped onto the stage and walked toward her.

His heart froze, realizing that the fireball would hit the human along with the Ghul.

-No!-

What have we done?

He watched as the woman looked from the Ghul toward the approaching ball of fire. Time seemed to slow as the ball expanded and spread outward, tendrils of flame touching the people, the ground, and eventually flaring in an explosion when it caught the stage. The hakimah had leaped forward, pushing the Ghul off the stage, taking the blast across her back, thrown off the stage by the release of power.

Krazack let out an otherworldly howl, flames jumping away from him and catching people around him.

He felt a piercing pain in his leg. Looking down, he saw the younger man, who had helped the robed man, stepping back. There was a nail in his leg. It pulsed and burned, surging. He wanted to punish the man.

Bang! Bang! Bang! Bang!

Shots rang out as police reacted to his presence. He attempted to shift into the wind but couldn't. Iron! He dove behind a large piece of equipment, a generator, losing sight of the people approaching him. He reached down and pulled the accursed metal out, his fingers burning at the touch, dropping it. Blood pooled from the wound. He shifted to wind and flew backward. Dispersing into a thin cloud, he flew toward the footbridge.

He didn't feel pain in his wind form, but he knew the wound would heal slowly. He felt the drain on his energy. How had they known to use iron? Not all humans had forgotten the old ways. He would have to be more cautious.

Krazack didn't travel too far away from the gathering, instead taking shape in a small copse of trees.

Is she alive?

-It was not our fault!-

We will follow cautiously.

-She saved the Ghul.-

The voices went silent at the realization. If she can love a Ghul, she can love him. She had saved him from a life of exile in a banished land. Would she accept him? Could she love him?

Chapter 45

Farid helped him up. Yusuf's hand hurt from his grip on the talisman, the iron ring leaving an impression on his hand.

"Sayyidi, are you alright?"

"Yes, Farid, I am. Did you see which way the Ifrit went?"

"No, I lost him when he jumped away. I was looking at you."

"I've seen his face. I'll not forget him. We need to get to Tanya."

"Security personnel have surrounded the stage."

Yusuf noticed the screaming around them. Farid held his ground, the people running away, splitting around them. He saw the lights of an ambulance behind the stage.

"The stage is ablaze," the younger man exclaimed.

"Help me. We must get to her before he does."

They pushed against the fleeing crowd. It became more difficult as many people were running away. He overheard them talking about the attack on the candidate. Her niece must have seen the attack, because she pushed the candidate off the back of the stage before the explosive hit.

"He threw a Molotov cocktail!" A man exclaimed.

"Did you see who threw it?" Another voice asked.

"No."

"It was the arsonist. I saw him on the news," a woman said.

Yusuf leaned into Farid as the people pressed closer. He held the talisman close to his chest. Should he have brought the blade? No, not to a political rally. He couldn't risk losing the weapon.

They slid through the crowd and to a police officer holding onlookers back.

"Sir, you're going to have to stay back."

"Officer, I am Ayatollah Yusuf al-Fortwani. Ms. Kavioni's niece, Tanya Janessy, invited me."

"I'm sorry, sir. I cannot verify your information. No one is getting through. If you are friends with the family, I suggest you contact them."

"At least tell me if they are okay."

"Several people sustained injuries, some severe. I cannot provide further information."

Yusuf nodded. "Thank you, officer. May God keep you safe."

The officer gave a slight smile of appreciation for the blessing. It was probably not what they usually heard.

He turned to Farid. "Ibni Farid, let's make our way back to where we met the Ifrit. I'm going to make a call."

They pushed their way back through the crowd, hearing similar speculation about the event on the way out. Many people had their cell phones out, recording.

"Farid, when we get back to the hotel, I need you to search social media for any videos of the attack. Once I talk to Reza, we should know what to look for."

As they made their way back to their original spot, they saw two ambulances leaving. A few minutes later, three more arrived.

"It must be bad. Let us say a quick prayer to Allah for the safety of those affected."

"O Allah, Most Merciful, Most Compassionate, we ask You to bestow Your protection, healing, and mercy upon Tanya and all those affected by this calamity. If they are among the living, grant them strength and recovery. If they have returned to You, envelop them in Your infinite mercy and forgive their sins. Guide us all through these trials with patience and faith. Amen."

He pulled out his phone and dialed a number. It would be seven PM in Qom.

"Wa Alaikum Assalam wa Rahmatullahi wa Barakatuhu, Yusuf. May Allah bless you. How are you, my son? Is everything well?"

"Assalamu Alaikum wa Rahmatullahi wa Barakatuhu, honored Shaykh. I hope you are in good health and under Allah's protection. May I have a moment of your time to seek your guidance?"

"Yes, of course," Reza said.

"I'm in Austin, Texas, with my student Farid Amirzadeh, who is with *us*. We have witnessed an attack on the young woman by the Ifrit."

"Are you sure?"

"I am. We literally ran into him, and he reacted to a talisman I was bringing to her."

"What happened? Spare no detail."

Yusuf filled in the details that he and Farid remembered from the encounter.

"It makes little sense. Openly displaying his powers would be foolish. Ifrit are chaotic beings, resembling the fire they are attuned to, but they are not careless. There must be something about the woman that frightens him. Has she said anything that might raise suspicion?"

"No, she insists she's not had contact with the Ghul. She did, however, inquire about the hakim. Now that I think about it, she passed it off as an innocuous question, something she saw in her research."

"That's an important piece of the mystery. She couldn't be a wise one, though. There hasn't been a confirmed hakimah in over a thousand years."

"Would that be enough to draw Jinn to her? How would they know what she is?"

"Those are insightful questions, Yusuf. The hakim are human, and while they could manipulate the weave, the Jinn might be attracted to her connection to the weave."

"I haven't been fully forthright with her."

"But you trust her?"

"I do, but I believe she is holding something back."

"Being a hakimah is a significant secret."

"To be honest, Reza, none of the texts I read mentioned the weave. Is this how Sulaiman could control the Jinn?"

"Yes, but he also had innate power. The ring provided by Gabriel was a gift from Allah. Extending his dominion over all living things, to include the Jinn, demons, and devils."

Yusuf shook his head. This was becoming more complicated. He believed nothing created by Allah could be evil, only the desires and choices of people and, apparently, Jinn, turned the good to bad.

"What should I do? I don't know what condition she is in after the attack. I need to find her."

"I agree. You need to secure her trust."

"Even if she's in contact with the Ghul?"

"Yusuf, my dear brother in faith, remember the words of our beloved Prophet Muhammad (peace and blessings be upon him), who was sent as a mercy to all worlds, including the Jinn. He taught us to approach the Jinn with the same sincerity and dedication as we do with our fellow human beings. It is our duty as scholars to follow in his footsteps and guide them with wisdom and compassion."

"Yes, Shaykh, I understand. I will follow the Prophet's guidance and approach this task with the dedication and sincerity it requires. May Allah grant me the wisdom to fulfill this duty."

"I'm going to send you two texts. Share them with the woman, Tanya. If she is a hakimah, she will need them to protect herself and those she loves. Peace and blessings be upon you."

Yusuf slipped the phone back into his pocket. His heart was in turmoil. He was concerned about Tanya and her aunt. He feared revealing too much and was afraid of the Ifrit.

"Sayyid, what did he say?"

"We need to find Tanya and trust Allah to help us protect and guide her."

Farid nodded in acceptance of the guidance. His faith was strong. He would be a wonderful teacher.

Chapter 46

Tanya lay in the hospital bed with various tubes attached, monitoring her breathing and heart rate and providing fluids through an IV, as well as oxygen through her nose. The nurse had wrapped her legs in non-stick burn bandages and administered pain medication.

Nafara stood by her bedside, seething. Lucy sat in the corner in a recliner, stealing glances at her phone. When Lucy twisted the phone to get a look, she tested Nafara's patience. Finally, she turned and snapped. "Lucy! Quit trying to disguise checking your phone. That's what you're supposed to do. It's why I brought you in."

"I'm sorry. Out of respect, I didn't want to appear insensitive."

"I'll take care of her. You focus on the campaign."

"Yes, Nafara." Lucy picked up the phone and began scrolling.

"How did he get so close? And then the foolish girl pushed me out of the way and took the blast. I don't know how it caught only her lower half. She should be dead."

"Is it because of her, you know?" Lucy wiggled her fingers, as if she were casting a spell.

"It could be. She needs more training. Her life is always going to be in danger."

"I have some good news. You have moved ahead of Garcia-Fernandez by one point five percent."

Nafara gave a cursory nod. Instead of risking losing control, she was exercising restraint to prevent any impact on the electrical systems. She didn't want any of the equipment in the room going out while Tanya needed it. She was hungry, and a distraction was welcome. Memories of their time together with Tanya's mother flooded her thoughts. *Hospitals provided a wide range of cuisine.* She grinned.

"I'll be back. When I return, be ready to discuss our strategy to remove the governor. Politically."

Nafara left the room and walked up the hall to the nurse's station. "Where can I find the cafeteria?"

The nurse, a young woman in subdued green scrubs, looked up, her eyes going wide. "Ms. Kavioni?"

"Yes."

"It's two floors down. Go to the end of the hall and take a left. The elevators are a little further down. Take them to the second floor. When you leave the elevator, there will be signs, but it's to the right."

"Thank you."

"Um, Ms. Kavioni. We'll take good care of your niece. Several of us support your campaign."

Nafara considered the woman's words. "Of those that don't, what's holding them back?"

The nurse paused, not expecting the question. "There are two big ones. Either they have always voted for one party, or they say you don't have the experience."

Nafara thought about it. "It's the older voters, right? They don't want to take a chance on something new."

The nurse cocked her head slightly, thinking. "Yeah, you're right."

"Thank you for your support, and for letting me know. I'll have to work a little harder." She took a card out and handed it to the nurse. "Call me if my niece wakes up and I'm not here."

"Yes, ma'am."

Nafara flashed a smile and followed the nurse's directions to the elevators. She studied the map on the wall outside the elevator.

She found the stairs and went up one floor to long-term geriatric care. When she reached the area, she saw it required a badge to get through the wide double doors. She ducked into a nearby staff restroom. Reaching behind the toilet, she pulled the pipe from the wall. Water sprayed against the back of the toilet, splattering all around and flooding the room. Exiting, she positioned herself just outside the room and waited. When a nurse came through the double doors, she flagged the woman down frantically.

"Excuse me, a pipe burst inside. I don't know who to report a leak to."

The woman grimaced, noting the water now coming from under the door into the hall. "Sure, let me look, and I'll call it in and get you some towels." She opened the door. Water splashed off the back of the toilet in a wide spray. "Oh my goodness!" She tried to back out, but Nafara shoved her in. The nurse slipped and then caught herself on the edge of the sink. "What the hell are you doing?" She turned back toward Nafara.

Nafara's hand flicked outward and scratched the woman across her cheek with a long, sharp fingernail.

Nafara shifted her appearance to that of the middle-aged nurse, with her blonde hair in a bun, wearing light blue scrubs and white shoes. She took the badge from the nurse's pocket, along with a set of keys. The nurse convulsed, blood and foam leaking from her mouth. "Such a waste. I hope you were voting for my opponent." Entering the hall, her presence was undeniable. She twisted the door handle and pulled the door, using her strength to jam it closed. She headed for the geriatric ward. All traces of water dissipated from her illusory clothing.

She strode to the nurse's station.

"I thought you left, Cheryl."

"I did, but realized I forgot my phone. I think I left it in a patient's room."

"I can help you look," the young nurse offered.

"No, I've got it. It won't take me but a few minutes."

"Okay. Good luck."

Nafara nodded, and walked down the hall and around the corner, entering the first room she came to. The sign read *Joseph Cavanaugh*. She strolled in, finding an older woman in the room with Mr. Cavanaugh.

"Are you the new nurse on shift?"

"Yes, ma'am. I'm just checking to make sure his room is clean."

"The other nurse was just in here. My husband is sleeping. We're good."

Nafara moved around the bed, stepping between the woman and her husband. "This won't take long. I'm glad you're here. He looks emaciated, not quite enough for a meal."

"Well, I never—"

Nafara hoisted the woman by the throat. Although she had a fiery temperament, she was a tiny woman. Holding the woman in the air with one hand, she used the other to open the private bathroom. She smiled as she laid the woman on the floor. Blood seeped from her pores. After draining the woman, she consumed the dried body. As she stepped out to finish the husband, the nurse from the station came in, closing the door behind her. She looked past Nafara and saw the blood covering the floor.

"Well, this is unfortunate," Nafara sneered.

The nurse screamed. The lights went out, the room was dim, lit only by the light creeping in from the side of the closed shades. Nafara grabbed the nurse and threw her into the bathroom. Her body made a wet sound as it hit the wall, cracking and shattering the tiles. Nafara looked around. The door had closed behind them. With the power out, the medical staff would check on all the patients. The man was still asleep in bed. She needed to move fast. The nurse was groaning in the bathroom. Nafara stepped out of the room, running into someone walking fast down the hall past the room.

"Cheryl, what's going on?"

Nafara kept a calm look on her face. "I'm not sure. Mr. Cavanaugh's sleeping. Keep checking the rooms. Hopefully, they get this sorted out soon." The hall was lit by emergency lights. She could take them all out if she wanted but decided against it.

"Yeah, okay." He hesitated, then moved to the next room.

She went to the double doors and pushed them open, hurrying to the stairs. She rushed down to the second floor, and stepped out, back in her Nafara Kavioni form, heading to where the nurse had shown her to the cafeteria. The lights were functioning normally down here.

Chapter 47

Tanya woke to the sound of the alarm outside her room. She didn't know where she was, and her mind was foggy. With great difficulty, she opened her eyes and felt a weight in her arms. She tried to tell whoever was in the room that she needed water, but her voice was weak and raspy. She sipped the ice water through a straw that someone held to her mouth. The wave of cold passed her lips, and she felt it go all the way to her stomach.

"Tanya, honey. Relax. The nurse will be here soon."

"W-what's going on? I can't turn off my alarm clock."

"You're in the hospital. Do you remember what happened?"

She tried to focus, but her eyelids felt heavy. "I don't know."

"Nafara should be back soon. She went to the cafeteria."

"No, ugh, the alarms. Not the cafeteria. She, my mom, was in the hospital." Her memories were fuzzy. She wanted to say more but couldn't concentrate. She took another drink of the water.

"Drink as much as you need."

She heard the door open behind a privacy curtain, and Nafara stepped through. Her aunt hurried to the bed, taking Tanya's hand. "Tanya, you're okay. What were you thinking?"

"You weren't looking. You were in danger." Her thoughts were becoming clearer.

"You could have been killed."

"I know. I tried to disperse the fireball."

"You were successful. The upper half flared outward at impact, dissipating the heat."

"The Ifrit attacked you." Her words trailed off as her eyes closed.

Nafara extended a fingernail, flicking it across Tanya's wrist. After a moment, her eyes shot open. She was awake and full of energy, and in severe pain from her legs. She cried out. Nafara reached under the covers. She felt her friend's hand slide across her back, and a scratch along the spine. The pain went away.

"What did you do?"

"Haven't you observed me? It's all toxins or chemicals."

Tanya knew about Nafara's control of toxins but hadn't considered she could use the effects in ways other than killing people. *Good and evil, the choice is hers.*

The door opened again, and a nurse stepped through the curtain. "Is everything okay in here?"

"Yes, we're as good as can be expected. What's going on?"

"There was an emergency on another floor."

Nafara feigned surprise. "I hope everything is okay."

"They haven't told us what happened. If everything's good here, I need to check on the other patients."

When the door closed, Tanya gave Nafara a stern look. "Is this you?"

"Maybe a little."

"With the Ifrit on the loose, don't you think we need to be more careful?" Tanya's hands were shaking. She felt like she had gotten an adrenaline shot.

"I'm not losing my closest friend." Nafara looked earnestly toward her. Tanya wasn't sure if she believed her. In the scope of what they were trying to do, losing Tanya would be catastrophic to their efforts to release her people. She took the Jinn at face value. "Thanks."

"The chemicals I gave you will last through the night, but you need to heal."

"How do I do that?"

"I don't know. For us, it's natural, much faster than humans. You'll need to manipulate the weave and coax your body into healing itself."

Tanya wanted to challenge her aunt, but it wasn't worth it. Her mind started going through everything she knew and reached the conclusion that she needed to manipulate the cells to repair the injury. She would have to think about it. After the koi incident, she was hesitant to manipulate anything alive, certainly not her own cells.

Nafara paced in the room. "One thing for sure is that I need to find the Ifrit and kill him."

"Isn't there any way you can contact him? Maybe bring him to our side. He must want to see your people freed, wouldn't he?"

"I think that's irrelevant. He attacked me. I won't tolerate anyone getting in my way."

Despite the attack, there was something about the Ifrit.

Nafara stopped at the foot of the bed. "After you pushed me off the stage. What did you do to the fireball?"

"I tried to pull it apart. I've been practicing with the weave. I know the theory of what goes into fire, so I tried to entice the flames with better targets." As she spoke the words, the realization of what she had done hit her, and her expression shifted to one of horror.

"No, no, no. None of that, Tanya, I'm proud of you."

"But I hurt those people. I urged it to seek others. I did that!"

"There are over nine billion people in the world. You need to be focused on our goals."

Tanya glared at her friend. "You know that's not how I work. Even all of that," she pointed toward the door, implying the alarms, "is not what I want."

Nafara looked at Lucy. "I'm pretty sure they weren't voting for me." Which garnered a stiff laugh from Lucy.

Tanya closed her eyes. She knew Nafara was going to do whatever it took to open the portal. She wanted to be disappointed in her friend, but she couldn't. It was in her nature. And she loved her. "Fine. I won't bring it up again. But you know how I feel about it."

Nafara took her hand, rubbing the back with her thumb. "I do."

Tanya saw sincerity in the Jinn. Was it genuine, or had she been practicing? "Okay, back to our problem, then. How did the Ifrit get close to us? I thought you could detect him."

"He's the first one I've experienced. He was downwind, and I didn't detect the scent among the others in the fires."

"Do you think he tracked you from the fire in Oak Hill? If he saw you, he had to know that you were trying to find him. Maybe he sees you as a threat, which is probably why he attacked the rally, and at your neighbor's house last night," Lucy added.

"I must admit that I didn't expect him to track me home. But it makes sense."

"We could lay a trap for him," Lucy suggested.

Nafara looked at Tanya. "No. I'll hunt him at night. The team doesn't need distractions."

"I know you want to win, but with all of this, is it necessary?" Lucy asked.

"It is. There are plans in motion that need to occur in a specific order. Becoming governor is one of those steps. Don't get me wrong, I'll be governor at the end of all this. Getting elected and having the support of the citizens makes other steps easier."

Tanya thought about Nafara's words.

The room phone rang, and Lucy answered. "There is a Yusuf Al-Fortwani here to see you."

Tanya looked at Nafara. "He can come up."

Nafara rolled her eyes. "I'll leave you to it, then. I have no desire to hear speculation from that man. Lucy, come with me. He'll speak freely if it's just the two of them. Maybe Tanya can coax something useful out of him."

She hesitated. "How much do you want me to tell him?"

"Only what you must, and nothing about me. Be creative. Try to get him to do all the talking."

"I will."

Nafara went to the door. "Let's go. I need you to get me on a flight to Mexico tonight."

"Yes, ma'am." Lucy followed Nafara out of the room.

Chapter 48

Yusuf pushed the door open, knocking on the door frame behind the privacy curtain.

"Hello, Tanya, is it okay if we come in?"

"Of course."

His heart skipped a beat at the sight of her bandaged legs and the wires and tubes connected to her. "This is my assistant, Farid Amirzadeh."

Farid stepped from behind Yusuf and nodded his head in acknowledgment. "Hello Tanya."

"I wish I could get up and greet you, but it's nice to meet you in person."

Yusuf stepped to the side of her bed. He wanted to comfort her, but with propriety. "We were there. We arrived just before the Ifrit attacked."

"It's probably better that you did. If you had tried to do anything, you might be right here with me."

"We saw the Ifrit."

"You did? Where was he?"

"Near the back, behind the crowd. He was focused on your aunt and ran me over, getting into position to attack."

"Did you see him actually throw fire? The news is convinced he's using pyrotechnics and chemicals."

"He threw a ball of fire at your aunt. He molded it in his hands. I'm sure it was nothing more than fire."

Tanya looked out the dark window. "I saw it as soon as he threw it."

"You're lucky to be alive. I feared the worst. If it weren't for our institute's connection with the police, I didn't think we would find you."

Silence hung in the air as Tanya struggled with what she wanted to say next. "I have to tell you something, and I feel bad about not telling you earlier, but I was afraid of how you might react." Her gaze shifted back to his. Fear coated her expression like a veil.

Yusuf and Farid quietly waited for her to finish.

"I'm different. I see things others don't."

"What do you mean? Because of what happened in Cedar Ridge?"

"I think I might be a hakimah. It's hard to describe to someone who doesn't see what I see."

"I had my suspicions after you asked about them. It may actually explain some things."

Tanya, sitting up in bed, laid her head back on the elevated pillow. "No one knows, of course. They'd think I'm crazy."

"I hope you don't mind, but I notified an old friend in Qom. He is sending an old text with information about the hakim."

"Is there anything to send? I haven't been able to find anything. It's all hit or miss wild speculation." Her excitement died down, and she became somber again. "Did you see the story about the small ponds at the Taniguchi Japanese Garden? It's on YouTube. I turned the water to blood and killed all the fish."

Yusuf shook his head. "You need to be careful. Have you considered that your learning, tapping into the weave, is what's attracting the Jinn?"

232

"Sayyidi," Farid said respectfully, handing him the talisman. The deep red knotted thread looked like the frills that would hang down from a carpet, capped with an ornate knot, and encircled by an iron ring.

Yusuf took the item and handed it to Tanya. "Take this. It will protect you."

"Are you be sure?" She looked skeptical, raising her arms with all the tubes and attachments.

"Had we not encountered him at the rally, I wouldn't have been. The Ifrit fled the moment he saw it."

"Will it keep other Jinn away, or just the Ifrit?" Her expression became neutral.

It was an odd question. Was she in contact with more Jinn? The Ghul?

"It should work against all, Jinn. You can also invoke the name of God in a prayer of protection. That's up to you and your beliefs."

"Thank you."

The room dropped into an uncomfortable silence. Farid shifted his stance, unable to find a comfortable position.

Tanya broke the silence. "Do you know why this is happening, besides the possible hakimah connection?"

Yusuf looked at her, concern in his eyes. "I'm not sure how much you know about the story of the Jinn, but colleagues of mine think that the events are building toward something significant. The Jinn are active after thousands of years of living in the shadows."

Tanya averted her gaze. "My aunt believes they're all just children's stories. She said that people are always looking for something to blame for their own faults."

Yusuf and Farid both nodded. "I thought the same thing until we encountered the Ghul. I'm more convinced now, though, that something is happening and we're not ready for it."

"What do you mean?" she asked.

"It's a feeling. We don't know yet if there is a connection between the hakimah and the Jinn. Maybe when the texts arrive, we'll have a better idea."

"And then what?"

"We need to stop the Ifrit and whatever his plans are."

"I won't be much use. They haven't told me when I might leave."

"I don't like that." His eyes glanced at the window. The blinds were drawn. "You are vulnerable."

"My aunt can make a call and increase the security of the hospital."

"You know, while the Christian Bible doesn't talk about wise ones beyond the three who visited the Prophet Jesus, there are stories from the Bedouins of hakim able to do miraculous things, similar to what Moses did in Egypt. You say you see the world differently. Maybe you can change things."

She lowered her eyes as her shoulders slumped. "I need to think about all of this, and I'm feeling a little tired. I'm sorry."

He patted her hand. "Don't be my child. Allah will watch over you."

She nodded as his hand retracted from hers.

"If it's okay, I'll check on you tomorrow. Maybe say hello to your aunt. I think we got off on the wrong foot."

"I will. She's worried about me and the campaign. She feels she can do the most good as governor."

He nodded. "Okay, we'll get out of here. Call us if anything happens. Farid doesn't say much in the beginning, but once you get to know him, he'll be a big help." They pushed their way through the curtain, leaving her alone with her thoughts.

Chapter 49

Krazack stood in the shadows across the multi-lane road in front of the hospital. This was where the woman was. It was his fault that she was injured. She tried to defend herself, but her control of the weave was clumsy.

-We must find her and make things right.-

She will be angry.

-It doesn't matter, she will see our grief.-

[We should take her from this place.]

No. The Ghul would come for us.

[We can kill the Ghul.]

-No. We must break the bond.-

Krazack silenced the voices and shifted to the wind. He kept the dancing flames that occasionally appeared close, pulling them to the center of the vortex. Now wasn't the time for destruction. Night fell, and the roads lay empty. An ambulance had arrived earlier. He flew upward, above the streetlights, and approached the hospital. Moving across the building and upward, he searched for the calm that came over him in her presence. Finishing the front of the hospital, he moved around the side, repeating his search until he found her room.

He moved closer, looking through the glass at the woman sleeping in the bed. The room was dark, but he could see her in the illumination provided by the small lights in the room. He inched closer, controlling the heat in the swirling wind to melt the glass. He was careful not to shatter it or to allow the heat to progress into the room. When it was clear, he moved through the opening and took his natural form. He was hesitant to move closer, taking in the sight of the young woman. He didn't know the extent of her wounds but felt the residual energy of his fire on her legs. His heart was heavy. How could he have done this to her? She found him, called out to the city, and saved him.

Krazack stepped closer. Her eyes opened, and she tried to move, but she was held in place.

"This is my fault." The woman relaxed a little, but he could see her muscles were still tense. "Do you understand me, Hakimah?"

"Yes," Tanya replied.

His mind was more at peace than it had been in years. "I am Krazack, former commander of the Ifrit Legion."

"My name is Tanya. Why are you here?"

"I am pained by what I've done to you."

Her eyes remained focused on him. "What of the others?"

"Inconsequential."

"Not to me, or their families."

Krazack stared at her. He did not want to answer or respond, as he felt no remorse for anything else he had done.

"Why did you come to me, then?" Her eyes pierced him. She is strong and determined.

"I came to see you. To help you."

"How?"

"You are a hakimah, but you lack experience. Let me teach you how to heal. Allow me to right the wrong I have done to you."

"You tried to kill my aunt."

"You are not Jinn. I know she is a Ghul. She may have mastered the deception of humans, but she is a novice compared to those in the city."

"The City of Brass?"

He saw the interest flicker in her eyes. "Yes. All races of Jinn are there."

She looked as if she were thinking. After a moment, she spoke again. "How can I heal myself? The burns are significant. My doctor said that it would take a long time to heal."

"Yes, for a regular, soft human, but you are hakimah. You can manipulate the weave."

"I'm learning, but you're right, I am inexperienced. Can you show me?"

"Your Ghul should have told you we cannot manipulate the weave as you can. We don't see what you see. It has been several centuries since I studied the works of the ancient wise ones. My mind is not what it once was, but you calm my spirit. My mind is at peace." He looked away. Why would he feel these emotions? She is human, frail and short-lived. He turned his gaze back to her and felt a stirring when their eyes met. It seemed odd, out of place, a cozy warm flame.

"Ifrit center themselves on the element of fire. A flame is destructive, capable of incredible damage, but it is also the energy of purification and cleansing."

Tanya nodded. "Like a wildfire, destroying everything in its path. Afterwards, the earth recovers."

"Yes!" She was quick to understand. "The fire that burned you remains in you. Can you feel it?"

"No. They have given me medication for the pain."

"It's there. You need to force the medicine out of your system, moving the chemicals as you would if they were dangerous to you."

She seemed to relax. Her breathing slowed. A look of concentration and strain dominated her face. Tears formed in her eyes and flowed down her cheeks as her lip quivered. His heart ached at the pain he had caused her.

"I believe you feel the pain of the fire. Can you see it?"

She nodded.

"You'll need to take control of the fire and use it to cleanse the wounded area. It'll hurt. As you do, pull in the elements of earth and water to strengthen the area and move toward rebirth."

"I understand, but I'm afraid of what I might do if I make a mistake."

"Faith in yourself and your strength of will is the binding force for controlling the weave. It's the essence of aether. You must believe and make the change occur. How did you partially extinguish the fire?"

Tanya strained, sweat forming on her brow. Her tears stopped, pain twisted her face. "I knew I had to save her. I made the fire seek other sources."

"You used air to manipulate fire."

Tanya strained with effort, her breathing increased as she tried to do what he asked. The heart-rate monitor shrieked. She continued to strain, ignoring the high-pitched tone. The door flew open, and a nurse pushed aside the curtains, saw them, and screamed.

Krazack moved to attack the woman. The veins on his arm glowed. He felt something cool and unfamiliar on his arm and looked down to see her hand on his arm. "Please, no."

He paused, hearing footsteps running in the hall behind. He turned and shot across the room, jumping out the window. Another nurse came in.

* * *

"What happened?"

238

The first nurse pointed at the molten edges of the window frame, still hissed with heat.

Lifting her radio, she keyed the mic. "Security alert, fourth floor."

"Help is coming." He comforted the first nurse, helping her to a chair. He hastened to her. "Ma'am, are you okay?"

"I don't know."

"Security is on the way. I'll stay here until they and the doctor arrive."

Tanya nodded.

An almost robotic voice came across the loudspeakers in the hall outside her room.

> *"Attention staff and visitors: This is a security alert. Attention staff and visitors, we are implementing a lockdown on the fourth floor. For your safety, remain in your current location until further notice. Do not attempt to enter or leave the fourth floor. Security personnel are responding to the situation. Please follow all instructions from hospital staff and security. Thank you for your cooperation."*

Tanya lay still, waiting for Nafara's return.

Chapter 50

Tanya dripped water from her glass onto her bandages and focused on her burnt legs. Wishing she had her flute, she hummed the notes of a song, reached into the skin, pulling on the filaments until she found the remnants of the fire. Nudging it, she guided the heat, but under control. Focusing on cleansing, she imagined her legs as swaths of forested land and moved the fire through them. She could feel the chaotic, destructive side trying to slip through, but her concentration was strong, despite the burning pain she felt along her right calf.

Slowly, she moved the fire higher, burning away the damaged skin, muscle, and nerves. She focused on pulling the water toward the exposed wound. By pushing the cells in the area, she drew in the water from the bandages, and pulled nutrients from the nearby blood vessels, encouraging growth. Tanya remembered the filaments from her garden and searched for the essence of life. Finding the filaments, she strengthened them, lending her will to them, letting the music strengthen them.

"What are you doing?" Nafara's voice broke her concentration.

She blinked away the vision of the weave and brought her friend into focus.

"I'm trying to heal."

"Do you want to tell me what happened?"

"It was getting hot in the last room, so I decided a change of scenery was in order."

Nafara sneered. "Are we getting snarky now?"

Tanya's smile faded. "No. I assume you know what happened."

"From secondary sources, but I'm asking you now. You were the only one who really knows."

"The Ifrit was here."

"I know that. But why?" Her aunt's response surprised her, as if she expected him to come.

"He said that he felt guilty about what he had done to me."

"What else?" She fixed her face in a stern expression, pressing her lips together.

"He gave me insight into fire and how to use it to cleanse and heal."

"Why did he attack?"

"I think he was after you. He knows I am a hakimah."

Nafara paced across the bottom of her bed and rounded it to the side, taking her hand. "Apparently, everyone is figuring it out. He wants to break our bond."

Nafara squeezed her hand. "He believes that if he removes me, he can take my place."

"I didn't get to ask him much. His name is Krazack. He mentioned the City of Brass, and that he was," she thought back to the conversation, trying to remember exactly what he said. "He was a leader of something called the Ifrit Legion."

"How did he get here?"

"What if I released him?"

"He came through the portal." She smiled.

"You're not mad?"

"That you let a crazed Ifrit into our world? No, because it means that you understand the concept. You can do it again, and as many times as we need until we can stabilize it."

"What if they all react like Krazack when they get here?"

Tanya's vision shifted. She saw a swirling golden maelstrom of light within a sphere. On either side were two supports made of a dark gray, almost black metal with curved spikes. The right, side spike curved upward, and the left support's spikes curved downward. The ball of combined elements flowed toward the spikes. As she watched the spinning energy, mathematical formulas filled her mind. She read each one, following the links between each. It wasn't a portal. It was a nexus for connecting realms. She recognized the elements on the right support. They were from Earth. The elements on the left were similar, but different.

Nafara came back into focus.

Tanya struggled to sit up. "I had a vision. I saw the gateway!" She felt her heart racing. She described the vision to the Jinn.

"We need to move faster."

"I saw the design for the supports needed to hold the nexus open, but I don't understand how the elements come into play."

"But you did it before, without a proper structure."

"Yes, and I almost died after Krazack came through."

"We have work to do. I need to give the campaign a little push, and you need to heal."

"I agree." She let her head fall back onto the pillows.

Tanya reached under her covers to rub an itch near the burns on her calf. She flipped the covers aside, exposing her right leg. She turned to the side, grimacing through the pain of the burn, rubbing against the non-stick gauze. Nafara leaned in to get a closer look. She scraped a piece of dried skin aside, and it fell away, showing a one-inch length of skin underneath that was pink but not scarred.

"That's going to be too hard to explain. I think we need to get you to Eunoia."

"Yeah, that's a good idea."

Nafara turned away from the bed and moved toward the window. "I have a story that will work."

"Okay, what do you need me to do?"

"We're going to say that you are being moved to Eunoia, which has a fully functional medical unit, so that I can oversee your recovery. We're going to use the Eunoia device to help you cope with the trauma of the attack."

"The press will think you're just being protective."

"Yes, they will, which will play nicely with the family-centered voters."

"Except we will not put that device on me, right?"

"Maybe one that is nonfunctional. If I trust it to help my only family, others will trust it for theirs."

"It shouldn't matter. It's safe, right?"

"Of course, it works exactly as it's designed."

"What if the Ifrit follows me to the facility?? He could destroy the whole place and kill everyone."

"I don't think he will. You already told me what he wants—you. But he can't have you until I'm gone. He'll have to come for me."

"Nafara, I'm worried. I know what you can do, but he grew up among your people. I suspect he knows more about your powers and limitations than you know about him. What if he knows vulnerabilities you aren't aware of? He could catch you off guard."

"Tanya, are you worried about me?" Nafara smiled playfully.

Tanya didn't take the bait. Instead, she let her emotions show. "This isn't a game! He wants to kill you." She worried Nafara would be angry with her. Instead, her friend's expression softened.

"You're right. I'll be careful. The prophecy is clear. I'll be there."

She moved toward the door. "I'm going to arrange your transfer. You keep working on healing."

"I will."

"And no more visits from strange men." Nafara gave her a sly grin.

"No promises." Tanya returned the look.

The response drew a stern look from Nafara before she let another grin escape.

Chapter 51

It was late morning when Nafara's extended black Escalade pulled up to the Fernandez Estate. The large, ornate wrought-iron gate extended between two tall stone pillars and upwards in an elaborate pattern of elegance and exclusivity, supporting the house crest of the Fernandez family. Large hedges lined the road all the way to the roundabout driveway in front of the home. Jacaranda trees on either side were in full bloom, their purple flowers contrasting the green landscaping and white classic Mexican colonial home.

The gate split open, drawing the driver's attention to the elegant scene before them. The large vehicle drove forward slowly, pulling around to the front entrance. As the party exited the vehicle, Nafara spotted Marcia Garcia-Fernandez walking a step ahead of her more homely husband. She had a friendly face, and her figure was full and rounded, with hips that swayed as she walked.

"Nafara Kavioni, to what do we owe the pleasure?" Her voice was warm and soft, a trait that often put others at ease.

"Marcia, I brought you a gift that had to be delivered in person, and I want to discuss the race, of course."

"You haven't pulled away yet. I am within three percentage points in the latest polls."

"Marcia, I think we can agree that we both want what's best for the people of Texas. Let's concentrate on our aligned policies, such as education, homelessness, and infrastructure."

"Come inside. The paparazzi have gotten more creative in how they capture images we probably don't want taken." Marcia looked up, searching the sky for drones.

"That would be wonderful." Nafara turned and nodded to the driver, who opened the back door on the opposite side of the Escalade. A ragged man, with hints of being handsome hidden behind malnourished cheeks and sunken eyes, got out. The man's trembling was not from the air or nerves, it was the tremble of a man dragged back from the edges of hell. His clothes hung on a skeletal frame, his eyes darting to every shadow, every unseen threat. For a moment, Nafara thought he might bolt.

Marcia gasped and ran around the vehicle. "Luis! Luis, my baby brother, how are you here?"

The man was shaking, his eyes locked on Nafara until his sister hugged him. Luis jumped at the contact but relented after a moment of recognition.

Marcia stepped back, tears in her eyes, and looked across to Nafara. "How did you get him released? We've tried for the last year, and the State Department said there was nothing they could do. Carcel del Desierto is off limits, controlled by the cartels."

"Let's discuss this inside. Perhaps your brother would like to clean up. Unfortunately, we didn't have time to allow him to do so before returning him to you. We only just got back from Mexico."

"El engendro del infierno," Luis whispered, his voice cracking. His eyes returned to Nafara.

Marcia hesitated, hearing the words. Her smile faltered, confusion flickering across her features. But she swallowed whatever fear threatened to rise. Trauma, she told herself. Delirium. Her brother was safe now.

Nafara shook her head. She saw Luis caught her meaning, and he dropped his eyes to the ground. "It was a disturbing, grotesque pit of despair. I'm sure his time there was anything but pleasant. In time, he may recover from the trauma. But for now, we need to talk."

Marcia walked her brother to a pair of house staff, who took him and led him into the house. She then signaled the others to lead them into the house. It was beautiful inside, decorated in warm earth tones accented with vibrant colors, spaced apart to allow each display to draw the eye as you progressed through the home. The guide led them to a sitting room with high-backed upholstered chairs on a beautiful red, gold, and green carpet.

Nafara sat next to Marcia and accepted a cup of tea.

"What's this going to cost me?" Marcia asked.

"Let me give a little background. You are familiar with the recent attack at my rally?"

"Yes, such a tragedy. Forgive me for not asking how your niece is."

"She's doing better. She's a resilient girl. We moved her to one of my research centers that has specialized medical equipment and additional security."

"Have the police been able to tell you anything?"

"Unfortunately, no." She gave the impression that she was hesitant to say anything else. "It's just that with our system of traffic cameras, we should have more information than we do. I'm not one to believe in conspiracy theories, but some have implied that the governor is slowing the investigation. Some individuals have gone to the extreme of suggesting that the arsonist, who supports the governor, may be influenced by what the man says in his speeches."

Marcia laughed. "You don't believe that, do you?"

"Of course not. But once a rumor is out, it's tough to put the genie back in the bottle."

"If the truth came to light, he would face the consequences of ruining his career and going to prison." Marcia set her cup of tea down on a saucer on the small table to her left.

"As I was saying, the arsonist has only attacked areas that affect our campaigns, first a homeless camp, and then a suburb that has shifted away from his policies in the last few years. What bothers me

249

are the attacks on or near my home. I believe the arsonist is targeting my family."

"Because they have not attacked me or the governor."

"Yes, I'll be honest with you, Marcia. I know you wouldn't do anything like this, and if he gets away with it, possibly kills me, then you would be next. I have prerecorded a message that would encourage all my support to you in case of my death."

"That seems a little extreme."

"It is. But it comes with a catch. I want you to leave the race and your party and join me."

"It would be political suicide."

"Marcia, I know you have aspirations outside the state. I do too. I assume this is just between us."

"Of course."

"Good. I've provided you with an out. Your brother has returned to you, and you need time to be with your family and help in his recovery from the barbaric conditions he endured."

"How does this help me in the future?"

"When I win, I'll appoint you as the Health and Human Services Commissioner. After two years, I'll move you to oversee the Board of Education. You'll have direct control over two of your platform positions. Unless you're only selling the message to the people."

"No, I mean what I say. What if you lose?"

"If I lose, I'll fund your campaign in four years."

"How much of it?"

"All of it."

"You don't expect an answer now, do you? This is too much to take in."

Nafara let out a hearty laugh. "No, of course not. Watch the news cycle and take your time thinking about it."

"What about my brother?"

"Enjoy the time you have together. I'm happy to have brought him home. One favor, though. If someone asks, please leave out my involvement."

Marcia squinted her eyes, the wheels turning. She should understand that some things are best left off the books. Nafara waited for a response.

"Of course. Thank you for bringing him back. I'll give your proposal consideration."

Nafara rose and reached her hand toward her opponent. "I look forward to hearing from you."

Chapter 52

Yusuf opened the door to the shared offices, his leather satchel hanging over his shoulder, and a metal briefcase in hand. The lights were on, and he smelled spiced tea in the air.

"Farid, are you here already?"

"Of course, Sayyidi, there's work to be done."

Bags were present under Farid's eyes, and his shoulders were slumped. His student's dedication heartened him, but he feared that the new knowledge of Jinn and their proximity to the threat might affect him. "Farid, you look exhausted. Have you slept?"

"I've gotten some rest. Not enough though."

"Is it the Ifrit?"

"Yes. I know I should be stronger and follow your example, but it is difficult."

"Talk to me. The knowledge we share is a heavy burden to carry. You must have questions. Perhaps you feel your faith is being tested, and it is."

Farid's shoulders slumped further, and he ran a hand through his hair, not looking up. "Had the Ifrit decided to kill us, he could have, with no effort."

"That is true."

"And it doesn't worry you?"

"No. And I'll tell you why. You've heard me quote the Prophet, may Allah's blessings be upon him, about the tests He presents to us."

"I do, and I believe, but that doesn't lessen the impact of knowing that I could die at any moment."

Yusuf's laughter faded into a gentle smile. "Ibni Farid, the body is but a vessel, a temporary home for the soul. Our true essence, the soul, is what Allah cherishes most, and it's eternal. The trials we face in this world, even the threat of death, are mere moments in the grand journey Allah has set for us. Fear not the end of this life, for it is just the beginning of a greater one. Trust in His wisdom and embrace your faith, for it is our souls that matter most in His eyes."

Farid nodded. "Thank you, Sayyidi. I will work harder."

"I wanted to show you—" Yusuf laid the metal case on the desk, "these."

"What is it?" Farid came around the desk to stand by his mentor.

"Gifts from Qom."

Yusuf laid the wrapped metal case on the desk, carefully cutting away the paper. Beneath it was a second metal box, nearly identical to the first but missing a combination lock. Instead, a small slot gleamed in the center. He pulled his necklace over his head and fit the seal into the slot. A faint whir sounded as the mechanism unlocked.

"That's pretty advanced. Is it the same as the other one?" He nodded toward the case Yusuf had brought in.

"No. These must be more important, which is hard to believe."

"Is that the weapon?"

Yusuf didn't look up. The case concealed another compartment. There was a button on the side closest to him. He took his seal, which was held in place, half exposed. He turned and opened the other case, which looked like it was designed to carry a handgun. It was the dagger Reza showed him in Qom.

He took the blade out of the case. The dark gray surface was simple, almost unremarkable, save for the faint etching of the Seal of Sulaiman near its base. Yet as he turned it in his hand, he felt an unsettling weight beyond its physical heft, as if the dagger carried a presence all its own. "This is my first time touching it. It's heavy for its size. Reza told me it was crafted from meteoric iron. Legend says it was collected from a star that fell in the Negev Desert. There is a known meteor impact, the Haluza Impact Crater, but there isn't a reliable connection between the strike and the creation of the dagger."

"How could you possibly know that?"

Yusuf smiled. "I want to say wisdom of the ancients, but Reza mentioned it in the letter that accompanied the dagger."

Farid shook his head, a reluctant smile tugging at his lips. "You know I would have believed you."

Yusuf passed the small dagger to Farid. His student took the blade and examined it, turning it over, looking at all sides. "Besides the darker color, it looks like an ordinary dagger. Not everyone would identify the symbol as the Seal of Sulaiman. There isn't anything written on it."

"Maybe we need to hold it up to the moonlight."

"Okay, I know you're joking." Farid gave his teacher a sidelong glance.

Yusuf chuckled. "I had to try, and I know you enjoy those fantasy movies."

"Now let's see what's in here." He pressed the button, and the lid slid apart, revealing an ancient text. The book binding was smooth leather, with no title or sign of what it was. He opened the book, and it was filled with symbols and drawings that looked chaotic at best. He perused the pages, revealing more of the same. The card stated:

For the hakimah. -R.A.

"He's a man of few words." Farid observed.

"Not usually. He could go on for hours about the ancient world and the Jinn. I believe his brevity regarding these implies simply that there is nothing else necessary. I'll keep the dagger and give the book to Tanya. Hopefully, she can make sense of it."

"When are we going back?"

"Tonight. You don't have to go. It would be helpful to have a contact away from what's going on, to keep Reza and the Society informed."

Farid looked at him, shaking his head slightly. "No. I need to be with you."

"Alright, you'll need protection. In the wooden box behind you on the shelf are two more talismans. Take one and keep it with you. If the Ifrit, or any other Jinn, comes near you, hold it up and recite the prayer from Surah Al-Falaq. Do you know it?"

"I seek refuge with the Lord of the daybreak, from the evil of what He has created, and from the evil of darkness when it settles, and from the evil of those who practice witchcraft when they blow on knots, and from the evil of an envier when he envies."

"Very good. May Allah watch over us."

Chapter 53

Tanya clenched her jaw as the nurse inserted the IV into her arm. The needle slipped in, and she barely felt the pinch. She was in a private room at Eunoia Labs, secluded from Austin. Nafara was sure the Ifrit wouldn't be able to follow them, and the distance should prevent him from sensing where they were. A hint of unease had crept into Nafara's demeanor after she told her what Krazack had said about her not being as strong as those in the City of Brass. Nafara was on a video call with Lucy to the side of the room.

When the call ended, Lucy disappeared, and the Kavioni logo replaced her.

"Is everything all right?" Tanya adjusted in her bed.

"Yes, we're up another point in the polls. We took it from Marcia. Unfortunately, Jerimiah took two points from her and is still seven points ahead of us."

"Texans don't want their state to be purple. They like things done the Texas way. It's almost a nod to the federal government that they could survive independently. It's the last bastion of wild west mentality in the South."

"I'm impressed. That's quite an insightful comment from someone not interested in actively taking part in the campaign."

"It was Lucy, and you told me to focus on my training."

"Well, that makes sense." The nurse left with a nod to Nafara. "I thought you might have figured out how to control your visions of the future. Lucy would be out of a job."

"No, though I hope to figure out when and why they happen so that we *can* use them. I might stop getting injured." Tanya chuckled.

"I think it's time I went on the offensive."

"Why? You said he can't track us here."

"He can't, but he's not stupid. Eventually, he'll find out where we went. It takes only one person from the hospital to say something."

"He said he doesn't want to hurt me. He's after you."

"And yet he has nearly killed you twice."

She had seen the concern in his yellow eyes. He looked remorseful, but Nafara was right. "I can't argue with that."

Her phone buzzed on the nightstand, and she quickly glanced to see who it was.

"Who is that?"

Tanya swallowed. She had been thinking of how to broach the subject with the Jinn. "That was Yusuf."

"The holy man? You're not going to find anything useful there."

"I know you don't like him, and I'm thankful you haven't killed him, but I think he can be a valuable ally."

Nafara turned to face her. "Ally?! You can't be serious. He's a threat to me, our plans, everything!"

"Maybe. But he has information that will help us, specifically me."

"What do you mean?"

"I told him I might be a hakimah." As the words left her lips, she could see an immediate change in Nafara's posture. Tanya fought the instinct to recoil. There was a rawness to Nafara's movement, a glimpse of something ancient and dangerous beneath her polished human guise.

"You told me I could tell him what I needed to," Tanya challenged, but softened her tone at the end.

The response didn't seem to lessen her anger.

"I'm not suggesting bringing him in on everything. I would never tell him about you, the portal, or the City of Brass. As far as he has surmised, the reappearance of a hakimah has drawn the Jinn to me. A Ghul and now an Ifrit."

Nafara seemed to relax a little. "That's a plausible excuse. What do you propose?"

"He's driving up from Houston. I'd like to bring him here. He's bringing an ancient book that he believes contains knowledge of the hakim."

Nafara's posture straightened, and her harsh expression softened. "And where did he get this book? I have traced down every auction and religious conspiracy theory about the wise ones over the past five years."

"I don't know. He mentioned friends in Qom, Iran."

Nafara, more relaxed, took in the information and appeared to think about the revelation. "Now it makes sense. Qom holds significance in politics, history, education, and religion for Shia Islam. It could hold several ancient works relevant to my people. His contact there must be someone of influence to provide a text this valuable. Get a name."

"I'll try. Maybe there are other writings I could ask him about."

"No, don't do that. We can't reveal too much. We need to keep him focused on helping you, not on me."

Tanya noted the change in how Nafara talked about him. She was going to let them work together. "There may be an issue. He was bringing a talisman to me at the rally. He encouraged me to have salt and iron around as a ward."

Nafara cocked her head slightly. "Defense against evil," she whispered. "That's not entirely accurate, but somewhat effective against us. I think it's a trick of God to make us susceptible to being injured by coming into contact with salt and then giving humans a nudge toward adding it to all their food. Iron, on the other hand, depends on the type and purity."

"Do you know why?"

"No, but now we know that there are two repositories of information out there. Which means there could be more. We're going to have to get control of those texts. If that information got out, it could be devastating." Her focus was distant, as if she were thinking of something else.

"So, I can bring him in?"

"Yes. We need to know what he knows and where he gets his information."

"What about the talisman?"

"I should be okay unless he shoves it in my face and starts reciting prayers."

"If you're just my skeptical aunt who cares about her niece, there should be no reason for him to do so."

"I'll play my part."

Tanya picked up her phone. "Great, I'll send him the address. I hope the book is authentic. I need to figure out which metal the nexus frame requires. I can feel it, but I can't see it yet."

"You will. I'm going to leave for a moment. I need to work with Dr. Gutierrez on the Eunoia. Just so you know, a few dozen people have already taken up my offer to help test the device. Soon, it'll be hundreds." She smiled as she left the room.

Chapter 54

Nafara strolled into the control room, her eyes finding Dr. Gutierrez. "Hector, how is the testing going?"

Hector turned from his discussion with one of the lab assistants and made his way to Nafara. "The device is performing better than expected. In fact, trauma patients volunteering in the study show a greater capacity for returning to what they view as normal. The device learns and helps reroute the neural pathways away from traumatic memories."

"As designed. What about removing the memories?"

"Things are moving more slowly in that area. Despite the pain caused, only seven percent of volunteers want memories erased."

"The theory is sound, though, right?"

"It is. The breakthroughs we're making are changing the field."

"Have you heard from our lobbyist in Washington?"

Hector looked uncomfortable. "There is little support for our device. While we are getting good press from our work with the VA, and your offer to help the residents of Oak Hill, most Congressional and Senate members are taking a wait-and-see approach."

"It's worse than that," Lucy said, popping her head up from a nearby cubicle. She got up and joined the pair. "The governor's team was unhappy with the implication that he has something to do with the attacks in Austin and against you. I'm hearing he pulled a few strings, and any support we had is drying up."

"Damnit!"

Hector and Lucy jumped at her exclamation, having witnessed her wrath imposed on some unfortunate soul.

"Relax, both of you. I need you for the time being. Let's take inventory. Marcia will drop out of the race soon, and when she does, we need to be ready to move. How is your work with Camila Navarro going?"

"Very well. There's a reason she's the queen of morning TV in Texas. She is all in. Once I give the word, she will shift all her stories, highlight the flaws within the current administration and the harm he has caused to Texans."

"What did you promise her?"

Lucy looked at Hector before answering the question. "What you and I discussed."

"She's a crafty woman who knows what she wants. I like it."

"If you don't need me, I'll get back to work. I need to leave a little early. My son has soccer practice." Hector said nervously.

"Is our meeting set up with Army R&D?" Nafara turned her attention back to Hector.

"Yes, we have a meeting in two weeks. They're very interested in the nonpublic capabilities."

Nafara grinned with an evil glint. "I knew they would be. No one has what we have. Imagine soldiers remaining completely calm on the battlefield with no stress or jitters. Calmly killing the enemy with relaxed precision."

"That's a little way off. It will be more difficult with the barriers being put up."

"Once the Department of Defense wants something, it gets much easier. But enough. You take off and enjoy your time with your son."

"Thank you."

"Lucy, let's head back to Austin later. Be ready to brief the numbers on the drive back. How are we doing with fundraising and events?"

"We have events scheduled in Houston again, as well as in Corpus Christi, El Paso, Fort Worth, and San Antonio. There are smaller venue events sprinkled in between. It's going to be a busy few months."

"Okay. Get everything ready. I'll let Tanya know that we'll be gone for a few days. Is my five o'clock appointment ready?"

"He is waiting in your office. I'll take care of everything."

Nafara left the lab and went to her office. The rectangular room had a conference table, a desk, and three chairs arranged in a semicircle in front of the desk. All the ancient art was Persian. In the office, there were fourteen artifacts displayed on pedestals, with glass protection and individual illumination for each artifact. Her collection of jewelry, tablets, texts, and carvings would make a museum curator jealous. A large man sat in the center chair and didn't get up as she entered and walked around to her desk.

"I'm sorry to keep you waiting, Mr. Callas. Are you comfortable?"

"Yeah, and you can call me Richard." He removed his glasses and cleaned them off with a rag from his pocket. He had a large, bushy mustache, and a few days of growth on his beard. The smell of fire was still on him.

"Richard, I understand you have some concerns about the treatment. You realize this is all voluntary."

"I do, and it all sounds pretty good. What I was wondering was whether your device can help with trauma further back. You see, I lost my family a while back, and it's just me now. I had to sell my gator farm in Florida before I moved here. So, I'd like to let go of all of it if I can. I've been working my whole life. I think it's time I let it all go and just enjoy my last days."

"We should be able to do something for you. Follow me." She went to the wall opposite the door and triggered a panel in the smooth bronze metal wall to slide to the side.

Richard worked himself out of the chair and lumbered close by. "That's a fancy door."

"Yes, it is, and it saves me having to walk all the way around the building."

They stepped through into a room of similar size to her office. A thin line of lights, a foot off the floor, bathed the dark room in light.

"I'm sorry, the lights should have come on. The doorway's in the opposite corner."

Richard chuckled nervously, peering into the blackness. "Uh. . .you sure this is safe?"

The door behind them slid closed, and the lights went out.

"What happened? I can't see."

Nafara shifted form, taking her natural shape. Her eyes glowed like burning coals. She turned. His reaction brought a smile to her face.

"What the hell? Help! Someone, can you hear me?"

Nafara grinned, despite his not being able to see anything but her eyes. She moved closer to him, his excessive shape visible to the Jinn's eyes. She seized his wrist, clawed his arm, and administered a neurotoxin that would induce a burning sensation in his skin.

He screamed, rubbing his arm and then his chest to ease the pain. "What did you do to me?" he yelled into the dark. "No, noo, noooooo!"

His screams continued to fill the air as she scratched him a few more times. When he finally collapsed into a crying defeated ball, she kneeled, placing her hand on his chest. Her hand shimmered, and his screams intensified as the blood drained from his body. When all that remained was a dried husk, she pressed her hand onto him, breathing in the ash from his corpse as it spun in the air toward her mouth. She closed her eyes as the ash entered her mouth, savoring the sensation like a sommelier appreciating a rare vintage.

He may hold us over for a few days. We'll see.

Chapter 55

"Argh!" His primal scream resonated through his makeshift home.

Krazack's veins were glowing hot white. He had reinforced his home by piling more cars around it. The walls he had formed and smoothed with the fire were now dripping metal into molten pools around him.

-She's gone!-

The Ghul took her. Hid her away.

[Find her! Kill the Ghul!]

-We need the hakimah!-

Krazack bent over, clutching both sides of his head. Spikes of pain were shooting through his head and radiating down his spine. He stumbled and reached out, putting a hand on the hot metal to steady himself.

[Burn it all!]

She wants power.

-Draw her out. Burn that which she seeks.-

The palace?

[Everything!]

She's a Ghul. Let her rule the dead.

The Ifrit crawled through the tunnel, pushing a car aside that concealed the entrance. The temperature was scorching. Perfect. He looked toward the buildings illuminated in orange from the setting sun. He took off at a run toward the city.

Krazack waited out of sight in an alley. People crowded the street across from the convention center. He turned away in frustration and went down the alley. As he passed the trash bins, flames leaped out, embedding themselves in the trash, smoldering.

He stepped out, joining the rear of a group crossing the street toward what they called hotels. Looking up, he saw they must hold hundreds, if not thousands, of people. He heard the names Hilton, Marriott, and Embassy. They must be powerful merchant families. Many people were here on business. They complained about the tourists, people on vacation. He thought about the word, the meaning. He was on vacation. People have fun on vacation. He grinned. It was about to become a lot more fun.

He made his way around the center of the city, avoiding the police. Several small fires had erupted in his wake, marking a large circle around the palace of Texas, the Capitol building. He took a worn hat and torn jacket from a homeless man and walked out into the night to look at his objective. His mind calmed as he focused on his strategy to draw his enemy out.

Krazack sat on a bench facing the Capitol building. This was his enemy's goal. She wanted power over these people. What would she trade to get it?

The hakimah.

[Burn it all down!]

-Silence! We are the commander of the Ifrit Legion!-

His vision blurred as the pain intensified. *No!* I must focus. *I must understand the strategy, make plans, disrupt her alliances and logistics.* He felt a chilling pain trickling down his spine, an icy feeling. *No!* He got up and staggered toward the west. There were more places to hide, to disappear, until…. "The pain!" he said through gritted teeth. He crossed the street and ducked into a tight alley. He wasn't close to any of the fires he had started. Each one was small, just enough to test the fire responders. They had eventually put them all out.

He smelled garbage. This world was exceedingly wasteful. He gritted his teeth and followed the smell to a gate around the garbage dumpsters. Opening it, he slid between the two and sat with his back to the wall. He closed his eyes to rest. For a fleeting moment, he remembered what it was to sit beneath living trees, among brothers who called him friend.

Images flashed in his mind. He walked across the devastated area of the battleground. Jinn lay dead all around him. The smell of their burning flesh filled his nostrils. He remembered. His forces had assaulted the City of Brass. The battle was supposed to end the war. His army had betrayed him, turned on the gathered allies. The betrayal had shattered his mind.

The betrayer is trapped.

-Locked in the City of Brass.-

267

[Let them rot there.]

The hakimah opened a doorway.

-She freed us.-

We must have her.

-She is of strategic value.-

No, she is a pawn of the Ghul.

[She is a pawn to be used.]

-No. It would break her.-

-She is not afraid of us, not ashamed.-

If she were ours, what then?

*-Peace. She brings us together, soothes
the pain.-*

Why does this happen?

[It does not matter.]

-It does matter, she could...-

What?

-Love us.-

What of her loyalty to her people?

-She protected the Ghul.-

He opened his eyes at the sound of a bottle bouncing and breaking close by, followed by shuffling feet. The pain in his head had subsided enough for him to move normally. It was getting worse, accelerating. He needed to eat. It had been a few days since his last meal. He rose and strode out. The person stopped, then took a step back.

"Oh, hey. I didn't know this spot was taken."

Krazack took a step toward the man. He sniffed the air. He smelled something like sulfur, but not quite. It had a delightful smoky scent. He focused on the man's face, not emaciated, his stance on edge. His hand was behind his back. He smelled the adrenaline, noted the tension in his muscles. *Warrior!*

He straightened, rising above the man.

"You are not what you appear," Krazack challenged.

"And you are who I thought you were. Keep your hands where I can see them." The man drew his pistol, aiming at the Ifrit.

Krazack smiled at the man, spreading his arms, holding his hands palm up. He would incinerate him.

[Come closer.]

"You're under arrest for arson, murder, and a dozen other crimes. Turn away from me, lie on the ground, and place your hands behind your head."

"No." He heard a click.

"I will shoot you," the man said, his gaze never faltering.

Krazack stepped closer.

"I'm serious. Don't take another step." The man's eyes remained locked on him.

Krazack considered the man. Their weapons had been ineffective. He stepped closer.

269

Bang!

Pain erupted from his thigh. It wasn't like before. This was different. Iron. He panicked, trying to shift to the wind, but could not.

[Attack! Move now!]

He leaped forward, turning to the side and gripping the man's wrist and neck. He released fire into the man equivalent to the pain he felt. Fire erupted from his hands, engulfing him, the gun clattering to the ground, the burning man beside it. Did they know what he was? Were there other Jinn? There must be. How else could they have weapons of iron? This changes things. He had to be careful. He examined the wound. It was small. He could feel the fragments inside, each splinter burning.

-His unit will miss him.-

Someone will come for him.

-We need to move. Find a more strategic position.-

Krazack headed in the direction the man had come. He moved slow. One good thing about the injury was that the pain in his leg kept the pain in his head at bay. He could plan his attack on the Ghul.

IFRIT

The Ifrit are born of smokeless fire. They are fierce and proud, bound by oaths yet unyielding in wrath. In the tales of old, they were chained by Sulaiman's seal, but fire never sleeps, it waits.

Chapter 56

Tanya read through the scientific paper Nafara and Hector had published on the theories behind the Eunoia device. It was still completely beyond her understanding. She had made it further through the document this time before skipping to the findings and potential applications. One part grabbed her attention.

She hit the nurse-call button.

A nurse popped his head in the doorway. "Yes, ma'am. How can I help?"

"Terry, I've told you to call me Tanya."

"I understand, ma'am," he said, his voice calm.

She smiled understandingly. Dr. Gutierrez, Hector, had likely given the order.

"Could you check to see if Dr. Gutierrez is available?"

"Will do."

At least he hadn't ended it with *ma'am*. So, there was hope for him.

Hector knocked on the doorframe as he entered the room. "Good afternoon, Tanya. How can I help today?"

"Hector, I tried getting through your dissertation and initial proposal for the Eunoia concept, and while I made it most of the way through, I have a few questions."

She observed the stress on his face and believed he had more important things to do. She also knew that Nafara had instructed him to ensure she was fully taken care of. Tanya knew he was within the inner circle and knew what Nafara was, and he may have witnessed what she could do to a person.

"Nafara tells me that the testing has gone better than expected."

"That is what we tell the public and the staff, but the theory itself is sound. Your aunt's unique abilities allow her to troubleshoot the device's functionality better than any machine we have."

His face was impassive. His answer, however, had revealed something that she didn't know about her aunt.

"How does she do that?"

"It has something to do with her species' ability to manipulate the minds of humans, similar to how she can change her appearance. We've seen Nafara change her appearance. Our mind knows that she isn't actually changing, but she can keep the illusion active in our minds, like a really powerful suggestion. Her species of Jinn can read us biometrically, which allows her to produce the myriad of chemicals that can affect us."

"That makes sense."

"Yes, well, I can't find a scientific explanation for it. I asked to examine her, but she declined."

"Back to my question. I've seen the next-generation device, the prototype small band that sits on the side of the patient's head, and I want to try it."

"Why would you want to do that?"

Tanya tilted her head, looking at the right side of his head. "You did it."

"That's hardly a reason. You know I always wear the latest version. It helps sell the volunteers."

"You could fake it, they wouldn't know."

His eyes shifted, becoming distant. "No, it's more believable if I tell my story."

Tanya was familiar with the story of his parents and siblings being killed on vacation in Mexico. It was a case of the wrong place and time, and he was supposed to be with them, but he had bowed out for a ski trip with his friends. The situation became worse because he didn't ski. He had shared with Nafara that he was at a point where he couldn't spend any more time with his family. A rebellious teen. He had survivor's remorse.

Tanya hesitated. If it worked, maybe she could learn how it controlled others. Maybe she could learn how to defend against suggestion. "Okay, well, you know my story: I had an abusive father who murdered my mother and was stalked by a serial killer, so I'd say there's plenty of room for traumatic healing."

"I need to check with your aunt."

"No, you don't. I'm an adult, and I know what her directives are. If it can help me heal faster, I want to try. I'll sign all the waivers."

He laughed. "You know that if something goes wrong, she won't care."

"C'mon, Hector, I trust you. Can we do it today?"

He looked past her, his eyes moving back and forth as if he were reading something. "We definitely cannot get everything done today. What we can do is develop your profile. We have to run an MRI and DTI, Diffusion Tensor Imaging. Then, over the next week, we can start the neural mapping. We might be able to have you fitted in a week or so."

Tanya cocked her head to the side. "That's BS, and you know it. The latest prototype allows you to skip the mapping and modeling."

"Tanya, I cannot afford it. My life is literally on the line if I do something that harms you."

"Fine, I order you to do it and not tell my aunt."

He sighed. "You know she won't care. Why are you pushing so hard on this?"

"I'm tired of having nightmares every night of my father standing over my mother's blood-soaked body," she lied.

He held her gaze, considering his options.

"You can remove it, correct?"

"Yes, but it is a more complex process, and there is a potential for side effects. Once your brain gets used to the process, it doesn't like to give it up."

"There's an addiction?"

"It varies from person to person. We've only had a few ask for it to be removed."

"What happened? Are they all right?"

"They seemed better. Calmer. Like they were finally healing. And then, within a week, they were gone."

"Do you know why?"

"We've been unable to determine a cause. They all seemed healthy when they left. But within a week of leaving the program, they committed suicide."

"I hadn't heard that."

"Your aunt and Lucy have been able to keep it under wraps."

"If it's a danger, then people need to know."

"Not if it would interfere with your aunt's plans."

Tanya thought of her pledge to Nafara. Maybe she thought the devices might be necessary for her people. Being locked in a cage for a few thousand years qualifies as a traumatic experience.

"Okay, so it's permanently on. Fine. I still want it."

He nodded, giving in. "Alright. I'll have you prepped. We should be able to start in about an hour. The procedure itself takes a few hours."

"Sounds great. You don't have to worry about my aunt. She has a dinner tonight and a rally in the morning. She already told me she wouldn't be back until tomorrow."

The mention of Nafara returned his worried look. "The staff will be in to prep you shortly."

> Tanya: I can't meet today. Can you come in the morning?

Yusuf: The morning is fine. Are you well?

> Tanya: As well as I can be lying in a hospital bed trying to heal.

Yusuf: At least you're conscious.

> Tanya: Good point. I can't wait to see you tomorrow.

Yusuf: We have news you will want to hear, and reading material.

Chapter 57

Tanya's head was killing her. Her throbbing headache reminded her of a Sunday morning hangover in college. It hadn't happened often, only once a year, around her mother's death anniversary. Each time, she hated herself the following day, not taking anything for the pain, telling herself she deserved it for how things played out. It was her ritual alone. Nafara didn't know.

She resisted the urge to touch the bandage on the side of her head. Dr. Gutierrez told her they had attached the devices and were picking up the signals from her brain. The AI was already mapping her thought patterns and neural pathways. Like learning her abilities as a wise one, she would have to dedicate time to looking at a few thousand photos. She hadn't told Dr. Gutierrez why she really wanted the Eunoia device.

The large screen display in her room showed a detailed 3D model of her brain. She could see the colors shift with her thoughts and emotions. She didn't know what it all meant and couldn't tell if her brain was being rewired, but she was hopeful. It wasn't quite like other brain-machine interfaces she had read about. The ones that were supposed to give access to the internet, help regeneration of sight and hearing, or even reverse paralysis. She didn't need to hide her trauma. It gave her focus. She had made a choice to do something different.

"Knock, knock!" The Ayatollah and his assistant stood in the doorway.

"Yusuf! Farid, come in."

"Thank you, and may the Lord's blessings be upon you while you heal."

"I'll take all the help I can get. Are you staying nearby or in Austin?"

"We're nearby, in a hotel. We've actually been here for almost an hour. Your security for this place is substantial."

"That's just what you can see. My aunt is a little paranoid about spying."

Yusuf looked at the side of her head. "Is that from the attack?"

"No, that's something else. Most of the damage was to my legs. I'm making progress, though."

"How?"

"He came to see me."

Yusuf stepped back as if slapped. "Who? The Ifrit?" he lowered his voice to a whisper.

Tanya nodded.

Yusuf stared at her, concern on his face.

"The Ifrit felt sorry for hurting me. He said I saved him and wasn't the one he was after. My aunt was his target."

"Why? That doesn't make sense."

"I don't know, but he said I was a hakimah and that he could help me learn to heal."

Yusuf sat down in one chair in the room.

Farid stood near the foot of her bed, looking at her with concern. "Did you?"

"Heal?"

"Partly, but what he told me works. It's like a wildfire clearing the land and the land recovering afterward."

"Fire is a cleansing element. Many cultures use fire rituals to cleanse the spirit, such as fire walking. I'm learning that there is usually more to these old tales than initially thought."

"It's a lost art."

Farid jumped, reaching down to lift the metal case with the book. "Not completely lost, hopefully."

Yusuf nodded, noting that Farid should go ahead.

Farid laid the case on the couch and opened it, took out an old book, and handed it to Tanya. "This is the book sent from Qom. I hope you have some kind of insight, because, well, you'll see."

Tanya took the book. It didn't feel magical. She didn't know what to expect. Some pages made her skin crawl. Others drew her in. It wasn't just the ink. She could feel the *intention* behind it. Maybe this was the key. Reading the book with the sight of a wise one. See the words, but sense the true intention.

"Is it useful?"

"I'm not sure. I'll have to try to read it and see if anything looks familiar. It's hard to explain. Hopefully, this will help. Do I need to keep it in the case?"

"If you leave here, I would ask that you do. I don't know if there are other copies in Qom."

"I'll take care of it."

"Where's your aunt?"

"She's on the campaign trail. And before you judge her, I insisted. This election is important, and I can't be a distraction that costs her."

"Your devotion is commendable."

"Do you know why the Ifrit is here?"

Yusuf nodded, not dropping her gaze. "I am afraid that a Jinn is seeking to open the gateway between their city and our world. I have not seen the full prophecy myself, but those who have claimed it speaks of the Jinn's return to Earth."

"And you believe this is a doomsday prophecy?"

"That's a tough question to surmise without a Jinn to discuss it with. But thanks to Farid, I have watched more science fiction movies about aliens and first contact than the average person, and my intuition tells me they are dangerous. Remember the Ghul and now the Ifrit. Imagine tens of thousands of these beings here on Earth, each with supernatural powers."

"*Independence Day.*"

"Yes! Like the movie, but with shapeshifting and abilities from our nightmares. Once a species understands it is dominant, it will resist all moves by the weaker species to return to the status quo."

"But from what you've told me. This was their planet first."

"And they were cast aside, expected to bow before God's greatest creation, humans."

"But we're just guessing, right? There isn't any proof of this? You said yourself that you haven't seen a prophecy. Maybe they are the last of their species, and they only came out because of me being a hakimah."

"Tanya, I don't think you are taking this seriously enough. You are in danger."

"I'm taking this very seriously, but I think I can connect with him. Maybe we can find out what's going on. My aunt wants to kill him for what he did to me. But I'm telling you, there was something in his eyes."

The pain in her head flared up, and so did the pain in her legs. She put a hand to her temple and squeezed her eyes closed. One machine beeped in a steady rhythm.

Dr. Gutierrez rushed in. "I'm going to need you two to wait outside."

"What's happening?"

"It's normal, an aftereffect of her surgery, but we're going to need to sedate her and let her rest."

"Okay, if someone shows us out, we'll call later."

Dr. Gutierrez waved for an assistant to show them out.

"Sayyidi, you didn't tell her about the knife."

"She's not ready. You heard her. She thinks she can reason with him."

"Shouldn't she make that choice? What if something goes wrong?"

"Then we'll have to stay close, just in case." *And pray we won't have to use it.*

Chapter 58

Nafara listened to the phone ring over the car speakers. Anyone in her inner circle failing to answer by the third ring annoyed her greatly. She waited for news from the facility, afraid Krazack had found Tanya. She didn't know precisely what the Ifrit Legion was or how many he had commanded, but it put her on edge. He was military and may have commanded forces in battle, Jinn forces. She had researched the term legion and found it meant a few to half a dozen thousand men, according to the Romans, but it could also stand for an overwhelmingly large number. She wondered if the rank was earned or ceremonial. Her instincts told her to err on the worst case, which meant he was strategic, careful, and focused on accomplishing his mission, which was to kill her, and possibly Tanya. Everyone else was expendable. Her gaze shifted to the person across from her.

Lucy was on her phone, texting away, making plans, tracking numbers, and doing everything she could to help with the campaign. Lucy had seen her kill someone. It was a rite of passage to determine whether they could be trusted, and as a test of their mettle. Later, she had killed Lucy's sister and her family, and the woman didn't show the least concern. Not a tear, not a flicker of pain. There was only ambition in her eyes.

"Hello, Nafara."

"Tanya, how are you doing? I was worried."

"I'm getting there. Most of the external damage has healed. My muscles are tender, but Hector has me on the treadmill. Which is why I couldn't rush over to get the phone."

"That's good news. I miss you."

"I miss you, too. I thought you were coming back."

"You know Lucy, she's got me running all over the state doing rallies. The numbers look good. I'm on the way to meet Marcia at her ranch near San Angelo."

"Good news?"

"I hope so. This has dragged on longer than expected."

"Listen to her."

"I always listen."

"You know what I mean. Listen and consider it before you do anything. That's my recommendation for any additional news you might get."

"You know me. Have you made any progress with the book he brought?"

"The short answer is yes. At first, it looked like a random collection of drawings, geometry, and symbols in an unknown language. But now I can *read* it."

"What do you mean?"

"It's hard to explain. The author infused the ink with the weave. Linked filaments, base elements and meanings interwoven with whatever the meaning and intent were."

"You're not making any sense. Is it the language of the wise ones? Something you can read?"

"Not quite. It's more like a book of theories based on implications, meaning, and intent. I know it sounds like a chaotic philosophical explanation. The theories have to be based on concepts from your people because the implication goes beyond the understanding of science. It links concepts that your society must have had before humans were created. For example, alchemical manipulation at the base level is closer to what we would describe today as quantum mechanics, but from a perspective different from what we understand."

"Okay, I'm not the one to get into all of that. You work on manipulating the weave, and I'll stick to people."

"Deal."

"The key question is whether it is helping you understand what you need to open the portal, stabilize it, and then keep it open."

"It is. In my last vision, I saw the device, and I believe that I have been over complicating it. Opening a portal requires an enormous amount of energy because we are attempting to establish a permanent link between the two dimensions. To create a nexus, one needs less energy but has to work with areas on the planes that already cross or are linked. A nexus takes input from all connected realms. If I can find the right location, it means I don't have to force the portal open. I can *coax* it into place, like striking the right chord to open a door."

"Well, that sounds promising. We're pulling up to Marcia's ranch. We can continue our talk later."

"Wait, one more thing. I am pretty sure I identified the metal we need."

"Okay, order whatever you need. Have Hector's team get it."

"Okay, I hope your meeting goes well."

"It will, one way or another."

"Remember what I said!"

"I will, bye."

The large gate swung open, and the car pulled through. Nafara felt a queasy feeling in her stomach. Iron.

Lucy read the text on her phone. "They're wrapping up another meeting. Marcia wants to meet us by the stables."

"That's odd. Why?"

"They didn't say, but they asked if you had ridden before. I said yes."

It was a test. They must have gotten the story of her brother's release, and wanted to see if she was the devil or an evil spirit. They believed in the old superstition that a horse can detect a demon and refuse to allow it to ride. "Of course I've ridden. This should be an interesting meeting."

They got out of the car and the stable manager, an older gentleman who was directing his team attending to six horses, greeted them. They were magnificent creatures. She felt the old urge to show them what a Jinn could do with a horse, not just ride, but *become one with it*, thought for thought. While humans believed they domesticated the horse, her people had done it long before, forming bonds that allowed the creatures to react to the rider's thoughts.

"Nafara, thank you for meeting me here."

Nafara turned to Marcia's voice. "Marcia, I'm happy to oblige."

"Lucy told me you rode. I hope you don't mind."

"Not at all. I love riding. It has been a while. I've found myself so busy in recent years with taking in my niece that I've had to put aside many things I love to do."

"I'm glad to hear it. Pick anyone you want."

"They're beautiful creatures."

"These are Andalusian. Do you know them?"

"It sounds familiar, but I don't know them." She knew the horse breed and had ridden them for many years in another guise in Spain before moving to America. Better to let Marcia have the upper hand in the conversation, for now. She considered taking the lone black horse to poke at their superstitions, but settled for a light gray stallion.

"That's Lluvia." Nafara noticed Maria watching her as she moved to the horse, running her hand along its muzzle, taking time to allow her calming pheromones to soothe the animal. The horse dipped its head, allowing her to scratch along the side of its head, below the ears. "He likes you." Nafara noted her host relax, a stress dismissed.

Nafara turned, stepped in the stirrup, and threw her leg over the saddle, adjusting for comfort that was irrelevant. She took the reins from the stable hand and held the horse steady. "Well, I'd say that Lluvia is a superb judge of character, wouldn't you?"

Marcia smiled and gave a slight nod. "I suppose he is." She took the reins of the black mare, and Lucy, another staffer, and three security personnel, mounted the other horses. Nafara chuckled to herself, noting the three security guards carried pistols and had a rifle in their saddle. They were probably good security against humans.

Chapter 59

Nafara rode beside Marcia. Their pace out of the gate had been comfortable, building to the gallop they were now in. She grinned, aware that Marcia was trying to push her, to see how fast she was willing to go. With each burst of speed, Nafara urged her horse to remain alongside. She guided the horse, remaining close. She didn't fear a fall as much as the human woman would. The others had struggled to keep up. Lucy had fallen behind, as did all but one of the security personnel. They would group and meet the pair at their destination.

She missed this freedom, racing across the land with no responsibilities beyond staying alive. In her younger days, she had struggled in the barren mountainous region of Persia. She fought her nature, refusing to become what society and culture had deemed her place to be. She worked to fit in and live among humans, watching them, and learning their nature. Before their deaths, her family passed down tales that she now recalls. Over time, her purpose became clearer, and she began to focus on releasing her people from their imprisonment.

She adjusted to match Marcia, slowing her horse to a gentle trot. Nafara could sense the exhilaration in both animals. The extended run was a treat for them.

"Up ahead, in that copse of trees."

Nafara followed her along the path, stepping down and securing her horse to an old-fashioned hitching post. The meeting place was not what she expected. It was remote from the house and barn, lacking modern conveniences, or so she thought. The camp area was built of stone and included a large open but covered pavilion complete with large ceiling fans. A large bar extended along the back, and a full stone fireplace and outdoor kitchen were to the side. There were two large round tables, with seating for eight.

"Well, this is cozy," Nafara said.

"It's our little getaway." Marcia pulled a chair from the table nearest the kitchen and bar.

"I hope this is an opportunity to celebrate."

Marcia smiled but remained silent.

Nafara noted the security was off his horse, and moving around the structure, a rifle in hand. She wondered whether her opponent intended to ambush them. She looked around and saw it hidden in a decent-sized grove of trees. Difficult to see from any approach, not invisible by air, though.

"While everyone catches up. Let's get a drink. I'd like to hear from you about what happened in Mexico."

"It's a longer story than you'd expect."

"We have time. Are you okay with bourbon?"

Nafara nodded as Marcia poured half a glass of the brown liquid.

"Thank you." As expected, she raised the glass, sniffed its contents, and took a drink. She savored the strong, smoky flavor. "It's good." She held the glass up in honor of her host. "As I was saying, the story started a few months back. Before I entered the race, I did my research so I could understand you and Luis. Your story was interesting. You and your brother grew up inseparable, with wonderful parents and family life until you left for college. Your brother's life took a turn. As your life improved, his declined. Run-ins with police, arrests and other accusations led to his earning the ire of the El Cártel del Sol Oscuro, Dark Sun. Apparently, he made someone angry. Luckily, your father passed before the last part, but the damage was done. I checked with the State Department and found that your family had made several requests to have him extradited, to no avail."

"That's a significant amount of research."

"I try not to underestimate anyone. Once I understood the situation, I thought I might use some of the recent influence I had gotten from my company and our research to appeal to people on the other side of the border."

"The cartels?"

"Yes, they're concerned about the implications of my research. Some people have connected the dots with our paper on mapping neural pathways and trauma and realize that the theory also applies to addiction. What if we can help addicts remap the way they think, blocking off the parts of the brain responsible for cravings?"

Marcia looked to the side, as if thinking, and followed it by drinking her entire glass. She looked back at Nafara and refilled her glass. "It would put them out of business."

"It will put them out of that business."

Marcia's eyes narrowed. "Did you make a deal with them to slow progress?"

Nafara laughed. "No. I gave them a warning, an opportunity to change their business model before I put them out of business. I simply asked for your brother's release as an act of goodwill on their part."

"I'm surprised you're still alive."

"My security is strong."

"What was their response?"

"While Alejandro Montes may be a businessman, he was less than receptive to my business advice. He had us escorted out and told me that if I ever insulted him again, he would have me, and my niece, killed most unpleasantly."

"Which left my brother in prison."

"It did. I then made arrangements, for his release."

Marcia gave her a look that belied disbelief. "That is very much an understatement."

Nafara took a drink of her bourbon and held the glass up, letting a stray beam of sun illuminate the contents. "It is. I sent a team in to free your brother and send a message to Alejandro, making myself very clear that I am not a person to be fucked with. To be blunt."

"My brother said there were over five hundred prisoners in there, and almost a hundred armed guards."

"That sounds about right." Nafara gave no reaction, as if five hundred souls were merely background noise.

"Who did you send in?"

"Why is that important?"

"He has nightmares. When I talk to him, he says that he saw the devil reclaiming all the souls of evil men. The scenes he describes are very disturbing."

"I wanted the message to be clear. Messy, disturbing, and very clear."

They sat in silence for a while until the sound of approaching horses broke it. Marcia refilled her glass until it was half-full and did the same for Nafara. She raised her glass in a toast. Nafara clinked glasses.

"Here is to your successful campaign, Ms. Kavioni. I will make an announcement tonight. I am indebted to you for bringing my brother back. If it isn't too much of an inconvenience, would he be eligible for one of your devices to help with his urges?"

"For you, of course. In fact, when we win, I'll let you lead the charge to end the plague of addiction in Texas, as head of the State Health and Human Services Department."

"It would be my honor."

Nafara smiled. "We all have our roles to play. Some earned. Some chosen."

The two ladies enjoyed their drinks as Lucy and the others finally arrived.

Chapter 60

Tanya peeled the last of the scar tissue from her leg. Hector was surprised by her progress, but he refrained from speculating and instead made comments about its implausibility. He was in the room, sitting in a chair midway between her bed and the large monitor on the wall they had installed to watch her brain activity.

"I don't get it. Even with the treatment, you aren't avoiding the trauma. I know where it lives in your memory, and if anything, the pathway has been reinforced. I'm at a loss."

"Don't be, I forced it."

He spun his chair around, his mouth open. "You strengthened the ties to your trauma?"

"I did. Once you explained the colors and what they represented. I did what you said, and the AI learned where my pain points were. What I did, though, is focus on a desire to feel pain, loss, and emotion."

"You're the first person to do that. Why would you do it?"

While he was privy to Nafara's true identity, they had kept her role as hakimah away from him. The nexus was a closely guarded secret. "It makes me a better musician."

"It's fascinating. We hadn't thought of what the impact would be on creativity. Especially if the trauma were the source of inspiration."

"If Eunoia works and everyone uses it, it would mean the end of jazz and the blues." She struggled to keep a straight face.

He looked shocked at the revelation.

"Hector, I'm kidding, mostly. The device still works, but now we know it can go both ways. It can help relieve the pressure of the trauma or increase the strength and influence. Give me a sec." Tanya took her phone and searched for something before looking up. She swung her legs off the side of the bed and stood up.

"Careful."

"It's okay, I'm fine. Are you an Adelle fan?"

"Probably casually. I know her hits when they come on."

"Do you feel emotions when you hear them?"

"Nothing stands out."

"Okay, close your eyes and listen. Let me know if and when you feel anything."

"Alright."

He closed his eyes, but there was a look of skepticism on his face.

Tanya started the music and began singing *A Million Miles Away*. She sang the opening stanza of the song, remaining as neutral as possible, but hitting all the notes. As she started the second stanza, she thought of her mother and how much she missed her. She watched the screen shift colors as the regions involved with her singing and memory became active. As she pressed through, she added on the times her father had abused her mother, and how sad that her life ended abruptly. Once she made the connection, she closed her eyes and poured her feelings into the song, strengthening the sound, imbuing the notes with her emotion in the weave.

When she finished, she caught sight of Hector looking at her, his eyes brimming with tears, and a solitary streak running down his cheek.

"That was amazing, and I was prepared for it. I could feel you in the song. This is a significant breakthrough. What I don't know, though, is whether you are using the device to tap into your pain to draw the emotion out affected me, or whether my device detected my grasping for the emotion once it presented itself and intensified the experience. I need to collect my thoughts. Do you mind?"

"Of course. I'm fine." She could see the excitement in his reaction, which was uncharacteristic. He had been an introvert since she had met him. She had asked Nafara if he was depressed.

"Would you mind closing the door? I'm going to sing, and I don't want to entertain the whole lab."

"No problem. I'll let the staff know to leave you alone until you open the door."

After he left, she sat down on the floor, crossing her legs. Her muscles were stiff and sore from the injuries, and she didn't want to attempt anything further for fear of something getting out of control. Images of the pond water changing to blood and the dead fish flashed in her mind. She shuddered.

She took the Compendium of Weave Essence from the stand next to her bed, opened it to the section she remembered reading, and realized that her previous understanding of how the book was used was a misrepresentation. The book showed not spells, but the theory behind the weave and how to manipulate filaments through intention, emotion, and understanding. While holding the book open, she had to open her eyes to the weave, and then carefully inspect each filament on the pages as they were intricately woven into the images and words, which usually bore no relation to what she felt. Ignoring what she saw while trying to perceive the intent of the filaments felt like her mind was being torn apart.

Bzzt! Bzzt! Bzzt!

"Hello?" she answered her phone in video mode, keeping herself open to the weave.

"Tanya, how are you doing?" Yusuf was close to the camera, Farid just behind him, leaning in. She couldn't see the weave on the screen. Their appearance, essence, sound, nothing. That was something she hadn't thought of.

"Yusuf, I'm studying."

"You've figured out the book?" A sense of incredulity crept into his voice.

"I think so. That doesn't mean I'm on my way to fully understanding it all."

"Is there anything about the Jinn?"

"Not really. Like I said, I'm figuring it out." It wasn't as easy as flipping through or looking at the table of contents. There had to be a logical flow to the way the book was 'written,' but she hadn't discovered it yet. She had started at the front and read through, but it was slow going. The section she was in dealt with alchemy, which she believed was important to building the nexus, but not connected to the Jinn. It was confusing.

"Okay, I wanted to check on you. I'm waiting for a response from Qom. They have been scouring their collection for any information that may help with the Ifrit. I also raised your concern about the Jinn focusing on you and whether your abilities were something detectable, but they have said nothing."

"Thank you for asking. If I find anything here. I'll pass it to you." She brought the book into view.

Yusuf and Farid waved goodbye, and the feed ended.

Tanya watched the large screen, the over-simplified colors representing her thought process. She had associated red with rage, violet with grief, and the glimmering white she saw earlier with focused will, though Hector said the meanings were still being mapped.

Turning to the next section, she found it titled 'Medium.' As she delved into the information, the realization hit her. A wise one's medium was the method by which the hakim could manipulate the weave. Art spoke to some, the written word to others, but music was her passion. A hakimah could influence the filaments of the weave through their chosen medium, drawing the necessary energy from their emotions to perform the action. She was sure that she would have made the connections necessary to gain control of how she manipulated the weave. Eunoia sped up the process. It would ideally quell Nafara's anger at finding out she had the device connected.

Someone knocked on the door before opening it. He burst in, went to find the remote on her nightstand and changed the large screen to a live feed from Austin.

"…is believed to be the work of the serial arsonist, who is still at large." The scene cut from the fire to Mayor McWilliams on the steps of City Hall.

"We're applying all available assets to control the fire and rescue as many people as possible. Local and national law enforcement have been called in to assist with the search for the individual responsible."

The scene shifted to an aerial view of the convention center engulfed in flames. Tanya's heart sank. *Please don't be full of people.* She watched as the black smoke from the large complex rose into the sky. In the background, another building burned.

If the Ifrit was there, then he wasn't hiding anymore. He was sending a message. And this time, it wasn't to her.

Chapter 61

Krazack watched from the rooftop in stoic observance of the helplessness of the humans in the wake of his destruction. The city's firefighters were being brought in from around the entire city. As he looked over the city before him, seeking tactical advantage points, sharp spikes shot through his mind. His pain was increasing in intensity and becoming more frequent. His patience had reached its limit. He had to gain control of the hakimah. He needed to draw the Ghul out, and this was the way. She appeared during or after the fires he started. Looking to his right, he saw the battleground he had selected and shaped. He became the wind and moved in the opposite direction from the burning convention center.

Death will draw her out.

-She wishes to lead these people.-

But she is afraid to use force.

[She is weak.]

-She hides her nature.-

Fire will draw her out.

[And then we will kill her.]

-The hakimah will be ours.-

He reformed out of view of any onlookers. The black smoke was dominating the eastern sky. He altered the appearance of his clothes to match those of the surrounding students. Dozens of groups had formed, looking into the distance. Speculation was rampant, with no group knowing what was going on.

-Keep your enemy in the dark.-

He made his way to the first building. The limp slowed him down as the wound from the iron shards refused to close. He had dug out the metal, but the damage was done. It fueled his anger. The hakimah could heal him. He would rule these people. Krazack approached the front entrance. He walked straight toward the doors, bumping into a large man, and knocking him to the ground.

"What the hell? Hey asshole, don't walk off."

Krazack ignored him, stepping inside. People stood in line as a pair of armed security personnel directed them through a rectangular piece of technology. The time for stealth was past. He pushed his way forward, gaining the attention of the two guards. A wide smile spread across his face as the veins in his arm glowed. Grabbing the nearest person, he released fire, engulfing them in flames, and tossed her into the two guards. Screams erupted around him as he released fire from his hands, engulfing the whole atrium in fire. He moved through the building, working his way to the top floor, spreading flames and chaos, and sparing no one.

From the rooftop, he transformed and flew across the University of Texas campus, setting the ground on fire below him. His next target was the museums. He sensed they were protective of the sacred artifacts and would put forth a significant amount of effort to save them. He melted the doors and moved in, releasing his fury into everything around.

-Anger the enemy commander. -

Put fear into the people's hearts.

[Show no mercy. Make them cry out for salvation.]

He scattered flames across campus, targeting buildings unpredictably to keep them guessing. When he heard the sirens of their police approaching, he left the campus, traveling south. He struggled to contain the flames aching to be released. He recognized the importance of the highway passing through and surged upward as a blast of searing wind. Vehicles lined both sides of the highway, stopped in traffic. He searched for a suitable target, finding two tanker trucks separated by a few hundred feet.

Bang!

Something hit his shoulder, moving him forward. The wound hurt, but healed quickly. Krazack turned to find the source. It was a man, not police, or dātabara.

Bang! Bang!

Two more rounds hit him with the same result. He suffered injuries and felt pain, but his body immediately started healing itself. Another person, a woman, held a pistol up.

What is this?

Non-soldiers using these weapons?

-Show them the futility.-

No! Another may have iron rounds.

He pulled the thought from their minds. He dashed toward the first tanker. Taking shape on the opposite side. He pushed heat into the truck until it exploded, covering all lanes of the highway, causing vehicles and people to ignite. He drew the inferno into himself, willing his flesh to absorb the heat like breath. It overwhelmed his senses, power and pain in equal measure. It disoriented him, but he didn't have time to refuel his body as normal. His pain intensified as the heat poured in. Shifting again, he destroyed the second truck, spreading fire across both sides of the highway, sending people running.

-Stay focused!-

[Burn them! Chase them down.]

No, others may have weapons.

-Continue the attack as planned.-

The Ghul is the goal.

[Yes! Yes!]

He resisted the urge to chase the people down and instead continued to his next objective.

Krazack sat on a park bench looking at the state capitol building. The conflagration they faced outmatched the capabilities of the emergency crews. He had encircled his objective, sending a message to his foe. *I will destroy that which you seek.* Despite the sirens in the distance, a sense of peace filled the surrounding air. The ring of fire surrounded him. Two buildings had collapsed, and others would follow. The drain on the water supply had already caused shortages, impacting their efforts to control the fires.

Will she hate us for what we've done?

The question gave him pause. This was a military campaign. A battle, she the prize.

But will she hate you for killing her people?

-No, she would see me for what I am, her champion. I do all of this in her name. I am saving her from the Ghul's manipulation.-

He heard approaching vehicles, a dull roar from the air. He stood and turned to watch the flying vehicles, helicopters, touching down behind the fire line. Krazack transformed and flew forward, stopping short of the whirling blades. Their technological solutions to their shortcomings impressed him. His sudden appearance must have startled the warriors, who raised their weapons toward him. This was their army.

"Freeze!"

He was in danger. He became a fiery tempest as the roar of their weapons filled the air. Their rate of fire was incredible. He dissipated, spreading his presence, and still felt the sting as rounds flew through. Krazack was relieved not to feel the sting of iron. Still, if the humans discovered the Jinn's weakness to iron, the weapons would be devastating. Was this why the Ghul sought to lead these people? With an army such as this, she would cut through the Jinn ranks. Initially. Eventually, the Jinn forces would overcome these new weapons, adapting as they always have, to bring victory.

He swirled faster, guiding the blazing inferno around the soldiers. He fed fire into the swirling wind, feeling the flames circle around, the temperature rising fast. The gathered warriors dropped their weapons, trying to get away from the wind that was blistering their skin. Surprisingly, their clothing resisted the heat. He coalesced his essence into a small, fiery tornado as the sound of another helicopter approached.

The Ifrit shifted direction, moving toward the next group. His mind focused on the battle.

Chapter 62

"Farid, pack up, we have to go." Yusuf gathered the box and his satchel.

"Yes, Sayyidi. I'll be ready in five minutes."

"Good, knock on my door. It will take me a little longer."

"May I ask where we are going?"

"We need to meet with Tanya briefly, then head into the city. Are you watching the news?"

"I have, and I have prayed for those caught in the destruction. That has to be the Ifrit."

"Inshallah (God willing), I believe so. There is no time. I don't understand his motivation for this destruction except, perhaps, to test us. Only Allah knows what the Ifrit hopes to achieve. This will only increase the pressure to find him."

"Maybe that's what he wants. That level of destruction is unimaginable from one being. Could he create a spectacle large enough to garner the attention of the politicians?"

Yusuf thought about it, his eyes scanning his room, going through the checklist of what he needed to do. "Let me finish packing. We can discuss it on the way to see Tanya."

Beep!

He looked at the phone and recognized the Iranian prefix. "I need to take another call."

"Okay, I will be there shortly."

Yusuf accepted the call, ending his call with Farid. "Hello?"

"Yusuf. May the blessings of Allah be upon you. This is Sheikh Ali al-Ridha."

"Yes, of course. Is everything okay?" Yusuf recalled the spectacled sheikh at his induction ceremony. He hadn't had time to stay, rushing off afterwards on an errand for Reza.

"It is not. We are watching the news from your part of the world. Is this a wildfire?"

"No, I believe it is the Ifrit."

"We were afraid of that. Reza has left Qom and is unavailable. Do you have the blade? *Forsaken?*"

"I do. He knows this."

"He left instructions. You must give it to the hakimah."

"She is just recovering from an attack. She isn't strong enough."

"If the blade is wielded by a wise one, the death of the Ifrit will be permanent. Anyone else will only wound the Jinn. Yusuf, trust her to be what she must."

Yusuf didn't like the idea. He didn't know if Tanya would have the strength to fight the Ifrit. "I'm not comfortable with this. I've faced a Jinn before. If I could weaken him, perhaps she could finish him."

"Reza was quite insistent."

Yusuf shook his head. "I will do as directed. May Allah bless her and give her the strength to succeed."

"May His hand guide her to accomplish His will."

"I am on my way to meet with her. What should I tell her?"

"The truth."

"I hope she is ready for it."

"One more thing, Yusuf. Our group has dispatched members to the Republic of India to investigate a plausible report of Jann activity."

"Jann?"

"Yes, search on YouTube for Flying Monkeys in India."

"I will. Are these signs of the prophecy Reza spoke of?"

"We cannot say for sure, but there has been more credible activity in the last five years than there has been for over a thousand years. A saving grace is the belief that the videos are AI-generated. The same goes for the Ifrit."

A feeling of dread crept over him. "A Ghul, Ifrit, and now Jann. Powerful forces are on the move. We must make sure the gate never opens."

"Yusuf, we're scrambling to understand. This sudden surge in activity has caught the Society of al-Batin off guard. I'll keep you informed. May the blessings of Allah protect you in this conflict."

"Thank you, Ali."

Yusuf hung up the phone, his mind a whirlwind of disconnected thoughts. Something was going on. Despite Indian reports, he questioned whether uninformed individuals witnessed other global Jinn events. He was uncomfortable passing the blade to Tanya. She had been through so much. Why must they add this responsibility to her? She had faced death and suffered injury. She was not proficient in her ability to protect herself. Was he sending her to her death?

"Allah, please grant her the strength, fortitude, wisdom, and knowledge to achieve the goals you have set for her. Protect her on her journey. May Your blessings be upon her."

He started emptying his drawers and gathering his belongings. Farid would be here soon. He took a moment to don his official robes, the ones he had worn in Qom. Now wasn't the time to hide behind Western dress. If he were to face this threat, he would meet it head-on. He wondered whether Gabriel would save him again.

Yusuf and Farid entered Tanya's room and were surprised to find her up and about, stiffly gathering her things.

"Yusuf! Farid, it's good to see you. I'm sorry this will be a brief visit, but I have to get into the city."

"Tanya, it is good to see you up and about. You've healed remarkably fast."

"Well, it feels better, but the process is exhausting. The book, which is named *The Compendium of Weave Essence*, by the way, contained useful information."

"Do you understand it?"

"Oh, no. It's not like reading. It takes time to really understand what it says."

"You've seen what's going on in Austin, I presume," Yusuf asked, pulling his satchel up and in front of himself.

"I have, and I need to go. My aunt is worried that the Ifrit is going to target her, and she refuses to back down."

"What about you?"

"I need to talk her out of doing something rash."

"Tanya, you have to convince her that this is a supernatural being. She saw what it did to you, and you were able to deflect the worst of the fire. She won't stand a chance."

"I know, but she is stubborn, which is why she continues to campaign despite the threat."

"About that." He glanced around before pulling the metal case from his satchel and laying it on the bed. "I need to give this to you." He opened the case to reveal the dark gray blade.

"What is it for?"

"You put the pointy end into the other person," Farid offered, offering a shaky smile.

"*Princess Bride*?" Tanya looked at Farid.

"*Game of Thrones,* I think."

"Ibni Farid, this isn't the time for games," Yusuf said.

"Of course, Sayyidi." Farid lowered his eyes, taking a step back.

She gave a slight smile. "May I?"

"Of course," Yusuf said.

She took the blade, rolling it over in her hand. It seemed to be a comfortable size for her grip. She flipped it over, looking at the six-pointed star. "This is?"

"The Seal of Sulaiman."

"Is this the actual seal?" Her interest piqued.

"No, that appears to have been lost."

"Do you expect me to kill the Ifrit?" She held the blade steady, but her fingers trembled. This wasn't research anymore. This was war.

"It takes a wise one to kill a Jinn. Otherwise, they can come back, heal."

"Wait, that doesn't make sense. There are stories about people killing Jinn?"

"Yes, with weapons created from a special type of iron, and those tales may have been altered to downplay the role of magic because of society's fear." It wasn't necessary to go into the entire story.

Tanya's expression changed. Her posture shifted at the news, her shoulders slumping. "I don't even know where he is."

"But you said he came to you. Perhaps you can get close again."

He could see the doubt in her eyes. Fear gripped her. Her hand tightened around the hilt of the blade. The dagger wasn't heavy, but it might as well have been. She didn't know how to fight. Knife scenes in movies always turned her stomach; too close, too real.

Yusuf lowered his head to look into her lowered eyes. "We could go with you. If you prefer, I could try to wound him to make it easier."

"No! If this is what I have to do, I'll try," she said, her voice firming as she tightened her grip on the blade. "But I don't want you in danger because of me."

"But—"

"No, thank you for this. I'll do my best. I've got to go. My aunt needs me."

"We'll accompany you to your aunt."

"I suppose saying no isn't an option."

Yusuf shook his head and placed a hand on her shoulder, the weight of responsibility heavy in his heart. It felt as though he was sending his friend to her death. He prayed she would survive. But in his heart, he feared he had just handed her a weapon and said goodbye.

Chapter 63

Nafara stood on the penthouse balcony looking over the burning city. The smoke-filled sky glowed orange in the light of the setting sun. The dry Texas summer made it easier for the Ifrit. Nafara's jaw clenched in frustration at the damage the Ifrit had caused. The smoke was an annoyance, focusing her on the threat. It made little sense that he would bring the unwanted attention to himself, all to get to her. Was this a message? Or a threat?

What is his goal?

"Social media is blowing up, literally. The only thing in your favor is that scared, running people have a hard time holding a camera steady. Most people still believe he's using firebombs and pyrotechnics, but there are some claiming he's an alien." Lucy continued scrolling on her tablet, a grim expression on her face.

"Not Ifrit?"

"Not here. American culture is egotistical. If we didn't make it up, it's not important enough to worry about."

"That'll change. Give me some good news."

"Unfortunately, I don't have any. With Marcia dropping out, the first polls show frustration among the voters. Texans like their traditions, and while they liked Ross Perot, it is hard for independents to gain a majority. Maybe a third of her voters have switched to you, but the rest of them are divided between voting for the governor or choosing to stay home."

"How far back are we?"

"Eight percent."

"With Marcia dropping out, it would look suspicious if he had an accident, even if I had full deniability."

"The state legislature would appoint a commission, and you'd have to go back through it all again, with conspiracy theories dragging you down."

"We need another approach. There has to be a way to spin this." Nafara paced.

"It's going to be difficult. This is a national story now. 'An American City is burning' and the governor has mobilized the national guard to assist." Lucy used air quotes to highlight what she was saying. "He is showing leadership in the face of a crisis, and as the incumbent, voters will be less likely to drop him. Maybe if you got out like you did for the Oak Hill fires."

"I don't think it would be enough, and people have already seen it."

The door opened, and Tanya came in, taking a straight path to the balcony to join the pair. She was walking better, but still with a pronounced limp. She wore loose pants and a T-shirt, her hair back in a ponytail. Her eyes were wide, and she pointed toward the fires.

"What are we going to do about that?"

"*We* aren't. I need to face the Ifrit and end this and do it in a way that gains favor with voters."

"Voters? How can you worry about the election while so many people are dying?"

Nafara turned abruptly, her anger flashing for a brief second before she regained control. "You know why! Everything seems against us right now. But becoming governor is a vital step in the plan. If I don't win, it'll be more difficult. We need to win. Your vision confirms we are on the right path. You saw the nexus in the Capitol building—"

She turned back toward the fires, focusing on the building surrounded by flames, and laughed.

"What?" Tanya said, exasperation clear in her voice.

"The fires. I understand. Look at the pattern. What's at the center of it all?"

Tanya moved to the edge of the balcony and saw the reddish dome of the Capitol building. "He's put a ring of fire around the Capitol building?"

"He's figured it out. You said he was a military commander, correct?"

"Yes, Commander of the Ifrit Legion."

"It's a trap. He surrounded the building with fire. He's inviting me to come to him to settle this. If I don't confront him, he'll destroy the thing he believes I desire."

"Let me go. Maybe he'll listen to me."

"No! I don't want you anywhere near him."

"You know he won't hurt me. He wants me on his side."

"It's too dangerous. If anything happens to you, I can't open the nexus."

"Nothing will happen to me. Maybe I can reason with him. If he knows the plan for your people, we may turn him into an ally."

An Ifrit would prove helpful, but Krazack seemed peculiar. His focus was on killing her to take Tanya as his own hakimah. Was there something she didn't understand? Some part of their relationship that was not apparent. She admitted her limited knowledge with hesitation and considered the possibility that he knew something she didn't. What had he learned during his time here? If anything, he was more brazen, daring humans to do anything to stop him.

There was something strange about the Ifrit's obsession with Tanya. Something she didn't fully understand. Perhaps it was power. Perhaps something else. Either way, knowing more was worth the risk.

Nafara looked at the Capitol, an idea forming. "Fine. I agree. He'd be a potent ally, but you need to get him out of the city. With the military here, we can't risk his getting caught. He needs to understand what is at stake."

"I'll do my best."

"I know you will." She reached over, taking Tanya's hand, and squeezed it gently. "Are you sure you're up to it?" Something about Tanya made her uneasy. She couldn't place it.

Tanya held her gaze. There was no hesitation. "I am. I have better control now."

"Okay." She let go of Tanya's hand. Tanya turned to leave. She adjusted her posture, her shoulders pulling back in confidence.

"Tanya."

Her friend stopped and looked back. "Yes."

"It'll be easier once it's dark."

"Thank you for trusting me."

Nafara nodded once before Tanya turned and left the suite.

"I can't believe you let her go," Lucy said.

"I hope she takes my advice. And she's not going alone. It'll be dark soon, and that's my time."

"What are you going to do?"

"I'm going to follow her in, and when he's at his most vulnerable, I'm going to kill him." Nafara's eyes flared.

"If you're wrong about this…" she trailed off, eyes locked on the fire.

"Then we'll make sure the narrative outlives the fallout," Nafara replied.

"I'm listening."

"I need you to get in touch with Camila. She's going to have the exclusive of a lifetime."

"Ooh, she's going to like that."

Nafara smiled at Lucy, then turned back toward the burning city. As the sun slipped beneath the horizon, the fire became their only light. The city burned, and the future waited in its shadow.

Chapter 64

Tanya made her way toward the Capitol building. Thick smoke filled the air and abandoned vehicles obstructed the streets. The fires lit the sky, giving the city an eerie glow. The National Guard was in the city, but their resources, and those of every firefighting team, were stretched thin. She had heard on the radio that casualties were high, and the police were out, trying to enforce evacuation orders.

The buildings in front of her, once at the edge of the financial district, formed a blazing wall. Nafara had given a speech a few months ago north of where she was now, in Waterloo Park. As she made her way forward, she stopped, looking up and down the street. No one was nearby. The fear of fire had kept instances of looting down. No one knew where Krazack would strike next. Someone had recognized the danger to the Capitol building and assumed that it was a 'Texit' group instead of a lone arsonist. The idea hadn't gained momentum.

Despite feeling the heat from the buildings she was passing between, she steeled her nerves and moved forward. Her vision shifted to the weave, and she sang the notes of an ancient Persian song. She wasn't sure the song mattered. She could have chosen Britney Spears. With a smirk, she envisioned Nafara and what a touch could do, singing *Toxic* to bolster the Ghul. She felt the heat increase in intensity and refocused her mind on manipulating the weave. Tanya surrounded herself with cooler air and pushed aside the heat, letting it flow around. She became a stone in a stream, the heat of the fire moving around her.

As she passed beyond the wall of burning buildings, she became aware of the quiet inside the fire ring. It mirrored the calm of a hurricane's eye. The orange light from the fires intensified the red stone of the building, illuminating it. She imagined this was what a building would look like in hell. As the pain in her legs intensified, she continued to sing and quickened her pace, which exaggerated her limp. She thought of Krazack and refocused the song inward. She kept her eyes on the building in front of her while visualizing the remnants of fire buried deep inside her leg, burning away the last of the injury. The purifying flames forged a path for her muscles and ligaments to rebuild. Instead of pushing the pain away, she embraced it, adding it to her efforts to heal.

She must have been a sight to see, a lone figure walking out of the fire. Plunging onward toward her destiny. She hoped she could connect with him. If he could control the flames, he could end all of this. Tanya didn't believe that he would turn himself in, and that wasn't what she wanted. If she could help him see what they were doing, she could convince him to join forces. Nafara only wanted to free their people.

Tanya passed several burning helicopters surrounded by charred bodies. She wondered what whomever thought they were in charge had reported back. Likely the governor, but they wouldn't know what was happening because they wouldn't believe what they saw. Outside of the movies, no one man could have caused this much destruction.

She was surprisingly calm. Perhaps it was the music, something she loved, that provided strength despite the inferno raging around her. She stopped before going up the steps to the south entrance and looked at the wall of fire around her. The emergency teams weren't making progress.

She opened one side of the double doors and walked in, the door banging shut behind her. It was dark and eerily muted. The emergency lighting was on, providing illumination along the walls, arrows pointing the way to the exit, and battery-powered lights showing the doors. She walked toward the rotunda, moving through the walk-through metal detector. Shadows from the lights extended from her in multiple directions around the large, round room. Should she call out? Was he even here? She looked for traces of him and saw nothing she remembered from their last meeting. She looked around and was greeted by the many portraits of previous governors and presidents of the Republic of Texas.

A brief shift in the light behind her caught her attention, a whisper of movement too low to be smoke. She ignored it.

"Where is the Ghul?" The familiar voice came down from the balcony. She looked up, searching the dark for him, and saw his glowing gold eyes.

"She's not here. It's just me." Tanya repositioned herself to face the Ifrit.

"I don't believe you."

"I asked her to stay away so that we could talk." She tried to focus on him but found it difficult to see any part of him but the glowing yellow eyes.

"You don't understand the nature of the Ghul. They are manipulative and cunning. Always making plans within plans, focused on their goals."

"And that's why you started the inferno outside? To lure her in by threatening her goals. You've injured or killed hundreds of people."

"What do you care, Hakimah? You betray your people by serving her."

That stung. He had thrust a dagger into her worries, opening the wound wide for her to see the truth of what it was. "She's trying to save your people."

"That's a lie. Ghul are unsympathetic to anyone but themselves."

"I came here to ask you to join her. A peace offering so that you can help your people come home."

Krazack laughed. His voice echoed and filled the rotunda. "You're already under her spell. She is using her pheromones or poisons to cloud your mind. Ghul don't make friends. What you believe is a fantasy created by her to manipulate you into doing her bidding."

Was he telling the truth? Are all Jinn manipulative? How would she know? Was the truth part of the weave? It had to be. What did it look like? If she could spot the truth, she could see lies. "I don't believe you. Since we met, she has always been there for me."

"Most likely in a scenario of her own design. She'll betray you when you no longer serve a purpose. Break your bond and join me, and I will guide you, bringing you knowledge you cannot gain from this world."

And there's the offer. "But what about your people?"

Krazack raised his voice, and she saw the glow on either side of him. "My people abandoned me. They deserve to be locked up!"

Tanya looked helplessly up at the Ifrit.

"I warned you he couldn't be bargained with," the smooth voice of her aunt came from the shadows behind her. Tanya looked over her shoulder and saw Nafara in her true form. She towered above Tanya, her ebony skin blending in with the darkness. Tanya could make out the blue wrap top cinched at the waist, and flowing around her hips, ending above her knees. Her burning eyes pierced the darkness.

"There you are," he growled, golden eyes flaring. "Let's finish this."

Chapter 65

Yusuf followed Tanya, moving from cover to cover as she approached the Capitol building. He worried she looked too calm, walking toward her death. He didn't know if she had the blade, but if the Ifrit saw him, it wouldn't matter. Each time he paused, he searched the surrounding area for any sign of the Ifrit. It took little effort to hold the image of the man in his head. His complexion and glowing eyes were like those of the Ghul. Was it a coincidence?

The images he had seen in the text showed diversity similar to that of humans. That observation alone raised more questions than he had time to consider. Although he had lost her, he assumed she was heading towards the south entrance. He didn't want her to know that he had followed and didn't want to interrupt her. His task was to observe and report back to the Society. He crept to the right, staying in the shadows cast by the fires burning around them.

As he neared the building, movement caught his eye, and fear gripped him. He froze, pressing himself against a tree. He glanced around. The shadows from the trees, dancing because of the billowing flames, played tricks on his mind. He saw people moving all around his position. He listened for anything that might tell him they were real, but the sounds of the emergency response vehicles came from all directions.

Yusuf slowed, wondering if the Ifrit was watching them both make their way toward the building. Tanya told him that the Ifrit didn't want to harm her. His presence was unplanned in the Ifrit's mind. He had killed plenty of people already, without reason. Yusuf felt doubt creep in, and Gabriel's image flashed into his mind. *Allah alone decrees what will strike us. He is our protector.*

The Capitol building loomed above him to the left. Despite his having been in Texas for over two decades, he had never taken the time to visit. It was impressive. The style was like the national Capitol building. He still preferred Persian architecture, with its flowing curves, parapets, and domes. He moved along the side of the building. Normally, this entire area would be lit up, but with the fires, the power was out, making the impressive structure appear sinister.

He made his way to the north side of the building. Two destroyed helicopters lay here, surrounded by the soldiers' remains, mirroring the scene on the other side. If he wasn't careful, he would end up like them. He crept to the doors, his intent clear. He opened the door and held it until it closed behind him.

Stepping into the lobby area, he heard the squeak of his shoes on the polished floor. He froze, afraid to make another sound. Stooping, he slipped his shoes off. He heard a woman's voice echoing ahead of him. It sounded like Tanya. He moved around the metal detector and inched to the corner of the passageway to the rotunda. He tried to stay in the shadows, hoping the emergency lighting wouldn't throw his shadow and give him away.

Looking into the rotunda, he saw Tanya talking to someone above her.

"I warned you he couldn't be bargained with," came a voice from the shadows. His heart skipped a beat when the Ghul from his nightmares appeared behind Tanya. He heard the shift in the Ghul's tone to the voice from years before. He hadn't forgotten how she had mocked him and left him to die.

No, his mind screamed. Tanya had lied. *I'm a fool.* She's been working with her the whole time, and he had given her the blade. The only weapon that could kill a Jinn, and she knew it. His hand flew to the small scar on his neck where she had scratched him, then to his arm and hand marred by the botulinum toxin. He retreated around the corner. Sweat formed on his brow as his heart raced. *I'm going to die.* He pulled his phone from his robes and sent a single message to Farid: "She's with the Ghul. Blade delivered. Await my word."

"Release the hakimah and vow never to return, and I will allow you to live, Ghul," the deep voice of the Ifrit echoed through the chamber.

"Hahaha, you think your fire scares me? I'll leave you paralyzed and give your corpse to the humans. You can't imagine the torture they'll inflict on you. They're quite creative."

The Ifrit continued to talk, but Yusuf couldn't make out what he was saying. He seemed to argue with himself. Tanya moved away from the Ghul, coming closer to him. Maybe this was her plan. Hope attempted to creep in, but he brushed it aside. If the two Jinn fought and weakened each other, it would be easier for her to strike. He shifted his thoughts to his research in Qom. Jinn engaged in battles amongst themselves. Even in the story of Sulaiman, it described rebellious Jinn who fought against the Prophet's Jinn forces. They were like humans with their own cultural wants and needs, and of those that fought regularly were the Ghul and Ifrit. His hope strengthened.

This had to be her plan. Pit the enemies against each other to weaken each. Both Jinn wanted her alive. She was the prize. If one could kill the other, she could kill the victor. His hope grew, not in her magic, but in her mind. If anyone could survive this, it was Tanya.

Chapter 66

Tanya felt the tension in the air and moved back in anticipation of the gathering energy. The eerie silence hung in the air as the two Jinn, legendary enemies Ghul and Ifrit, dared the other to make the first move. Tanya shifted her gaze. Nafara danced with a kaleidoscope of energy swirling around her form. She was drawing energy from the Earth. Had the Ifrit made a mistake confronting her here?

Krazack radiated heat. It swirled around him, the tendrils coiling around his arms, pulsing with the chaos of a dancing flame in a whirlwind. The banister in front of him glowed. It was a sliver of orange light growing in intensity until the entire metal frame glowed. With the paint cover burnt away, something distracted the Ifrit. He stepped back from the heated metal. She hummed a song for battle, a militaristic march. As she focused on the metal, she understood his distraction. The second-floor frame was made of iron.

Nafara moved when he stepped back, shifting to her shadow form, passing around the metal, and reforming with claws extending from her fingers. Her hand shot out as she continued to move around him, scratching down his arm. Where she split the skin, glowing fire erupted from his veins, spraying her arm. Her poisons went to work, flowing into the wounds. The toxins mutated, trying to find a weakness in the Ifrit. His arm shook.

He became a fiery wind shooting forward to envelop Nafara, her skin blistered under the attack. She shifted to shadow, and the swirling tornado of energy created a maelstrom of shadow-flame, neither Jinn gaining the advantage. The dark energy dissipated. Krazack reformed.

"Where are you, fiend!"

Nafara's voice came from the shadows above and across from him. A rainbow of green hues bubbled from the dark. The filaments of the living organisms floated faster outward, thickening the air with an earthy smell. The air felt damp, cooler. Tanya continued to hum the song, reaching out to identify the threat. Mold, bacteria, mildew, and fungus appeared. First in small patches, then exploding to cover every surface in sight. Spores filled the air as the surface became covered.

A whisper coiled through the threads, not in any voice she knew, each syllable stretching like molten glass....*walk in flesh... burn clean...*

She blinked hard, shaking the sound from her mind before it could take root.

Krazack coughed. His anger grew, feeding his building power. He raised his hands and directed fire to flow across the rotunda, erasing the shadows and illuminating the growth-covered expanse. He coughed again, then broke into a fit. Spreading his hands, he set everything around him on fire.

"Impressive. Your people could have used someone like you. Maybe you could have saved them."

Nafara grinned in return, channeling her power upward toward the sprinkler heads. The system may be down, but there should still be water in the pipes. A rattling erupted from above as the sprinkler heads burst outward, not only with water, but a twisting, sprawling tangle of vines. Fed by the abundance of water in the sprinkler system and guided by Nafara, the plants grew at an exponential rate, thickening, and moving to cover everything in their path. Tanya moved further toward the west end of the round room.

The flames surrounding Krazack weakened. The spider plants were driving up the humidity in the room, which they in turn, used to sprout new growths. Krazack coughed as the spores took advantage of the diminishing flames, working their way into his lungs. His eyes flared, and he roared, fire swirling around him. He leaped across the rotunda toward Nafara. She shifted, leaping down to the second-floor balcony. Krazack didn't respond to Nafara's move. He raised his hands and projected focused flames toward the largest growths, evaporating the moisture in the air and causing the plants to wither. He continued to send flames upward, destroying the plants, and turning the remaining water to steam. Spinning, he shot flames downward, catching Nafara in the chest. She screamed and fell back.

"No!" Tanya yelled. Nafara staggered to her feet in time to greet the Ifrit's leap downward toward her. He grabbed an arm, his veins glowing as her skin bubbled, smoke rising. She shot her other arm forward, sinking all five claws into the side of his chest. Both Jinn struggled, enduring the full might of their foe, attempting to outlast the other, their energies pouring into the other.

Krazack squeezed her wrist, snapping the charred hand off.

Nafara screeched. Tanya saw the swirling green energy flowing into the wounded Ifrit. The Ifrit was stronger. The disease and poison injected into his side wounded him, but his heat burned away the toxins faster than Nafara could change them.

Krazack reached up, grabbing Nafara by the neck. Fear gripped Tanya. *This can't be happening.* The Ifrit lifted the Ghul and threw her with all of his might down to the center of the circular floor. She hit hard with a wet snap. Tanya rushed forward as Krazack jumped down to land nearby.

"No! You can't kill her. Please!" she pleaded, pushing Nafara's hair out of her face. The Ghul lay still, her chest quivering with each breath.

"Hakimah, I'm freeing you from her."

"I can't lose her. Please don't." Water dripped down around her.

"She must die."

Tanya stood, placing herself between the Ifrit and Nafara. She held one hand back toward the Ghul. "Wait, I'll go with you. I'll do whatever you ask." Tears were streaming down her cheeks now. The thought of losing Nafara tore at her heart.

Krazack stopped before her. His gaze softened.

"Do it for me," she pleaded.

His muscles relaxed, eyes locked on hers.

She stepped forward and reached up to place her left hand on his cheek. "Please."

Conflict tore at him. She could feel it. Something held him back.

She brought her body close to his, her right arm rising before she pressed the blade into his chest with all her might. His eyes filled with pain and betrayal. He fell to his knees before slumping over. His breath slowed as he continued to hold her eyes in his. He fell to the side, pulling her onto him as she kept her grip on the blade. His blood was hot, but he didn't burn her. It flowed from the wound, over her hand. She pulled the blade out.

"I'm sorry."

"You were . . . the last light I saw."

Her tears fell on his face as the fire went out of his eyes. She sobbed.

"Tanya! Are you okay?"

She looked up. "Yusuf? What are you doing here?"

"I was worried about you. You have to finish this."

"It's finished. Krazack is dead."

"Not him." His eyes went to Nafara. "She is weak."

Tanya scrambled to her feet, moving between the two. "No, you don't know what you're saying."

"She's a Ghul. You could end it all here."

"No, I won't. I owe her." She raised the blade toward him and saw the pain in his eyes.

"You don't have to do that."

"I won't let you kill her."

"I can't force you, but your decision will bring pain and suffering to us all. You're my friend. I'll pray for you to be guided by the will of Allah. You don't have an enemy in me. I want you to know that."

She saw her friend as a threat, and this tore her apart. "You need to go. I have to help her."

"I'll do as you ask." He lowered his head and left through the north entrance.

Bzzzt!

"Hello?"

"Tanya, we've got it all. I need you to help her out the south entrance." Lucy sounded eager.

"What are you talking about? She can't."

"The military is moving in. The helicopters just took off. You know you can't let them get her." Lucy was right, she needed to get them out of here. "I'll try."

"Hurry." The call ended, and Tanya took a few breaths to calm down. She opened herself to the weave. Beginning with the song that bound her to the Ghul, she sang. Tanya opened herself to the emotions. Fear of losing the Jinn strengthened her resolve. She manipulated the filaments as the Ifrit had taught her. First, she attacked the worst injuries. She continued to sing, lost in the music while working on the filaments to repair what she could. Tanya poured all her emotions into the song.

"Tanya," Nafara's voice was weak.

"Nafara, you're going to be okay. We have to get you out of here."

"Everything hurts."

"I know. I'm sorry, I'm trying."

"It's okay. Help me up."

The pain in her leg flared. She struggled to help her friend. Tanya gritted her teeth. Nafara's wounds were healing faster. She watched, amazed, as Nafara's body resumed what Tanya had tried to begin. The repair came slower, but deeper.

She supported Nafara, now in her human guise, toward the south entrance, opening the doors as the first pair of helicopters were landing. The first boots hit the pavement, not military, but media. Camila Navarro stepped through the smoke, camera crew in tow, eyes locked on the wounded woman in Tanya's arms.

Chapter 67

Nafara groaned as the Black hawk helicopter banked to the left in approach to the Eunoia research facility. The concern for her aunt overshadowed the fear of her first time in a helicopter. Nafara insisted they take her to the research facility despite the army medics' insistent claims. The physician's assistant, a tall, thin captain, had stormed off in a fit of anger at Nafara's refusal of medical treatment.

The helicopter flared as it approached the landing area, settling onto the pad. Hector and members of his team greeted them and took Nafara into the facility. They moved quickly, rolling her through to the private room. Tanya had to walk fast to keep up. When they got her to the room, they helped her onto the bed, which was extended. Hector dismissed the others except for one nurse. She was older, bright-eyed and meticulous in her work. With Tanya, she carried out all prescribed treatment on time and precisely, according to Hector's specifications.

"Irene, close the door, and help me extend the bed." Tanya stepped back and let the pair work. They moved all the electronic equipment to the side, knowing it would be useless on the Jinn.

"Nafara, how are you feeling?"

The Jinn shifted to her natural form, filling the elongated bed. "I hurt like hell, and this sucks." She held up the arm, burnt at the wrist and missing the hand. Tanya noted Irene hadn't reacted to the change. She didn't know everyone holding Nafara's secret, but she knew those who did were completely devoted to the Jinn.

"We could contact the top prosthetics companies. They're making significant progress."

"No, Hector, that won't be necessary, and anything with electronics would fail. I need you to keep everyone away except those on my list. Tanya will help me. Lucy should arrive soon. Send her in immediately."

"Of course. We'll leave you alone."

"One more thing. I'm going to need a volunteer or two." Irene looked at the doctor, her lips pressed together. She knew what Nafara meant.

"Of course. We'll send them to your office."

Tanya wanted to feel sorry for the victims, but in the end, it didn't matter. Nafara had to eat. The Ghul would need her strength to heal. The battle was the first time that she had observed the Jinn through the weave. Her vision blurred.

Tanya stood in the rotunda. The damage from the battle was still present. The scorched spider plants were growing again, fed by the sprinkler system. Water dripped all around her. Krazack was gone. She was alone. Two blocks of dark metal sat in front of her. They rippled across their surfaces. Each mirroring the other, shifting their form and taking the shape she had seen before, the nexus. A low hum filled the air as she heard the pillar on the right vibrating. She sang, focusing on the emotions of someone finding the family they thought lost long ago. She reached out to touch the arching right half of the nexus, its vibration now holding the song she had sung. Blood dripped from her hand, but she wasn't injured.

Krazack. She had killed the Ifrit, his blood was still there. She reached into the weave, touching the filaments of the blood. They were different. Math equations appeared and disappeared in her head. The formulas for plotting vortices, quantum entanglement, and understanding the earth's resonant frequency resonated in her thoughts. The blood was from the City of Brass. It was the key.

She stumbled forward, bracing herself on Nafara's bed, the treatment room coming back into focus. "I have it."

"What do you have?"

"The key to the nexus. I understand how to open a stable link between here and the City."

"What do you need?"

"The metal. The location will be the challenge. We need to be in the rotunda where you fought Krazack."

"That's going to be difficult if we don't win the election."

"You're right. The last time I saw the nexus was in the house chambers. Now it's different."

"Visions reveal likely outcomes, but they are never set in stone."

Tanya thought of the other visions, the military command center, the White House. Maybe she could change them, finish Nafara's plan without so many people dying.

"Tanya." Nafara sat up in bed, swinging her legs over the edge to touch the floor. She reached out, waiting for Tanya's hand.

She stepped closer, taking the offered hand. "Yes."

"Where did you get that blade?"

"Yusuf gave it to me. He told me I had to be the one to kill the Ifrit. The blade in the hands of a hakimah makes it permanent, otherwise, your people heal."

"May I see it?"

Tanya reached behind her back and pulled the blade from its sheath, showing it to Nafara. The Jinn recoiled.

"That is made from Jinn steel."

"What do you mean?"

"Put it away, please. That's Jinn steel, not just iron. It was forged to end us."

"Yusuf told me that his friends in Qom insisted I be the one to use it."

Nafara paused in thought. Tanya almost mentioned that Yusuf wanted her to kill Nafara as well, but didn't want her to go after the old teacher.

"You could have used it on me." Nafara raised her eyes, locking her gaze with Tanya.

"I know, but I never will. You are my friend. My family. I would never hurt you."

Nafara looked troubled. "I should ask you to destroy the blade, but I won't. Keep it. You have my trust."

"Nafara, I need to ask you a question. It's about something Krazack said."

"*You* may always ask me anything."

"Have you altered my thoughts or feelings with pheromones, spores, or anything like that?"

"Not you."

Tanya looked into Nafara's eyes and saw her love. "Thank you."

Chapter 68

Yusuf sat in the passenger seat as he and Farid drove south. He didn't grasp the extent of the prophecy. Ali had insisted that she be the one to kill the Ifrit. He had doubted the decision, but it passed. She had remained outside the fight as the two Jinn battled. Their capabilities were beyond anything he had studied. When he returned to the Institute, he would lock himself in his office to record everything he had witnessed.

"Sayyidi, are you alright?"

"Ibni Farid, I know He'll protect us," Yusuf replied, his eyes fixed on the horizon. "May He continue to bless us in our task." He paused, his throat feeling dry. "When we return to the Institute, I'll contact the council of the Society. I believe there's more going on here than we understand."

"Why are the Jinn returning now? It's been thousands of years."

"They were the first to fall. Many were banished, locked in the City of Brass."

"But—" Farid stopped.

"Say what you're thinking. Now isn't the time to hold back."

"The City of Brass is not in the Quran. It's a story passed down in legend, ancient stories. Sulaiman was said to have chained the disobedient."

"If the Jinn were the first created by Allah with a choice of good and evil, and their civilization fell. Should we believe they could not have progressed as far as humans? These thoughts take leaps of faith. Is Allah all-powerful? And I'll quote from Ayat al-Kursi, *The Throne Verse*, 'Who is it that can intercede with Him except by His permission? He knows what is before them and what will be after them, and they encompass not a thing of His knowledge except for what He wills.' All power and grace are His."

"You believe in the City's existence?"

"How can we not? There's so much we don't know. Maybe the answers are locked away in a mythical city in the desert, Rub' al-Khali. Perhaps they, the Jinn, were chained in place, unseen by human eyes, just outside our ability to detect them. Whatever the case, Jinn are returning to Earth, and that cannot be good for us."

"Sayyidi, what can we do against them? Look at the damage one Ghul and one Ifrit caused."

"Have faith, Ibni Farid. We need to understand the prophecy. The purpose of our society is to prevent the return of the Jinn. For thousands of years, the Society has stood guard, and in the last five years we have failed twice."

"But the Ifrit is dead, and the Ghul disappeared. That's a success."

But the Ghul is alive. Yusuf wasn't ready to admit his failure to convince Tanya to kill the Jinn. Her role in both instances meant something. She told him she was a hakimah, a wise one. What was the significance? She was protective of the Ghul, and from what he could tell, it was a willing devotion, despite the pain and suffering she had caused. Tanya stepped between him and the Ghul and would have protected her from him. It still hurt him, but there was something between the Jinn and the hakimah. She cared for the Jinn. He saw it in her eyes.

"Yes, but at what cost? Hundreds dead. Austin in flames. Is that success?"

Farid blew out a long breath. "We haven't encountered a Marid or Si'lat."

Yusuf's shoulder drooped. "True, and what I've seen of their abilities to control the base elements is far beyond our understanding. The prose and exaggerations of the tales from the Bedouin do not measure up to what I've witnessed. Imagine the destruction a hundred Jinn could cause."

"Sayyidi, we must inform the government, the military, law enforcement, whomever can help."

Yusuf chuckled in a fatherly manner, trying not to dismiss Farid's recommendation. "I'll bring it up with the Council. At least there are others who believe. But, they've kept the secret for thousands of years, and even when I sent a report of my encounter with a Ghul, they didn't take any action."

"But the threat is real. Something is going on here. They have to listen."

"I believe they will. This isn't a secret society as popularized by western media, there is no conspiracy. The Society of Al-Batin works within the borders of the Quran. Reza is a Grand Ayatollah and a scholar of occult studies. Reza's title is well known, and all scholars can access his portion of the library at Qom. The concept of Jinn is accepted. Granted, there are more texts that are held by the society, but the general knowledge is available."

"Are we stuck behind politics?"

"We're bound by the teachings of the Prophet and the word of Allah."

"I understand and will follow your lead."

"I'm sure Reza will have answers if he has returned. If not, the others should provide guidance."

They sat in silence, passing through the ranches and open land between the cities, each lost in thought. *Ya Allah, guide us along the difficult road You have set before us. I place my trust in You, knowing that Your wisdom will aid us in this journey. Grant Farid, and those who may join our cause, the strength and patience to endure what lies ahead. We seek Your mercy and protection in every step we take, for You are the All-Knowing, the All-Powerful.*

Bzzt!

Yusuf glanced down, seeing the message 'Caller ID blocked.' He was thinking about the events of the past few hours and didn't want to lose his train of thought. He looked at Farid, who wore a look of concern.

He hit decline. Whatever it was could wait. He had enough doubts in his heart already.

Chapter 69

Tanya left the cafeteria, heading toward Nafara's office. The treatment was going well, though she found the process to be full of trial and error. Apparently, Jinn were more attuned to their bodies. Nafara had guided her in assisting through the healing, but Tanya's inexperience had caused more harm than good in their first session. Nafara had explained the Jinn's unique alignment with base elements, something she had to respect.

She leaned into the camera. The light turned green, and the door opened. The minimalist office always intrigued her, so different from her own at home, where keepsakes of Sheri, Amara, and her mom surrounded her, as if they were watching over her.

"Faith, open the garden, please."

Opening garden. To what level would you like it opened?

"Fully opened."

As you wish.

"Thank you, Faith."

Faith, the upgraded AI, was a step up from the previous version. Tanya had worked with Dr. Gutierrez to carve out part of its functionality for her personal use. Tanya knew Nafara's distrust of technology, but believed it crucial for her development, especially given the difficulty in deciphering ancient texts and scrolls. So far,

Faith hadn't provided groundbreaking insights, but it had taken meticulous notes.

As the garden's retractable roof opened, sunlight filled the room. Tanya knew this was where Nafara fed, and the lingering filaments of death hung heavy in the air. Pushing aside her discomfort, she focused on the task at hand.

"Faith, I am going to manipulate the weave. Please observe, record, and analyze."

Yes, Tanya.

The room became illuminated, transforming from a dark, moss-covered oasis into a vibrant space filled with exotic plants. Mist drifted from above, bathing the edges of the room in a cool haze, while the center remained dry and mossy. Tanya took her place, sitting in the middle as the sunlight touched her skin.

She opened her eyes to the weave, where the multicolored filaments of the plants filled the air. Taking a breath, she reached out, touching them delicately, feeling the familiar scents of jasmine and lavender, the essence of Yasmin and herself. Singing a Persian melody, she began manipulating the filaments, filtering them until only the ones she needed remained.

Her mind shifted to the residual pain in her leg, and she let memories flood her thoughts: her mother's murder, Amara's family, and finally Sheri's necklace. Her heart ached, and her voice deepened, her song imbued with sorrow. The plants seemed to react, as if sharing in her grief, but the sensation slipped away before she could fully grasp it.

She pulled the song back, focusing on the pain in her leg, searching for remnants of the cleansing fire. When she found a faint spark, she carefully lifted it, guiding it into her palm. The tiny flame flickered, chaos burning within. She fed her sadness into it, watching it grow in intensity, but as the fire strengthened, it faltered. She had nowhere to keep it.

Closing her eyes, she visualized the tendrils of her own being, the weave that connected her. The image was unsettling, with tendrils spiraling outward from her core, delicate yet vast. And then it came to her: Sheri's necklace. The sapphire.

She sang once more, weaving a yearning into her melody, searching for the stone. When she found it, the sapphire's filaments appeared different: knotted, thick, and unyielding. Tendrils crept from the knot, slow and deliberate, as if they moved through a gentle current. She hadn't sensed this before. Her curiosity piqued, she reached out, and a chill of sadness swept over her.

Tears spilled down her cheeks, and she felt the full weight of the memory behind the pendant. Sheri's father handed it to her after her mother's funeral. The sorrow, the love, and the bittersweet joy intertwined in the sapphire threatened to overwhelm Tanya, but she steadied herself, grounding her emotions in the pain she'd drawn from earlier.

The knot of filaments around the stone was strong. As she struggled to untangle them, her frustration grew. The flame in her hand pulsed with heat, and she brought it closer to the stone. After what felt like an eternity, she found a small gap in the knot and pressed the flame inside.

The sapphire reacted. It pulsed as the knot tightened, and tendrils of light sprouted from the stone. The memory wrapped around itself, strengthening the weave as elemental power flowed into the filaments.

Tanya released a breath she hadn't realized she was holding. When she finally looked down at the stone in her hand, it glowed, warmth radiating from within.

"Faith, what did you observe?"

You were meditating, singing a lovely Persian song.

"Did you notice anything that is out of the ordinary?"

No.

"We need to research the latest innovative sensors and get you upgraded. If you're going to help me, I need you to see what I see."

An analysis of your brain patterns during the process is available. Would you like to have the results forwarded to you?

"Yes, thank you, Faith. You can close the ceiling."

The room darkened, lights along the walls illuminating the space as the room closed itself off. She left the room, looking forward to describing the session with Nafara.

Chapter 70

Nafara sat in a large recliner in the corner of her room. The wide burgundy chair supported the Jinn in her natural appearance. She was across the room from the monitors for the latest patients receiving the Eunoia device.

"The latest group includes the candidates from the Department of Defense. We have volunteers from the Army, Navy and the Marine Corps," Hector said.

"What's our test population up to, and what's the timeline for FDA approval?"

"Well, the initial results are positive. The AI is learning with each group. The next generation is smaller, and more effective. Average time to remap the pathways is down to a few weeks."

"What about the walling effect?"

"That takes longer. Sometimes patients have been able to change a neural pathway after developing a new one. It's very rare, less than point two percent."

"Are there any patients here now who have done this?"

Hector nodded, fidgeting as he looked at Tanya standing just inside the doorway.

"I did it," Tanya said. Nafara noted Hector relax at her admission. Which did nothing to quell the feeling welling up inside.

"You don't have Eunoia."

Tanya turned her head and pulled her hair apart to show the small rectangular devices. "I meant to tell you before the Capitol. But everything moved so fast."

"We talked about this. How do you know it won't interfere with your other projects?" She sat forward, her lips pressed together. She shifted her gaze to Hector, who took a step back.

"Don't get mad at him. I used the authority you gave me, and I told him I would let you know."

"But you don't know if it will interfere."

"If it did, then I would have it removed, but it hasn't. In fact, I believe it has enhanced my ability to see and manipulate the weave. I also need to feel the emotions from my trauma. It helps me focus. I need the pain."

She considered what Tanya had said. "How did you manipulate the mapping algorithm?"

"I focused on strengthening the pathways to the memories of my mother."

"And the device detected the path of least resistance, assuming it was linking to happy memories."

"I don't know about that. Faith reworked the code for me."

Nafara stood up. "You had a test model AI change the code that affects the way you think and feel? Are you insane?"

Tanya shrank a little at the rebuke. "No, I just thought that maybe it would help. It does, by the way. I've made more progress. It's been helpful in the past few weeks as I've tried new things. I don't have to remember exactly what I was thinking, singing, or feeling. It feels more natural, even when I shift my sight."

Knock-knock-knock!

Lucy opened the door. She looked around at everyone and stopped. "Am I interrupting?"

"Yes, but nothing we can't finish later." Nafara shot her one more stern look.

"Nafara, I'll check with you later." Dr. Gutierrez excused himself.

"Thank you, Hector. I'd like to make sure we remove the ability to change the code in future versions. For safety purposes. We don't need the liability of something going wrong because of a hacker or someone in the Department of Defense poking around in areas they don't understand."

"Of course." He headed for the door, slowing to look at Tanya, though she couldn't see his expression. Still, she nodded at his words.

"Well, that was tense. But I bring good news." She walked to the nightstand by the bed and picked up the remote. "May I?"

Nafara nodded. Tanya went to stand by the Jinn.

Governor Baker has made a statement denying his involvement in a conspiracy to affect the election.

The image on the screen showed the governor in his signature jeans, button-down shirt, sport coat, and boots. He never wore a tie unless he was at a fundraiser or in Washington.

"These claims are a fabrication of someone or some group seeking to sully my name and that of my family. I have the utmost respect for my opponent and have never stooped to underhanded tricks to win an election. I wish a speedy recovery to Ms. Kavioni."

"Governor, we have the serial arsonist on tape stating that your reelection team hired him to kill or scare off your opponent. Do you deny this claim?" Camila Navarro held the microphone toward him.

The governor stared into the camera. "That's a lie. I'll not have my family's name dragged through the mud. Let me know when you're ready to do some real journalism, not throw about silly conspiracy theories."

"So, your response is that everything in the capital is silly? Is that the response to the hundreds of Texas citizens that passed away, or the thousands now affected by the fires?"

"Mrs. Navarro, you know damned well that's not what I said." He took a menacing step toward her.

She stepped back, within view of the camera and turned away as if to fend off an attack. A state trooper next to the governor touched the governor's arm before ushering him off stage.

Camila, looking shaken, straightened her jacket and took a deep breath before continuing. "Folks, we will continue to investigate the failures of the governor's team and their ties to the arsonist in the coming days. As a Texan, I am worried. Before today, I'd never have believed that the challenge of a strong woman shook the governor, but you saw what I just experienced. Bullying is unacceptable in any setting." She shuddered. "I'm going to need some time to process what just happened. Many of you know I've interviewed the governor before. Each instance was pleasant. Something was different this time. I will not speculate if the governor is involved in targeting Ms. Kavioni. Stay tuned for more information." The camera stayed on her a moment longer, catching her putting her hand over her face with a slight shudder. Someone stepped in, putting their arm around her before the camera shut off.

"Oh my, she is good," Nafara said.

Lucy beamed. "I know."

"Do you think Camila went too far?" Tanya asked.

"She's riding the edge. That's where the power is."

"What was on the video files?"

"You're trying to talk the arsonist down. He attacked you. Tanya jumped in to save you. In the end, he had a moment of realization of all the bad things he'd done, and confessed that the governor payed him to kill you or drive you out of the race."

Nafara was pleased. "That's all?"

"Basically, his last words are his confession. It was so sad." Lucy frowned, feigning a look of concern.

Chapter 71

Yusuf checked his email. He had sent an encrypted report to the Society but had yet to receive a response. Ali had gone silent after informing him that the reports of Jann in India remained unconfirmed. The lack of contact with the Society bothered him.

He pushed back from his desk and took a sip of tea, wincing at the chill. Looking out the door to the larger office, he saw Farid's jacket was still hanging on the wall near the door, but he didn't see his protégé.

Yusuf picked up his phone to call Reza. Should he bother the teacher? His silence could be a sign of more trouble. *I have to know they received my report.* He clicked the Ayatollah's number.

"Salam, Yusuf. May the blessings of the Lord bring health and protection to you. It is good to hear from you again."

"Reza, may the Lord's peace be upon you as well, wherever your travels take you. Your silence worried me."

"Forgive me, my friend. Much is happening. Ali told you about the Jann in India?"

"Yes, but he said the reports were unconfirmed."

"It's confirmed. Things are moving faster than we expected. I'm traveling to investigate another instance. How are you doing?"

Yusuf hesitated for just a moment before answering. "As mentioned in my report, the Ifrit has been dealt with."

"With the blade?"

"Yes. The hakimah killed him" The question unsettled him. Reza knew that only the blade could kill the Jinn. He made a mental note to revisit this later.

"I saw the media coverage. It's horrific, the damage he caused."

"It is. But there's something I left out of the report. I ask your forgiveness."

"There is no need for that. All that we do is guided by Allah. Nothing is insurmountable with His blessings upon us."

"The Ghul lives."

"I assumed so."

"Reza, I urged her to kill the Ghul, but she refused, shielding the Jinn. We may have lost our advantage. I saw it in her eyes. I don't think she'll trust me again."

"You did what you had to do. The wise one must live. She has an important part to play."

"In the prophecy?"

"If the prophecy is accurate and the Jinn are released upon the Earth, then yes."

"I don't want to see her harmed, but wouldn't her death prevent them from escaping?"

"As with all prophecies, it is uncertain."

"I'm relieved, but her relationship with the Ghul worries me. I've seen what she can do."

"Your report was thorough. Her ability to control and influence plants and use toxins is worrisome, but there are defenses in the old texts. Have you considered whether it's the hakimah that influences the Ghul? Remember what the Quran says, 'Say (O Muhammad): It has been revealed to me that a group of Jinn listened, and they said: *Indeed, we have heard a wonderful Quran, guiding to the right way, and*

350

we have believed therein.' The Prophet was sent as a messenger to both humans and Jinn."

The reminder humbled him, and he took it as a rebuke, although that wasn't the intent. His responsibility was to pass on the teachings to all people.

Yusuf bowed his head slightly. "Your wisdom always brings clarity, Sayyid Reza. May Allah continue to preserve your insight. My fear sometimes clouds what I know to be true. Thank you for reminding me of the path."

"We're all students. Only Allah holds all wisdom. I have one more question, Yusuf. What happened to the body of the Ifrit?"

"I don't know. I left the girl, Tanya, with the Ghul as she asked. Perhaps I should contact her again and reassure her we are not enemies."

"That's a prudent course of action. I dislike having to ask you so soon after inducting you into the Society, but we need you to remain close to the hakimah."

"I'll try." He felt despair at the request. He felt as if he had broken Tanya's trust, and it sickened him. She'd done nothing to counter his beliefs.

"Yusuf, I need to go. I'll be in touch. May Allah bless you in all endeavors."

"Thank you. Blessings upon you as well, my friend." An announcement played in the background, but he couldn't understand it.

Putting down his phone, Yusuf stood and stretched, trying to relieve the stiffness in his lower back. Picking up the half-empty cup, he left his office and headed to their sink. He made a fresh cup of tea and went to the window, looking down on the open grassy area. The steady rain was welcome, but kept the students inside. He didn't want to imagine what would happen if the Jinn escaped. The fight between the Ghul and the Ifrit played again in his mind. The powers they used were more frightful than anything he had seen in a Hollywood movie. What could they do to stop them if they joined forces? Would humanity know peace?

351

Knock! Knock!

The door opened, and a man and a woman in similar gray suits entered.

"Hello. Ayatollah Yusuf al-Fortwani?"

"Yes. How may I help you?" His voice was wary.

The pair stepped into the open office area, closing the door behind them. The woman was tall, brunette, hair tied back firmly. The man had a short, cropped haircut. Their clothing was professional. The man carried a thin briefcase.

"Mr. Al-Fortwani? I'm Special Agent Hent, and this is Special Agent Brooks. We'd like to ask you a few questions," the woman stated. Both extended their credentials.

He waved them off. "Yusuf is fine, and yes, of course. May I ask what this is about? Please sit if you'd like." He invited them to the small conference table. "I hope you don't mind if I sit. My knees aren't what they used to be." He sat in a chair opposite the door, instinctively rubbing his right arm.

"Of course." The woman took the seat nearest to him. The man sat next to her and pulled a green folder from the briefcase. He pulled a few photos out, spreading them on the table. They showed him exiting the Capitol building with a timestamp. "First, I'd like to state that you're not under investigation or suspected of a crime."

He relaxed a little and let an uneasy chuckle escape. "That's good to know. How may I help?"

"Have you seen the released video coverage of what occurred within the State Capitol building?"

"Yes, I have."

"Do you have anything that you would like to add, or correct?"

"I'm not sure I have anything."

She leaned forward. "Yusuf, a candidate for governor, was almost murdered by a serial arsonist. These images show you leaving the scene. Now, the other witnesses have corroborated the video, and neither mentioned you."

"I'm friends with Ms. Janessy. I talked to her earlier in the day. Afterwards, I had a feeling that she might do something rash, so I followed her."

"What did you see?"

The scene replayed in his head, the larger Ifrit standing over Tanya, stepping forward to kill the Ghul. The fiery glow of his veins broke up the dark skin on his arms. He saw Tanya move the blade from behind her back and stab the unsuspecting Jinn. He gripped his injured hand, trying to steady the tremor.

"Yusuf, are you okay?"

"Yes. I was replaying it all in my head. The video is accurate. The arsonist had beaten Ms. Kavioni, and I believe was moving closer to kill her. Ms. Jenessy talked to him long enough to distract him before I believe he stabbed him."

The man cleared his throat. "Yusuf. Is there anything you noticed about the suspect? How he spread fire, or maybe the chemicals he used?"

"That is outside my area of expertise. I'm sorry."

"Where were you specifically during the encounter?"

"Entering the building from the north, I heard the noise from the rotunda and tried to creep forward without being seen. I didn't want her to see me."

Agent Hent spoke up. "Weren't you worried about her safety? The man is enormous."

"Yes, of course I was, but I didn't have time. By the time I entered the rotunda, Ms. Kavioni was already hurt, and Tanya, Ms. Janessy, was trying to help her. I didn't want to startle the suspect while she tried to get control of the situation, and then she stabbed him to protect her aunt."

Agent Hent smiled and reached into her jacket, taking out a cardholder. "Thank you, Yusuf, Ayatollah. If you think of anything else, maybe something that seemed out of the ordinary, call us." She slid a business card across the table.

"Of course."

The agents got up and excused themselves. He closed the door behind them. They were fishing for something. It had to be the Ifrit. If they had the body, and he was certain they did, would they find organs? Bones? Or something alien? Nothing he read described Jinn as being any different from humans. He couldn't imagine what they might find in the autopsy. He went back to his desk to send an update to the council in Qom.

Chapter 72

Tanya and Lucy stood to the side as Nafara paced. Her Jinn form was an imposing sight. Her bones had mended and the scar tissue had sloughed off. Tanya trusted the Jinn's metabolism to regenerate limbs, but injuries from other Jinn or iron proved insurmountable. The blade of star-iron would further impede regeneration. She tucked away that fact, showing that they were not impervious to being killed or hurt.

Nafara held her left arm up, turning it while she examined the deep scars that remained. "I think this is going to help me. While it might not be as significant as a veteran's wounds, in the people's view, a corrupt politician and a broken system injured me."

Lucy looked up from her phone. "I agree. While he's still on the ballot, the polls have shifted significantly in the last week. In the public's eyes, he is guilty, and there are no other witnesses to counter the argument. Texas judgment. Early voting is going well, though we won't know anything official until the polls close on election day."

Nafara paused her pacing to look at Lucy.

"Well, official results aren't available, but indications from people we are in touch with show you double digits ahead of the governor."

Nafara smiled a full, genuine smile, something she rarely did.

"That is good news."

"I've booked you on Camila's show at the end of the week. Are you okay with that?"

Nafara's form shifted, and she was in her human body. Her hair was short, and the scars on her neck reappeared. Her arm was in a sling, with a clean white bandage. She had circles under her eyes, but a fierce resistance in her look. "I think my arm is going to hurt like hell for a long time. Damn that fire, it still burns under my skin. What do you think?"

Lucy stood and walked over and around her, clapping her hands. "Oh, I like it. You look injured, but resilient. Noble qualities in a leader."

"Why are we doing this?" Tanya jumped in.

"The United States is the perfect place to make a peaceful transition. Their resources and influence are immense."

"Over any other country in the world?"

Nafara tilted her head in question. "Actually, yes, it is. The decline in religious influence, coupled with the youth's search for relevance and purpose, makes it a very appropriate location. Along with the strength of the military."

"I get it. I guess I'm trying to understand the bigger plan. What happens after we open the nexus?"

"The inquisitive hakimah. I love it." Nafara moved to her and took her hands. "Once my people are freed, they will heal this world. They will teach humanity how to nurture the land and bring back its natural beauty. The prophecy is about restoring balance."

"Yes, but you could accomplish all of that without taking over, couldn't you?"

"We could, but that would be like leaving a disease in place. It's counterproductive. I'm not suggesting we abandon all technology, just the ones that damage our home. Why are we talking about this now, on the verge of opening the nexus?"

Tanya hesitated, letting go of Nafara's hands. She turned and walked toward the monitor. "Krazack."

"What of him?"

"He believed you were manipulating me, and before you say anything, I know you're not. But what about all the other Jinn? We don't know what their mental state will be like. What if they are all angry or crazed at being banished from their world? What if they all hold a grudge against humanity? Can you control them?"

"I can control them, because I'm the one releasing them. The prophecy states that the one who releases the Jinn from their prison will rule over them, bringing about several millennia of peace and prosperity."

"The Jinn Prophecy?"

"Yes, and you play a critical role, as do all of my trusted advisors," she motioned toward Lucy.

Lucy nodded and looked relieved. She didn't like it when they shifted to a discussion of the plan for humanity. Tanya wondered if there was a little guilt, quickly tossing aside the notion. Lucy wanted power and influence. She had no family and blamed the mismanagement of society for many of the world's problems. The Jinn were just as likely to fix what humanity had broken.

"It's fine. I'm just curious." She glanced at Lucy. The woman's expression showed concern. She flashed a supportive smile when she caught Tanya looking at her. What did she believe? All of Nafara's trusted advisors had their own goals and motivations, but none was willing to share. Only she could question Nafara in this way. Their friendship was genuine.

"Tanya, you have nothing to worry about. You're an integral to the prophecy. I'll always protect you. Not because you're a hakimah, but because of our relationship. You said it yourself, we're family."

"I'm fine. I just wanted to understand." Nafara's eyes were sincere. A quick shift of her sight showed no pheromones in the air. She wanted to believe the Ghul, but a spark of doubt remained. It would have to be enough. "I think I need to rest."

"You should. You've been throwing yourself into the weave for hours at a time. We don't know what your limits are, but there must be a cost. There always is." Nafara stared at her. "Are you worried about the governor?"

"No, Lucy showed me the information she dug up. He's lucky. If Marcia got wind of his 'work' with the cartels, he'd have some hard questions to answer."

"Exactly, everyone has dirt. We're the ones holding the hose."

"We are."

Lucy jumped in, "I have good news. Camila can get you on the show tomorrow if you're up for it."

Nafara stretched, shifting back to her natural form. "I think we can make that. Do you want to go, Tanya?"

"No, I'll stay here. The titanium arrived, and I want to test it." The images of the dead soldiers in the military bunker and the White House flickered in her mind. Were they predetermined? She didn't know. If they were, she was worried, because that meant a war was coming, and it would be harsh for humanity. How much ruin could be justified in the name of healing? And what if it wasn't enough?

Chapter 73

Nafara moved within the shadows. The smell of fire and oil lingered in the air. The night was cool, with a breeze blowing through the city. She paused, resting against a tree as she gazed at the boxy home, reminiscent of an old southern plantation. Smiling to herself, she was pleased with the outcome. Texans had a long memory, and the arson attack from almost fifteen years before was still fresh in many of their minds. They accepted the possibility of an arsonist attacking their great state, this one trying to outdo the one that had damaged the governor's mansion.

She moved forward, flowing up to the balcony. Reforming into her natural shape, she opened the door, stepping silently onto the wooden floor. Nafara didn't expect there would be any supporters here. Once she knew the governor's career was over, she wasn't shocked by how easily she gathered information about him. They cast him aside, and the lieutenant governor distanced herself in an attempt to set herself up for the next run.

The Jinn made her way through the house to where she heard his voice.

"I can't believe that bitch is going to get away with this."

She heard something hit the wall, followed by the sound of glass breaking.

"I've served these people for two terms. It was never about political lines. I made life better for everyone," Jeremiah said, his Texas drawl coming out.

"Honey, calm down. We believe in you. We'll get through this, prove the video is fake, and take her down."

Nafara assumed it was the governor's wife.

"Jeremiah, Carlene's right. I've got friends at the NSA examining the video."

"Damn her. This is bullshit. I swear to God, I'm gonna—"

"What are you going to do, Jeremiah?" Nafara stepped into the room in her human form, wearing a light gray business suit and skirt. Her eyes were defiant.

"How the hell did you get in here? Jack! Get security!" Jeremiah Baker, the current governor of Texas, stepped between Nafara and his wife. The other person in the room was Ed Stone, his chief of staff and campaign manager.

Nafara waited until the pair of state troopers on duty entered the room, their weapons drawn.

"Put your hands where we can see them!"

"Now that's rude," Nafara said, raising both arms to shoulder height, one missing a hand.

"I don't know what games you're playing, Kavioni, but you just threw this election to the wolves. Breaking and entering the governor's mansion, threatening my family. I don't care how many tears you toss to the media, Texans won't accept it."

"Jeremiah, you assume the public is going to know about this. How are they going to feel when they find out what this stress did to you? I mean, murdering state troopers, your best friend, and a missing wife? I almost feel sad. Almost." She bit her lower lip.

"What the hell are you talking about?" His face reddened. He took a step toward her.

Nafara shifted form into a shadow in the blink of an eye, shooting backward between the state troopers. She materialized in her natural form, scratching one, then the other, until each toppled forward. She smiled at the shocked looks on their faces. His wife had dropped to her knees and was praying for salvation from the demon that had just appeared.

"What the hell are you?" His bravado disappeared.

She walked toward him as he backed away, her long strides cutting the distance faster than he could retreat.

"I'm your new governor." She flicked her hand, leaving a slight scratch on his neck. He collapsed on the floor, his eyes open.

She stepped over him and did the same to his wife and campaign manager.

Nafara kneeled beside the other man. "It's a shame to waste a good meal, but appearances need to be made."

The Ghul turned his wife over on the floor, looking over at the governor to make sure he had a clear view. Nafara laid her hand on the woman's chest and focused, coaxing the blood out of her body. Something like a troubled squeak escaped the governor's mouth as he watched his wife wither to a dry husk. Once the process was complete, her hand glowed, and the body turned to ash, swirling over the body and into the mouth of the Ghul. When she turned to the governor and wiped the side of her mouth, she smiled wickedly.

Nafara stood and went to the troopers, holstering one gun and taking the other. She walked to where the governor had been standing and shot each trooper in the head. She turned and shot the paralyzed campaign manager. Kneeling down, she placed the pistol in the governor's hand and fired two shots out the window behind his friend. Lifting the governor, she sat him on the couch.

Stepping back, she looked at the disheveled, now-drooling man sitting limp on the couch. She held up her arm and looked at where her hand had been. "It's a small price to pay for what's coming. Don't worry, I hear the state has fantastic facilities to take care of you. Of course, you'll probably be like this for the rest of your life. I'd say I feel sorry for you, but I don't, not in the least." She went to the door, looking back before she left the room. "Someone should be by in the morning to check on you. I know you won't forget this, Jeremiah. I'll stop by from time to time to see how you're doing." She winked at him, noting the tears rolling down his cheeks from terror-filled eyes.

Chapter 74

Nafara looked out at her gathered supporters filling the ballroom through the mirrored window. Her loyalists were among those seeking power and influence.

"I can't believe this night is here already," Tanya said. She had paced a path onto the carpet as they watched the results roll in from the various districts across the state.

"Everything's good. The governor's downward spiral paved the way for Nafara's win." Lucy sipped from a glass of champagne.

Nafara shook her head. "The man was under so much stress with the investigation, it's no surprise he snapped." She shook her head.

With the final districts now reporting, we project Nafara Kavioni's election as governor of Texas.

"Woo-hoo! Cheers, Nafara! Congratulations." Lucy held her glass high.

A loud knock at the door drew their attention.

Nafara tensed, shifting into her natural form, nails extending from her hand. A spike extended from her arm. It looked like twisted roots pulled to a fine point. "Get back!"

Tanya shifted her sight, moving behind Nafara. Lucy leaped up, rushing to the small kitchenette to the side.

"Enter," Nafara commanded, her voice projecting power.

The door opened. A tall man dressed in traditional Islamic scholar robes with a black turban stepped inside, a genuine smile on his face. He did not appear to be fazed by Nafara's form or threatening stance.

"There's no need for that, sister. My name is Reza Al-Majlisi. I've been waiting for you." He leaned over to get a look at Tanya. "Both of you." His form shifted, flowing like water, his skin turning a deep blue.

"You're Marid."

"Yes. And I've waited a long time to meet the two who would change everything."

Tanya stepped out from behind the Ghul, examining the Marid. His form was distinct. The essence of the filaments emanating from him were water based.

"Please, Hakimah, I mean you no harm. You can attest to my honesty?"

Tanya looked from Reza to Nafara. "I don't know how to do that."

"Tanya, let's not share secrets until we know his intentions." She stepped to the side again, placing herself between Reza and Tanya. "You're supposed to be arrogant and aloof."

"And you are supposed to be diseased, decrepit, and roaming in graveyards."

"What do you want?"

He turned and locked the door behind him. "I'm here to assist you."

"How are you going to do that?"

"However you see fit. More specifically, I am here to advise. I do not know what you know or understand, but if you'll indulge me, I'll tell you what I've surmised."

Nafara relaxed a little. "Enlighten us."

"Nafara Al-Hiyal, you are the last of your family. You have been roaming the world for at least a thousand years, looking for her, Tanya, I presume. You discovered her five years ago. Since that time, you have sought knowledge to help her understand her gifts. Now, you seek to open a pathway between the City of Brass and Earth."

"If you surmised all of that, then the abilities of your kind are grossly underrated."

Tanya stepped into the open again, sidestepping Nafara. "You know Yusuf!"

The Marid nodded. "Well done." He bowed.

"That doesn't explain everything," Nafara insisted.

"You're right, it doesn't. My role, and how I know Ayatollah al-Fortwani, is that I am the senior scholar of occult studies at the Qom Islamic Seminary. Who did you think forwarded the texts you have? Once Yusuf shared your belief that Tanya was a wise one, I increased the scrutiny of anyone seeking ancient texts and ensured they made their way to you."

"So, you've been guiding us the whole time," Tanya said, her voice a mix of awe and suspicion. "You sent him the blade, *Forsaken*. Why?"

"The prophecy states the hakim will be a slayer of man and Jinn."

Tanya recoiled. "I haven't killed anyone except the Ifrit." Her mind raced. Nafara had killed. Was she guilty by association? Her heart rate increased, and she felt unsteady. *That couldn't be it, could it?*

"Do you know the prophecy?"

"Only pieces. I will share what I know, because that is my role in the liberation of our people. The first step was to find the wise one who is bound to the one destined to lead. The next step is to open the pathway."

"And after that?"

"After that, will be a time of turmoil as our people are brought together again."

Tanya wanted to ask more, but a knock at the door interrupted them. Nafara and Reza shifted to their human forms. Reza unlocked the door and opened it at Nafara's nod.

A young man in his early twenties, with an enthusiastic grin, burst into the room. "Governor-elect Kavioni, everyone is downstairs waiting for your acceptance. The news crews are ready." He looked at Lucy, who was standing now in the kitchenette.

"Thanks, Jason, she'll be right down." He nodded and left, closing the door behind him.

Nafara straightened her jacket and moved toward the door. She turned to make sure Tanya was following. "I don't want to keep them waiting. Now more than ever, we must keep up appearances."

Reza nodded. "As you should. I'll await your return and answer any questions you may have."

Nafara gave him a slight nod and waved Lucy over to follow. "It might be a little while. Make yourself comfortable."

Chapter 75

Tanya strode into the rotunda of the State Capitol Building. Her heels clacked on the smooth stone floor. She was one of the handful of people allowed inside. She marveled at how quickly Nafara's team had restored the building's interior after the fight. Nafara had removed all traces of the plants before journalists could enter. The building was closed for longer because of reports of black mold and other toxins in the air.

She walked through and down the hall to the basement stairs. The bottom level was stark in contrast with the rest of the building. Downstairs offices existed yet remained undecorated. Nafara, as the governor-elect, has made the ground floor off-limits. Air samples continued to pick up hazardous spores, and the environmental engineers hadn't located the source. The good news was that they would open all the upper levels soon.

The round room under the rotunda had eight columns spaced to form an octagonal pattern that supported the floor of the rotunda. Tanya walked to the center of the shape and kneeled, running her finger along the stone floor.

"What do you need me to do?"

Tanya jumped, despite recognizing the voice of the Jinn. "You scared me. I didn't hear you behind me."

Nafara smiled. The edges of her lips curved, but her eyes remained distant. "I didn't follow you. I've been going through the rooms down here. Everyone has moved out. I just want to make sure our story to keep everyone away is sound."

"I think the mold is the best solution." Tanya remembered seeing the spores from the fight with Krazack filling the air, getting into his lungs, and causing problems until he recognized what was happening.

Nafara crept toward her. She moved without making a sound. There were no filaments of sound coming from the floor. Was she even touching it?

"This is interesting." Nafara reached for the pendant but stopped. "Did you change the stone?"

"No, or I suppose yes, it depends on what you mean."

"The sapphire looks different. It is still deep blue, but it looks like there is a flame dancing inside."

"It's one of a kind. Apparently, while alchemy, or manipulation of matter, is possible, it is far more difficult with precious stones. Their structure is rigid and resists changes."

"Yet you could do so. This would be priceless."

Tanya shot her hand up to touch the pendant. "I wouldn't sell it. It was Sheri's."

"I wouldn't ask you to."

Tanya held her gaze for a moment longer before turning and showing the area inside the columns. "I know we can't weaken the ground under the columns, but can we transform the inner area with a thick growth of soft, clean, green moss?"

Nafara nodded and held her hand up, palm down, over the center of the floor. She stood for a moment before lowering her hand. I'm going to need Reza to help."

"Is he here?"

"No, I'll have Lucy get in touch with him. Is there anything else you need besides those?" She pointed at the two cubes of metal.

368

"This space is larger than the one you had below the Vulture House. Could you recreate that atmosphere here?" She thought of the lush growth and atmosphere of the small grotto.

Nafara smiled. "A woman after my heart. I know I haven't shared everything, and I have my reasons. Please know none involves trust. But I will share with you one thing I want to do, and that is to create a set of gardens that would rival the legendary hanging gardens of Babylon. Of course, I never saw them, but I remember the stories from when I was young. Passed down through the ages. I can close my eyes and imagine them exactly as described."

Tanya couldn't help but admire Nafara's ambition, but the words carried an undertone of nostalgia. This transcended mere beauty, it recovered a lost artifact, something out of place in this era.

"Well, no need for you to wait around here. Let me talk with Reza, and I'll let you know when it's ready."

"Okay. I'll start work on the nexus."

Nafara flashed a quick grin before heading down the hall and upstairs.

Tanya sat between the blocks of titanium. She slowed her breathing, reaching out to the filaments filling the room, the stone floor, columns, metal in the frame along the ceiling, and the bricks in the walls. She could see the electrical currents flowing in the wires and lighting, and in the outlets surrounding her. Focusing, she minimized the intensity of everything but the titanium. Recalling the image of the nexus to her mind, she visualized the finished shape. She felt something was off. There was no support structure at the back. Calculations filled her mind, forming a vortex and the connection to the other plane. The image spun in her head, allowing her to examine the shapes of each arch, the support, and the spinning energy field.

Tanya sang, improvising in the style of ancient Persian music. She adjusted her tone and took hold of the filaments of the titanium. Its firmness yielded to a supple undercurrent. She detected a low hum. Focusing on the hum, she pinpointed its frequency. She could feel the clash between the ancient hum of the Earth's core and the buzzing of modern electricity. The weave encompassed both, allowing her to manipulate them as one, a delicate balance between the natural and the engineered. Her memory brought up the vibration of Krazack's blood. She created a second melody to intertwine with the original but of the new hum. The metal, while resistant to blunt force, was more susceptible to manipulation of the music or the emotion of the song.

Tanya's voice took on a muted characteristic as the reverberation in the round room canceled out portions of the sound. The song felt flat. She drew from her pain, each note sharpened by loss. Sheri's face flashed in her mind, the memory of her pendant burning against her skin. Weaving her grief into the gaps created by the room's unforgiving shape, she fortified the music. She didn't know how long it took her, but the metal cubes felt ready to change their shape. She increased the power of the dueling frequencies, adjusting for the room. The cubes quivered before beginning to change. In place, the cubes appeared to spin. The cubes themselves did not move. It was the corners beginning to swirl, one to the right, the other to the left. It took a steady effort to continue spinning until cylinders replaced the cubes. A dot formed in the middle of the top, and rose into the air, dragging behind a smooth rod of the metal. In her mind, she shaped the metal, pulling it into place, each hand working its own side, in perfect mirrored unison. The arches rose seven feet into the air, arching toward the other, but not touching.

She could hear two distinct hums. She brought out the spikes from the metal as she had seen in her vision, and with realization extended a longer spike from each arched pillar, on the right, the longer spike curved upward, and around the back, the spike from the left curved downward, mirroring the one from above. As the spikes extended from the arches, the air seemed to thicken, vibrating in tandem with the frequencies she had woven. A faint warmth radiated from the titanium, like the first breath of a forge, as the metal obeyed her commands. She examined the frame and saw that it would cradle a sphere of energy, which would be the nexus.

Tanya stood, her muscles ached. She pulled her phone and checked the time. Exhaustion hit her. It was just past two in the morning. She had lost herself in the weave for over seventeen hours. Nafara must have left directions for her not to be bothered. If anyone came down now, they would believe the frame was a new piece of art brought in by the new eclectic governor. To most, this nexus will look like "modern sculpture" when it is, in fact, the gate to a new age.

She spun around, confirming she was in the center of the room, and sang without the weave, and she could hear the difference in sound. She had never felt this sensation before. Of course, she didn't remember standing in the center of a round room and singing. It felt unearthly, which was maybe the point of this location. She thought about delving deeper into the weave, into the realm of electricity and currents, but thought it better to explore another day. Now she was equally hungry and tired.

Chapter 76

Yusuf shifted in his seat in the office of the United States Special Operations Command, SOCOM. He had been 'cordially' invited after the visit by FBI agents. Apparently, his responses hadn't provided the answers they wanted. They knocked on his door early in the morning, and unlike in the movies, they gave him a little time to pack a quick bag before rushing him to the airport to catch a military flight to MacDill Air Force Base in Tampa. His guide, an army major, confiscated his phone and refused to let him tell Farid his location, promising to return his phone later.

He felt out of place in his robes and turban, sitting in this office. Add to his dress the fact that he was born and raised in Iran, whose public statements hadn't been positive toward the United States in several decades, and he worried. *Allah, protect me, and give me strength to face this test. Show me the way, and I will follow You.* He repeated the prayer until he felt his body react.

An enlisted man entered, carrying a tray with a teapot and cup. He smelled familiar spices. *Of course they knew.* He smiled at the sight of this young man, with veins popping along his arms, very fit, who was serving an ayatollah tea in the headquarters of one of the deadliest military groups in the world. He felt the tension disappear.

"Sir, the admiral apologizes for the delay. He'll be a little longer. He wanted us to make you comfortable."

"Thank you. It smells wonderful."

"I made it myself. I've picked up a taste for the stuff during my first deployment."

The mess specialist placed the tray on the end table and left him alone again. Yusuf poured himself a cup and raised it, smelling the fresh tea. He took a sip. It was commendable. After another fifteen minutes, the door opened, and a large black man entered. He looked like an American football player. He had close-cropped hair on the sides and short hair on top. His full mustache contributed to his intimidating demeanor.

"Ayatollah Yusuf Ahmed Al-Fortwani. It is a pleasure to meet you. I'm Admiral Otis Tolbert. How was your flight in?" The admiral strode in, shook hands, circled his desk, and sat down before he could answer.

"It was good. I'm not sure why I am here."

"I think you're a smart man. Top of your classes in Qom, moved to the US, rose to lead a large congregation in the DFW area before transferring to the newly developed Darul Hikmah Institute. Your specialty is in occult studies."

Was there anything this man didn't know? He straightened himself, understanding the situation he found himself in. "You seem to know quite a bit about me, Admiral. I assure you my interest in the country is purely based on faith."

"I have no doubt. You're here because I have questions, and despite having brilliant analysts, there are too many unknowns. That was until I received a classified brief from the FBI, identifying you as a witness to the terrorist arson attack in Austin."

"I answered the questions honestly."

The admiral's eyes seemed to bore right through him. He leaned forward on his redwood desk, crossing his arms and resting them on the polished surface. "I'm sure you did. I don't think they asked the right questions, Ayatollah." Yusuf didn't feel intimidated using his title, but the admiral's intensity was palpable.

"I'm happy to answer any questions I can."

"Great. What do you know of the entity that was killed in the Texas State Capitol building?"

"Entity?"

"Yes, because he's not human. He looks human, but the autopsy shows he isn't."

Yusuf looked at the admiral. The fate of the Ifrit's body was now clear to Yusuf, and he was thankful it wasn't lost to a local coroner's office. "Admiral Tolbert, I'm hesitant to answer."

"Trust me, I have a wide-open mind right now."

Yusuf exhaled and rubbed his injured arm. "I am going to tell you what I think. I am certain of what I believe, but there will be many who will not support my assessment." The admiral held his gaze, waiting for him to continue. "I believe the entity is an Ifrit, a Jinn."

The admiral didn't appear fazed by the answer. If anything, his glare appeared sterner. "A Jinn, like a genie?"

"That is the westernized word for them, but yes, a Jinn."

"And this Jinn is an Ifrit. Is that a subclassification?"

"Think of the Jinn like humans, a species, an Ifrit is a race, like you or me. There are several races of Jinn."

"Are they all as deadly as this one?" He paused. "It was one, correct?"

"Yes, Admiral. It was a single Jinn. And I presume they are each as deadly."

"Do we know where this one came from?"

"Not for sure. In Islam, it is believed that most of them were banished to a mythical City of Brass in the Rub' al-Khali, southern Saudi Arabia."

"So, this one escaped this legendary city."

"Maybe I don't know, and I never actually interacted with him."

"Okay. Why did he want to kill the governor-elect of Texas? She was a candidate then."

"I don't have an answer for that. My concern was for her niece."

"Given the destruction caused by this Ifrit, how do you explain its death at the hands of her niece?"

"I wouldn't have thought she could. The Ifrit was interested in her, but he didn't make his intentions clear. I don't understand where she got the strength. Perhaps that's what disarmed him. I couldn't hear everything that was said, only that her voice was calm and soft. She approached him, and then you've seen the video."

"Yes, she got lucky. Between the ribs and into the heart. The problem is that there are too many unknowns in this case, and in my line of work, unknowns get people killed. I can't say we got lucky. Hundreds dead, and over a thousand injured, a scar burned across the landscape of a major US city."

"Admiral, I think you are on the right path."

"What do you mean?"

"I don't believe this will be an isolated incident."

"And that's why I brought you here. I want to bring you on board as a consultant."

"Admiral, I don't think I can leave my position. My loyalties lie with my faith."

"I understand. But it's hard to be a shepherd when you have no flock. I'm not asking you to move here, only to take my calls, and occasionally meet with experts I send to you. If these Jinn are a threat, then I need my teams ready."

"I will seek guidance and let you know. If that is okay with you."

He checked his watch. "I have another meeting. Major Garret will take you home and will act as our liaison if you decide you can help. I appreciate your flexibility, Ayatollah Al-Fortwani. I would ask that you keep this between you and me. We don't need to cause a panic."

"My sentiments exactly."

"Good." He stood and came around the desk, offering his hand. Yusuf shook his hand, and Admiral Tolbert showed him to the reception area, where Major Garret was waiting.

"Sir, follow me please."

Yusuf followed the major out to the airfield. His thoughts drifted to Tanya and the Ghul. He had protected their secret, but why? Where were his loyalties?

He whispered a prayer into the wind, uncertain whether he sought guidance or forgiveness.

Chapter 77

Tanya swiped her badge at the recently installed card reader that granted access to the bottom floor of the Capitol building. They asked her to stay clear of the floor while they added additional security to the other entrances and from the main floor above. Her heels clacked on the stone steps, and more so on the wood floor of the wide hallway. The thick glass walls and security door, which resembled an airlock more than a typical door, guarded one of the state's most exclusive gardens. She paused there before turning toward the nexus room.

With a swipe of her badge at the second reader, the door slid open. Stepping through, she let the door close behind her. When it did, the door in front of her opened. She stepped into the humid garden, kicking off her shoes and placing them in an empty cubby. Over the past month, they transformed the round room. The floor was a thick, soft layer of green moss that reminded her of pictures from Scotland. Flowers were in long planters around the outer wall. Vines crept up and covered the eight columns. It was too perfect. She thought it was a movie set. In the middle of the octagon, contained within the columns, sat the nexus frame.

She walked up, running her fingers over its surface. It was a work of art. The lighting was dim because someone had replaced them with LED lights. They should be controllable. A fine mist drifted down from the outer wall to the abundant flowers.

A door that hadn't been there before slid open, letting Nafara and Reza into the room.

"What do you think?" Nafara asked as she went to Tanya's side.

"It looks good. We have the four major elements: earth, water, air, and I assume the braziers extending in from the columns are for fire."

"You're missing an element."

"Aether," Tanya said. "I've been trying to understand it, but the book you sent isn't clear."

"Aether is the essence of reality."

Tanya looked at him, waiting for more information, which wasn't coming. She chuckled. "Oh, that's it?"

Reza cocked his head to the side. "I believe so."

Great, just give me a second and I'll summon some reality. What did that mean? How would she find the essence of reality? She didn't know where to start. Her mind raced with ideas of what it could be.

"You look perplexed. I wish I knew a Si'lat, but I don't."

"What is a Si'lat?"

"Another of our race. Their base element is aether. They are masters of illusion and shapeshifting."

"All of you can shapeshift though, can't you?"

"To an extent, but they are undetectable, even for most wise ones. As you grow stronger and better understand the weave, you will see the true nature of things. Which I implied when I told you about knowing the truth from falsehood. The Si'lat are the best among us at manipulating their appearance."

"Tanya, you described what you see when you open yourself to the weave as a world of threads, providing the essence of everything, right?"

"Yes. All the senses we experience exist as threads, or filaments, in the weave. More complex things have base threads. If I focus on it, I can see the strands that make up the thread. Living things add to emotion and feelings, which are also filaments."

"What is the essence of a filament?"

"Well, it's, um." She hadn't looked at them in that way. She assumed the filaments extended from the characteristic elements. Were the filaments potential? Everything she had seen, heard, smelled, touched, and tasted had base elements to them. Were there empty filaments, or did filaments come into existence with the creation of the object? No, the universe was in balance. The filaments held the basis of reality. They were the reason we experienced life in the way we do. In creating the gateway to the city, she had touched the aether before. She brought it into existence with her belief that she could, but it took the other elements. She thought back to the ritual she had performed in their house many months before.

"I think I understand."

"Good. Are we ready then?"

"I don't think so."

"What?" Nafara looked confused. It was a look she hadn't seen on the Ghul.

"I think I know how I opened the gateway to the city, but it was only for a moment. Krazack was waiting for it to open again, and he jumped through. It collapsed. If I am correct, I will need something from the other realm, the City, to keep on this side, otherwise, the nexus will only be opened as long as I hold it open."

"I'll go," Reza said.

Nafara's posture straightened, and she turned toward the Marid. Tanya recognized the Ghul's defensive stance. "For what purpose?"

Reza held his hand up. "Of the three of us, I'm the logical choice."

Nafara thought for a moment before relaxing. "Let's assume that's true. What are you planning to do, and how much time do you need?"

Reza ran his hand through his beard. "I need to contact whoever is leading our people. It's been a very long time. We don't know what's changed."

"That's a good point. I told Krazack that we were trying to save your people, and he didn't care," Tanya said.

"Still, I have to try."

"It would be beneficial to have some understanding of our people's situation before opening the gateway, or nexus." Nafara added.

"A month. Give me a month."

Nafara nodded.

Tanya took a deep breath. "Okay, let's see if I've got this. Once you pass through, I'll wait a month before opening it again."

Tanya stood in front of the portal and opened herself to the weave. She drew on the four elements, pulling them into the frame. She sang, letting the melody flow along with each element as she wove them into a swirling sphere inside the frame. The elements stubbornly resisted each other in their original forms, making it challenging. She looked into the essence of each, separating the supporting filaments. As she delved deeper, she found softer filaments without specific traits. She shifted her tune to a longing melody and coaxed the potential filaments out and wove the distinct elements together, binding them in a web around the sphere of swirling elements. With stability, she tapped the pendant's fire, instantly locating and clarifying the city's image.

She had formed the nexus.

"Good luck, Reza Al-Majlisi. The fate of our people is in your hands. I will prepare a home for them here."

"Blessings upon you as well, Nafara Al-Hiyal." Reza stepped into the swirling sphere of energy. He disappeared as he walked into the sphere, as if fog had closed around him. Tanya held the nexus for a moment longer before allowing the sphere to dissipate.

"What do we do now?"

"You continue your studies, my hakimah. I'm going to get something to eat."

END

Acknowledgments

I want to thank the people who helped make Ifrit a reality.

First, as always, my wonderful wife, **Elaine**. Your support, your eye for continuity, and your exceptional editing make every story stronger. Your patience with my stubborn attachment to characters is a gift in itself.

George Engel, my go-to for all things horror. Your insights into mood, pacing, and character arcs are invaluable to the *Jinn Prophecy* series.

Cheryl Barger, thank you for racing through the pages, catching hidden innuendo, Easter eggs, and prophetic overtones that others might miss.

I'm also grateful to those who contributed to the creative process: **Suvajit Das** for the striking cover design, and **Maura Jacquinet** for her media marketing expertise.

And once again, to **Elaine**, for every phase of editing, for steadying me through the process, and for always believing in this world and its characters as much as I do.

Thank You

Thank you for stepping into *The Jinn Prophecy* and spending your time with Ifrit. I write to give you a world worth visiting and characters worth missing when you close the book. If this story moved you, chilled you, surprised you, or kept you up too late, I'm grateful.

Readers like you are how stories travel. A short review on Amazon or Goodreads (even a sentence) makes a huge difference and helps new readers discover this series.

Want to know when the next book arrives? Follow me on Amazon to get release alerts, and stop by my site to see what's coming next.

Until then, thank you for reading, and for believing in these worlds.

— D. L. Wilburn Jr.

Follow on Amazon:

About the Author

D. L. Wilburn Jr. is the author of *The God Protocol* trilogy, the prophetic horror series *The Jinn Prophecy* (*Vulture House* and *Ifrit*, with *One Nation Under Jinn* in progress), the YA adventure *Steve's Alien Rescue Club*, and the co-authored contemporary novel *The Meaning Between Us* (as Leilana Rae). His work spans prophetic horror, near-future science fiction, and heartfelt contemporary fiction, always centered on worlds where myth, technology, and human emotion collide.

Don is also the founder of W-III Publishing LLC, where he and his wife **Elaine** champion both their own stories and those of other authors. When he's not writing, he can be found coaching youth soccer in Texas, tinkering with new story ideas, or exploring the strange edges of science, mythology, and prophecy that inspire his work.

He is committed to building expansive, interconnected universes that resonate across generations—stories that entertain, unsettle, and linger long after the last page.

To learn more or explore upcoming releases, visit donwilburnjr.com

www.ingramcontent.com/pod-product-compliance
Lightning Source LLC
Chambersburg PA
CBHW021128260626
47169CB00005B/1501